tragic

LARK COVE
SERIES

USA TODAY BESTSELLING AUTHOR
DEVNEY PERRY

Editing & Proofreading:
Elizabeth Nover, Razor Sharp Editing
www.razorsharpediting.com
Ellie McLove, My Brother's Editor
www.mybrotherseditor.net
Julie Deaton, Deaton Author Services
www.facebook.com/jdproofs
Kaitlyn Moodie
www.facebook.com/KaitlynMoodieEditing

Cover:
Sarah Hansen © Okay Creations
www.okaycreations.com

Formatting:
Champagne Book Design
www.champagnebookdesign.com

dedication

To Carol Motschenbacher.
Your strength, humor and heart are an inspiration.
You were so loved.
You are so missed.

prologue

KAINE

ONE OR TWO.

"Kaine?" Mom's voice echoed off the cement walls as she stepped outside. The glass door swished as it closed behind her.

I didn't look at her as she stepped up to my side. My eyes were aimed blankly ahead as I wrestled with my decision.

One or two.

"What are you doing out here?" she asked. "We've been looking all over the hospital for you."

I wasn't sure how long I'd been standing out here. I'd told Mom that I was going to the bathroom and that I'd be back soon to talk with the doctors. But when I'd passed this exit door, hidden on the bottom floor in the back wing of the hospital, it had beckoned me through.

I'd needed a few moments away from the red-rimmed eyes and sniffling noses. I'd needed just a few seconds to pass without a single person asking me if I was okay.

I needed some quiet to decide.

One or two.

The parking lot ahead of me was shrouded in darkness. The night itself was pitch-black. There were no stars shining. There was no moon glowing. A thick fog had settled in, dulling the light of the streetlamps so their beams barely illuminated the few cars parked on the asphalt. The air should have been cold on my bare arms, but I couldn't feel it.

I was numb.

I'd felt this way for hours, ever since they took her from my arms.

One or two.

It was an impossible choice, one I shouldn't have to make. But because of *him*, it was inevitable.

"Kaine, I'm so sorry. What can I do?"

"I can't decide." My voice was rough as I spoke, the burn of rage and sorrow and pain making it nearly impossible to speak.

"Decide what?" she whispered. I didn't need to look to know that Mom's eyes were full of tears. Her dark hair had gotten a dozen new grays tonight. Her normally cheery and bright hazel eyes held their own fog of grief.

"One or two."

"One or two what?"

I swallowed the fire in my throat. "Graves."

One or two.

"Oh, Kaine." Mom began to weep and her hand reached for my arm, but I shied away. "Please come inside, sweetheart. Please. We need to talk about this. *He* needs to talk to you. Give him a chance to explain."

"I have nothing to say to him." He'd done this. He was the reason I had to decide.

"Kaine, it was an accident. A tragic accident." She hiccupped. "He—"

I walked away before she could finish. I walked right into the dark, wishing this blackness would swallow me whole.

Mom's voice rang across the parking lot as she called out, but I simply walked, my boots carrying me into the black.

One or two.

An impossible choice.

As if the heavens sensed my despair, the clouds opened. Rain poured down, soaking my dark hair. It dripped over my eyes and coated my cheeks. The water soaked my jeans, making them cling to my legs.

But I couldn't feel the water droplets as they streamed down the bridge of my nose. I couldn't feel the locks of hair that were stuck to my forehead. I couldn't feel the wet denim on my thighs as it rubbed my skin raw.

I was numb. There was nothing.

Nothing except the weight of four pounds, two ounces wrapped in a pink blanket resting in my arms as I said good-bye.

One or two.

What would Shannon want?

One. She'd choose one.

So I'd bury them together.

Then surrender to the black.

one

PIPER

"YOU'RE HERE!" THEA RUSHED ACROSS THE RUNWAY.

"I'm here!" I stepped off the last stair of my boss's private jet just as she threw her arms around me. The Kendrick family, Thea in particular, was arguably more excited about this adventure of mine than I was.

Montana, meet your newest resident: Piper Campbell.

I loved it here already.

The sky above me was blue with only a few wisps of feathered clouds. The sunshine was warm on my shoulders and the April air fresh in my nose. Any doubts I'd had about moving floated away in the mountain breeze.

Thea gave me one last squeeze for good measure, then stood back so her husband could take her place.

"Hey, boss." I gave Logan a mock salute as I infused the word *boss* with as much sarcasm as possible.

Logan chuckled, shaking his head as he came in for an embrace. His hug wasn't quite as enthusiastic as his wife's, but it was a close second. "It's good to see you."

"You too," I told him as he let me go. Then I gave him a diabolical smile. "It will be much easier to give you orders in person than over the phone."

"Maybe this was a bad idea." He frowned and looked over

my shoulder at his family's pilot standing on top of the plane's staircase. "Mitch, Ms. Campbell isn't staying after all. You'd better turn this thing around and take her back to the city."

"Ignore him!" I called over my shoulder to Mitch, who laughed and went back inside the plane.

I was Logan's assistant but gave him a hard time about who was really in charge. His ego could use a little razzing now and then. It was all in good fun because we both knew that I'd be lost without him. He was the best boss I could have ever asked for.

Logan took the backpack from my shoulder and slung it over his. "I'm glad you're here."

"So am I." I stepped around him, going right for the cutest little girl on the planet. "Charlie!"

She smiled and left Thea's side, rushing forward for a hug. "Hey, Piper."

"I've missed you, kiddo. I want to hear all about school and your soccer team."

"Okay." She smiled and took my hand, showing no signs of letting it go anytime soon.

Spending time with Charlie Kendrick was pure joy—except for the tiny pinch of longing that poked me in the side.

With her quiet voice and sweet nature, Charlie didn't act like a princess or a diva. She was a tomboy, much like I had been at her age. Instead of a tiara, she wore an old, faded baseball cap over her long, brown hair the same color as her dad's. There wasn't a stitch of pink or purple anywhere in sight.

If I could have had a little girl, I would have wanted one as precious and unique as Charlie.

I ignored the pinch and held out my free hand to fist-bump her little brother, Collin. "Hey, bud."

He gave me a shy smile but held fast to his dad's leg. Collin was destined to be beautiful, like his siblings. While Charlie took after Logan, Collin was the spitting image of his mother, with nearly black hair and rich, dark eyes.

I winked at him, then went over to the baby carrier where eight-month-old Camila was fast asleep. "I can't believe how much she's grown in four months," I told Thea as I looked adoringly at Camila's chubby cheeks.

"They always say time flies after you have children. It's the truth."

Another pinch, but I ignored it too.

I'd have to get over those now that I was living here. Whenever Logan and Thea had come to New York, I'd always volunteered to babysit the kids so their parents could have a night out, and I planned to do a lot more of that now that I was living in Montana.

I was determined to become Aunt Piper, blood relation be damned.

"How much stuff did you bring along?" Logan asked.

"Not much." I turned back to the plane as one of the attendants hauled a large suitcase down the stairs. "That case plus two more. The rest is in storage until I find a place here. Then I'll have it shipped out."

"All right." Logan smiled at Thea. "You guys get loaded up and I'll take care of the bags."

Twenty minutes later, my suitcases were in the back of Logan's beast of a silver SUV and we were headed down the highway toward my new hometown.

Lark Cove.

"It's so beautiful." My nose was practically pressed against the window as I soaked everything in. "It takes my breath away every time."

Tall evergreens lined the highway, towering above us into the bright sky. Past their thick trunks, the water of Flathead Lake rippled and glittered under the sun's rays.

Paradise.

"And now you get to live here." Logan smiled at me in his rearview mirror.

I smiled back, then returned to the scenery. "And now I get to live here."

My parents thought I was crazy for giving up my apartment in Manhattan to move to a small town in Montana I'd only visited once—maybe they were right. But I needed this change of pace.

I'd spent months grieving the death of my marriage. I'd come to terms with what I would and wouldn't have in my life. And when the dust had settled, I'd realized New York wasn't home anymore.

The only thing that had kept me in the city after Adam and I divorced had been my job. Working for Logan at the Kendrick Foundation, his family's charitable organization, was the best part of each day. But after a while, even work couldn't fill the lonely void.

This past Christmas, I'd confided in Thea that I was looking for a change and that it might involve me quitting. She'd passed it along to Logan, who had adamantly refused to accept my resignation. Instead, he'd offered to move me anywhere in the world to work remotely.

When he'd tossed out the idea of Montana, it had stuck. I could *see* myself living here.

I wanted empty highways instead of crowded city streets. I craved more space than the six-inch personal bubble people allowed me on the subway. I was sick and tired of seeing my ex-husband's face on every corner, plastered to buses and billboards.

So I'd waited out the winter, enduring the longest four months of my life while I hid behind the walls of my apartment.

Then I packed up my stuff, bid farewell to my family and friends and said good-bye to the city of my past.

Adam got to keep New York in our divorce.

I was taking Lark Cove, a town he hadn't ruined.

The thirty-minute drive from the airport to Lark Cove went by fast. While the kids laughed, Thea and I talked about her latest art project and how things were going at the bar she ran with her best friend. Logan tried to sneak in a few work topics, but his wife shut him down immediately, reminding him it could wait until the weekend was over.

And then, before I knew it, we were here. Home.

"Don't blink or you'll miss it," Logan teased as we passed a small green sign that read *Entering Lark Cove.*

My smile got wider, my dimples no doubt deepening. "It's better than I remember."

He drove slowly through the quaint town, letting me take in all of the businesses clustered along the highway. I saw things differently than when I'd come out here a few years ago for Logan and Thea's wedding. Then, I'd only been a tourist, excited to witness my boss get married.

Now I was a resident.

I was giddy at the prospect of grocery shopping at the small mercantile. Bob's Diner looked like my new favorite cheeseburger joint. When I went into Thea's bar, it would be as a regular patron.

And maybe one day, I'd meet a handsome man in town who'd be up for a casual, uncomplicated relationship.

The majority of the homes in Lark Cove were set behind the businesses along the highway. They were normal-sized homes situated in friendly blocks where everyone knew their neighbors.

On the other side of the highway, the lakeside, the homes were larger. They reminded me of the houses in the Hamptons, though not quite as big and more rustic lake house than beach chateau.

Logan turned off the highway toward the lakeside of town, following a quiet road that wrapped around the shoreline until he pulled up to a house that screamed Logan Kendrick.

It was all class, like the man himself: handsome, with its cedar shakes and gleaming windows and well-manicured lawn. The boathouse on the water was larger than most of the homes we'd passed in town. The loft above it was going to be my abode for the next couple of weeks or months, however long it took to buy my own place.

As Logan parked in the detached garage and shut off the SUV, Charlie hurried to unbuckle her seat belt. "Piper, do you want to see my fort?"

"You know it!" I told her, helping Collin free from his car seat. The two-year-old squirmed out and crawled to the front before I could stop him.

"Daddy! Daddy!" he yelled, then giggled as Logan swung him out of the car and tossed him into the air.

"Come on, little one," Thea said, opening the back door to get out Camila's carrier. "I bet you need a diaper change and a bottle."

Camila cooed at her mother, her tiny mouth forming a hint of a smile. The jury was out on which parent she took after, but I'd get a front-row seat to watch as she grew up.

I climbed out behind them all, deciding to leave my suitcases for the time being. I wanted to play with the kids some before dinner.

"When is the meeting with your realtor?" Thea asked as we walked toward the house.

"Tomorrow," I said as Charlie slipped her hand in mine. "He's got three places lined up for me to see."

"Want some company? Logan can watch the kids and I can tag along to give you the inside scoop on potential neighbors."

"You wouldn't mind? I'd love to have your input."

I'd thought of inviting Thea along on my house-hunting trip, but I didn't want to smother her. The last four months had been incredibly lonely, and since she was my only girlfriend in Lark Cove, the chances were real that she'd get sick of me soon.

"Of course I wouldn't mind," Thea said. "Though I should warn you, I'm probably going to become that friend who calls and texts too often. Have I mentioned that I'm really excited you're living here?"

She couldn't have known, but I'd really needed those words and the enthusiasm in her voice. Thea Kendrick was good people.

"Ready to see my fort?" Charlie asked.

I looked to Thea, just to make sure it was okay. She nodded and smiled. "I'll get Camila changed and fed, then we'll come find you. White wine or red?"

I amended my earlier thought. Thea Kendrick was *great* people. "White, please."

"You got it." She smiled and disappeared into the house with the baby.

"I'll take care of your suitcases," Logan told me as he set Collin down to go play in the yard. "You just relax."

"Thank you, Logan. For everything."

He patted my shoulder. "You're welcome. Glad you're home."

Home. I was home.

As he followed Collin to a stack of toys on the deck, I turned down to Charlie. "Fort time?"

She nodded. "Want to race?"

I slipped out of my four-inch stilettos. "Loser is a rotten egg!"

The next day, Thea and I were hiking through the trees behind the home my realtor had just shown us. This particular property was located in the mountains and had some acreage in the forest. So while the two of us were exploring, my realtor was back at the car, giving us a moment to debrief without him hovering.

"What do you think?" Thea asked.

"I don't know." I sighed. "That house is . . . there are no words."

She giggled. "I've never seen a house so dedicated to a decade."

"Ugh. Have you ever seen such hideous carpet? It was like the designer looked at an orange creamsicle and said, 'How can I turn this into a paisley shag?'"

"Exactly." She laughed again. "I can't get over those yellow cabinets in the kitchen. And that wallpaper? Lime green stripes should never be paired with beige."

I looked over my shoulder to the house and grimaced. It was an old-style rancher with three bedrooms, each needing a complete overhaul to bring them into this decade. Did I have it in me to take on such a large project?

This was our last showing of the afternoon. The first two homes we'd seen were in town. Both were nice, far better than this sixties monstrosity, but they were within twenty feet of a neighbor on each side.

I'd spent over a decade in apartment buildings and townhomes, sharing walls and public spaces with neighbors. I was ready to have some space.

"You're sure you don't want to look for something down along the lake?" Thea asked. "Something newer?"

"I just can't afford any of those listings right now." Only a few lakeside properties were on the market, and everything available was way outside of my budget.

Thanks for that, Adam. In a dick move, he'd contested our divorce, forcing me to spend a chunk of my savings on an expensive attorney.

So to stay within my price range, I'd have to purchase a house in the middle of Lark Cove or buy this one and do a complete renovation. The first choice was by far the easiest. But the latter option had its perks too.

This fifteen-acre property on the mountainside was gorgeous, and there was only one neighbor, a cabin about fifty yards away. It was close enough to run over in an emergency but far enough that I wouldn't have to see them unless it was intentional.

"I do like it up here in the mountains." Though Thea's lakeside home was peaceful, there was something enchanting about being surrounded by hundred-year-old trees. The forest smelled rich and mossy with a hint of pine spice in the air.

"It's a beautiful spot with your own hiking trail. You wouldn't have to worry about setting up a home gym. Just climb this every day and you'd be in killer shape."

"No kidding." I was breathing harder than I ever had in a spin class.

We continued our hike, going up the steady incline behind the house that led to a ridge at the back of the property. My realtor had pointed us in this direction, encouraging us to hike to the top.

He was a good salesman, that one. The farther away from the house we walked, the more I was willing to buy it just so I'd have this as my backyard.

By the time we reached the final stretch of the trail, my

thighs were burning. Sweat was beaded at my hairline and a drop rolled down my cleavage. I was comfortable in my cuffed boyfriend jeans and a casual T-shirt, but what I really should have worn was my gym attire.

"Almost there," I told Thea as the trees opened up and the ridge came into view.

We pushed through the last twenty feet and smiled at one another as the trail leveled off, turning to run along the ridge. We followed it, stepping into an open meadow filled with spring wildflowers.

"Wow," Thea whispered. "I'm starting to think a remodel is the way to go. Who cares what the house is like when you have this?" She held out her hands to the view.

"This is . . . unbelievable."

From here, the towering mountains were visible in the distance. The one we'd just climbed was no more than an anthill in comparison. The valleys below were green and lush. The horizon went on and on for miles, and nearly the entire lake spread out behind our backs.

"Let's keep going." I took one step farther down the trail, but Thea grabbed my arm, holding me back.

"Wait," she whispered, her eyes aimed ahead of us.

A momentary flash of panic hit. *Is it a bear?* I didn't want to get eaten by a bear on my first real day in Montana. Slowly, I turned and followed her gaze, my feet ready to bolt at the sight of a grizzly.

But it wasn't an animal that had caused her to freeze.

It was a man.

He was kneeling on the ground, about thirty feet in front of us. His head was bent and his eyes closed. His hands were pressed against his cheeks, his fingers straight as they steepled at the bridge of his nose.

Was he praying? Or meditating? Whatever he was doing, he was so consumed with it that he hadn't noticed us down the trail.

His shaggy brown hair curled around his ears and at the back of his neck. His jaw was covered in a dark beard that tried its best to hide the fact that its owner was likely quite handsome. His green shirt was strung tight across his biceps and broad shoulders. It showcased the corded muscles of his back.

Even from a distance it was clear that he was the quintessential mountain man, big and brawny.

My first instinct was to get closer. I wanted to see what his face looked like if his hands dropped. I wanted to see the breeze play at the curled ends of his hair. But besides his rugged appeal, there was something else drawing me in. Something that made me want to wrap my arms around his narrow waist and promise him it would be okay.

He had a tragic allure, one that screamed sorrow and loss. I knew that pain all too well. Recognition hit me in a flash and I spun around, hurrying back in the direction we'd come.

That man was up here to grieve, and we'd just intruded on his private moment.

Thea was right by my side as I hustled to the trees, doing my best to keep my footsteps quiet. I held my breath until we disappeared into the safety of the forest. Neither of us spoke as we hiked down the trail, retreating to the house.

"I hope he didn't hear us," Thea said.

"Me too. Do you know who that is?"

She shook her head. "No, I've never seen him before, which is strange. I know almost everyone in Lark Cove. I bet he's just visiting. We get a lot of tourists who come up and hike in the mountains."

I nodded as my realtor spotted us. "What did you think?

Nice spot, isn't it?"

"It's beautiful." Except when I took in the house's exterior, my face soured.

The house was a tribute to midcentury modern design with a plethora of windows and odd roof angles. It was as far from my traditional taste as you could get, and to renovate this into my forever home, I'd have to change everything.

My head ached just thinking about the construction bill.

"I can tell you the sellers are motivated on this one," my realtor said. "It belongs to a brother and sister who each live out of state. It was a vacation home for their parents, who have since both passed. It's been empty for about a year now."

Which explained the musty smell and the recent price drop.

"Can I think about it?" I asked him.

"Of course. Take all the time you need."

Thea gave me a reassuring smile, then got into the back of the car. I took one last look at the house, frowned again, then turned toward the trail we'd come down.

Find some peace. I sent my silent wish to the man on top of the mountain.

Pushing the stranger from my mind, I went to the other side of the car and got in the passenger seat. We drove down the long gravel driveway, then took yet another gravel road, this one wider and more traveled, that led back to the highway. With a wave good-bye from Thea's front yard, I promised my realtor I'd be in touch soon.

"How'd it go?" Logan asked the minute we came inside. Camila was crying as he rocked her in his arms and Collin was bawling into his leg.

"Uh, it was good," Thea said, eyeing her children. "What's going on here?"

Logan blew out a long breath and handed the baby over.

"These two have gone on a nap strike. While I was trying to get Camila down, Collin climbed out of his crib. He started crying and woke her up. It's been chaos ever since. Charlie escaped to her fort when the wailing started."

Thea laughed, then nuzzled Camila's cheek. "Come on, baby. Let's go cuddle."

Now that both arms were free, Logan picked up Collin and settled him on a hip. Collin rested his head on his dad's shoulder and his eyelids sagged.

"So did you find a place?" Logan asked, swaying his sleepy boy side to side.

I sighed. "There are options. Nothing is perfect, but I guess it never is. I was actually thinking about driving by them all again. Would you mind if I borrowed the Suburban?"

"Not at all." He led me to the kitchen and swiped keys off the counter, tossing them over. Then, as he headed toward Collin's room, I went outside and to the garage.

It took me the entire trip through town to get used to driving a vehicle two times the size of my Mini Cooper, but by the time I headed up the gravel road toward the mountain home, I'd gotten the hang of it.

The moment I parked under the tall canopy of trees, my gut began screaming, "This one! This one!" When I'd driven past the two homes in town, the only reaction I'd had was one burp.

I got out and surveyed the area again. This house might be hideous, but the location was serenity incarnate. I would have peace here. I would have quiet. I would—

A pained roar from across the trees startled me, and I looked toward the neighboring property. The moment my eyes landed on the log cabin nestled between tree trunks, a loud shout filled the air. "Fuck!"

I flinched again, then froze, listening for another sound. It didn't come. Was someone hurt? Should I go check?

There was a path between this house and theirs, so I took it, hurrying in case someone's life was at stake. I rushed right past ferns and forest bushes to the steps leading to the cabin's front door. Without delay, I pounded on the wooden face since there wasn't a doorbell. "Hello?"

Angry footsteps thudded on the floor. The entire porch shook and I backed up a step. My fist was still lifted when the door whipped open and none other than the man from the ridge appeared in its frame.

"What?" he snapped, planting his hands on his hips.

"I, uh . . ." Any other words I'd planned to speak fell away.

This man was even more handsome than I'd expected. He was tall, standing at least six inches above my five seven. His nose was maybe the most perfect nose I'd ever seen, straight with a strong bridge set perfectly in the center of his high cheekbones. But it was his eyes that swayed me sideways.

They weren't green or brown or gold, but this incredible swirl of all three. The ring around the edge was like melted chocolate.

I hadn't been with anyone since my ex-husband and I had separated over two years ago. A rush of desire, one I hadn't felt in a long time, rolled down my body. It pooled between my legs, curling in my belly as I raked my eyes over this man's thick chest and flat stomach.

The man's eyes flared as he looked me up and down. He tried to cover it up with annoyance, but there was lust in his darkening eyes.

"What?" he barked, louder this time.

I came unstuck, breathing again as I forced my eyes away from his soft lips. He had an old rag wrapped around one of his hands and blood was soaking through.

"I heard a crash so I thought I'd come over to see if every-thing was okay. Are you hurt?" I reached for him, but he jerked back.

"Fine," he grumbled. And with that, he spun around on his brown boots, stomped inside and shut the door.

"Seriously?" I whispered.

I gave him a moment to come back and be neighborly. I got nothing in return.

"Nice to meet you!" I waved at the closed door. "My name is Piper Campbell, in case you were wondering."

Nothing.

"I'm thinking about buying the place next door."

Still nothing.

"Great talk, uh . . ." I searched the porch, landing on a red and white cooler by the railing. *KAINE* was written on the handle in block letters. "See you around, Kaine."

My crazy was starting to show, so I turned around and walked back to the Suburban. The minute I hopped up into the driver's seat, I pulled out my phone from my handbag and dialed my realtor.

"Hi, it's Piper. I've given it some thought and made my deci-sion." My eyes stayed glued to the cabin across the way. "I want the mountain house. It's just what I need."

Some peace. The quiet forest. A project to throw myself into headfirst.

And maybe a hot, sweaty fling with my grouchy, soon-to-be-next-door neighbor.

He had no-strings-attached sex written all over his hand-some face.

two

KAINE

"**G**ODDAMN, SON OF A BITCH, MOTHERFUCKER!"
The hammer I'd just smashed into my knuckle fell out of my grip, dropping right onto my toe.

"Shit!" I chucked the chisel in my throbbing hand across the shop. It crashed into a stack of wooden dowels along the wall, rattling them before falling to the ground.

The noise outside was driving me insane, and I couldn't *fucking* concentrate.

I'd been in the middle of carving a notch into a maple board. The table I'd designed used various notches and grooves to fit together. Not only because they were sturdy but because they lent detail to this particular piece's unique design. It was like a puzzle and each piece had to be made with precision.

This particular board had ten notches. Right as I'd been about to finish the last, a loud crash had boomed outside and made me flinch. The hammer I'd just raised came down at the wrong angle, moving too fast. It hit the end of my chisel, sending it too deep into the wood before skidding off and bashing my thumb's knuckle.

Not only did my hand hurt, now I'd have to remake this piece and the nine other notches I'd just spent an hour carving.

I was already behind on this project because my client had

changed their mind on the type of wood three times. By the time they'd finally settled on maple, my supplier had been on back order. I was in a rush to finish this table by the deadline, and mistakes would only set me back further.

I'd been making stupid mistakes like this for a week, all because of the fucking noise.

All because of my *fucking* neighbor.

It had been a month since that woman had shown up on my doorstep. I'd spent two days after her arrival dreading the idea of company up here. I'd gotten used to living up here alone. Even before my former neighbors had passed, they hadn't been here much. So when she'd stayed away for weeks, I'd figured she'd given up.

I'd relaxed, glad I wouldn't have to share this mountainside.

Then a week ago, right as the May flowers had begun to bloom, an Airstream had backed into her driveway.

After that, a construction crew had arrived. They'd been making noise ever since, starting at dawn and ending after dark.

Another crash sounded outside, forcing me up from my stool.

"Fuck, I give up." I'd have to come back late tonight and pray I could focus.

I bent and picked up the hammer by my boot, taking it to my workbench, where each tool had its rightful place on the plethora of hooks and shelves. I hung up the hammer, then went to retrieve the chisel. It got placed in a drawer, third spot from the left.

My tools were priceless. I treated them arguably better than I treated myself. But along with my hands, they kept me fed.

When I'd finished trade school, I'd made the decision to invest in the highest-quality tools on the market. Like a painter used brushes and oils to craft beauty, I used calipers and carvers.

Planes and spokeshaves. Files and rasps. They were all top-of-the-line. And my power tools, the saws and shapers and presses, were worth more combined than my truck.

To use them all effectively, I had to concentrate. To concentrate, I required silence.

Three years ago, that construction crew could have made all the noise in the world and it wouldn't have bothered me. Back then, my shop had been in the middle of an industrial park. Traffic would continuously whiz by. Visitors from nearby businesses would stop by to bullshit and drink my strong coffee. I used to work with rock and roll turned up to eleven.

That was before.

Now, the only sounds I allowed in my shop were those from my power tools. I tolerated the forest's noise but would close the overhead door if the wind blew too loudly in the trees or the birds chirped obnoxiously.

I'd grown accustomed to quiet.

If they couldn't keep it down next door, I was going to lose my goddamn mind.

Maybe I already had.

What the fuck was she doing over there anyway? She had five guys over there, destroying the place. She was living in an Airstream with the generator kicking on and off at all hours. Was she trying to make my life a living hell?

Since work was out of the question, I shut off the lights to the shop and locked the door. No one ever came up here and I hadn't locked up in ages. But that woman and her minions made me nervous, and I'd decided last week not to take the chance that my tools would find themselves in the bed of someone else's truck.

Who knew what kind of people she'd hired? Or what kind of person she was? She obviously didn't have any boundaries.

She'd come marching over to my property without an invitation last month. Then when I'd sent her as clear a *get fucking lost* message as you could get, she'd shouted at me through the door I'd slammed in her face.

Who did that?

"I'm not crazy," I muttered as I walked up the small path that led to my house. "She's the crazy one."

My neighbor. The thought irritated me to no end. I hadn't bothered to get to know the previous owners. They'd been an older couple who'd come and gone for vacations, never once bothering to introduce themselves. Just how I liked it.

But then there was this one. What was her name?

Piper. Piper Campbell. God, even her name annoyed me.

Why? I wasn't sure. Probably because of how quickly *Piper* had gotten under my skin.

I glanced down at my palm. The scab that had reminded me of her for a month was nearly gone now. The day she'd come over, I'd just sliced a gash in my hand.

I was peeling an apple that afternoon, trying to remove the skin in one long spiral. It was something my mom had always been able to do. I was half asleep from too little sleep for too many years, and after a long hike that morning, my muscles were weak. The knife slipped, cutting deep into the fleshy part of my palm.

After throwing the knife and the apple across the room, I scrambled for a rag. The cut bled like a bastard, and I was trying to staunch the flow when Piper knocked on my door.

One look at her and the pain in my hand vanished. Her chestnut hair was long and full, parted in a perfectly straight line down the middle. It hung past her shoulders in thick, silky strands. Her deep-set eyes were the color of my favorite dark-roast wood stain.

Her lips were plump beneath the regal bridge of her nose. The green forest light illuminated her olive skin. Her classic beauty was out of place on my dusty porch.

My body responded immediately to the swell of her breasts and the lush curve of her hips. After three years of living in solitude with limited social interaction, I'd all but forgotten how quickly my dick could harden at the sight of a beautiful woman.

Or maybe it was just her.

My body's reaction only fueled my anger, so I shut the door on her stunning face.

Though the damage had been done. Every one of her features had been imprinted on my brain, and I'd been unable to block them out since.

I stepped up onto my porch, picturing her in this exact spot, and glanced over to her place. Was she remodeling it? Or tearing it down?

Curiosity got the better of me and I turned, retreating down the stairs I'd just climbed. The old path between our properties was overgrown but still passable thanks to the deer that kept it broken in.

I walked toward her property, not planning on getting too close. I had no desire to speak to anyone today—or any day. But when I saw the disaster this woman had created, my footsteps just got faster.

"You're fucking kidding me." I shook my head, gritting my teeth as I scanned the area.

The construction workers had brought in a large metal Dumpster. It was parked between our properties, overflowing with broken boards and sheetrock. Old ceiling panels stuck out of one end.

And what wouldn't fit in the Dumpster was now scattered on the ground.

There were Formica countertops crushing bushes. Yellow cabinets were stacked up against a young tree. Rolls of old carpet were scattered over the forest floor.

My forest floor.

Piper's house was built on the edge of her property, much like mine. The two places hugged the boundary line between our individual acreage. The logic behind that decision was a damn mystery. Maybe the people who'd originally built on these properties thought neighbors were a good thing.

But since I didn't, the proximity of our homes had always bothered the hell out of me.

When I'd first moved up here, I'd contemplated having my cabin relocated to the center of my fifteen-acre plot. But when I'd learned that my neighbors were never here, I'd decided to just let it be.

Big fucking mistake.

I should have moved my cabin. Better yet, I should have bought her property and guaranteed myself the seclusion. But since I was a furniture maker, not a billionaire, I hadn't had that option.

Funerals were expensive.

I'd been lucky just to pay for my own property and have enough left over to build my shop.

My savings account was slowly growing again because I didn't need much to live on. I didn't eat out or go to bars or buy new clothes. My only expenses were groceries, utilities and the cell phone I rarely used.

But as I reached the invisible line between our properties, I cursed myself for not taking out a loan to buy her place.

Trash was everywhere. I spotted more yellow cabinets and some scraps of lime-green wallpaper. Was that a teal refrigerator?

It was.

And it was on my property along with the rest, infecting my life with its hideousness.

I looked away from the mess and aimed my glare at the house just as the front door burst open. A stream of five workers barreled out, laughing and clapping one another on their backs. Now that they'd spread destruction all over my property, they were probably off early this Friday afternoon, ready for a beer at the Lark Cove Bar.

The workers piled into a line of trucks parked along the drive and, one by one, pulled away. Not a single one had noticed me. I stood, scowling at their taillights until all that was left was the distant rumble of engines.

With them gone, I went right to the Airstream and pounded on the silver door.

Piper's clown car was parked behind the camper. The car was too damn cute, too trendy to belong up here. My eyes were narrowed at the car when the latch to the door clicked open.

"I thought you all just left for the day." Piper was smiling as the door swung open. Her dimples were also too damn cute. They disappeared along with her smile when she saw it was me at her door, not a crew member.

My gaze roamed her face, picking it apart and searching for things I didn't like. But I came up empty.

Son of a bitch. I liked it all, from her big eyes to her narrow nostrils to her flat chin. I even liked her teeth that were too white.

"Can I help you?" She held the door open but didn't step down.

"What the fuck is going on here?"

She blinked, then her mouth turned down. "Excuse me?"

"What. The fuck. Is going on here?" I repeated, then pointed behind me to the pile of shit on my property. "What is all of that?"

She looked over my head to where I was still pointing. "That would be garbage. I'm renovating my house."

"Why is it on my property?"

Her eyes narrowed, though they were still too fucking big. "It's not on your property. It's on mine."

"No. It's on mine," I said through gritted teeth.

"You're wrong." She cocked a hip. "After I bought this place, I had the county come and stake out the property line. I was thinking of putting in a fence to keep the neighbors out."

Neighbors? I was her only neighbor. But if she wanted a fence, I wouldn't balk. Hell, at the moment, a fence sounded fantastic. Maybe it would block out some of the noise. Maybe it would be easier to pretend this beautiful, irritating woman wasn't so close.

Piper crossed her arms and moved down the metal steps, forcing me backward. "See those stakes, right there and there? The ones with the neon-orange ribbons on them?" She pointed to a stake at the back corner of her house and then at another down the hill in the trees.

I grunted, wishing I'd noticed the stakes before trudging over here.

"That is my property line," she declared. "And—now use your imagination here—if you pretend to draw a line between stake number one and stake number two, you'll see the pile of trash is on my property. As is the neighbor I'd hoped to keep out with the fence."

I grunted again.

It was a pitiful response given how badly I'd underestimated Piper.

She was standing close to me. Really close. Closer than I'd been to a woman in years. She was wearing a thin, white tank top. The neckline was cut low enough that the tops of her breasts showed. Two faint freckles dotted her creamy skin, just above her cleavage.

"Did you need something else, Kaine?" Her voice dripped with sarcasm as she drawled my name.

I forced my eyes away from her breasts. "Just . . . just keep your shit off my property."

"Fine."

"And keep the noise down. It's bothering me."

"Tough," she snapped.

"Tough?"

"Listen, *neighbor.* I'm paying a small fortune for this construction crew to work overtime and remodel my house. I don't give a rip if the noise bothers you. I'm living in a camper, right next to the noise, and working from a table that doubles as a guest bed. If I can deal with it, so can you."

"Keep it down or I'll call the cops."

She huffed. "And tell them what? That there are people working next door? I can hear the dispatcher laughing at you already."

"God, you're a piece of work."

"And it's time for you to run along." She flung out a hand, waving me away. "Go be grumpy somewhere else."

"Keep it down. I'm warning you." I stepped closer, using my height to intimidate her.

But instead of backing away, she locked her jaw and stepped closer. Those incredible tits nearly brushed my chest. "Or what? Huh? What are you going to do?"

That damn, smart mouth.

We stood there, glaring at one another. The inch between us was filled with hate, our mutual annoyance and frustration a tangible wall between us. And then, as a slight breeze swished over us, the wall just . . . blew away.

My breaths were coming in heavy pants, not from anger, but lust. My brain screamed for me to step away, but my feet were rooted to the gravel.

Piper was breathing hard too. Each time her chest rose, her breasts skimmed my T-shirt. The heat from her cheeks spread down her chest, tinting her creamy skin a pale pink. Her dark eyes flashed, melting from cool indifference to scorching lust.

She wanted me. That flash in her eyes was unmistakable and it flipped my switch.

Off to on.

I crushed my lips down on hers, swallowing a gasp, then a moan as her hands slid up my chest. My fingers dove into her silky hair, letting the thick, luscious strands weave through my fingers.

What the hell was I doing? I'd come over here to put my neighbor in her place. Not to kiss her. The smart thing to do would be to stop this and let her put up that fence. But as she moaned again, stopping was no longer an option.

I slid my tongue into her mouth, finding hers hot and wet. The intensity of our argument carried into our kiss, our tongues dueling as they tangled and twisted.

Piper gripped the cotton of my shirt, fisting it in her hands. She pulled me forward, forcing her lips harder into mine, pushing her tongue deeper.

She might want control of this kiss, but *tough*. She wasn't going to get it.

My fingers slipped from her hair, and I wrapped my arms around her back. With one fast tug, I smashed our bodies together. Her breasts were crushed between us.

Piper let out a tiny whimper, the sound filling my ears and drowning out everything else but this woman.

She was everywhere. Her taste flooded my mouth, a

mixture of mint and strawberry. The smell of her hair overpowered the musk from the trees, filling my nose with sweet florals and citrus. Her touch was electric, heating my skin in the cool spring air.

Her hands traveled around my waist, drifting lower. Her fingertips dug hard into my ass, and she used her grip on the canvas of my Carhartt pants to pull my hips closer.

I thrust my erection forward, pressing the entire length against her, making her breath hitch.

What were we doing? The question went in and out of my head in a fleeting second. Who cared what we were doing? It felt so fucking good—it had been so damn long—that I cursed myself for not taking this kiss a month ago.

"Kaine," Piper moaned, her hands gripping my ass with daring ferocity.

I returned the gesture, unwrapping my arms from her back so I could squeeze her luscious ass like a stress ball. I wanted to make her cheeks red as punishment for the smart mouth she'd given me earlier.

As I squeezed tighter, she yelped, then nipped my lower lip.

The sting in my lip drove me over the edge, sending me flying from lust to desperation. Step after step, I walked us backward toward the camper. For once, Piper didn't fight me. Her sandals shuffled over the driveway until her back hit the Airstream.

We broke apart as I pressed her against the shining aluminum, giving me a chance to take her in. Piper's cheeks were flushed rosy. Her lips were wet and swollen. And her hooded eyes were full of want, not a flicker of regret or shock anywhere in sight.

I was studying those puffy lips as the corners turned up in a smirk. Before I could make sense of it, her arm shot out to the side and she flipped open the camper door that had swung shut.

I ground my throbbing cock into her hip, making sure she understood that when we went inside that camper, there was no turning back. "How far do you want to take this?"

She didn't hesitate. "All the way."

Our mouths collided in another scorching kiss that sent us stumbling toward the door. My hands went under her knees and with one hoist, her legs were wrapped around my waist. Her pulsing hot center rubbed against my cock, making it weep.

It had been over three years since I'd been with a woman. My stamina was shot, and with the way she attacked me, this would be over not long after it started. But no matter how much I ached to come, I'd be sure she got there first. Maybe I'd surprise her by not being a complete asshole today.

I took the metal step into the camper with Piper in my arms. She held tight to my shoulders, letting her hair drape around us as her tongue licked my bottom lip like a lollipop. She did it again and I nearly exploded.

I growled and yanked my mouth away from hers, willing my self-control to hold. Then I took in the camper. The bedroom was at the opposite end, too far away, but the couch was just to my right.

One step in that direction and Piper knew our destination. She unwrapped her legs, dropping her feet to the floor, and immediately went for the button of my pants. While she tugged it loose, I reached behind my head, fisting a handful of cotton, and sent my shirt flying over my head.

"Get your top off," I ordered, needing to see her tits bouncing free.

She obeyed, whipping it over her head while I toed off my shoes and socks.

"Damn." My mouth went dry, seeing her before me in just

a pale-pink lace bra.

She grinned, then unhooked the center, setting herself free.

I staggered sideways, thunderstruck. Her full breasts bounced and swayed. Her nipples were hard and dark and begging for my tongue. Even as she unbuttoned her jeans, I kept my focus on those perfect globes just waiting to be cupped in my hands.

The second she kicked her pants free, I was on her, filling my palms. Her skin was smoother than the finest sawdust. The moan that escaped her lips was more intoxicating than my favorite malt whiskey.

She arched her back into my touch, her eyes drifting closed. She let out another moan as I massaged her curves, and in that sound, I heard it.

Starvation.

She was as deprived for touch as I was. How long had she gone without?

Her hands came on top of mine, pressing them deeper. Her hips rolled, searching for a touch. Was the center of those matching lace panties soaking wet?

My cock was aching to escape my zipper and rub against her soft flesh. As I leaned in closer, Piper took her hands off mine and let them drop to my zipper. I hadn't bothered with boxers this morning, so with a quick flick of her wrist, my dick was free and bobbing between us.

Piper gripped my shaft, stroking as I continued massaging her breasts and tugged at her nipples. Her thumb came to the crown, spreading the drop of pre-come around the head.

"Fuck," I hissed. If she continued, I'd come in her hand. "Get those panties off. Then get on the couch."

She dropped my cock, her mesmerizing eyes flaring as she

stripped bare. Then she laid back on the couch, her gaze zeroing in on my erection. "You're . . ."

Big. The unspoken word echoed in the camper.

The corners of my mouth turned up as her cheeks reddened. Her hungry expression boosted my ego, something I appreciated today since this wasn't going to last longer than ten minutes, fifteen tops.

I gripped my shaft, holding it between us as she tossed one leg on the back of the couch. She was wet, practically dripping, and the sight of her bare lips sent me scrambling toward the couch. I knelt down and inched close, then without delay, I positioned and thrust deep.

Piper cried out, her head digging into the couch cushion. I squeezed my eyes shut, not moving an inch for fear that I'd lose control and come.

This woman. Her pussy was perfect. She was tight and wet and hot. She clenched around me once, already close to coming, so I found her clit with the pad of my thumb and circled.

"Oh, god. More." She arched up her hips, sending me even deeper.

I pulled out slowly, my thumb never stopping, then slammed in hard. Piper cried out as another spasm rocked through her core. The squeeze was unbearable, incredible torture. My teeth clamped on the inside of my cheek, biting down hard. The pain distracted me just enough to endure the rhythm as I pounded into her.

We fucked hard and fast. Piper braced her arms on the wall above her head and met my strokes one after the other.

A slight gasp and a shudder were the only warnings she gave before her inner walls bared down on me and she detonated. Her torso jerked off the couch, her body at the mercy of her orgasm.

When she started to come down, I left her clit and cupped her breasts, letting them fill the emptiness of my hands. Then I unleashed, hammering into her until I couldn't take it anymore and tipped over the edge.

White spots burst behind my vision and every muscle in my body shook as I sent stream after stream into her tight body. My heart was thundering and my hands shaking when I finally felt my release subside.

Piper was flushed and beautiful, staring up at me with those big damn eyes. Some of the lust had disappeared, revealing their normal color. They weren't just brown, but a unique mixture of chocolate dipped in honey.

A man could disappear into those eyes. He could get lost and never want to be found.

Outside, a hawk screamed. With his piercing cry, the situation I'd put myself in came rushing back. I'd just fucked a perfect stranger on a camper couch with thin cushions and scratchy upholstery.

I'd just fucked my new neighbor.

Without a condom.

"Son of a bitch." I slid out and stood, going straight for my pants.

"What's wrong?" Piper sat up and wiped the hair from her face before swiping her shirt from the floor to cover her chest.

What's wrong? I didn't need this complication. I didn't need my neighbor's noisy distractions. I didn't need her constant temptation.

I stepped into my pants, tucking away my still-hard cock. "We didn't use a condom."

"Damn it." She sighed and closed her eyes. "I'm clean. And I'm protected against, um . . . pregnancy."

Thank the fucking stars for that. "I'm clean too."

"Good." She nodded, still not looking at me.

I wasn't sure if she was giving me an out or if she needed a moment of her own to regret fucking her neighbor, but I didn't ask. I gathered my shoes, socks and shirt, then bolted out the camper's door.

three

PIPER

I FUCKED MY NEIGHBOR.

Honestly, I never thought it would happen. Was I intrigued by my sexy neighbor? Sure. Did casual, hot sex with a man who had muscles upon muscles sound appealing? Absolutely. What recently divorced, single female wouldn't want a guy like Kaine to make her see stars?

He was the unintended perk of picking this house as my forever home. From day one, I'd hoped to get to know him intimately. I'd earmarked him as a potential Post-Divorce Fling.

But I'd never *really* expected it to happen.

And certainly not the week I'd moved in.

At thirty-two years old, I'd been with two men. One was my high-school boyfriend of three years. The other, my ex-husband who I'd met in the dorms our freshman year of college. We'd dated for four years before getting married after graduation.

I hadn't flirted with a man in over a decade. My skills at picking up a man weren't just rusty, they'd never existed in the first place. So the fact that I'd just had sex with my neighbor was more than just shocking, it was unreal.

If not for Kaine's semen sticking between my thighs, I would have sworn I'd fallen asleep after lunch and had one hell of a wishful dream.

When my marriage had imploded, I'd thought about going down to a corner bar and finding a random hookup. But I'd never had the courage. Now I was glad that I'd stayed home all those lonely nights.

Kaine had been the right choice for my first foray into casual sex.

I stared up at the camper's ceiling and ran my fingers over my lips. Kaine's beard had rubbed the skin around my mouth raw. My nipples had suffered under the rough calluses of his fingers. And my vagina would be sore for a day.

It was the best I'd felt in years.

I searched for a tinge of regret but came up empty. My only wish was for a bathtub instead of the camper's narrow shower.

I sat up and fished for my panties with a toe. I stood, then gathered the rest of my clothes scattered across the floor. Carrying them down to the bedroom, I paused as I passed the large window by the dining table.

From here, only the corner of Kaine's log cabin and its green tin roof were visible. But just that small glimpse made me smile because he was in there, hiding from me.

"That was either the dumbest thing I've done in years or the smartest." I touched my lips again.

Smartest.

My ex and I'd had a great sex life. At least, we had at the beginning of our marriage before the scheduled sex took the fun out of it. And I'd always considered Adam an incredible lover.

I'd been missing out. Kaine and I might have gone quick, but that fifteen minutes was the best sex I'd had in my life.

I wanted to shout it to the treetops and scream with glee.

Sex with Kaine was just another reminder that the love I'd thought would last my lifetime, the love I'd thought ran bone-deep, really just stopped under the surface.

For months, I'd been single. For years, I'd been separated from my husband, waiting for our divorce to go through. And though signing divorce papers had been a milestone, the legal declaration of my single status, today had been the turning point.

I wasn't just proclaiming that I was over Adam—words without action always felt empty. Today, I'd taken action. I'd had sex with another man. I'd jumped off the boat into new waters.

I was swimming with fast, sure strokes into a future of my own making.

Dumping all of my clothes into the hamper, I went to the bathroom and turned on the shower. While the water warmed, I went to the mirror and giggled at my flushed cheeks. Kaine might regret what we'd done, but he'd left behind a look of utter satisfaction on my face.

Steam filled the room quickly and I hurried into the stall. I didn't get luxuriously long showers in my Airstream, but the hot water was enough to relax away the stiffness in my shoulders.

When I stepped out and tied up my hair in a towel, I met my own smile in the mirror. Should I be this happy? Shouldn't there be *some* worry rattling around in my brain after having sex with a stranger? I searched again for a ping of shame.

And again, I came up empty.

Wearing only my towels, I went to the fridge and got out the chardonnay I'd put in there last night. I poured myself a healthy glass and sat on the couch. As I sipped, a grin tugged at the corners of my mouth.

Kaine had run out of here so fast, he'd probably pulled a muscle in one of his bulging thighs. He'd been so angry when he'd stormed over here earlier, so sure that my renovation trash had encroached onto his property.

The look on his face when I'd pointed out those two

property-line markers had been priceless.

A giggle slipped loose, followed by another. Then the dam broke, sending me into a fit of hysteria as I set down my wine and laughed so hard there were happy tears.

I'd missed laughing. I'd missed feeling carefree.

I'd missed being . . . myself.

Kaine couldn't know, but what he'd done for me this afternoon had broken the chains I'd wrapped around my heart these last few years.

With each negative pregnancy test, I'd wrapped a chain. With the test results from our fertility doctor, I'd added a lock to the chains. When Adam had admitted to kissing his costar, I'd added an anchor.

Those chains had become a shield, one I'd retreated behind years ago.

Slowly, I was casting them away.

My phone rang on the counter by the sink and I got up, holding my towel secure to my boobs as I answered Thea's call. "Hey!"

I'd missed her earlier today when I'd gone down to work for a few hours with Logan in his home office. She'd already been off to work at the bar.

"Hey! Want to come down to the bar for dinner? Logan is at home with the kids, and there's a pretty good after-five crowd in here so it could be fun. A few of your construction workers just walked in."

As tempting as it was to go down and gorge myself on pizza and an amber ale, I wasn't up for it. I wasn't a *leave the house make-up-free with wet hair* kind of woman, and I didn't have the energy to do myself up. I wanted to spend the rest of the evening relaxing and reveling in my postcoital bliss.

"I think I'm going to pass tonight. I'm wiped. Rain check?"

"Of course. I'll be here." There was a smile in Thea's voice. She didn't need to work, not with Logan's vast fortune, but she loved being part owner of the Lark Cove Bar. It was her passion.

Just like working for the Kendrick Foundation was mine. It wasn't glamorous. I was on the stage crew, watching from the curtains as men like Logan and our CEO got the standing ovations for the work we did to change people's lives. But I wouldn't have it any other way.

"Okay, I'll see you tomorrow?" Thea asked.

"Yes. Logan and I have a conference call with the New York crew at ten. I'll stop and get us all lattes from the hut."

"Have I mentioned how happy I am that you're living here?"

I smiled. "Once or twice."

"Bye."

I said my farewell, then set down the phone on the counter. With my wine in hand, I went to the bathroom and unwrapped my hair. I'd been blessed with a head of thick, silky hair, but it required a hair dryer to keep straight.

Air-drying was not an option if I didn't want to wake up with kinks on one side and a flat spot on the other. So I got out the blow dryer and went about taming my tresses. The generator kicked on with my hair dryer, and I gave myself a diabolical grin in the mirror.

Could Kaine hear my generator? Did it annoy him too? Maybe he'd get mad about the noise again and come over for another round on the couch.

As I dried my hair, I saw dimples each time I caught my reflection. The grouchy man next door had turned me into a smiling fool, and I didn't even know his last name.

Kaine had left here in such a hurry, there was no way he felt the same about our encounter. But after the shock subsided, I hoped he'd feel differently.

When I'd seen him on the ridge last month, he'd been shrouded in agony. He'd shown up at my camper with the same tortured heart—pain lurked behind his colorful eyes. It rippled over each of his muscles, floating underneath his skin.

My only regret from earlier was that our sex had been so fast and consuming, I'd missed the chance to give him one tender touch.

Kaine had helped me over a hurdle today. In turn, I wanted to erase a bit of his pain, even if it was only a pinch.

With my hair dry and resting over my shoulders, I put my hair dryer and round brush away just as my phone rang again from out in the kitchen. If it was Thea, I'd have a harder time saying no to an evening at the bar now that my hair was dry.

The task was always a feat, but with it done, it wouldn't take much to summon the energy for makeup. I was contemplating eye shadow palettes as I picked up the phone.

Adam.

When would he stop calling? Hadn't we said all there was to say?

I hadn't seen my ex-husband in person since the day the judge had finally granted me a divorce. Though, it hadn't stopped me from seeing his face throughout the city. Adam was the star of a hugely successful Broadway play, so his chiseled jaw, blue eyes and blond hair were plastered all over Manhattan.

They popped up on my screen with every one of his phone calls.

God, I wanted the ability to ignore him. I wanted so badly to hit decline and block him out of my mind. But I'd never declined a call from Adam. Not once.

I'd missed some calls over the years. I'd let some go to voicemail if I was heading into a meeting or if my hands were full. But I'd never made the conscious choice to actually decline, not even as we'd been going through the divorce.

Why was it so hard to cut him out of my life? Less than an hour ago, I'd thought I was over this and moving on. But with just his name on the screen, the ache from our failed marriage was creeping its way back in.

My finger hovered over the red circle to decline. *Push it.* As it came down on the green circle instead, my heart sank. I pressed the phone to my ear. "Hi."

"Hello." Adam's smooth voice rolled over my skin like oil. For years, I'd called him just to hear his hello. His voice had once been the balm to soothe my hurting heart.

Kaine's voice was the exact opposite. It was deeper, gruff and unrefined. He'd only spoken to me twice, both times with anger, giving his tone an additional bite. Yet I couldn't get it out of my head. It overpowered Adam's greeting.

"Piper?"

"I'm here."

"How are you?"

I was good—on the road to fantastic. At least, I had been until this call. "What do you want, Adam?"

"I was just checking in. Wanted to see how your project is going."

My project. I slid into the bench seat at my small table and looked out the Airstream's window to my future home. "It's coming along."

The construction crew had nearly completed demolition. They'd ripped out all of the old finishes, carpet, cabinets and countertops. They'd already torn out one of the walls I was taking down between the kitchen and living room to brighten up the space. And they'd marked out places where we could add windows so the forest's magical light would seep inside.

I smirked at the pile of trash next to the property line. The crew had gotten on a roll with demo, and rather than stop and wait for the industrial-sized Dumpster to be emptied, they'd piled junk beside the full one. My plan was to turn that area into a flower garden, so the bushes and shrubs in that area were getting ripped out anyway.

Kaine was averse to yellow cabinets and old carpet. How would he react to rose bushes?

"Are you happy with the crew you hired?" Adam asked.

"Yes." I might be unable to decline his calls, but I didn't feel the need to elaborate with long sentences.

"Are you, uh . . . seeing anyone?" Adam asked.

I rolled my eyes. He asked me that question every time we spoke.

Though I was tempted to say yes just to hear his reaction, I answered honestly. "No. I'm not seeing anyone."

"That's good. That's . . . great." He was overly happy about it, victorious even. "Listen, I ran into Gin Kaneko a couple of days ago. I mentioned to him that you're renovating a house. He offered to make you a dining room table."

"Really? I'd lov—" I stopped myself.

Out of habit, I'd nearly accepted the offer. Gin Kaneko was a well-known furniture designer to the wealthy elite. He'd done a few pieces for our home at one point, and his current waiting list was six years long.

As a local celebrity, Adam had connections all over New York, so getting elusive material items wasn't hard for him. There was no such thing as a waiting list. Whether it be clothing or art, he used to come home every other week with something only available to people who ran in the right social circles.

The *rich* social circles.

And normally, I'd jump so fast at Gin's offer my head would spin. But not today.

Gin's style was minimalistic with an Asian flair, true to his roots. His pieces were stunning and had gone beautifully in the modern home I'd shared with Adam. The museum with white walls, white floors and white ceilings.

Except I wasn't going for minimalistic or modern in my new home. I was going for rich and colorful. I wanted beautiful pieces full of details. I craved a life full of messes and dirty dishes and piles of laundry.

"Please give Gin my deepest appreciation," I told Adam. "But no, thank you."

"W-what?"

"It's not the style I'm going for in this new house."

His frown was audible. "You love Gin's work."

"Yes, I do. But I'm doing something different with this home. Something . . . me."

Not me and Adam. Just me.

"I didn't realize my style was so different than your own," he snapped. "Many seem to share my tastes."

"I'm going for something different. Something warmer." I got up from the table and went down the short hall to the bedroom.

For too many years I'd protected his ego, stroked it even. This would have been the point in previous conversations where I'd spend ten minutes complimenting his style. But we weren't married anymore, and his ego was no longer my problem.

So I let him huff as I pressed the phone between my ear and shoulder. With it wedged tight, I stripped off my towel and slipped on some clean panties.

"Warmer," he repeated, his tone full of disdain.

"Yes, warmer."

Adam's mother was a well-known architect in New York. She'd become quite famous over the years, designing expensive homes and penthouses for the city's social climbers. And she'd imprinted her style on Adam from an early age.

He probably took my critique as a snub to his mother.

But since she'd all but disowned me during the divorce, after years of telling me I was the daughter she'd never had, I didn't care if I offended either of them.

"I want a house that's cozy," I told him as I hiked up some leggings. "One where you can tell that people actually live there. I might even get some magnets for the refrigerator. I don't know, I, uh . . ." I needed both hands to get my breasts covered. "Hold on a second."

I didn't miss his huff before I tossed the phone on my bed and stuffed myself into a sports bra. My breasts had developed early and hadn't stopped growing until my junior year in high school. I was a solid double D, too big to avoid underwire most days, but I'd found a few high-end sports bras that gave the girls a good lift and had a cool crisscross pattern on the back.

I wasn't going to be a women's fitness model any day, but my curvy hips and great bust looked pretty damn good in spandex.

After tugging on a slouchy green tank, I went back to the phone. "Okay, I'm back." And I was done with this conversation. "Was there something else you needed?"

"No. I just wanted to talk. I'm sorry about the furniture. I didn't realize you were so unhappy with the style we'd picked for our home. If I'd known, we could have done something different."

Damn him. He'd annoyed me with his attitude, so much that I'd been ready to hang up. But then he said things like that and in rushed the guilt.

It was no secret he hadn't wanted our divorce. He'd wanted to stay together to work on our marriage. I'd called a lawyer.

"Adam—"

"Are you okay? Everything good?"

I nodded, hating the heartbreak that laced his voice. I hated knowing I was the reason he was lonely right now.

"Piper?"

"Yes." I cleared the lump from my throat. "Yes, I'm good."

"I wish you were still here. I was craving a hot dog for dinner, but I can't go to Gray's Papaya without you."

That restaurant had been our spot in college. Any time one of us had an important exam, we'd go there afterward to celebrate. Except as soon as Adam had turned twenty-five, he'd deemed hot dogs contraband. Our home hadn't just been devoid of color but junk food too. I'd brought home a bag of Cheetos once and he'd acted like I'd brought in the bubonic plague.

"You don't eat hot dogs anymore, remember?"

He chuckled. "I would have been willing to break a rule."

My eyes closed and I sank down to the edge of the bed. "Did you get the key?"

"I did. Though you could have given it to me directly."

"I forgot."

We both knew I was lying because I never forgot anything.

I'd brought the key to our home, the one where Adam still lived, with me to Montana. I don't know why I hadn't just left it with the doorman. Or why I hadn't set it on the counter when I'd moved out. But I'd taken it with me during both moves, keeping it on the same keychain it had been on since we'd bought the place.

The day I'd closed on my home in Lark Cove, I'd mailed the key to New York.

"What if you want to come home?" he asked softly. "How will you get in?"

I sighed. "I'm not coming back."

"But Pip, you love the city."

I cringed at the nickname, one that he'd given me our first year together. While we'd been happy and he'd been my Good Guy, I hadn't minded when Adam called me Pip. But things were different and he didn't get to use old nicknames.

"Piper," I corrected.

He grumbled something into the phone, chasing away the softness in his voice. "I can't believe this is where we are. You've thrown everything away because of a kiss."

"Me?" Rage ran through my veins, burning away the guilt. "You did this. Not me. You threw us all away when you kissed another woman."

"She was a costar."

I shot off the bed. "Were you on set? Were you rehearsing? Because as I recall, you were out to dinner with her at *my* favorite restaurant and got caught kissing her in a back booth by an overeager fan with a selfie stick."

The fan had snapped the photo with herself in one corner and Adam and his costar in the other. They hadn't noticed with their mouths fused. A herd of elephants could have trampled the restaurant to the ground and they would have been found in the rubble with their lips still locked.

As Adam's Number One Fan, I'd stalked his social media accounts regularly, never wanting to miss someone bragging about my husband or overlook a picture a fan would post of him signing an autograph.

That was how I found out my husband was having an affair. Via Instagram.

And it had shattered my already broken heart.

"I'm sorry," Adam whispered. "For the millionth time, I'm sorry. It meant nothing. It was *one* kiss."

"And that is what you still don't understand. It was one *kiss*."

I knew that when I'd started dating Adam, he'd often be

physical with other women during his performances. I'd sat front row at his first college play, and when he'd kissed his co-star, I'd about fainted. It had taken me a week to decide if I could handle it.

But even as a freshman in college, I'd decided he was worth it. I'd learned to compartmentalize that part of his job. It wasn't my Adam with another woman, it was his character. In my mind, they were two completely separate human beings.

Except the kiss in the restaurant wasn't him playing a character. It was *him*. My husband. The man who'd vowed to stick with me through good and bad had shared something intimate with another woman.

And he'd done it a week after we'd found out that I couldn't bear his children.

The photograph of them together was burned in my brain. It kept company with a slew of images I'd conjured of the pair together, all of them naked in bed.

"Did you sleep with her?"

"No," he insisted. "I've told you that over and over. It was just that kiss."

Yet I still asked because the pit in my stomach screamed there was more to his story. "It doesn't matter. The kiss was enough."

"This isn't all my fault," Adam declared. "You weren't the only one devastated by the doctor's news. That was a game changer because I wanted kids too."

I flinched. Not once had Adam held my infertility against me. But here he was, taking my greatest insecurity and using it to justify his infidelity.

So for the first time in my life, I hung up on Adam Hall.

It hurt knowing I'd let Adam down. It hurt knowing I was unable to give him a family. It hurt knowing that someone I'd once loved with my entire being was in pain.

But he'd kissed that woman. Instead of dealing with our problems, he'd found solace with another.

This is not my fault.

Yet here I was, suffocating with guilt.

The air in the camper was too thick, so I stepped into some tennis shoes, not bothering with socks, and rushed for the door. The minute I burst outside, my lungs filled with the May mountain air and my legs took off.

I took the trail to the ridge at a near sprint but slowed to a jog as my thighs protested the steep incline. About halfway up, my throat was on fire and I tasted blood. But I refused to give in to the pain and pushed on, hiking faster and higher. I tripped on an errant rock and again on a fallen branch, but I didn't stop.

I climbed until the trees broke and the world opened.

And then, I walked to the same place in the meadow where Kaine had once sat and dropped to my knees.

Then I let it all go.

four

KAINE

"WHAT THE FUCK WAS I THINKING?" I MUTTERED TO myself, not for the first time since I'd come home from Piper's camper.

I ran a hand through my hair. It was still damp from my second cold shower, but with the way my dick was filling out my boxer briefs, I'd be due for another in five minutes.

I'd gone years without the desire for a woman. My hand and I had gotten along just fine. But now that my dick remembered how it felt to be inside a woman, I couldn't get the damn thing to soften. Piper's face popped into my mind every few minutes, and each time, blood would rush to my cock.

"Goddamn it." I made an adjustment. "Knock it the fuck off already."

I really had lost my damn mind. I'd been talking to my cock for the last hour like it was a person. Not that it was listening.

Since the showers hadn't worked to cool me down, I walked out of my bedroom and toward the front door. Maybe a hike and some fresh air would burn off my pent-up energy and help me regain control of my body. My arms felt restless and my legs itched for some exertion, so I went outside, refusing to glance at Piper's camper as my long strides took me up the mountain trail.

What the fuck was I thinking?

Instead of saying my piece and leaving my new neighbor alone like any sane man would do, I'd kissed her. I'd turned into some kind of hormone-driven maniac, attacking her with my mouth and tongue. Then I'd fucked her, hard and fast, without so much as a thank-you on my way out the door.

The son my mother had raised was truly gone. She'd be appalled to learn how I'd treated a woman. Though I was sure my actions had been appalling Mom for the last three years, so maybe today's actions wouldn't be as shocking as they seemed.

Guilt settled heavy in my gut. I was ashamed of the way I'd run out of Piper's camper like a coward, but oddly enough, I didn't regret being with her.

Sex with Piper had been phenomenal. The best I'd ever had, edging out the one time in my early twenties when I'd hooked up with a couple of girls who'd been eager to experiment. Just thinking about the way she'd clenched around me as she'd come had me rock-hard again.

I picked up the pace on the trail, chasing away the images of her beautiful face. By the time I hit the junction where her trail and mine merged into one, I'd broken a sweat and my body felt more like my own.

Had Piper ever come up this trail? I'd been the only one to hike up this ridge for so long, I considered it my own. Would we run into each other in the woods? As long as it wasn't soon, I'd deal with the company. I needed at least a few weeks, maybe months, until I was ready to see her again.

The image of her face seemed to be permanently stuck in my brain as it was.

Her construction crew could make all the noise they wanted. She could light that house of hers on fire and I'd steer clear.

No matter what happened on her side of the property line, I'd be staying on the other.

After today's hike, I'd be sticking close to home, where it was safe.

The air was chilly beneath the trees and cooled the drops of sweat as they beaded on my temples. I preferred hiking in the spring when the grasses were neon green and the wildflowers were in bloom. During the summer months, I tended to cut back on expeditions, especially since the last couple we'd been plagued with smoke from forest fires.

But when the weather turned, the autumn breeze would beckon me outdoors to watch the leaves change and the animals prepare for winter.

In the time I'd lived here, I'd hiked all over this area, exploring my own property as well as the national park land at my far border. Walking through these woods, breathing in the mountain air and listening to nature's symphony had become a coping mechanism to deal with stress and pain. That, and working in my shop.

Three years ago, I'd traded family for towering evergreens. I didn't need friends when I had the raw earth to keep me company.

So I'd thought.

I was questioning my choices now that I seemed to have forgotten the norms of social conduct. Normal men didn't kiss their sexy neighbor just because she gave them sass. Normal men didn't haul a stranger into a tricked-out Airstream to fuck her on the couch. Normal men didn't run away from a woman ten seconds after coming inside her body.

"Fuck." My curse bounced off the nearby trees.

I looked down to the bulge behind my zipper. *This is all your fault.*

I wouldn't be staying inside my own property lines after all. I owed Piper an apology—if she'd even speak to me.

And I'd have to adjust to sharing my mountain with a neighbor.

I didn't leave my place often. I went into town once a week for groceries and household supplies. The only visitors I had were delivery truck drivers from the lumberyard.

Maybe solitude hadn't driven me crazy. Maybe this was only a one-time, bad reaction to a sudden change.

Eventually, I'd get used to seeing Piper around. Right? Within a couple of weeks, I'd be used to the added noise and activity. The next time I saw her, I'd behave.

There'd be no kissing against the Airstream or romps on its couch.

My cock twitched, liking the idea of a repeat couch session. Though, having her in an actual bed, where we had space to maneuver, would no doubt be incredible. I pictured her beneath me, with her hair spread out on a white pillow and those dark eyes squeezing shut as I thrust inside.

I was throbbing again, my dick practically dripping at the image.

In the distance, a bird chirped, though it sounded more like a cackle. The damn thing was laughing at me. There'd be no bedtime play in my future.

When I showed up at Piper's door to apologize, I fully expected her to slam it in my face.

If, or when, that happened, I'd just shout my apology through the thin camper walls. Since it was just her and me on this section of the mountain, I wasn't worried about another neighbor overhearing me grovel.

The closest house to mine was miles away. The neighbor on my opposite side had built his home on the far edge of his own fifteen-acre plot. And on Piper's side, there was nothing but trees all the way to the gravel road that led down the mountain.

She'd hear my apology, whether she wanted to or not.

As I hiked, I rehearsed my apology, perfecting it by the time I was cresting the ridge.

Hi, Piper. I'm sorry for how that played out earlier. I'll adjust to the noise and stay out of your way. Though if you could tell them to keep it down, I'd be grateful. Thanks.

I'd shake her hand if she let me, then be on my way. Neighbors didn't have to see each other much. I'd say sorry and keep my distance. Maybe I'd order some of those noise-canceling headphones.

I focused on the trail, pushing my body hard the last twenty feet of the steep, rocky incline, then stepped on top of the ridge, breathing easy as the trail flattened and the world opened up.

This view never failed to take my breath away.

I scanned the mountain ranges, savoring how the blue got lighter and lighter as the ranges disappeared over the horizon. Then I turned down the trail, planning to walk through the meadow a bit while I caught my breath.

But my feet stopped cold as a whimper carried across the wind.

In my same resting spot, the place where I always knelt to send up my silent words, sat Piper.

Her face was buried in her hands, and her shoulders were hunched forward, shaking violently as she cried. But I'd recognize her hair anywhere.

My hand drifted to my sternum, rubbing it hard as a deep ache settled in my chest.

Was this about me? Had I done this to her? Had I made her cry?

Son of a bitch. I was scum. I was the lowest form of filth to hurt her like this. The flimsy apology I'd practiced wouldn't be nearly enough.

My feet shot forward, propelling me in her direction.

She must have heard or felt my boots thud on the ground, because when I was about twenty feet away, her entire body jolted. Her face snapped up with a look of pure terror. But once she recognized me, her shoulders relaxed.

There was a mixture of shock and confusion in her eyes as I got closer. The tears hadn't stopped rolling down her cheeks. But she wasn't afraid as I knelt by her side.

She didn't shy away as I pulled her into my arms.

Her body was stiff for a few moments but then she melted. Her frame sank into the embrace and she burrowed her head into my neck as the sobs returned.

My arms were tense, unsure of how tightly I should hold her. The last crying woman I'd held had been my mother. The memory of Mom, clinging to my arms in the hospital, rushed into my head, and I nearly dropped Piper on the ground.

What was I doing? I didn't want personal attachments. My mind screamed to let her go, but my arms refused to listen.

Let her go.

I hugged her tighter.

Her sobs were full of such pain, I wanted to take it away. I wanted to meld it into my own. I kept so much inside of me already, what was a little more?

I shifted off my knees, sitting on the ground so I could pull her into my lap and rest my cheek on the top of her hair. Then we sat together, her clinging to me, me clutching her until she'd cried it all out.

"You okay?"

"Oh my god. I'm so sorry." She leaned away from my chest, swiping at her eyes. Even with red eyes and blotches on her face, she was stunning.

"It's all right."

"No, it's not. I got *slobber* on your shirt." Embarrassment flushed her cheeks as she dabbed the wet spot over my heart.

"It's fine." I trapped her hand under mine, but she refused to look at me.

I bent my head, trying to catch her gaze. When it finally flickered to mine, I gave her a small smile. At least, I think it was a smile. I hadn't done much of that in three years either. Even just a small uplift at the corners felt strange.

She shook her head, pushing away from me to stand. "You must think I'm crazy."

"I don't." But since I was crazy myself, what the hell did I know?

I stood too, watching as she brushed the grass and dirt from her black leggings. They accentuated every luscious curve of her ass and legs, and I shoved my hands into my pockets to keep them away.

"I'm a mess," she muttered.

"No, this is on me. I'm sorry. The way I ran out on you was, well, I'm an asshole. For all of it. Coming over. Getting pissed at you. The, um . . . kiss. I didn't mean to do that. I didn't come over expecting, uh . . . sex."

This was the worst damn apology in the history of mankind. What happened to the mediocre one I'd just memorized? Jesus. *Sum it up already.* "I'm just . . . I'm sorry. I didn't mean to make you cry."

Piper gave me a sideways glance, then shut me up with a smile.

My heart skipped and my hand went back to my sternum. She was as beautiful as she was dangerous. Just minutes around her and I was unbalanced. When was the last time a woman had made my heart skip?

"Don't worry." Piper laughed. "You aren't the reason I was crying."

"I'm not?"

She shook her head. "No, those tears belonged to someone else. What happened between us earlier was the craziest thing I've done in a long, *long* time, but I'm not upset about it. I don't regret it."

"I don't either."

"Are you sure? Because the way you bolted out the door makes me think otherwise."

"I'm sure." As much as it was messing with my head, as much as *she* was throwing me off-center, that was the best time I'd had in years.

She smiled wider, enough to get the dimples. "Can I confess something?"

"Uh, okay?"

She turned away and spoke to the mountains in the distance. "That first day when we met, when I came to your cabin, I'd been up here earlier. My friend and I hiked up here to check out the ridge. I think my realtor thought it would sell me on the place, which it did."

I took in the view. "It's beautiful."

"Yes, it is," she said. "I saw you up here, in this spot. You were kneeling here."

The muscles in my shoulders went rigid as a flurry of feelings swirled in my head. I was ashamed that she'd seen me at my most vulnerable moment. I was angry that she'd intruded on something not meant for anyone to see. I was relieved that it was her who had seen me and not someone else.

In the end, relief drowned out the other two. *Huh.* I would have put money on anger.

"Were you praying?" she asked.

"No."

I didn't pray. Not anymore.

I waited for the inevitable question. *Then what were you doing?* But it never came. Piper stood quietly, staring off into the distance, satisfied with my one-word answer.

Another strange sensation rolled over me. The short answer might have appeased her, but it didn't sit well in my gut.

"I was talking to a ghost."

Her face tilted up to study my profile. "A ghost?"

I nodded but kept my eyes on a bird circling a tree in the distance. Eye contact would reveal too much. "A ghost."

I came up here and talked to the precious spirit somewhere in the heavens. I told her the things I hadn't been able to during her short life.

All because of *him*.

Three years later and I still went into a rage when I pictured his face. When I thought about all he'd taken from me with his betrayal. The anger burned my throat as fire spread through my veins. My hands ached for something to throw or squeeze or punch.

Piper was standing too close and I took a step away, not trusting myself with this much fury building inside. But just as I was about to take another step back and head down the trail, to disappear into the forest with punishing footsteps, her voice rang through the blood rushing in my ears.

"I'm Piper Campbell."

The red cleared from my vision. "What?"

"Piper Campbell." She shot her hand between us. "It's my name."

I studied her long fingers for a moment before taking them in my own. "Kaine Reynolds."

"Nice to meet you, Kaine Reynolds."

"I, uh . . ." *What the fuck?* She was like a fire extinguisher. My hand enveloped hers and the burn just died. "Nice to meet you too."

"That was kind of random." She laughed, slipping her soft hand free. "But I felt like we needed to start over. I know we've already had sex and you've seen me bawl my eyes out. But I'm kind of a stickler for knowing someone's last name before they see me naked and since we already broke that rule, I figured it was long overdue that I properly introduce myself."

My jaw slackened. Piper was either the craziest person I'd ever met or she saw right to my core, distracting me before I could give in to the rage.

"Sorry for that crying jag," she continued. "Sometimes you just need to cry, you know?"

Not really. Even after everything that had happened in my past, I hadn't cried. Not once.

But there was no way we'd be psychoanalyzing my past today. Or any day. "Don't mention it."

She took a long, deep breath and blinked, letting her eyes stay closed a few seconds. When she opened them, she smiled. "You were probably up here for some peace and quiet. I'll leave you to it. And, um, thanks. Sometimes you just need a hug."

As she stepped around me and headed for the trail, I eyed the path going in the opposite direction. It went on for about fifty feet through the meadow, then curved back into the trees. From there, it wound along a thick forest trail for about a quarter mile before opening up into a meadow twice as large as this one.

It was another favorite spot and one I always visited this time of year.

The step I took was to follow Piper. "Wait up."

She glanced over her shoulder. "You can stay."

"I'll come back down. I'm hungry."

I wasn't, not where my stomach was concerned. My cock on the other hand was starving, begging for another taste of her. It swelled as I caught a whiff of Piper's shampoo in the air. The citrusy, floral scent overpowered even the surrounding juniper bushes.

Don't even think about it. I ordered my cock to stand down with a quiet growl. Then I focused on the trail, keeping an eye on Piper as we descended the steepest part of the climb.

The path widened as we crossed the tree line, and I stepped from behind Piper to walk at her side. Otherwise, I'd probably slip and break a leg because I'd be too busy staring at her ass in those second-skin leggings.

We walked for a few yards until Piper broke the silence. "I was—ahh!"

Her ankle rolled and her shoe skidded in the dirt. Arms went flying, feet scrambled, as she tripped, flying headfirst down the hill.

I reacted fast, grabbing her around the waist before she could fall. One arm wrapped around her hips while the other banded around her ribs. Her ass pressed against the bulge in my groin. Her breasts heaved against my forearms as she breathed.

Piper tilted her chin, her wide eyes staring up at me. Her lips were so close, all I'd have to do was bend down and take them.

I swallowed hard, summoning every ounce of willpower. Then I let her go. "Are you okay?"

"Yep. All good." She nodded, smoothing down her clothes, though they weren't out of place. "Thanks."

I nodded.

Nothing good could come of another hookup. Right? It

was better if we forgot all about what had happened earlier in her camper.

"So, how's your hand?" Piper asked, taking a careful step down the trail.

"Huh?"

"Your hand." She pointed at the hand I'd cut last month.

"Oh, um, it's fine." I flexed my hand, the scab from the cut gone and now just a small red line.

"What happened?"

"I was cutting up an apple, and my grip slipped on the knife. It sliced right into my palm. Bled like crazy but it didn't hurt all that bad."

She grimaced. "Ouch."

"Eh, it's not the worst cut I've had. My hands tend to get banged up on occasion with my work."

"What kind of work do you do?"

"Woodworking," I told her. "Mostly custom furniture pieces."

"Really?" She laughed. "That's ironic."

"What's ironic?"

"Oh, nothing." She waved it off. "I was just talking about a furniture designer earlier today. He made some pieces for me in New York and offered to make me a dining room table. But he's got a unique style, very sleek and simple. I'm going for a different style with this house."

"Like what?" I asked, my interest sparked. Dining room tables were my specialty, and I was curious what kind of table a woman like Piper wanted in her home.

"I don't know." She shrugged. "Something rich and warm. Rustic even. I want a table that is beautiful but functional. I don't want to worry about spilling wine or using glass cleaner every other day just to keep the fingerprints down."

A design came to me immediately, flashing into my mind with such clarity, I knew exactly what I'd make for her.

I'd use walnut for its strength and its beauty. The wood's grain variation came to life under my favorite dark brown stain. Instead of four legs, I'd do two wide square posts to give the piece a sturdy flair. Seven feet would be large enough for a good crowd at the holidays but not so long that she'd feel like she was sitting at an island when she was eating alone.

I mentally sorted through the slabs of wood I had in the shop, the ones I'd collected over the years that were just waiting for the right project. I'd narrowed it down to one of three pieces by the time we reached the split in the trail where she'd take her path home and I'd continue on to mine.

"I guess I'll see you around. Neighbor."

I nodded. "I guess so."

"We'll try to keep the noise down."

"Appreciated."

She waved and stepped down her path.

I let my gaze linger on her ass for just a moment before turning down my own trail.

"Hey, Kaine," she called.

"Yeah?"

"Would you like to come to dinner tomorrow?"

The smart answer here was no. There was too much chemistry between us to be confined to her camper. And I didn't trust myself to keep my hands off of her.

But instead of declining her invitation and sticking to my original plan to keep some distance, I called out, "Sure."

"Six o'clock."

I nodded and we both went on our separate ways. I glanced at my cabin as I walked by but didn't stop as I hustled to the shop.

By midnight, the project I'd been working on earlier had

been tarped and pushed to the side. I'd dug out a raw, magnificent slab of walnut from my stash. It was resting on two sawhorses in the center of the room. And I'd just finished sketching the design for Piper's table.

A dining room table that looked exactly like the one I would have made for myself.

five

PIPER

"Stupid sweat glands." I fanned my armpits, taking a few breaths to calm my racing heart.

I was so nervous for this dinner with Kaine that I'd been sweating profusely for an hour. My hands were clammy, and I'd put on three layers of deodorant so far tonight. I hadn't been this nervous for dinner with a man since my first date with Adam in college.

I wasn't exactly sure why I'd invited Kaine over tonight. Maybe because he'd been so nice to me on the hiking trail. Maybe because I hadn't expected him to accept. But he was due at any moment, and I didn't want to be dripping when he arrived.

Thankfully, he hadn't come out of his cabin yet, so I had a few moments to breathe and cool down as I kept an eye on his house through the window.

It was Saturday so I'd spent the morning cleaning the camper. Then I'd gone to the local grocery store, where I'd questioned my menu choice at least a hundred different times as I'd wandered up and down all eight aisles.

Finally, I'd settled on a meal that a burly man with bulging muscles would enjoy: steak and potatoes. Though, I'd grabbed some chicken too in case he didn't eat red meat.

I'd come home and spent my afternoon in the kitchen. I'd

prepped my favorite scalloped potatoes, which were currently in the oven. I'd cooked and shredded the chicken for my backup meal of barbeque sandwiches. But since scalloped potatoes went great with steak but were too fancy for barbeque, I'd made a homemade potato salad.

When I'd realized he might not like potatoes, I'd dashed into town for more groceries. I had coleslaw, fruit salad and corn on the cob crammed in my refrigerator.

It was when I'd finished cooking that the anxious sweating had started.

The only thing I was certain he'd like was dessert. I was going all out and making my famous skillet cookies.

I'd found these mini cast-iron skillets a few years ago. I would press chocolate chip cookie dough into the bottom and bake them until they were just past gooey. Then I'd top them with an enormous scoop—or two—of vanilla ice cream, drizzle them with chocolate and caramel sauce and dig in.

Even after Adam gave up sugar and processed foods, he'd indulge and split one with me.

Everyone loved my skillet cookies.

And even though my own skillets were in a storage unit until my house was remodeled, I'd found a skillet to use temporarily at a sporting goods store in Kalispell a couple of weeks ago.

If Kaine didn't like sweets, I had no problem eating the entire cookie myself.

Life was too short to skip dessert on Saturday nights. And my curves wouldn't maintain themselves.

A loud gust of wind rolled over the Airstream, and I glanced out the window. The wind had been steadily picking up all afternoon, and the treetops weren't just slow dancing now, they were doing the polka.

Not wanting the camp chair I'd set up outside to go blowing

down the mountain, I hustled out the door to fold it up.

"Hey." Kaine's deep rumble caught my attention.

I spun around to see him striding along the path between our homes. The chair slipped from my hands.

"Hi," I breathed, raking my eyes over sheer magnificence.

Kaine wore his signature tan pants—Carhartts, I think they were called. The sporting goods store in Kalispell where I'd bought my skillet had racks and racks of those thick, canvas pants. Apparently, they were a staple in Montana menswear because of their durability.

I knew from tugging them off his narrow hips that they were heavier than jeans. I knew from watching him leave my camper, shirtless and still glossy with sweat, that they accentuated his incredible ass.

I tore my eyes away from his beefy thighs flexing beneath my new favorite brand of pants and forced them upward, over his flat stomach.

He was wearing a hunter-green Henley and had bunched up the long sleeves, baring his forearms. They were tanned and snaked with veins. His biceps pulled tight at the thermal weave, and since he'd left the buttons undone at the collar, it hinted at the chest hair that covered his pecs.

My gaze drifted higher to his face and I licked my lips. Not even my skillet cookies were as mouthwatering as Kaine Reynolds.

The color of his shirt made the green in his eyes stand out and the gold flecks darker, more like copper. He'd trimmed his beard today. It was still thick, but he'd cut it back enough so I could see the contours of his square jaw.

My god, he did it for me. Head to toe, Kaine Reynolds was magic.

Just the sight of him made my lady parts quiver and my

heart do a funny flip. Even when we were in love, my heart had never flipped for Adam. I refused to think about what that meant.

Instead, I pictured Adam wearing Kaine's clothes and stifled a laugh. Adam would have looked like a fool in those clothes, an imposter portraying a rugged character. He lacked Kaine's natural grit and edge.

My neighbor's long legs ate up the distance between us quickly, and before I was ready to stop gawking, he was standing in front of me.

"Hi," I repeated. "How are you?"

"Good." He bent down for the chair I'd forgotten, folding it up and propping it against the camper.

"You're right on time. I'll get dinner started but I forgot to ask what you liked yesterday. Are steak and potatoes okay?"

He nodded. "Great."

"Okay. Would you like a beer or wine? I have red and white." Along with sparkling water, milk and three kinds of soda in case he didn't drink.

"Beer's fine."

Why did he keep grunting short answers? I was sweating again but smiled, hoping to put him at ease.

He had this odd look in his eyes, one I'd seen a couple of times over the last day. His mouth turned down on one side, not a complete frown, but the beginning of one. His eyebrows slanted together at the center, creating a deep crease above the wide bridge of his nose. And his eyes seemed to go in and out of focus, like he was being torn between past and present. The swirls of gold and brown and green dulled to a muddy mixture of all three.

I wanted to hug him.

But instead of wrapping my arms around those broad shoulders, I did the only thing I could think of to steal his attention.

I rambled.

"Did you ever see the inside of this house?" I pointed to my future home. "It was a shrine to the sixties. I'm having to remodel the entire thing because it looked like a psychedelic rainbow puked in there. I've never seen anything so hideous in my life."

He blinked, his eyes refocusing, and glanced at the house. Then he turned to my garbage heap by the Dumpster. "If those yellow cabinets are any indication, I'm glad I was spared the experience."

I giggled. "It's forever burned into my brain. For your sake, I'm glad too."

"How's the remodel going?"

"Slower than I'd like." I sighed. "But the crew has nearly all of the demolition done, so now they can start putting it all back together. Luckily for me, the house is structurally sound so they aren't having to fix a ton of fundamental problems."

Making it beautiful was tough enough. In addition to my floor-to-ceiling cosmetic updates, I was removing a few walls to open up the living room and kitchen area. And the master bathroom was going to be rearranged completely to give me more storage space.

It might be just me, but I liked to have an abundance of bath towels on hand. One day, I hoped to meet a guy who'd want to come over and occasionally spend the night. My future lover deserved plush towels after his morning shower too.

"Maybe after dinner you can give me a tour," Kaine said.

"I'd like that. Come on in." I led the way into the camper as Kaine followed close behind.

The moment the door shut behind him, the air turned heavy. My eyes landed on the couch and my cheeks flushed. Just yesterday he'd had me on that couch. Just yesterday he'd been inside me, making me lose all control.

When I looked over my shoulder, his eyes were locked on the couch. The colors burned bright and clear. They were electric. His chest heaved with short, shallow breaths. Yesterday's escapades were fresh in his mind too.

Could Kaine be the guy who used my spare towels? My brain screamed *Danger! Danger!* and I shut out the image of him emerging from my future shower, naked and dripping wet.

I cleared my throat. "Make yourself at home."

He blinked, then shied away from the couch to sit at the table instead while I went to the fridge and got out his beer.

With a quick flick of his hand, he unscrewed the top and tilted the dark glass to his lips. His Adam's apple bobbed as he took one long pull.

I about combusted on the spot. Drinking beer was not supposed to be sexy. But the way he held that amber bottle in his large hand, the way his wet lips barely touched the rim, was scorch-the-earth hot.

"Need any help?" Kaine set his beer down, causing me to flinch.

"No, I'm good." I spun around for the fridge, busying myself by unloading the steaks.

Get a grip, Piper. If I kept staring at him, he was going to think I'd just invited him over for sex. Maybe subconsciously, that had been the real motivation for my dinner invite.

Kaine's addicting scent filled the camper, and I frowned, knowing the food would soon drown it out. He smelled like wood and spice, something I rarely came across with city men.

I went back to the fridge, getting out my potato dish just so my hands were busy. His hair was a little too long and curled at the nape of his neck and around his ears. My fingers were aching to find out if the hairs were soft or coarse like his beard.

Yesterday's couch time hadn't been about learning or

exploring. It had been all about relieving the tension and scratching the itch.

But the problem was, that itch was back, nagging me more than ever.

I turned on the oven and lit a burner on the stove, pushing away the urge to say screw the steaks, I'd rather screw Kaine. I got out a frying pan, ignoring the feel of Kaine's eyes dragging up and down my backside.

I'd worn my favorite cuffed jeans tonight, the ones that did great things for my ass and highlighted my slim waist. I'd also worn a simple black tank top with thin straps. The tank dipped low in both the back and front, showing off some skin.

"How do you like your steak?" I asked over my shoulder.

He ducked his head to his beer. *Busted.* "Medium rare."

I smiled and went about my cooking, occasionally glancing backward at Kaine. We'd make eye contact, instant heat sizzling between us, until one of us would find the courage to break away. When I went to set the table, I brushed his arm accidentally and he nearly came out of his seat.

The electricity between us was at ten thousand volts by the time I plated our meal and sat across from him. The room was so stifling with sexual tension, I was barely able to fill my lungs.

Every breath was a pant. Every heartbeat a boom. Every movement intensified the throbbing between my legs.

What the hell was going on? It was like years of repressed sexual desire had finally caught up with me. Sex with Kaine had awoken this intoxicating need for more and more and more. Not even the glass of red wine I'd had while cooking had mellowed it out.

And it appeared I wasn't the only one in this predicament.

Kaine's beer bottle had long since been drained, and he'd almost polished off his second. His hand was gripping his steak knife so hard, I worried it would snap in his fierce grip.

"Enjoy."

He nodded, cutting into his steak and forking a bite. I cut into my own but froze as he lifted the bite to his mouth and chewed. His jaw flexed. His lips moved, just slightly.

Chewing? *Chewing* was sexy now? I recrossed my legs, concerned I wouldn't make it through this meal without a spontaneous orgasm.

I set down my fork and knife, closed my eyes and took in a long breath.

If we were going to survive this meal, I needed a distraction. We needed to move past the chemistry and into something more like friendship.

"So you design furniture," I said.

He nodded, still chewing.

"Do you like it?"

He nodded again.

"Good. It's important to love your job." I picked up my utensils and went back to my steak. "I love my job. I work for Logan Kendrick. His wife Thea runs the bar in town. Do you know them?"

Kaine shook his head. "I don't get into town much."

Why did that statement not surprise me? "He moved here a few years ago from New York. That's where I met him. But then he moved out here for Thea. This is actually their camper. They weren't using it this summer and let me borrow it."

Logan and Thea had tried to convince me to stay in their boathouse until the remodel was done. But once I'd bought my property, I hadn't wanted to delay living here for a single minute. I'd planned to find my own camper to rent for a few months, but once Thea got wind of that idea, she'd insisted on me taking the Airstream. When I'd asked to pay them for using it, Logan had threatened to fire me if I brought it up again.

"Logan and Thea are two of my favorite people on the planet," I told Kaine. "Logan's family has a charitable organization called the Kendrick Foundation. I've been working as his assistant there for years."

"What kinds of charities?" he asked before diving into the potatoes. A small hum of appreciation came from his throat.

"Their portfolio is varied, but since they were founded in New York, they dedicate a lot of resources to inner-city programs. Logan's got a soft spot for children's charities, so over the last few years, he's really focused on pulling more of them under the Kendrick umbrella."

And now that he was living in Montana, more of those charities were being added from the West Coast. For decades, the Kendrick Foundation had been city-centric, but Logan was expanding their reach. I was proud to say that my efforts were helping to make us known nationally.

"They own the children's camp here in Lark Cove," I said as Kaine continued to devour his meal. "Thea's partner at the bar, Jackson Page, is married to the director. Do you know them? His wife's name is Willa."

Kaine shook his head again. "Never met them."

And again, I wasn't surprised. If I had to guess, I'd venture that Kaine's social circle consisted of the small herd of deer I'd seen walking around our mountainside over the last week.

"They're all wonderful people."

Willa was sweet and shy and as genuine as they came. The way Jackson looked at her made me swoon every time. He'd get this dreamy look in his eyes whenever they settled on his wife. And when they made eye contact, the rest of us went out of focus.

It was the same with Logan and Thea.

I wanted to believe that Adam and I'd had that once. That we'd been so in love, the two of us would get lost in each other's gaze for hours and hours on end. But the more time I spent around my friends in Lark Cove, the more I realized I'd been pretending for a long time. My marriage had always been missing that sense of completeness.

Or maybe we'd just lost it along the way.

We had started our relationship at such a young age. After college, we'd each concentrated on our careers. I'd gone to work for the Kendrick Foundation right after graduation, working as an assistant to one of the lower-level vice presidents. Then I'd worked my way up until I'd eventually become Logan's assistant. He was chairman of the board and the most powerful man in the company.

And I was his right hand.

My grandfather had thought "assistant" was a glorified word for secretary, but the day after I'd sat down and explained all of my responsibilities, he'd bragged me up to all his friends. Years later, he never missed the chance to tell his golf partners in Arizona about my accomplishments.

My job was my pride. It was my passion.

Helping various charities get up and running made my pulse race. I loved weeding through proposals and pitching the ones I felt most strongly about to Logan. It was empowering, being in the inner circle, helping make decisions that would put a vast fortune to good use.

Nothing went on at the Kendrick Foundation that I wasn't privy to. But seating myself at Logan's side had taken work. A lot of hard work.

And while I'd been climbing my ladder, Adam had been climbing his. He'd landed his starring role on Broadway the same year I'd been promoted to work with Logan.

Ever since Adam and I had separated, I'd been carefully inspecting my failed marriage. Had he ever looked at me like I was the very oxygen keeping him alive? My subconscious was whispering *no*.

I wanted *the look*.

"This was delicious. Thank you."

Lost in my own introspection, I hadn't noticed that Kaine had finished his plate. "You're welcome."

"It's been a long time since someone cooked for me."

"My pleasure. It's nice not to eat dinner alone."

Even though we hadn't visited much, just his company was nice. Especially once the sexual tension had eased.

I'd spent months eating alone in New York. I'd avoided restaurants for fear of running into Adam or his family or our former friends. He'd convinced them all I was depressed, and that was the reason why I'd filed for divorce. Whenever I ran into an old acquaintance, they'd say hello, then spend the next ten minutes convincing me to give marriage counseling a chance.

Adam loved me, after all.

Everyone seemed to have gotten memory loss about Adam kissing his costar.

The press had scandalized him, but it had blown over quickly. His costar was soon seen on the arm of another New York elitist. And Adam had made a public apology for his infidelity that the media had eaten up like candy.

At times, it had felt like all of Manhattan was judging me for not running back into my grieving husband's open arms.

It had been easiest to stick to my apartment after that. I went to work. I went home. On occasion, I'd go see my parents or my brother. But they were busy with lives of their own, so I'd spent most evenings at my dinner table for one.

And though I loved being in Lark Cove, there were lonely

nights here too.

Thea and Logan would have me over for dinner every night, but I was trying not to wear out my welcome. I often ate lunch with them when I went down to work with Logan. If Thea was at the bar, we'd often take breaks and eat with her there. But they needed their family time, so even when I was crashing in their boathouse, I'd leave and eat dinner alone.

"I'm a slow eater," I told Kaine, though he'd probably figured that out already.

"I inhale my food. Take your time."

As I ate, he looked out the window and over to my house. Then he inspected the camper from his seat. What he didn't do was make eye contact.

My table in the RV was small, technically a four-seater, but only if two of those four people were small children. And Kaine was a big guy. His knees came well past the halfway mark, and as I shifted slightly, our knees touched. Beneath us, our feet were close. His tan boots were within a mere inch of my wedge sandals.

Testing the distance, I moved my foot ever so slightly. The second our soles touched, his eyes snapped to mine. The heat from earlier came back with the force of a blazing wildfire.

It wasn't a look of utter devotion and worship, but this look from Kaine was a close runner-up.

Any second now, I was expecting him to rip the table between us off its hinges and out from between us. His eyes bored into mine, holding me captive, then skimming down my nose and to my lips.

The intensity of his stare made me dizzy. My tongue, acting on its own volition, darted between my lips and licked the bottom swell.

Kaine's eyes flared before his long lashes drooped, hooding

his lust-drunk gaze.

My heart was missing beats. My fingers ran across the edge of the table, unable to hold still. But Kaine sat rigid and stiff, moving only to breathe and flick his gaze across my lips.

I wanted his tongue on my mouth, not his stare. I wanted to feel it sweep inside and have him for dessert.

My breath hitched when his foot next to mine twitched. It came up my bare ankle, and though the sole of his boot was rough, he used the slightest touch. The friction shot tingles straight up my leg, past my knee and right to my core.

Was he playing footsie with me?

I tested him, lifting the toe of my sandal up his ankle. He didn't pull his foot away.

Any other day, any other man, I'd laugh at this situation. We were playing footsie and it was utterly erotic.

Having sex with Kaine again would only complicate things. My body was all in, but there was a tiny warning bell ringing in the back of my mind.

Was this just a rebound? Was I transferring feelings from Adam to this man, simply because he was here?

No.

This wasn't a rebound or some kind of revenge fuck. This was pure, unfettered attraction. This was two people whose chemistry was explosive. This was me wanting Kaine. And him wanting me right back.

If we agreed this was casual, then what was the harm? Awesome sex between neighbors didn't have to get messy. When I'd moved here, I'd hoped to eventually find an easy relationship. So it had happened a little sooner than expected.

If we set some ground rules, there was no reason Kaine and I couldn't enjoy one another's bodies.

"I have dessert." Our feet kept playing beneath the table.

"It's this huge chocolate chip cookie in a cast-iron skillet. I put ice cream on top and then drizzle chocolate and caramel sauce over it all."

"Sounds fucking incredible." His gravelly voice made my core pulse.

"They are. I'll make one for us." I didn't make a move to get up. I was too busy enjoying the feel of a rugged man's work boot kissing the soft skin of my ankle.

We both knew this conversation wasn't about the cookie.

His boot went higher up my calf. Heat pooled between my legs and I spread them apart.

"I'm not looking for a relationship," I told him.

He nodded. "I'm good with casual."

"No expectations?"

"Not from me."

"Okay," I whispered, reluctantly taking my foot away from his so I could slide out of my seat.

I cleared my plate to the sink, but before I could turn and get Kaine's, his heat was at my back. He reached around me, setting his empty plate on top of mine. Then he pried the steak knife and fork out of my hand, dropping them into the sink with a clank.

My heart raced. My breathing stopped. My hands shook with anticipation of what he'd do next.

Slowly, deliberately, he lowered his mouth toward my neck. His breath hit my skin first in a warm whisper before his soft lips pressed onto my bare skin.

Then came his hands, drifting slowly up my arms from my wrists. His square fingertips glided over my forearms and the sensitive skin on the undersides of my elbows. Nerve endings ignited and singed as his trail continued up my biceps.

By the time his hands made it to my shoulders, I was

trembling. I lost my balance and swayed backward into his hard chest.

The moment we collided, his movements changed. Gone was the slow, torturous caress. His large hands gripped my shoulders before sliding palms across my collarbones. His fingers dug into the tops of my breasts, kneading them until I was on fire.

"Kaine," I moaned, so close to coming from his lips and hands alone.

But before I reached the peak, Kaine spun me around, hoisted me up in his arms and carried me down the short hallway to my bedroom.

He tossed me onto the blue quilt and came at me with the same ferocity as he had yesterday on the couch. But this time, we savored. We worshipped. We discovered.

Kaine Reynolds was a master with his hands, among other appendages. He had sensitive nipples and liked it when I tugged them between my teeth. His hair was soft and threaded perfectly between my fingers.

And despite our first go on the couch, the man had stamina.

Long after the sun had gone down, Kaine and I shared a big cookie. Then he got dressed and went home.

I watched from the doorway as he navigated the path home in the moonlight and laughed to myself, muffling it with a hand.

Of all the neighbors I'd had before, and there had been many, Kaine was far and away my favorite.

Six

KAINE

A CAR DOOR SLAMMED OUTSIDE, AND ITS ENGINE HUMMED TO life. I ditched my bowl of cereal on the coffee table and stretched over the couch to peer out the window. I was just in time to watch Piper peel out of her driveway in her tiny black clown car. A Mini something.

It would be shit to drive in the Montana winter, especially up the road to her house. The county wouldn't plow these side roads until the highway and streets in town were clear. She needed something with higher clearance and four-wheel drive.

But it wasn't my business what kind of car she drove. We were fuck buddies, not best friends. I wasn't her Montana lifestyle coach. If she got stuck just once, she'd figure it out herself.

Though if she did get stuck, she'd probably be pounding on my door, begging for help. I'd have to haul out my towrope from the shop, then drive to wherever she got stuck and drag her car back home. She'd probably ask me to take her up to Kalispell and go car shopping. What a pain in the ass.

"She needs a new car," I told the glass, then went back to my cereal. I'd talk to Piper about it before the end of the summer.

I scowled at the other vehicles in her driveway. Besides the camper, three trucks were crammed in by the house. Her construction crew had been banging and crashing around since six thirty this morning.

I wasn't sure how she could fucking stand it. I wasn't going to ask.

It had been three days since she'd had me over to her camper for dinner, and I'd been avoiding her property line like the plague.

Piper had this way of stealing my ability for rational thought. When she was near, my brain got muddled. Simple conversation was difficult because I was too busy thinking about kissing her or touching her or finding some way to get inside her luscious body.

So I'd kept my distance, not trusting myself to get close. We'd agreed on casual sex. That, I could do. But she was the type of woman I'd want daily. Hourly. Seeing each other that much would be too risky. She might develop feelings. She might confuse sex with love.

She might? That was bullshit. I was really worried about myself. So for casual sex to stay uncomplicated, I couldn't see her as often as my body would have liked.

But even though I'd stayed away physically, my mind crossed that property line at least ten times a day. Piper had rooted herself in my thoughts.

Every morning, I'd sit in this exact spot, eating my cereal on the couch. I'd tell myself not to look when she left for work. But just like today, every morning, I looked. I'd never looked out my living room window as much as I had in the last three days.

Besides the spying, I wondered about her constantly. Was she having a good day at work? Had she eaten lunch? What was she doing for dinner?

It was pathetic. *I* was pathetic.

I'd had girlfriends come and go all through high school. I'd had plenty of women afterward, all casual relationships, and never had a woman stuck like Piper did. Not even work could keep her from sneaking into my mind.

I normally got lost in my projects, completely enveloped in the wood and the design and working with my hands to shape something beautiful out of a raw element. No matter how good the sex was, a woman had never come between me and my craft.

Until now.

A loud crash sounded outside, and I turned again to the window. The crew seemed to be ripping out doors today. A young guy hauled one out the front door and threw it in the Dumpster that had been emptied yesterday.

The huge bin was full again because the crew had cleared away all of the trash they'd piled outside the house. Had Piper asked them to do that for my sake?

Another guy came out carrying another door. It was tossed in the Dumpster with a cracking boom.

"Son of a bitch," I grumbled.

This morning was going to be a disaster of noise and distraction. And as much as I wanted to work on Piper's table, I still hadn't remembered how to work amid all the racket. Though, the noise from her crew wasn't the only reason progress had been slow.

The night after our dinner, I'd come down to the shop and worked until sunrise with the smell of her still lingering on my skin. Since then, every time I'd gone to the shop, I'd start to work only to find myself lost in thought hours later, holding a tool that I hadn't actually used.

Why her?

Answering that question was like an unsolvable puzzle.

Any man on earth would say Piper Campbell was breathtakingly beautiful. The sex was incredible. When I'd orgasmed the other night, it had been my first out-of-body experience.

But besides the intense physical attraction with Piper, there was something else about her I couldn't put my finger on.

She didn't ask about my past, and I didn't ask about hers. And even though we didn't know much about one another, the undercurrent between us was familiar. My mother would have called us kindred spirits.

Or maybe we were both just needy. Piper ached for my touch as much as I craved hers.

It had been three years since I'd touched another person. Three years of no handshakes. No hugs. No nothing.

For three years, I'd avoided all physical contact because I never wanted to forget the last person I'd held in my arms. I didn't want to forget how her little body had rested against my chest. How her weight had felt in my arms.

I still felt her. I still felt that ghost.

But I felt Piper now too.

And that scared the hell out of me.

Another door landed in the Dumpster across the way and I pushed off the couch. There'd be no work in the shop today, so instead, I decided to do something I'd put off for too long.

Clean.

It had been over a month since I'd done any kind of tidying up in the cabin. It was an old place that would always have a slight hint of must, and most days, I didn't care. But after eating dinner in Piper's Airstream, I'd taken a more critical eye to my own home.

Her camper was brand-new with top-of-the-line finishes. She kept it spotless with gleaming countertops and crumb-free floors. I wasn't sure if she kept it that way because it was her boss's rig or if it was just her—probably her.

I'd caught a glimpse of her closet the other night while we'd been lying in her bed, recovering from the third or fourth orgasm—I'd lost count after the second had nearly left me blind. Everything in Piper's closet was either folded or hung, the wardrobe color coordinated and the hangers evenly spaced.

When she ate, she set her fork down pristinely on the edge of her plate between bites. She dabbed the corner of her mouth with her napkin, not wiped, then gently returned it on her lap. Her glass of wine was sipped, then placed right back on its coaster.

Aside from sex with me, Piper didn't seem like the type of woman to act on whims and impulses. She was so orderly and proper. So . . . restrained.

Was that how people acted in the city? Was that how she'd been raised to behave? Or had she learned those habits from practice?

Whatever the answers, they all added to her allure.

Even her movements were a mystery, one I was already trying to solve. Why did she tuck her hair behind her left ear but not her right? Why did she absently rub the small scar at the top of her hand? Why did her stare make me want to stay inside of her bubble and never leave?

Why her?

"Fuck if I know," I muttered to the empty room.

I stood, taking my cereal bowl to the sink. I set it down without rinsing it out and turned away. But not two steps out of the kitchen, I sighed and turned back.

My conscience, something that sounded a lot like my mother's voice, told me to do the damn dishes. Usually, I left them until every single piece I owned was dirty and I had no other choice but to wash.

I went back and rinsed out my cereal bowl of the leftover milk, then put it in the dishwasher. I did the same with the plates and utensils I'd stacked up over the last two days. When the sink was clear, I towel dried my hands and surveyed the cabin.

When had I become such a slob?

A visible layer of dust coated the television. Dust bunnies were breeding like, well, rabbits in every corner. As I took a deep breath, I smelled the foul odor coming from the refrigerator.

I'd been playing a little game these last two weeks, opening the fridge door as quickly as possible, retrieving my target with a lightning-fast strike before slamming the door closed and trapping the smell inside.

"It's got to be those damn eggs."

How old was that carton? I'd bought those eggs thinking I'd swap out my morning cereal for something with protein. But it turns out, I hadn't miraculously learned how to cook eggs, and I didn't like them much to begin with.

I plugged my nose, sucked in some air and held my breath as I braved the door. The expiration date on the egg carton read three months past edible.

The smell had gotten steadily worse and worse, but I'd been too lazy to deal with it. That voice in my head came back, but this time it sounded like Piper's gasp of disgust. So I got out a garbage bag and cleared away the rotten eggs along with all of the other expired items.

There wasn't much left at that point, so after taking the trash outside, I emptied the refrigerator shelves and cleaned until the foul odor had been erased with bleach.

That one simple task sparked a cleaning rampage.

My bathroom was atrocious, with beard clippings on the countertops stuck in toothpaste-spit splatters and soap residue. I was ashamed of myself for letting the tile in the shower become so coated with grime. It took me an hour to make it clean enough that I wouldn't be embarrassed if a certain neighbor stopped by.

From there, I tackled the rest of the kitchen and the living room.

The only articles in my house that didn't need a thorough scrubbing were all of the wood pieces I'd made over the last few years. Nightstands. My coffee table. The small, round dining table that I rarely sat at with its pedestal base. Those I oiled and kept dusted on a regular basis.

Everything else got a long-overdue scouring. It took all day, and like work had been the last few days, thoughts of Piper kept me company. Though unlike in the shop, those thoughts didn't distract me from my progress. Instead, they fueled me forward.

I pictured her stepping inside my house, scanning each room with those brown eyes. I cleaned so there wouldn't be a cringe on her features if she did stop by. I didn't want her to flinch at the home I'd let go.

By the time I was ready to tackle my bedroom at the back of the house, I'd already washed two loads of laundry. The first load had been my bedsheets. Clean linens hadn't been a top priority for me in the past, but that was before I'd started screwing my neighbor.

Stripping my bed, along with doing the dishes, would become a regular chore.

I stopped by the laundry room to grab the clothes I'd shoved in an hour ago. The timer on my dryer didn't work and if I let it, the thing would run for days. I filled a basket full of ratty T-shirts, briefs and socks.

Then I brought the basket to my bed, tossing its contents out on the ugly, pea-green quilt.

Not much thought had gone into decorating this house. That quilt was the first one I'd touched at the home store, so I'd bought it. The same was true with my towels and sheets. I'd furnished this place in under twenty minutes at a department store in Kalispell, shoving items in my cart and getting the fuck out of that hellhole.

Nothing matched. The colors were dull. And before today, I hadn't given a shit.

But then Piper's face flashed in my mind. She looked at my bed and grimaced.

This woman. She was ruining me.

I'd never cared about matching things. As long as I was warm at night, the color of my bedding was irrelevant to how I slept. I hadn't even cared what color Shannon had picked out for the nursery.

Pain slashed through my chest, stealing my breath, and I sank onto the edge of the bed.

When was the last time I'd thought about that nursery? When was the last time I'd even let myself think Shannon's name?

A year. Maybe two.

I'd blocked it all out. I'd spent years refusing those memories.

My eyes drifted slowly to the closet. At the top, shoved in the farthest corner, was a box I hadn't opened since the cardboard flaps had been closed.

Of all the belongings in my former life, that box was the only thing to come with me up here, except for the clothes on my back and the truck that had carried me away. Everything else had been left behind and forgotten.

I stood and stepped to the closet, taking down the box. Then I went back to the bed, collapsing on the edge with shaking knees. With the box on my lap, the log-and-mortar walls closed in. The air was too thick to breathe.

Before my brain could throw up roadblocks on this trip down memory lane, I jerked one flap open, sending the rest popping free.

Pink. The inside was full of pink.

The color stung my eyes.

While one hand trapped the box flaps open, the other carefully reached inside. My fingertips grazed cotton.

I jerked my hand free, and my entire body jolted like I'd just been pricked by a needle.

With more force than was necessary, I shut the box, practically throwing it into the closet. Only when it was shoved away could I breathe again. The walls pushed back, giving me space. I fisted and unfisted my hand, shaking away the sting.

I never should have started cleaning. I never should have worried about what Piper would think of my house. I never should have opened that fucking box and let the memories trapped with a pink baby blanket escape.

Damn her. This was all Piper's fault.

No, not her. This was all *his* fault.

My roar filled the room as I swatted the laundry basket off my bed and onto the floor. I picked up the lamp on my nightstand next, ripping the cord from the outlet. My arm was cocked, ready to send the lamp flying across the room, when someone knocked on the front door.

I threw the lamp onto my bed instead of into a wall, then I stormed down the hallway. My boots boomed on the wooden floor as I marched straight to the door, ripping it open so hard all three hinges moaned.

"What?" I shouted.

Piper's dimples didn't falter. "Is that how you always answer your door? Or is that greeting just for me?"

"I, uh . . ."

She stood there, grinning, as I looked her up and down. Her hair was tucked behind that one ear. Her eyes were laughing. And in her hands, a cake sat on a white platter rimmed with scallops.

She'd brought me a fucking chocolate cake.

Piper balanced the plate in one palm while her other hand pointed a slender finger past the porch. "Is that your shop? I hadn't noticed it before, and I can't see it from my camper. It's enormous. After we eat some magic cake, maybe you could give me a tour."

I blinked at her once. Then twice. The burning fire that had been coursing through my veins moments ago was just . . . gone. Somehow, she'd smothered the flames before they'd been able to take on a life of their own.

How did she do that? It wasn't the first time either. What was so goddamn special about Piper Campbell that she had that kind of power over me? Until I got a handle on those answers, I should tell her to take that cake and go the fuck home.

I stepped back, waving her inside without a word. The smell of her hair hit me as she passed by. My eyes raked over the fitted, sleeveless dress she wore that hugged each of her curves. It was a deep khaki color, a few shades darker than her naked skin.

Her smile curved higher on one end as she crossed the threshold. She scanned the living room on the left, then the kitchen on the right without a grimace or a flinch in sight.

A rush of relief hit that I'd chosen today to clean. It irritated me how happy I was. Piper's reactions were controlling too many of my feelings.

"What's your stance on cake for dinner?" She set the cake down on the dining table situated close to the door.

"I'm not against it."

"Good." She nodded. "Where are your forks?"

I pointed to the drawers along the far wall of the kitchen. "Middle drawer."

Her ass swayed on her tall heels as she strode across the

kitchen like she owned the place. The front of her shoes were made up entirely of olive-green straps, all balanced on a thick heel in the same shade. They were sexy, like her dress, but I had no idea how she'd walked over here on the rough dirt trail without tripping.

But Piper had this grace in the way she walked, a surety with every step. She looked as comfortable in those chunky heels as I was in my boots.

"Plates are—"

"No plates." She turned from the silverware drawer and waved the forks in the air, shaking her head as she walked back over. "Magic cake doesn't need plates."

Magic cake?

Before I could ask, she took a seat at the table, set down my fork in front of the other, then dug in.

She didn't start on the outside, placing a dainty bite on her fork like I would have expected. No, she *dug in.* She scooped a piece of cake right out of the center, one so large I was sure it wouldn't fit in her mouth. But somehow, she balanced it on the fork so it wouldn't fall and then she shoved it past her lips.

Her cheeks bulged like a chipmunk. Her lips were covered in cake crumbles and creamy frosting. Piper's eyes drifted shut, her head lolling to the side. Then she let out a moan that was nothing but sheer pleasure, like the ones I'd coaxed from her in the camper's bedroom.

The sound sent a jolt through my veins, stirring the lust I'd been fighting for days.

She finished chewing, opened her eyes and went back to the cake for another gigantic bite. But before she brought it to her mouth, she paused to look at me and raise an eyebrow. Then she pointed to my fork with her gaze.

Right. Cake. For dinner.

I unglued myself from the door and pulled out the other chair to sit. Following her lead, I scooped a bite from the middle of the cake.

"Jesus Christ," I groaned as the flavor exploded in my mouth.

Piper grinned as she chewed. "Magic cake."

This cake was magic. Any remaining anger or frustration or irritation evaporated. It was just me, Piper and the best cake I'd ever had in my life.

The texture of the cake was fluffy and moist. The flavor of the frosting was rich but not too sweet. It was like happiness in physical form. This cake had actual healing powers. I hadn't felt this good since . . . well, since I'd last had sex with Piper.

I swallowed the first bite quickly, needing more. I scooped another heap from the middle of the cake, letting another groan loose as soon as I'd fit it in my mouth.

Across the table, Piper giggled with her mouth full.

We ate with abandon. There was nothing prim or proper about how we attacked the cake. She didn't take tiny bites. She didn't ask for a napkin. She just wiped the crumbs away with her fingers if she couldn't catch them first with her tongue.

This cake brought out a relaxed and carefree side to Piper I'd never seen.

Magic cake.

Piper and I demolished the cake until all that was left was the outside ring with a hollow crater in the center.

"Please tell me you have milk." She stood from the table and walked to the fridge.

As she opened the door, I gave myself a mental fist pump that it no longer smelled. Then I stood and went to the cupboard for glasses.

She poured from the carton and we each downed a glass.

When her glass was empty, she set it down and leaned on the counter, smiling with a sigh. "I love magic cake."

"You have a milk mustache." I stepped closer to wipe it away.

The moment the pad of my thumb touched her skin, an electric shock ran up my arm. She sucked in a sharp breath, holding it in her lungs as I dragged my thumb from one corner of her mouth to the other. Her gaze was locked with mine.

Blood rushed to my groin and my heart rate spiked. Instead of my thumb, I wanted to kiss that milk away. I wanted to devour those lips and see if they tasted like chocolate.

I leaned in, seconds away from hoisting her onto this counter and fitting myself between her legs. But then she blinked, tearing her eyes away and aiming them at the floor.

"I, um . . ." She blew out her breath. "How about that tour of your shop?"

I dropped my hand and took a step back. Then another. The smell of her hair and the heat from her skin made me lose my mind, and I needed some distance to think straight. I took a few breaths to get my racing heart under control. I ignored the sting to my ego that she'd just shut me down.

We'd been seconds away from a hot, sweaty night in my bed, but she'd put on the brakes. If she didn't want to go there tonight, I'd respect that. Though we needed to get far away from my bedroom and to a place where nothing reminded me of sex.

"A tour sounds good." I turned and crossed the room, taking the shop key off a hook by the door. With my back to her, I made a quick adjustment to my stiff cock, then held the door open for her.

Her heels clapped on the floor as she went outside. "I like your porch. I'm surprised you don't sit out here."

My eyebrows came together. "I do."

"Oh." She shrugged. "I just assumed you didn't since there

aren't any chairs."

"Huh." I guess there weren't.

Normally, I just sat on the railing, leaning against one of the posts. The porch ran along the entire front of the cabin. From here, I could see through the trees and down the slope of the mountain. I'd sit out here and spy on deer or other animals.

A year ago, a black bear had come through here every now and again to scratch her back on one particular tree. A different summer, there'd been an eagle that had built the beginnings of a nest in one of the trees before giving it up to relocate somewhere else.

Maybe some chairs would be a nice addition.

I was mentally sketching a design by the time I walked down the steps and joined Piper by my gray truck parked in the narrow gravel driveway.

I didn't have a yard up here so there was no mowing or maintenance. It was all natural, including the footpath I'd worn between my house and the shop.

"Can you make it in those shoes?" I asked.

"I'm good."

"You sure?" I could carry her down if I needed to, though that might be dangerous for us both. I'd probably get so distracted by her in my arms I'd trip and crash us both.

"I'm sure." She waved me off. "I've had years of practice in shoes like this. I'm just as steady on heels as I am in sneakers."

I scoffed. "Uh-huh."

"I am! See?" With that, she skipped down the trail. She fucking skipped, like a little kid. Her hair bounced on her shoulders. Her arms swung at her sides.

I about had a damn heart attack, running to keep up just in case she slipped.

But she made her point, arriving safely at the shop without

so much as a hint of a wobble on those shoes. I scowled at her smug grin, then unlocked the shop.

We went in through the side door since I used it most. The front of the shop was a large garage door, but I opened it rarely for deliveries or in the summer afternoons when I needed a breeze to chase out the heat. It was nice to have open, but I didn't want to risk having a squirrel or bird sneak inside and make my shop their new home.

I flipped on the panel of lights by the door as I stepped inside. Like always, my first breath was a long one, dragging in the smell of sawdust and lacquer.

Piper came in behind me, her eyes tracking everywhere as she took in the walls and tall ceilings. "Wow. This is quite the place."

It was my haven. A place only a few had ever stepped inside, not once a woman.

The exterior of the building was made of two-tone steel, the bottom rimmed with dark brown while the rest was tan. The roof and garage door matched the darker color. I'd paid extra for a nonwhite building, but it had been worth it so the shop blended in with the trees.

Still, it was simple. It was a steel box that didn't have a lot of exterior charm.

The inside was a different story.

The tool benches on the wall beside the side door were as high quality as you could get, more expensive than what you'd find in most mechanics' garages. I'd made the shelving myself to hold larger tools, as well as the large racks at the back of the shop that I used to sort and store wood. I'd added extra lights to ensure that even in the dead of night, I could be here and it would feel like high noon.

The center of the vast space was where I kept works in

progress. There were two tabletops out now, each stacked on sawhorses. One of the projects was Piper's table.

"You're an organized one, aren't you?" Her eyes were locked on the pegboards along the wall, where every tool was hung in its own precise location.

"I take care of my tools."

"And your house. It's the cleanest bachelor pad I've ever seen."

I coughed to cover a laugh.

"What are you making?" She walked over to her table.

"These are both dining room tables."

She nodded, her hand going out to the walnut wood, skimming over the top to test its texture. "This is beautiful."

So are you.

My lips barely managed to keep the words from spilling out.

This was casual. We were having some sex, enjoying one another. This thing between us would just get complicated if we gave out compliments like we were more than lovers.

"Who is this table for?"

"Just a lady." It wasn't a complete lie. But if I told her the table was hers, that would just lead to questions about why I was making her a table.

Before I answered those, I had another to solve.

Why her?

seven

PIPER

WHEN I DIED, I WANTED TO BE BURIED IN SAWDUST.

My parents were New York natives, so were their parents and their grandparents. City blood ran through my veins. I loved living in Montana, but I'd be lying if I said I didn't miss the noisy traffic, bustle of energy and potent scents from metropolitan streets.

But the smell of Kaine's shop was paradise.

It erased the homesickness I'd been feeling for the last few days. It soothed away the worries that I'd made a mistake by moving here. The smell was like being wrapped in a warm blanket after walking five blocks in a snowstorm.

It was almost as magical as my cake.

I splayed both hands on the tabletop in front of me, pushing down hard to see how sturdy it was on the sawhorses. It was like a rock, so I leaned a hip on the edge.

"What's left to finish this piece?"

Kaine came closer to the table. He touched the raw edge, then brushed away a loose wood shaving. "It's all sanded and ready to stain. Once I do that, the grains will really come alive. Then I'll build the base."

"Is the edge going to be like this? Or will you cut it off so it's straight?"

"I was going to leave it like this. It's called a live edge. It's not for everyone."

"I love it." At the edges, the bark was still attached. Along its edge, the wood had a lighter tone, almost yellow, where the rings were newer. The contrast between the darker center, the black knots and the bright edges was stunning. It wasn't just a table, it was art. "I want a table like this for my place."

Kaine's mouth broke into a smile, blinding me with his white teeth. I hadn't seen anything more than a slight grin from him before. His eyes sparkled with something new. Humor, maybe? Amusement?

Whatever it was, he dazzled me.

"Are you actually smiling?" I teased. "I didn't think you knew how. Where's my phone? I need to take a picture."

I patted my dress pockets, pretending to search for my phone. And that's when I got the good stuff. Kaine's laughter echoed in the shop. It wasn't a doubled-over, booming laugh, but I'd take it.

I hid my own smile by turning away and pointing to the other project he had set up in the middle of the room. "What's that over there?"

"That's a custom table for a guy who lives in Utah. He's giving it to his wife for Christmas."

"That's sweet."

He walked over to the table, touching the round top. "This is just the framework right now. I'll mount this to a tooled and spun pedestal. Then once I get it all built and shaped, I'll be putting a design on top."

I was frozen in place as I watched him run his large hands across the table. He was gentle with the wood, caressing it like he had my skin.

"It's basically these thin wooden pieces, like an overlay," he said. "My client wants to try and have the design match this quilt of his wife's grandmother. I guess they were really special to one another. So I'm recreating the design with different wood colors in the pattern on top."

My mouth fell open a bit as he spoke. Maybe the sawdust smell worked magic on Kaine too because that was more words in a single stretch than I'd ever gotten from him.

"That's amazing." *He* was amazing. "Your work is . . . breathtaking."

He shrugged and ducked his head. Was he getting shy? He turned his back to me, but before he hid his face, I swore I saw a blush. He *was* shy. My god, that was sexy.

Not wanting to embarrass him, I scanned for other pieces in the shop. When my eyes landed on one by a stack of dowels, my jaw dropped. I had no place to store it, but I needed it for my new house. "Tell me that one isn't sold yet."

"Sorry. I've got a guy picking it up in a couple days. I'm just waiting for the epoxy to cure and then I'll seal it. But it turned out nice."

"Nice?" I mocked. "It's stunning."

He'd taken what looked like a swath from a huge tree and mounted it onto three legs to serve as an end table. The top was full of cracks and breaks from how the tree had grown. Kaine had filled them all with some kind of blue plastic, making them look like streams of water running through the honey-colored wood.

This man was so much more than he let people see. He came across so rough and cold, but in this shop, I saw an entirely new side to Kaine Reynolds. He was full of hidden passion and bursting with creativity. He'd poured his heart into these pieces.

Kaine inspected part of the table, testing the blue epoxy. He was wearing jeans today, and as he bent down, they hugged his thighs and ass. It was the first time I'd seen him in something other than Carhartts. He was delicious.

We'd been so close to kissing in his kitchen. If I hadn't suggested the shop tour, we would have ended up having sex in his bedroom.

I wasn't ready for that.

I wasn't ready to share his bed.

Over the last few days, I'd thought constantly about Kaine—more than I should have for a casual, no-strings, strictly physical relationship. So I'd decided to put up some boundaries.

There would be no sleepovers. Cuddling would be kept to a minimum. And I didn't want to get used to having sex in each other's beds.

The camper bed was the only exception. Because it was a temporary home, not my *real* bed, it didn't count. Though the couch would have been the safest bet, Kaine was just too big to make that cramped space comfortable for either of us to do some exploration.

If we kept sex to casual places, I'd be able to maintain some emotional distance. The camper was safe. Even this shop could work.

Along with the location boundaries, I was also setting some limits on the amount of time we spent together. I was forcing myself to stay away from Kaine for at least three days between hookups. Three days.

I'd barely made it.

When I'd gotten home from Logan and Thea's place early this afternoon, I'd decided to take the rest of the afternoon off and make a magic cake.

Because I was homesick.

My family was busy in New York. I'd been busy too, but when I'd lived there, they'd only been a train ride away. I'd taken their closeness for granted. Leaving the city after my divorce had been the right decision. I didn't regret coming to Montana. Still, I missed my family.

So in an effort to cheer myself up, I'd decided to make the chocolate cake my aunt had taught me how to make in high school.

I wasn't sure if it was the high butter and sugar content or the dark chocolate I bought for the frosting. But it had never once failed to lift my spirits. I'd deemed it magic after it had soothed my broken heart when I'd gotten dumped by my high school boyfriend two days before junior prom.

Magic cake had helped me through the hardest nights of my divorce when Adam's pleas to reconcile had worn my emotions raw.

I'd made the cake in the camper's tiny oven, then frosted it once it had cooled. I'd debated eating it all myself, but then I'd realized my three-day limit was over. My feet had just carried me over to Kaine's, cake plate in hand.

When he'd answered the door shrouded in the grief he wore like a gray mist, I'd known visiting was the right decision. *Magic cake to the rescue.*

After more calories than was healthy, the anger and sadness on his face was gone. I'd even earned myself a smile.

Kaine was still lost in his end table, so I took the quiet minute to study the benches and shelves I'd only just glanced at before.

There were hooks and drawers for everything. The larger machines all had their place. The shop was right up my alley, organized and structured to the point of near compulsion.

"I think the way you keep your shop organized is . . . sexy."

That got Kaine's attention. He stood from where he'd been hunched, momentary surprise on his face. Then he schooled his features into what could only be called a smolder.

The heat in his gaze melted my core, sending a rush of desire between my thighs.

Kaine stalked toward me like a mountain lion would its prey. His long legs closed the distance between us in a flash, bringing with him the heat we'd sparked in the kitchen. Only now it had magnified tenfold.

He didn't stop when he crossed into my space. He didn't give me any breathing room. Instead, he crushed his chest against mine, then gripped my hips and hoisted me onto the table at my back.

"Whoa," I breathed.

"I want to fuck you."

"Yes," I moaned.

"I want to fuck you with those shoes digging into my back."

My sex clenched, on the verge of a spontaneous orgasm. I nodded, now panting against his bearded cheek. He had yet to kiss me or make his move. Instead, we just breathed the same air. We let the fire between our bodies melt together.

The skirt of my dress was hiked up my thighs, the material stretching over my hips. My Montana work attire was mostly jeans and a cute top with sandals, but I'd opted for a dress today. Probably because I'd been a bit homesick and wanted to dress like I would have in the city. Even baking my cake, I'd kept on the dress and heels.

I mentally high-fived myself for being too lazy to change.

All Kaine had to do was reach between us and he'd find the center of my panties wet.

Which was exactly what he did. He wasn't careful or soft as he dove under my skirt. He went for the gusset of my panties like an arrow finding the bullseye.

"Oh, hell," I moaned, letting my head go limp toward my shoulder as two of Kaine's fingers yanked my panties aside and thrust inside my slick heat.

He curved them, finding the spot that made me squirm. I tilted my hips closer, desperate for some attention on my clit. But he wouldn't touch me there. He wouldn't kiss me. He just plunged his fingers in and out, breathing against my mouth.

I leaned forward, angling my lips for his, but he backed off an inch and shook his head. "I want to watch."

I nodded, panting even more as I wiggled closer. I spread my thighs as wide as the stretch of my skirt would allow. With one hand gripping the edge of the table to keep from falling, I used the other to drag the hem up even farther.

The rough denim covering Kaine's legs scratched against the sensitive flesh of my inner thighs, all while his fingers kept plundering.

"Touch yourself," he commanded, his eyes catching mine. "Show me."

I held his eyes as my free hand went between my legs. It slipped into the waistband of my panties and found my aching clit.

"Fuck." We moaned the curse together as I let my finger swirl over the hard nub.

I wanted to close my eyes. I wanted to just disappear, shut out the world and let the pleasure consume me. But I kept my focus on Kaine and the changing colors of his irises. I watched as the gold flared and the green got swallowed by the brown.

It didn't take long until I felt my orgasm swell. My finger swirled faster as he stroked my inner walls. Then the explosion came, rolling over every muscle, pulse after pulse.

Kaine groaned as I clamped down on his fingers. I barely heard the slide of his zipper as I rode out my release. Though I did catch my own whimper as he pressed his crown to my entrance.

With an easy glide, he replaced his fingers with his cock, stretching my sensitive folds around his width. Just like all of our other times together, he didn't hold back. He used those powerful hips to leave me breathless on every thrust.

My legs wrapped around his waist, pulling him close. Then I dug my heels into his ass, earning a hiss.

Kaine returned the sting by yanking me forward with his meaty grip. His fingertips held a bruising grasp on my ass. That hint of pain mixed with the sensation of his cock thrusting inside had me barreling toward another orgasm.

It was like falling down a hill. The more you rolled, the faster you went, and there was no holding myself back from coming hard. He'd paralyzed my vocal cords, so all I had was an open mouth as I silently screamed through my release.

Not Kaine. He let loose the loudest roar I'd ever heard. The sound waves echoed in the cavernous shop, ricocheting off the metal before soaking into the wood.

As I fought to find my senses, I wrapped my arms around Kaine's neck and sagged against his chest. He took all my weight, holding me on the slightest edge of the table until I'd finally filled my lungs and calmed my racing heart.

"Wow." I leaned away and cracked my eyes open.

Kaine's eyes were waiting, staring at me with such intensity that I squirmed on the table. His expression was full of lingering lust and some hesitancy.

Had sex in the shop been a mistake? Had we just tainted his sacred ground? Or did his worries match mine?

Was casual sex going to ruin us both?

We'd only been together a few times, but this fling was exhilarating. It was exciting to look across our shared forest, hoping to catch a glimpse of him as I went in and out of the camper. It was a thrill to see how long I could stay away from his temptation.

And learning little things about him was an adventure.

Like tonight, I'd discovered that his refrigerator was clean but nearly empty. I'd fallen in love with the furniture he made for others.

"I hope the owners of this table don't mind that we just broke it in for them." A giggle escaped my lips as Kaine's chest heaved with a silent laugh.

He smirked, giving me the same look he had earlier, like he knew something I didn't.

"What?" I asked.

"Nothing." He shook his head. "I'm sure the owner of this table won't care that we just fucked on it. But I'll keep that info out of the care instructions, just in case."

"Good call." I giggled again before he slid out and tucked himself back in his jeans.

He backed up and held out a hand, helping me down from the table. As I righted my dress, he zipped his fly and fixed the black T-shirt that I'd pulled crooked at some point during our escapades.

The overhead lights buzzed as silence descended on the shop. I shuffled on my sandals, not sure where to look. Kaine ran a hand over his beard, avoiding my space.

Should I leave? Should I say something? Thank you, maybe? Clearly, I wasn't good at the after part of casual sex. If we were in my camper, he would have already been out the door at this point. But I needed to get my cake plate from inside his cabin. It felt weird to just wave good-bye and walk out the door.

"Where'd you get that scar?"

Kaine's question surprised me and I looked up from my feet. He was staring at my hands where I'd absently been rubbing the scar on top of my right wrist.

"Oh, I, um . . . I cut it on some glass." That was the short version of a long story.

I'd been distraught after I'd learned that Adam had kissed his costar. That night, I left our apartment in a daze and walked around the neighborhood block. I made the loop three times as tears streamed down my face.

When the shock passed, I got so angry that I decided to go to the restaurant and confront my cheating husband.

Furious and heartbroken, I wasn't paying much attention to traffic as I walked. About five blocks from the restaurant, I stepped out into the crosswalk—I swore the walk signal was on. I swore it. But I stepped right in front of an oncoming taxi. They swerved, missing me by an inch, and crashed into a light pole. Glass shattered everywhere. Most of my skin was covered, except for my hands. One shard sliced deeply into the back of the hand I used to shield my face.

I was lucky. The driver of the car sustained a concussion.

I spent the next two hours in the emergency room, getting the cut cleaned up and assuring the doctor I hadn't stepped into traffic on purpose.

When I finally got home, Adam was upset I'd missed his calls. He was worried.

I apologized for worrying him, then asked for a divorce.

"It was a nasty cut and I have always been bad about picking at scabs." I shrugged, tucking a lock of hair behind my ear. "My mom used to cover me in Band-Aids because it was the only way to keep me from picking at my skinned knees or elbows."

Kaine stepped closer, touching the shell of my left ear. "Why do you tuck your hair behind this ear but not this one?"

"It's silly." I sighed. "My right ear is bigger than my left. I guess I got used to keeping it covered a long time ago."

"Huh?"

"It's true." I held my hair back so he could see both ears.

"When I was a teenager, I never wore my hair up. I got over that eventually, but the tucking thing is just an old habit."

He looked from one ear to the other, then shook his head. "They're the same size."

"No, they're not. Trust me, I spent hours in the mirror as a teenager comparing the two." That had been my favorite pastime as a seventeen-year-old learning to accept the things about her body she could not change.

Kaine turned and walked over to the wall with all of the tool chests. He opened a drawer, pulled out a tape measure, then came stalking back.

"Don't move," he commanded as he proceeded to extend the tape a few inches.

"You're really measuring my e—"

"Shh."

I clamped my mouth shut, pulling my lips between my teeth to hold in a smile. Then I stood stoically still as the metal tape whispered across my ears and Kaine's face narrowed in concentration.

He didn't just measure the height of my ears, he measured the width, the distance they were from my nose. It was a more detailed inspection than I would have expected from a plastic surgeon's office.

When he was done, he stepped back from my face with a smug grin and his tape measure. "Your right ear is an eighth of an inch smaller than your left."

"What?" I gasped. "No way!"

He nodded. "It is."

"Are you kidding?"

"All this time you've been hiding the wrong ear, Dumbo."

"Hey!" I smacked him playfully on the shoulder, then broke out into hysterical laughter.

To my surprise, he did too. Kaine's laughter was deep and hoarse, almost like he hadn't used it in so long that it needed to have the rust broken free.

But it was beautiful as it filled the shop, making the already-bright space shimmer.

And the sight of his smile, wide and white underneath those soft lips and between those dark bearded cheeks, was more breathtaking than even the ridge on our mountain.

He was dashing.

I refused to blink, not wanting to miss a moment of that rare laugh. And I vowed, then and there, to make him smile more often.

A sense of pride filled my chest, squeezing out the pain from past memories. Knowing I was the cause of his smile and laugh was empowering. I did that. Me.

I made Kaine smile.

He made me forget.

Now I had to make it three days without him. Three days. I'd force myself to wait those seventy-two hours because being around him was too good. It was too dangerous.

Could I make it three days?

With the way my heart was sprouting wings, I'd better try and make it four.

Two days later, a fist knocked on the Airstream's door, making me shoot out of bed. It was dark, and after a quick glance at my clock, I saw it was after midnight.

My heart raced, my mind immediately imagining the worst. Was someone here to kill me? Would they feed my body to a bear? I grabbed my phone and dialed 9-1-1, ready to hit send, but

I hesitated.

As quietly as possible, I slipped out of bed and ducked low. Then I crouched, getting on my hands and knees to crawl out of the bedroom.

Logan and Thea had bought this Airstream brand-new. Its finishes were light and airy, and it reminded me a little of the apartment I'd left behind in the city. I couldn't have asked for a better temporary abode.

But at this moment, all I really wanted was a door with a deadbolt.

Why didn't I own pepper spray? Or a gun? Not that I knew how to shoot either. But they were both sold at the sporting goods store in Kalispell. All I had to defend myself was my cast-iron skillet.

I sucked at being a Montanan. I'd left all of my self-preservation tendencies on the subway in New York. If I was about to be murdered and fed to a bear, I had no one but myself to blame.

I continued to crawl, making it past the bedroom and into the kitchen. I couldn't reach for a knife without my murderer seeing me through the large front window.

The knock came again and curiosity overruled judgment. Carefully, I rose up on my knees and peeked past the table to the door. A lock of dark hair caught my eye first, followed by an arm of familiar, bulky muscles.

I sighed, breathing again as I slumped onto the wooden floor.

It was my sexy neighbor.

I pushed up off the floor, watching through the window as Kaine spotted me. His eyebrows came together, probably confused by what I'd been doing on the floor. I went right to the door, flipping the flimsy lock and opening up for him.

"You scared me," I hissed.

He winced. "Sorry."

"It's fine. Come in." It wasn't like I'd be going back to sleep after that scare. My hand rubbed at my sternum, soothing my still-racing heart, as I stood back so he could climb the step.

He reached behind him and closed the door.

Then to my complete surprise, he pulled me into his arms. One of his hands pressed the back of my head so my cheek was resting against his heart. With the other, he trailed a light path up my bare arm.

He was dressed in his Carhartt pants and smelled like wood varnish. He'd probably just come from the shop.

I was in my pajamas, a thin tank top and silk sleep shorts with a ruffled edge. Both were a pink so pale they were nearly white.

"What are you doing here?" I murmured into his shirt as I wound my hands around those narrow hips and tucked them into the back pockets of his pants.

"Thought I'd see if you had any cake."

I laughed. "I'm all out."

"Damn. I need something sweet." His arm left my hair, trailing down my back and to my ass. I didn't have pockets for him to use, so instead he slipped those callused fingers into the waistband of my shorts and palmed my ass, skin to skin.

A shiver broke across my shoulders and I tipped my head back. The moment I did, he captured my mouth in a desperate kiss.

"Sweet," he whispered against my lips before sweeping his tongue inside.

It had been only two days since the night in his shop and my magic cake. A part of me was glad that I wasn't the only one getting addicted. I wasn't the only one here aching for another taste.

The other part of me was disappointed because I'd been

counting on Kaine to keep his distance.

If he came over every two days, I was going to get attached.

No. I wouldn't let myself get attached to Kaine Reynolds. I wouldn't let myself believe that I could heal his broken heart. Or that he could heal mine.

One more night didn't mean this was love.

And next time, I'd go longer.

eight

PIPER

TWO WEEKS LATER, I WAS PERCHED ON A STOOL AT THE LARK Cove Bar with a paper boat of peanuts by one hand and a seasonal wheat beer by the other. Thea and Jackson were both working behind the bar, and I was here to hang out with them and Willa.

"How much of a pain in the ass is it to clean up all these peanut shells?" I asked Thea as I shucked another and let the shell fall to the floor.

She shrugged. "It's not so bad. At first, I tried to sweep them up all the time. I was so used to Manhattan bars where finger-prints anywhere were a capital offense. It made me twitchy to see them pile up. But then I got used to it, and now I just wait and sweep them up after closing."

"I love it." I popped the peanut into my mouth, crunching away. "It's so . . . chill."

She smiled just as a man walked up to the bar to order a pitcher of beer.

This entire place was relaxed. The Lark Cove Bar was may-be my favorite place in the entire town. It was unique because of its owners and their flair for charm.

Compared to most bars in the city, it was actually kind of dingy—but in a good way. The bar itself ran in a long L along the back and side walls. The booths by the front windows had been beaten and battered from years of use. The pool table had been re-covered recently, but the legs showed where it had been kicked or scratched throughout the years. There was even a legitimate jukebox that played country music so twangy it was like stepping back in time forty years.

The high ceilings were open, and the iron beams running from one side to the other were exposed. It had a rustic, industrial look, thanks to the scuffed wooden floors and the walls paneled to match. The barstools were all different, and the one I was sitting on wobbled slightly to the right.

Shelves of liquor were loaded against a mirror that stretched along the back wall behind the bar. The footrail my purse was sitting on had visible grooves from people resting their feet in the same place, year after year.

The walls were covered in neon and metal signs as well as numerous framed pictures. My first visit here, I'd spent almost thirty minutes inspecting them all. It was like staring at a living timeline, one that had been started by the original owners and continued by their daughter, Hazel, when she'd taken over the bar.

And now, this place was run by Thea and Jackson—Hazel's children for all intents and purposes. She wasn't their biological mother, but she'd been their role model for so long, they looked to her like a parent. And though they weren't related either, Thea and Jackson were basically siblings.

At least, they argued like brother and sister.

Being around them made me miss my own family, especially my younger brother Owen. The two of us had grown apart, like adult siblings do, but as a kid, he'd been my best friend.

I made a mental note to call him tomorrow. Then I added my parents and grandparents to my call roster too. Maybe if I was better about calling my family, the physical distance between us would seem like less than thousands of miles.

I'd go home to visit. Eventually. But not until Adam had more time to come to terms with our divorce.

What would he think of this place? I laughed to myself, picturing his look of horror.

Adam and I ran with a certain crowd of friends in New York, none of whom would be caught dead in the Lark Cove Bar. Our evenings out had always been spent in the same type of establishments. They were all clean and upscale. They were all on the cusp of the latest trends.

We went to the bars and restaurants so Adam could be seen.

But the Lark Cove Bar wasn't about being seen. It was about seeing people and friends and neighbors. This place was as much of a cornerstone of this community as the Statue of Liberty was a symbol of America.

Every time I came here, I noticed something new. That was just how much stuff was crammed into the nooks and crannies. My eyes snagged on a set of antlers in one far corner off to the side of a large flat-screen TV. A bunch of trucker hats hung from its horns and at the very back, I could make out a scrap of lace.

"Oh my god." I choked on my peanut, coughing and hacking. I grabbed a swig of my beer, chasing down the bite that had tried to murder me. My eyes were watering as I looked at Thea and then back at the antlers. "Is that a bra?"

Thea and Jackson both laughed, then shared a look before Jackson jumped in to explain.

"There was this woman in here about five or six years ago who was coming on to me," Jackson said.

"This should be enlightening," Willa muttered from the stool at my side.

"Come on, babe." Jackson came down the bar, leaning

across it to give her a soft kiss. "Don't get jealous."

She rolled her eyes but couldn't fight her smile. With her delicate frame, striking blue eyes and long blond hair hanging in waves to her waist, Willa was more angel than human. Or maybe that was because of how Jackson looked at her.

Thea had told me stories about Jackson, how he'd been a playboy for years. It wasn't hard to believe since the man was as handsome as his wife was beautiful. He had eyes the color of a cloudless Montana sky and the frame of a star quarterback.

His wicked grin and charismatic personality could have attracted any woman in this bar, but he was all Willa's. The day he'd noticed the shy woman who'd always had a crush on him was the day all other women stopped existing in his life.

She might grumble at old stories of women hitting on her husband, but we all knew exactly who owned his heart.

Those two were making gaga eyes at each other, so Thea jumped in to continue the story of the bra.

"So this woman was all handsy on Jackson. But he wasn't paying her any attention."

Jackson shrugged, still leaning on the bar in front of Willa. "It was a busy night. She was too drunk."

"Drunk?" Thea scoffed. "That is putting it lightly. We cut her off but she didn't leave. She just kept hanging around the end of the bar, waiting for Jackson to walk past. Every time he went to clear a table, she'd follow him around and try to grope his ass."

Sweet, gentle Willa let out a sound that could only be considered a rabid growl.

Jackson just chuckled and leaned over to give her another kiss.

"I can't remember exactly what happened, but this woman . . ." Thea rolled her eyes. "She was relentless! She followed

Jackson around all night like a little puppy, trying to nip at his heels and hump his leg."

Jackson's face flushed as he shook his head. "What happened next was not my fault."

Thea laughed. "She was so sad that he wasn't paying her any attention. So she decided to make a scene. She walked up to this group of guys who'd just ordered a pitcher. She swiped it off their table, shouted 'Wet T-shirt contest, woohoo!' then poured it over her head."

"Oh. My god." I snorted, laughing along with Thea.

Jackson groaned. "So I bring her one of the bar T-shirts we used to sell."

"Which happened to be white," Thea added.

"I get the shirt pulled over her head," Jackson continued. "And I'm thinking she'll take the opportunity to wise up. Or at the very least one of her friends, who'd been sitting in the corner booth, would intervene. But they didn't. Those bitches just sat there laughing and watching as this drunk chick struggled out of the drenched tank top she was wearing underneath the T-shirt I'd just pulled over her head. She threw the tank top across the bar—"

"And then came the bra." Thea finished for him.

"Landed right on the antlers Hazel's dad had hung up there thirty years ago."

"Why didn't you take it down?" I asked.

Jackson hung his head again as Thea kept laughing. "Things got worse."

Willa giggled. "How?"

"There was still another pitcher on the table."

My eyes widened. "Noooo!"

"Oh yes!" Thea nodded. "And that's why we don't sell white T-shirts anymore."

We all laughed, even Jackson, causing a ruckus in the bar. None of the other patrons seemed to care, and a couple of the regulars were even listening in.

"She came in the next day and apologized," Jackson said. "I've never seen anyone that green before. I asked her if she wanted her shirt and bra back, but she said she never wanted to be reminded of that night again."

"Obviously, we never did take down the bra." Thea shrugged. "I don't know. I guess I like it up there. It reminds me of all the fun times we've had in this place."

Jackson moved closer to her, wrapping an arm around her shoulders. "That was a fun night."

"Sure was." She patted his stomach, then stepped away, going around the bar to check on some customers in the booths.

Thea had told me that things were different at the Lark Cove Bar than they'd been years ago. It wasn't just her and Jackson working as Hazel's employees anymore. They'd bought her out a year ago, making sure she was set for retirement with her husband Xavier, the retired town sheriff. And because both Thea and Jackson had families, neither one of them wanted to be tied to the bar every night.

They had another bartender who covered most of the later shifts. They put a heavier emphasis on food items, making it not only a bar but a full restaurant to rival the one other in town. They'd turned an old beer and whiskey joint into a must-stop attraction on the tourist route around Flathead Lake.

Thea and Jackson had somehow turned a bar in the miniscule town of Lark Cove into a raving success.

A huge part of that success was simply because it was *fun*. Pure, unbridled, laugh-until-your-sides-hurt fun.

A lot of my moments in Montana had been fun.

It wasn't like I hadn't had good times in the city. But things were different here.

There were no expectations to keep quiet. If I stood on my stool and did a happy dance, people would cheer me on. No one cared if you got too drunk and made a fool of yourself. A bra was left hanging on the antlers so patrons could share a laugh years later.

Would Kaine like it here? Would he ever want to come down and split a pizza?

He popped into my mind, like he often did.

In the two weeks since he'd surprised me with his first late-night visit to my camper, we'd fallen into a routine. Every other day, he'd come over after dark. We'd have sex until the midnight hours and then he'd return home.

Two days was as long as we'd go without seeing one another. Like clockwork, he'd knock on my camper door just before the forty-eight-hour timer would run out, shooting my three-day rule right to hell.

I hadn't been back to his cabin or his shop in the last two weeks. We hadn't shared a meal, or conversation for that matter, so at least our relationship was limited to physical closeness only.

But I'd taken to staying up at night, waiting for his faint knock. I sat on the couch even on the nights when he wasn't due to come over, just in case. And during the day, he crept into my thoughts on an hourly basis.

Who was this man who'd swept into my life? What was his story? We'd agreed on casual, but feelings were beginning to stir.

Did he feel them too?

Spending time with him, kissing him and holding on to one another, was something I'd come to depend upon. I reveled in his company, his smell in my bed and his hands on my body.

Kaine chased away the homesickness. When he held me in his arms, I wasn't alone.

When he was in the room, I wasn't the loneliest person there.

He was.

Kaine never mentioned family or friends. I hadn't seen another person come to his house except me. But something had caused him to retreat inside himself. Something had caused the severe pain that lingered behind his eyes.

What had happened to him?

I doubted I'd get the answer to that question. Kaine kept his demons locked up so tight they were silently wreaking havoc on his soul. He seemed determined to fight that battle alone.

My wish for him was to find friends or confidants, like the ones I'd found here.

"I'd better get home and check on Roman." Willa drained the last of her water glass.

Her son was only seven months old and she was still nursing. Her mom had volunteered to watch the baby tonight so Willa could have a little adult time.

She'd come down to eat pizza with me and Thea—and because she liked to visit when Jackson was working. But dinner had long since ended and even with the fun we were having, I didn't blame her for wanting to get back home.

"I'll walk you out, babe." Jackson rounded the bar. "Thea, you good for a few?"

"Take your time," she told him. "I'll hold down the fort."

We all hugged Willa good-bye, and I waved as Jackson escorted her outside. As soon as the door closed behind them, Thea went back behind the bar.

She'd only come to the bar tonight for some girl time. It was technically Jackson's night to work. But that didn't stop her from serving customers or making drinks. Just like I couldn't go into Logan's office at their house and not jump into my work, Thea couldn't be in this building without doing something.

"So . . . I did a thing," Thea announced. "Made a thing, actually. In my workshop."

"Yeah?" My shoulders perked up, excited to hear about her latest art project. She wasn't just a successful business owner and wife to a billionaire philanthropist, Thea was also an incredibly talented artist.

If I didn't love her so much, it would be easy to be jealous.

"Do you remember that day we went to look at your house for the first time? And we hiked the ridge?"

"Sure." That was the day I'd seen Kaine for the first time.

"You know the man we saw up there?"

I nodded. *Intimately.*

"I kind of couldn't get the image of him out of my head. So I used it for a piece. I brought it tonight." She held up a finger and hurried down the length of the bar to the hallway that disappeared behind the bar to her office and the kitchen. It didn't take her but a moment to come rushing back out with an unframed canvas in her hands.

"I don't know why." She held the canvas back so I couldn't see the front. "But I just had to capture him. He was so . . . raw."

Raw. That was the perfect way to describe that moment.

She glanced at the painting again, worry settling on her beautiful face. For as talented as she was, she was oddly secretive about her art. There was no doubt she could make a killing, selling her unique pieces in high-end galleries. But for the most part, she did it for fun. It was her outlet. Even when Logan had offered to buy her a nice studio, she'd refused. She created her pieces in an old garden shed that was practically falling apart.

"Hand it over." I motioned for the painting.

"I'm not the best painter."

I rolled my eyes. "You're talking to a woman who can't

draw stick figures."

She smiled and reluctantly turned the canvas. The painting stole my breath away.

Thea had captured Kaine's pain and trapped it on that canvas. It lived underneath the oil colors, jumping off the painting to settle heavy on my heart.

"Wow," I whispered, unable to blink or look away.

It was a stunning piece, but it physically hurt to look at. Just like the day we'd seen him on the ridge, I had the overwhelming urge to hold him. I ached to take some of his pain away, absorb it like a dry sponge.

I swallowed hard and forced a smile. I didn't want Thea to think my shocked reaction was because it was a bad piece. It was beautiful. Achingly beautiful. "You did an incredible job."

"You think?" She tapped her finger on the bar.

"It's amazing. But I, uh . . . I have a confession." I sighed. "I know him."

I'd kept my casual relationship with Kaine a secret from everyone, mostly because I hadn't known exactly how to describe it. And because I hadn't known if it would last. But it had gone on long enough that I felt like I was keeping a secret from my friend.

"How?" Thea asked.

"He's my neighbor."

"Hmmm." She nodded. "I wondered if he lived up there."

"There's more." I set the painting down. "We're kind of . . . hooking up."

Her mouth fell open. "You are?"

"Yeah." I shrugged. "It's nothing serious. Just a casual thing."

"Casual?"

"I've never done that before. Have you?"

She shook her head. "I don't know if I'm capable of casual.

I mean, look at me and Logan. I tried casual with him, got pregnant and basically thought about him every day for six years."

Thea stared at me for a long moment before she smiled. "I think this is a good thing."

"You don't think it's too soon?" I asked, voicing one of the many worries about my encounters with Kaine.

"You've been divorced for months. You and Adam were separated long before that. I think finding someone new is overdue."

My shoulders fell with immense relief. I needed to hear those words. I needed to have someone I admired and trusted tell me it was okay to move on from Adam.

"Do you like him?" Thea asked.

"I do," I admitted. "Neither of us is interested in anything serious. We don't really know anything about one another, but that kind of makes it fun. It's all different for me. But for the first time in years, I don't feel like I need to act a certain way to impress him. It's . . . freeing."

Thea's smile widened. "And he is not hard to look at."

"No." I blushed. "No, he is not."

Her painting hadn't captured the details of Kaine's face, simply because his hands had been covering most of it. But during our nights together, I'd memorized some of my favorite features. Now that I knew what his nose looked like from all angles and how his mouth was ever so slightly off-center from his strong chin, it made the painting even better.

I couldn't stop glancing at it resting on top of the bar.

"Keep it."

"What?" My gaze shot to Thea. "I can't keep this."

"Why not?"

"Well, what if he sees it? He might think I'm a crazy stalker who painted him."

Thea waved me off. "Tell him I did it, then draw him one of

those stick figures you were just bragging about."

I giggled. "Good point. He'll know right away I couldn't make this."

"I'm glad for you. I think a casual fling with a handsome man is just what you need."

Handsome was an understatement. Kaine didn't have a classically perfect face like Logan. He didn't have a charming, playful appeal like Jackson. Kaine was too serious. But he was better looking than either of them in my opinion, especially when he smiled.

The door behind me opened and Jackson came back inside. His eyes didn't shine as bright now that his wife had left. Behind him, the evening light was fading through the windows.

"Okay, I'd better get going." I downed the last of my beer and fished out some cash from my purse. It was only eight thirty but I wanted to stop by the grocery store before going home, and they closed in thirty minutes.

But before I could pay, Thea waved it off. "Family discount. And I'd better go too. I want to catch Charlie before Logan tucks her in."

"Have a good night." Jackson waved to us both as we walked out the door. Thea and I exchanged a quick hug before she got in her car to go home, and I climbed into mine.

Then I drove the two blocks down the highway to the grocery store, rifling through my purse for the list I'd made earlier as I walked inside. I gave the owner stationed behind the one and only register a quick smile and kept on digging.

"Seriously?" I grumbled. Why did my purse always eat my grocery lists?

It was nowhere to be found, so I gave up the search and plucked a basket from the stack next to the pushcarts. With it resting on my arm, I went through the small produce aisle first, collecting a bunch of bananas and a bag of baby carrots. Then I went up and down each of the other aisles, picking things that I remembered writing down and a plethora of items that I hadn't.

By the time I made it to the second to last aisle, my basket was getting heavy, and I cursed myself for not getting the full-sized cart. I turned down the baking aisle to get some brown sugar but froze when I saw the man standing in front of the Betty Crocker boxed cake mixes.

Kaine was glaring daggers at the box in his hand.

I grinned, walking as quietly as I could in my cork wedge sandals down the freshly waxed floor. "White cake? If you're going to go for something other than chocolate, at least get the rainbow chip."

His face whipped to the side, the scowl disappearing as he recognized me. Kaine was wearing a navy baseball hat, pulled low on his head so you could barely see his eyes. The light sporty jacket he wore was zipped up all the way to his neck.

"Is there a reason why you're standing in the baking aisle looking like a criminal in hiding?" With a quick flick, I tipped up his hat, knocking it back so I could see his eyes.

His frown returned as he put the cake mix back on the shelf and mumbled, "I was goingtoaskyou . . ."

"Huh?"

He shuffled down a few steps, grabbing another box and studying it like it was made of pure gold. He wouldn't look at me. He wouldn't speak up. Was he nervous?

Yes! He was totally nervous. It was strange and oddly sexy to see Kaine Reynolds, the man who preferred to speak in three-word sentences, jittery because I'd surprised him at the grocery store.

"What was that you said?" I pressed.

He shrugged those broad shoulders, huffing as he swapped

out one yellow cake mix for another. "I was going to ask you to dinner."

That was when I noticed the contents of his own shopping basket. He had two pork chops and a tub of macaroni salad. There was also a bowl of precut watermelon and a bag of dinner rolls.

I held back a smile, wanting to play with him a little. "I already ate."

"Tomorrow. I was going to ask you to dinner tomorrow," he grumbled, swiping a can of vanilla frosting off the shelf.

Yellow cake and vanilla frosting? *Eww.*

My face soured and he took it as a no to his invitation. With an angry huff, he shoved the frosting back on the shelf. But before he could walk away, I grabbed his arm.

"Wait. I'd love to go to dinner." With one hand restraining his elbow, I reached for the right kind of frosting for yellow cake. Chocolate. "But only if you make that cake with this frosting."

His frame relaxed. "Okay."

The reality of what had just happened sank in, and my heart beat double time. Kaine had just asked me over for dinner. Was it a date? Did he want more than just casual?

I took a breath, not wanting to get ahead of myself. This was casual. *We* were casual. This dinner invitation didn't have to be anything other than pork chops shared between neighbors.

"Can I bring anything?" I asked.

"Dinner." He chuckled. "I'm a shit cook."

"Just don't mess up the cake and we'll be fine."

nine

KAINE

BAKING WAS NOT MY STRENGTH.

I ruined the first cake mix because of the piss-poor instructions on the damn box. It said to insert a toothpick until it came out clean. Betty Crocker and I had different opinions on what a fucking clean toothpick looked like.

Fifteen minutes longer in the oven than the box recommended and the toothpick still came out with a small crumb. The instructions should have read crumby, not clean.

But I got lucky because I'd baked that cake—or tried—before noon. Once I'd let it cool and tossed it in the trash, I'd gone back to the grocery store and started all over again.

The second time around, I baked the cake according to the median time on the box, then took it out. To hell with the toothpicks.

Why had I invited Piper over last night at the grocery store? *Insanity.*

I'd gone down for my weekly visit, and like always, it had been right before closing time. That's when it was typically the quietest. The first few times I'd gone to the store, I'd been waved at, talked to and welcomed to town. People were too friendly in Lark Cove.

So I'd learned quickly to go in late, wear a hat to shield my face and emit a *don't talk to me* attitude that made men give me the side-eye and women scoot their carts as far from mine as possible.

There hadn't been anyone but me and the clerk in the store last night, so I'd let go of my edge. Then Piper had surprised me in the baking aisle, and I'd blurted out my invitation without thinking it through.

I'd planned on asking her to dinner casually. I was going to walk over to the camper and say, *Hey, I made dinner. Want some?*

If I screwed up the meal, it wouldn't have mattered. I wouldn't have invited her over. But since I'd lost my mind at the store, now there was all this pressure.

Now, this felt too much like a date.

We'd been having a blast these last couple of weeks in her camper. The sex just got better and better. But the last few times I'd walked home after leaving her bed, worries had kept me company in the dark.

Did she think I was just using her for sex? Piper was an incredible woman, and I didn't want her to feel . . . cheap. When I left her camper every other night, I had nothing but respect for that woman.

Was she a friend? Not really. I didn't have friends, not anymore. I didn't want friends. Just like I didn't want to be in a relationship with a woman ever again. But Piper deserved a little extra effort on my part than she'd gotten so far.

I'd hoped a nice, neighborly dinner would show her that she was more than a willing and able body to me.

We could have sex and occasionally share a meal without becoming serious. The idea was solid, my execution a disaster. All because she'd snuck up on me at the grocery store.

Did she think this was a date? Because it wasn't, even though it smelled like one.

This isn't a date.

I ran a hand over my beard, staring at the cake sitting on the counter. I glanced at the clock on the microwave and knew Piper would be here any minute.

Once she arrived, I'd get the grill going for the chops. Everything else was coming premade.

Everything except this cake.

A knock came at the door and I took one last look at the cake, hoping I'd made it right. The frosting wasn't anything like the frosting on Piper's magic cake. Hers had been even and smooth. Mine looked too thick on one side and too thin on the other. In one corner, there were cake bits crumbled in.

And I called myself an artist.

Piper knocked again and I left the cake to open the door.

"Nice chairs." She nodded to the porch chairs I'd set out this afternoon after cleaning my house again.

I shrugged, side-stepping so she could come inside.

But she didn't move. "Did you make those?"

"Yup."

"They're beautiful. I love them."

Heat crept up my neck and my toes squirmed in my boots. "Come on in."

She narrowed her eyes and still didn't move an inch. "Do you not like it when people compliment your work?"

I grunted.

Piper frowned. "That's not an answer to my question."

"Are you going to come inside or not?"

"Not." She crossed her arms over her chest.

"Fine." I walked into the kitchen to get out the pork chops, leaving the door open.

She could stand out there all night if she wanted. But what we weren't going to do was talk about my work.

No, I didn't like compliments about my work. They made me twitchy. Some designers relished the praise. I just wanted to make the best furniture my hands could craft. Getting paid was a bonus.

Feedback on my work was hard to hear, even the good stuff. I didn't know why. Maybe because each and every project was something personal.

My furniture was my passion. My art. It came from deep within my soul and flowed through my hands into the tools. Clients may give me guidance or direction, but each piece was mine.

My mother had once told me that my extreme humility was endearing. She'd also told me I was far too critical of my own work. She told me I invented flaws.

She just couldn't see them. Hardly anyone saw the mistakes but they were there.

Like those Adirondack chairs. One of them was slightly shorter than the other by about half an inch. And on that smaller chair, the middle board of the backrest was slightly darker. It should have gone on the base, not the back.

When someone did point out a flaw, I didn't just get twitchy. I flew off my rocker.

The one and only time I'd had a customer tell me they didn't like what I'd built them, I'd told them to fuck off and sent them their deposit back. That piece was the coffee table in my living room.

It didn't matter if people loved or hated them. That's not why I built them.

"I like that you're shy about your work," Piper said from the door. "But I'm not going to stop giving you compliments. Your work is the best I've ever seen. You don't have to acknowledge my comments. You don't even have to say thank you. But I'm not going to stop telling you how much I love it."

My frame deflated. She was just trying to be nice and I'd left her standing at the door. Then she'd said exactly the right thing. I glanced over my shoulder and nodded. "Thank you."

"You're welcome." Her shoes clicked on the floor as she came inside. As I plated the raw meat, the door clicked shut.

She went to the living room, setting down her purse on my coffee table. She bent and skimmed her fingertips over the table's top, smiling as she admired the piece. But she didn't gush over it like I'd expected. She let those dimples and the way her hands lingered on the wood tell me how much she liked it.

"Want something to drink?" I asked.

"Sure." She sat down on my leather couch. "Whatever you're having is fine with me."

I washed my hands, then went to the fridge, getting out two bottles of beer. I popped the tops, tossing them into the garbage, then delivered one to Piper.

"I haven't tried this yet." She inspected the label before tipping it back to her lips.

"It's a local brewery. They're good." I took a drink from my own bottle, still standing in the middle of the room.

Should I sit with her? Make small talk? Getting too close was dangerous. We'd never make it to dinner once that spark ignited. And I hated small talk.

I swallowed another gulp of beer. "I'm going to get the grill going."

"Okay." She stayed seated, turning her attention to the end table at her side. Again, she smiled at my work, touching it gently, but didn't say anything.

I took it as my cue to escape outside and light the grill on the porch.

This isn't a date. I repeated it over and over as I drained the rest of my beer, then I trudged back inside. This wasn't a date. So there was no reason to avoid Piper. Right?

"Can I set the table?" Piper asked, standing from the couch as I went to the cabinet for my favorite seasoning.

"Sure." Maybe it would be easier if she was moving around and making this dinner more of a joint effort. "Plates are in the cabinet next to the sink. Silverware in the drawer underneath."

"Got it."

While she bustled around the kitchen, I seasoned the pork chops. With every shake of the bottle, I inhaled a deep breath. After the fourth, my shoulders began to relax.

"Want another beer?" she asked as she set a plate on the table.

"Sure." I glanced over my shoulder in time to see her guzzle the rest of her own beer. Okay, maybe I wasn't the only one nervous about this dinner.

She went to the fridge, getting us each another beer. She handed me mine as I took the chops outside to the grill. Piper followed me out, taking a seat in the smaller chair as I went to the grill and put on the meat.

"They're comfortable." She ran her hand over the arm of the chair, then she grinned. "That was a fact, not a compliment."

I chuckled. Her joke lightened my mood, and I crossed the porch. It was a risk to sit next to her, but one I took as I sank into the other chair. We sat quietly, looking out into the trees as we drank these beers more slowly than the first.

After about three minutes, the rest of my anxiety just blew away. My body relaxed into the seat. Sitting here with Piper was easy, like we'd done it for years, not moments. Nothing about this dinner needed to be awkward.

This was Piper. She wasn't some strange woman I'd asked on a first date. We both knew and understood our boundaries.

We were lovers. We were neighbors. Nothing more. When tonight was over, she'd go to her property while I stayed on mine.

"How goes the remodel?" I asked.

"Good. They're starting to put walls back in place so it feels like we're finally getting somewhere."

"And work?"

"Also good." A smile tugged at the corners of her mouth. "This was the best week I've had in a long time."

"Tell me about it." With the way her face lit up, I didn't want her to stop talking.

"Did I ever tell you that my brother is a veteran?" she asked and I shook my head. "Owen went into the military right after high school and served for about twelve years. He had a hard time coming home after his final deployment. A close friend from his unit committed suicide and it really affected him."

"Sorry to hear that."

"Me too. But he's in a lot better place now. He found a job working with an organization that helps veterans like his friend. The Kendrick Foundation donates to them every year. And it has sort of become my pet project, finding other organizations like his who help veterans."

Piper's eyes sparkled whenever she spoke about her work. I was so lost in her face, I nearly forgot the food on my grill. "Shit. One sec." I hurried to the grill and flipped the pork chops before they burned, then came back to my seat and nodded for her to continue.

"Not long after I moved here, I found an article in the Kalispell paper about this organization in Bozeman that helps veterans. They take them fly-fishing for a week and teach them a skill they can use to get some peace. I was skeptical at first, but their success rates are incredible. The testimonials from some of the participants are phenomenal. I pitched it to Logan, and today, we wrote them a million-dollar check to fund them for the next three years."

"Nice job."

She blushed. "Thanks. It was maybe the best donation we've made this year. Well . . . my personal favorite, I guess. If I hadn't moved to Montana, I never would have heard about them. Logan and I are planning a trip down there in a week to deliver the check in person."

"To Bozeman?"

"Yep." She nodded. "That's where they're located."

"Huh. I, uh . . . I grew up there." That was the first detail about my past I'd shared with someone in Lark Cove.

The admission surprised me for a moment, but I didn't regret sharing. Piper was a genuinely good person. While I found passion in my furniture, hers was supporting the causes she believed in most. I trusted her with a few minor details about my past.

"Do you still have family there?" she asked.

"My mom."

If Mom still lived there. I hadn't talked to her since I'd left Bozeman three years ago. She'd taken *his* side when everything had crashed, and I couldn't forgive her for that choice.

"Do you go back often?" Piper asked.

"No, I don't." My tone was short, and I stood from the chair, going back to the grill.

We were treading on dangerous territory now. Piper wouldn't learn about my family. I wouldn't be sharing the reason why I'd left Bozeman. She didn't need to know that I refused to return and that I'd blocked my mother's number years ago.

The life I'd had in Bozeman was over. Dead. I'd buried it in a single grave.

I tested the pork chops, then shut the grill to give them a

few more minutes. But I didn't go back to my chair. I used the physical distance to reiterate that the discussion about my past was over.

"Most of my family is in New York." She sipped her beer, taking the hint to let my past go. "My parents. Owen. Some aunts and uncles. They all think Montana is this wild and un-tamed wilderness where I'm most likely to be eaten by a bear. But I'm slowly convincing my parents to come out and visit this fall or winter. I think they'll love it."

"You grew up in New York?"

"Born and raised. I went to college at Columbia. Graduated and took a job working for the Kendrick Foundation."

"Why'd you move? For work?"

"No." She stared blankly at the label on her beer. "Divorce."

And just like I was done talking about my past, she was done talking about hers.

"How'd you find this place?" she asked.

I pushed off the railing and went back to the chair, sensing it was safe again. "I was looking for a place to disappear."

Of all people, I had a feeling that answer would resonate with Piper. She wouldn't ask why. She wouldn't need more de-tails. She'd understand that this was where I'd come to suffer alone.

I looked over to her profile and found her dark eyes waiting. *She came here for the same reason.*

Smoke from the barbeque drifted my way, and I forced my gaze away from Piper. "Want to grab the salads from the fridge and the rolls? I'll bring these in."

"Sure." She stood, taking our beers inside.

Then we got ourselves situated to dish up and dive into the meal.

"This is fantastic," she said after a few bites of her pork.

"What did you do?"

I shrugged. "It's a mole mix I made from scratch."

She almost choked. "And you said you couldn't cook."

I grinned and took another bite. "I can't cook much. But I rarely ruin my meat."

She laughed just as her phone rang from her purse on the coffee table. "Shoot." She tossed down her napkin and rushed across the room. "Sorry. I should have shut this off."

I waved my fork at her. "It's fine."

"I, uh . . ." She looked at the screen with indecision on her face. "I better take this. Do you mind?"

"Not at all."

She turned her back to me, taking a couple of steps down the hallway toward the bedroom and bathroom. My place was small, so no matter where Piper went, I heard her voice. I didn't mean to eavesdrop, but it was unavoidable as she hovered outside the bathroom.

"Hi." Her voice was strained as she spoke quietly. "I'm kind of busy right now. Did you need something?"

I chewed one bite, then another as Piper stayed silent. I glanced over my shoulder to see her shoulders bunched up to her neck. Who was she talking to?

"I'm sorry you had a rough day." She sighed. "I know it bothers you, but a couple of days off could be a good thing. I jus—"

The other person on the phone cut her off. I set down my fork, not even trying to pretend I wasn't listening.

"Fine," she clipped. "I'm sorry. But can I call you later to talk about this?"

She was quiet for too long to have gotten a simple *okay*.

I spun in my chair, my hackles rising as she hung her head. When her shoulders curled in on themselves, I nearly shot out of my chair. But I stayed put as she said a quiet, "Yes, I am."

Who was this? Family? A friend? Whoever it was, I didn't like how the air in the room had shifted. An icy blast from her phone was making our food cold.

I was seconds away from interrupting her when she snapped. "I'm not talking about this right now."

The voice on the other end of the line got louder and Piper held it an inch away from her ear. Then she put the end with the speaker to her lips and blurted, "I have to go."

I spun around to my plate as she turned and emerged from the hallway. She tossed the phone on top of her purse and returned to the table. Without a word, she grabbed her beer, tipped the bottom to the ceiling and drank it dry.

"Everything all right?"

She put a fist to her chest as the carbonation worked its way free. Then she grabbed her utensils. "My ex-husband hasn't quite adjusted to our divorce yet."

"I see." I stood from my seat and went to the fridge, getting her another beer. When I set it down by her plate, she reached for it immediately and took a long drink. When she went back to her food, the fork and knife shook in her hands.

Piper was normally so collected and balanced. The only time I'd seen her lose it had been on the ridge. So what had the ex said to get her so riled up? Did I even have the right to ask?

Curiosity won out. "What does the ex-husband do for a living?"

"He's an actor. He stars in one of the most popular shows on Broadway at the moment. It's a demanding job. He works constantly and performs nearly every night. Except I guess the director put in his understudy tonight. Adam is getting sick or something. I don't know. But he doesn't like having anyone in his spotlight. He was upset and his first reaction is still to call me."

"Hmm." The guy sounded like a spoiled bitch. Definitely not someone I pictured Piper marrying.

I was stereotyping based on his job as an actor, but I bet the guy spent more time grooming in one day than I did in a month. He probably got manicures and regular massages too.

They were divorced, and unloading his problems on her was weak.

She needed a strong partner. Someone sure. Someone as sturdy as the wood slabs in my shop. Not because she couldn't stand on her own, but because a weaker partner would pull her down. She needed someone to lift her higher.

Someone like me?

That thought sent ice through my veins. I wasn't the guy for Piper. Maybe I could have been once. If I'd met her years ago, I might have deserved her.

But things had just changed too much.

"Sorry."

"It's fine," she muttered, though it clearly was not.

We ate the rest of the meal in silence, each of us concentrating on our food rather than the company. Piper ate a few more angry bites but then lost her appetite, picking at her food while I finished the rest of mine.

"Want another beer?" I asked.

She dabbed the corner of her mouth, then gently set down her napkin. Her back was straight as an arrow, her shoulders poised. We were back to prim and proper now, were we? "No, thank you. This was a lovely meal."

Lovely.

I shoved my chair backward to clear my plate, but when I caught Piper's face from the corner of my eye, my ass slammed down in the seat.

The color of her skin was ghostly white. Her mouth was

turned down. The brightness in her eyes had vanished, and the rich color I'd memorized weeks ago in her camper had dulled to a gray mud.

"What's wrong? Are you sick?"

She shook her head. "What are we doing, Kaine?"

"Eating dinner."

"No." She shook her head, motioning between us. "What are *we* doing?"

Fuck. This was not the conversation I wanted to have tonight. "I thought we were just keeping things casual."

"Do you think casual is going to end well?"

"I don't know." I sighed. "Why does it have to end?"

Weren't we still having fun? Piper still crossed my mind all the time, but I'd finally figured out the answer to my question. *Why her?* Because she was special. I didn't analyze my emotions. I didn't dissect the way she made me feel. Over the last couple of weeks, I'd blocked all that out by focusing on the sex.

The routine we'd fallen into was working for me. And until thirty seconds ago, I'd thought it was working for her too.

"I wish . . ." She stared blankly at her uneaten roll, letting her words die in the room.

This dinner invitation had been an epic mistake.

"Let's have some cake," I offered. "Take it easy."

"Actually, I think I'd better go."

That stung more than it should have for a casual relationship. She stood from the table, lifting her plate, but I held out a hand.

"Just leave it. Just . . . leave."

She winced at my dismissal, then bolted from her chair.

I stayed in mine, clenching my jaw as she collected her purse, slung it over her shoulder, then left without another word.

The door banged shut. Her footsteps raced across the porch.

And then there was nothing.

Good. That's what I'd come here for, wasn't it?

I didn't need my neighbor distracting me with her sexy dimples and big brown eyes. I didn't need her temptation. What I needed was peace and quiet. Ever since she'd moved in next door, I hadn't had either.

I rose from my chair, taking our plates over and slamming them in the sink. One broke in half. The other in fifths. Then I piled the other dirty dishes on top. Maybe I'd clean them later. Maybe not.

Who was I trying to impress?

As I turned to the fridge for another beer, my gaze caught on the cake I'd spent all day making.

I swiped it off the counter and carried it to the garbage, where it got thrown inside, pan and all.

Fuck you, cake. And the woman I made you for.

ten

PIPER

STANDING IN THE MIDDLE OF WHAT WOULD EVENTUALLY BE MY living room, I surveyed the progress my contractors had made over the last couple of weeks.

Walls that had been demolished and moved were now drywalled, taped and ready for texture. The maple cabinets I'd chosen for the kitchen were in the corner, covered in a drop cloth and waiting to be hung once the walls were painted. The enormous island that separated the kitchen from where I was standing had been set in place.

My project was coming together. The demolition and reconstruction of my house had been time-consuming. For the last month, I'd wondered if this was a mistake, if attempting to tackle such a large remodel on my own had been the equivalent of shoving an entire pound cake in my mouth and attempting to chew.

But when I'd come over tonight to check on the progress, I'd found a slew of samples leaning against the island. Paint swatches. Carpet squares. Tile boards for the bathrooms and kitchen backsplash.

Finally, we were getting to the good stuff.

The foreman estimated that in another six weeks or so, I'd be able to abandon my Airstream and move into my *home*.

Though it had been draining, a part of me didn't want this project to end. What would I do at night when I didn't have colors to pick and flooring options to weigh? My neighbor certainly wasn't keeping me occupied anymore.

It had been two weeks since my dinner at Kaine's house, and I hadn't seen him once in that time. The first week, I'd found excuses not to be home. I'd driven to Kalispell for three impromptu shopping trips. I'd eaten at Bob's Diner once and the bar twice. At night, I'd taken to sleeping with earplugs so if Kaine ventured over in the dark, I wouldn't hear his knock.

Then last week, I'd simply left town, traveling south to Bozeman, where I visited the veterans' organization and delivered them a huge check. Logan had decided to stay home, letting me represent the company in his stead. I think he opted out of the trip because he wanted me to get all the praise for our donation.

It was different to be in the spotlight, and though I'd enjoyed my day being fawned over, I preferred to stay behind the curtain.

The rest of my trip had turned into a short vacation, exploring a new part of Montana. I'd driven to a quaint town called Prescott and spent a few nights there in one of the most charming motels I'd ever seen, The Bitterroot Inn.

That area was a bit more rugged than Lark Cove, though just as beautiful. Underneath the modern-day amenities, you got a small glimpse of the Old West.

After a few days, I'd left Prescott and taken a scenic drive through Yellowstone National Park, slowly making my way home and back to my corner of paradise.

The trip had been wonderful and the long drive exactly what I'd needed.

Sitting behind the steering wheel with nothing but the radio and my thoughts, I'd had time to think about everything that had happened in my life these last few months. The quiet drive had given me time to get some perspective on the dinner non-date that had toppled upside down.

I'd been so excited to have dinner at Kaine's. His invitation had made me feel like more than just his late-night booty call, and I'd taken it to mean he at least wanted some sort of friendship. That he'd wanted to get to know me as a person, not just a bed buddy.

It wasn't a date. I knew it wasn't a date. Still, the evening had started off awkwardly, like the blind date I'd had my freshman year in college that had lasted all of twenty minutes until the guy ditched me to go bowling with his roommate.

But when Kaine and I settled into those chairs on his porch, I felt a shift. A click. He was easy to sit beside.

Then he shocked me by opening the door to his past. I forced myself not to squirm in the chair as he told me about his hometown and that his mother still lived there. For a fleeting second, I thought he might actually confide in me. Maybe he invited me over to unburden some of the weight from his past.

Foolish thoughts.

Kaine Reynolds was the most closed-off person I'd ever met. In no uncertain terms, he made it clear. His past was his secret. *Check.*

As we sat on the porch, I refused to let his silence bother me. After all, he had invited me to dinner. That was something. Little wins were often just as important as the big victories.

So I told him about my job and my brother. I carried on a mostly one-sided conversation until it was time to eat.

Then my damn phone rang.

Why was it so hard for me to just ignore Adam? Of all the nights and times to call, he'd picked the worst. Yet still, like an idiot, I'd answered.

I always answered.

Adam immediately began bitching about his director. I listened. Whenever Adam was having a hard time at work, he came to me. For years, I was proud to be his sounding board. He couldn't afford to complain to coworkers or cast mates. The gossip mill on Broadway was worse than an all-girls boarding school. It had been my duty as his wife to listen.

Old habits died hard.

When I finally got a word in edgewise, I told him I was busy. Then came the questions.

Doing what? Are you on a date? You're not seeing someone, are you?

Was I seeing someone? One glance to the dining room table where Kaine was pretending not to listen and the *Yes, I am* just slipped out.

Adam exploded, and after the second accusation of betrayal, I hung up.

It took me the week of my vacation to realize I'd let Adam's feelings control me for too long. I had every right to see someone. I had every right to have casual sex with my neighbor. Because I wasn't married anymore.

Adam hadn't come to terms with our divorce, and I'd realized after about five hundred miles of open road, neither had I.

Too bad my realization had come weeks too late. I'd let Adam's phone call set me off-kilter. I'd retreated into myself and ended my fling with Kaine.

I owed him an explanation. Since I'd gotten back from my trip, I'd looked out my window toward his house twenty times, knowing I needed to cross the line. But I couldn't seem to force myself in his direction.

Instead, I'd walk out the door and into my house, inspecting every little detail of the remodel. Last night, I'd borrowed the crew's industrial vacuum and cleaned each bedroom of wood splinters, sheetrock dust and fallen nails.

The foreman had told me this morning it was unnecessary. I'd pretended not to hear him.

That vacuuming had distracted me for over an hour of thinking about Kaine. Of missing his late-night visits to the camper. Of missing his spicy smell on my sheets and the flecks of sawdust he often left behind.

I'd realized another thing on my road trip—I was not made for casual sex.

My bruised heart was on the line and it required careful relationships, not callous.

Friendship was the most I should offer Kaine.

My phone rang in my pocket and I dug it out. Mom had told me she'd call to catch up and I was excited to talk with her. But Adam's name flashed on the screen instead of Mom's smiling picture.

I hesitated over the button that would decline him. Then I pushed it.

"Ha!" I cheered with a fist pump. "Go, me."

Adam hadn't called me since my dinner at Kaine's place. I certainly hadn't called him. I'd been dreading it the first few days, and after a week, I'd let myself hope that maybe the calls were over.

I should have known better.

My phone rang again, his name returning to the screen. And once again, I hit decline, this time without hesitation.

I smiled to myself, though it turned to a frown when he called again. He would just keep calling, and as therapeutic as denying him was, I didn't want to be doing it all night.

Besides, ignoring two out of three calls was progress.

"Hello."

"Hey, how are you, Pip?"

I cringed at the nickname. "What's up, Adam?"

"Just calling to check in. See how your week was."

"Fine."

"That's it?" He chuckled. "Fine? You used to tell me all about your day."

"I did. When we were married. But we're not married anymore."

"That wasn't my choice."

"Yes. It was." My voice stayed cold and calm. "You kissed another woman. That was *your* choice. Surely there's a picture hashtagged out there somewhere." #cheatingbastard maybe?

"It was just a kiss."

"Was it?"

"I didn't—you know what? I don't want to fight. I just miss you. That's all. You live on the other side of the country. It's just a phone call to check in."

I sighed. "Okay."

"How is work? How's Logan?"

"Good. He's happy." Adam hadn't ever really gotten along with Logan. I think because he was jealous of how much I admired my boss.

"Great. That's great."

There was an awkward silence as I waited for the question I knew was coming. All the curiosity about my job and Logan was just Adam's way of biding his time. What he really wanted to know was if I was dating someone.

"So . . . who's this guy you're seeing?"

Called it! Adam was like a little kid and someone had just stolen his favorite toy. Well, Kaine hadn't really stolen me. But Adam didn't need to know that. "A man I met out here."

"Is it serious?"

"No," I admitted.

"Oh." He sounded too chipper. "I was thinking about coming out to Montana."

"What?" I gasped.

This was my place. My safe place. I didn't want Adam out here, filling it with memories of what I'd left behind.

"We should talk, Pip. Really talk. So much has happened, I feel like we need some closure. Or maybe even a fresh start."

I opened my mouth but no words came out. A fresh start? Did he actually think there was a chance for us to get past everything that had happened?

Our marriage had been riddled with problems, fundamental issues I'd ignored for much too long. And one by one, they'd revealed themselves since the day I'd asked for a divorce.

Adam had to be the center of attention. He'd rarely accompanied me to the foundation's employee functions because they were about me, not him. I'd begged him to attend three Christmas parties, and after listening to him yawn through each, I'd just gone solo from then on out.

His family's money meant we were always running in the elite circles. My parents weren't hurting for money, but we'd never been rich. I hadn't ever wanted to make Adam feel ashamed of me, so I'd acted as perfectly as possible. I'd gone so far as to take private etiquette lessons before our wedding.

Adam never criticized me or put me down. He was supportive of my job and loved my family. But I never *fit* into our lifestyle. His lifestyle. Most nights, I went to bed with knots in my stomach. I'd chalked up my constant stress to a demanding job, but that had simply been an excuse.

I'd been exhausted, trying so hard to make everything perfect. And somewhere along the way, Adam and I had fallen apart. From the moment we'd traded *I do*s, I'd labeled us as

Happily Married. Then I'd used that label as an excuse to put on blinders and ignore the things really happening between us. I'd disregarded the changes shaking our foundation. Our young love hadn't been strong enough to last, not without work—work neither of us had cared to do.

"What if I came out in two weeks?" he asked. "We've got a break in the play schedule. I could visit for a couple of days."

"Adam, I don't think that's a good idea."

"Why not?"

"Because it won't accomplish anything. I'm sorry you don't feel like you've gotten closure. I really am. But this *is* closed. And I think it would be best if you stopped calling me for a while."

"Piper, you can't mean that."

"I do," I said gently. "I'm sorry, but I do."

"We belong together. We lost our way, but it's always been you."

My heart ached with the pain in his voice. When was this going to get easier? He'd said the same thing all during our divorce. Every meeting with every lawyer, he'd always pull me aside to tell me he loved me.

I may have fallen out of love with Adam, but I still had love for him. Our lives were just no longer paired together. Our paths were no longer entwined.

"No, we don't belong together. We grew apart, Adam. Please find a way to accept our divorce. Please. I wish you all the best, but this is good-bye."

"Pip—"

"Good-bye." I pulled the phone away from my ear even though his protests were still coming through. Then I ended the call.

That was harsher than I'd hoped it would be, but that phone call was long overdue.

I'd asked for a divorce. I'd seen it through despite Adam's protests. I'd changed my last name back to Campbell and moved to the opposite side of the country.

If Adam wasn't able to recognize that as the end of our marriage, this phone call tonight should make it unmistakably clear.

Tonight, I'd handled Adam.

This weekend, I'd make peace with Kaine.

This would be my home for years to come, and I refused to have my sanctuary ruined because of a short-lived affair.

Now I just had to find an olive branch.

As I walked through the living room toward the dining area, an idea popped into my mind. Maybe he'd be willing to build me a dining room table.

Hiring Kaine might bridge the awkwardness. His furniture was a safe zone for conversation. My renovation was one too. Combining the two together could be the first step in a new relationship with my neighbor.

A platonic one.

It was Memorial Day weekend, and though I doubted Kaine had any big plans on a Friday night, I didn't want to go over so close to dark. I didn't trust my body around his in the twilight hours. One brush of his muscular chest against mine, one nudge from his bulky arms, and we'd find ourselves in bed.

Tomorrow, I'd put an end to the hiatus. From here on out, my interactions with Kaine would be limited to daylight hours.

I continued my inspection of the house, walking down the long hallway that led from the front door, past the kitchen and to my master bathroom. None of the work had started in there yet, but I still wanted to check, just in case the crew had done a little something extra.

The room was the same as I'd found it last night, except clean, since I'd vacuumed, so I continued down the hallway to the guest bedroom at the far end of the house. From the big window that overlooked the forest, I had the perfect view of Kaine's cabin.

He'd told me at our failed dinner that he'd come here looking for a place to disappear. It would be a lie to say I hadn't left New York to disappear too.

But while Kaine simply resided here, I wanted to grow roots deeper than the hundred-year-old trees shading my front door.

This house would be my forever home.

It would be full of happiness, even if it wasn't filled with children like I'd once dreamed.

Adam and I had tried to get pregnant for years, and every month, I'd cry over a negative pregnancy test. Finally, we'd gone in to see a fertility specialist and learned what I'd feared.

No matter how many ways we attempted to correct my hormone imbalances, I wasn't ovulating. Add to that my cervical abnormalities, conception had been impossible the old-fashioned way. Before Adam and I could talk about other options, like IVF or adoption, our marriage had imploded.

The only good thing about my divorce taking years was that it had given me ample time to accept that I wasn't broken. I wasn't defective. And I didn't need a husband or children to make me whole.

What I needed were things to love, like this house. Maybe once it was finished, I'd get a dog or a cat or both.

I bet a cat would love to sit in the large window of this guest room and stare outside.

I finished exploring the house and went outside, crossing the gravel driveway toward my camper. It was well past time for a large glass of wine and some meaningless social media surfing.

But as I reached for the door handle, the sound of an engine revved to life. It wasn't a car or truck, but something smaller like a lawn mower being started with a pull cord.

I took two steps backward and looked to Kaine's cabin. He was standing on the porch with a chainsaw in his hands. The engine idled for another moment, but then he hit the gas and the thing roared.

What was he doing?

His back was to me, but even from a distance, I saw that his movements were off-balance. He stumbled sideways, one foot tripping over the other. The chainsaw was still screaming, and the vicious blades spun dangerously close to his leg before he regained his footing.

Was he drunk? My heart lurched as he swayed again, and I dashed up the path between our homes.

"Kaine!" I shouted but he didn't hear me over the noise of the saw.

I ran faster.

He lifted the saw, bringing it dangerously close to his ear, then dropped it down on one of his porch chairs. The same chair I'd been sitting in two weeks ago.

Sawdust flew from the back of the machine. The engine strained as it sliced through the wood. With one cut complete, Kaine lifted the chainsaw and hacked at the chair again. His feet stumbled between cuts, but he managed to stay upright.

My heart was racing, my flip-flops sliding on the uneven earth as I hurried to his cabin, terrified I'd be just seconds too late. I had no idea how I'd wrestle the chainsaw from his grip, but I'd try.

"Kaine! Stop!" I yelled again, but he was lost.

The cuts got faster and as I approached the cabin, the chair was no longer standing. He'd cut apart the back and both arm-rests. All that was left was the seat resting in a mess of broken boards.

The saw went after that piece too, but instead of cutting it clean, a grinding, clamping noise filled the air. The chain on the blade had gotten wedged.

Kaine let off the gas, letting the motor idle. Then he dropped the machine on the porch. "Fuck!"

He stumbled backward, raking both hands through his hair. As he took one step, then two, he tripped on his own heel and dropped on his ass.

"Kaine!" I yelled again. If he heard me, he didn't turn.

He just rested his hands on his bent knees, staring at the chainsaw that was still idling on the porch boards.

I sprinted up the porch stairs two at a time, breathlessly falling to my knees at his side. "Are you hurt?"

He didn't answer.

"Kaine," I snapped, my hands and eyes scanning his body for cuts. "Are you hurt?"

His foggy and unfocused eyes drifted up to my face. "Piper?"

I took his bearded cheeks in my hands. "Are. You. Hurt?"

"Yup. Just like you."

He wasn't drunk. He was incoherent.

I didn't see any cuts and there wasn't blood anywhere, so I let my hands fall from his face as he breathed. Alcohol wafted off his body in waves.

I stood, going over to the chainsaw. I'd never seen one in real life before, but I searched the machine, looking for an off switch. Next to the handle was a small toggle and I flipped it, killing the engine cold.

The quiet was startling. My chest heaved as I stood, the adrenaline still pumping in my veins as I took stock of what Kaine had done.

He'd destroyed the chair completely. Sawdust and wood bits were strewn across the porch. He'd managed to saw uneven slashes in the porch boards too. He could have taken off his own arm. *Idiot.*

I whirled back to Kaine, fury taking the place of fear. "What were you thinking?" I shrieked. "You could have killed yourself!"

His eyelids drooped closed as he shrugged. "That chair was too short."

"Too short?"

He nodded. "Half an inch."

"I see." I frowned. "And that meant you had to hack it to pieces like a crazed serial killer? Should I call you the Chair Chainsaw Murderer?"

He chuckled, flashing me his white teeth. "You're funny."

"You're drunk."

"Meh," he muttered.

"Shit." I wiped a bead of sweat from my temple.

Kaine sat on the porch, disheveled but no less gorgeous. His words weren't slurred, but he was most definitely intoxicated.

"Just . . . stay there." I held out my hand in a stay gesture, though I doubted he'd get too far in his state.

I hurried inside the cabin, my feet skidding to a stop at what I saw. The place was filthy. There were dirty dishes all over the kitchen and even some in the living room. The foul odor hit me next, making my face sour.

Kaine had always impressed me with his cleanliness, both here and in his shop. But it was like he'd purposefully tried to trash his home over the last two weeks.

From the living room, I could see down the hall and into his bedroom at the rear of the cabin. His bed had always been made whenever I'd been here before, but now the ugly green quilt was on the floor. The blue sheets were in a tangled mess on the bed.

I went to the kitchen, gagging as the smell got stronger. I risked a glance at the overflowing sink. The plates at the bottom appeared to be broken.

Was this disaster because of me? I went to the cupboards, searching for a clean glass. The shelves were mostly empty, but I rummaged around on the top shelf and found a dusty beer mug.

I rinsed it out, then filled it with water, taking it back outside.

Kaine had scooted across the porch to the stairs and was propped up against a post. Both of his legs hung loosely down the steps, his booted toes pointing up to the sky at different angles.

"Here." I sat next to him and held out the mug. "Drink some water."

He blinked slowly, his face lazily turning my way. With an unsteady hand, he took the water from my hand and gulped. Dribbles fell down his chin, leaving droplets in his beard. But when the glass was empty, he handed it back.

"I threw it out," he muttered.

"Threw what out?"

"Your cake."

My cake? He had to be talking about the cake he'd made for our dinner. The one I hadn't tried because I'd been too busy running out the door when he'd ordered me to leave. "I'm sorry."

He waved a hand. "It's fine. Over now."

Yes, it was over now. "Are you okay?"

He let out a low groan that sounded like *no*.

But I didn't ask for more. I wasn't comfortable leaving his side, not with the chainsaw within reach, so I scooted over to the opposite post and leaned against the wood.

The evening sun was setting, and with the tall trees surrounding us, the light faded quickly. I let my eyes drift closed as I listened to the sounds of the forest and Kaine's heavy breathing. If he fell asleep out here, I'd have a hard time getting him inside. But I'd deal with that after five minutes of quiet.

"It was three years ago."

My eyes flew open. "What was three years ago?"

"They betrayed me."

Who? And what was their betrayal? I wanted to ask so badly, but Kaine was drunk. It wouldn't be right to push for information in his drunken haze.

"She died on Memorial Day weekend."

I winced. It wasn't just pain clouding his tone. It was misery. It broke my heart to see the anguish he worked so hard to hide, out in the open. I didn't know who she was, but I could venture a guess. Kaine had lost someone he loved, and that loss had created the shell of a man at my side.

"I'm sorry."

"I can't feel anything." He let out a long breath, then he shifted. He laid back on the porch boards while at the same time twisting so his head rested in my lap.

My body froze, waiting to see what he'd do next. But he sighed and relaxed, the weight of his neck and head on my thighs. Of their own volition, my fingers found their way into his silky, dark hair.

"I can't feel anything." Kaine's eyes held mine. "But I can feel you."

"I feel you too," I whispered.

He turned away, staring off into the trees. "I don't want to feel."

My fingers stopped threading his hair. His tone was sharp but it didn't sting. It was born of fear.

This would all be easier if we could turn off those feelings like the toggle on the chainsaw. But here they were, circling us with the evening air. There was nothing more to say, so I resumed toying with his hair and watching the sun's light fade.

Until Kaine and his broken heart fell asleep on my lap.

eleven

KAINE

I WAS HAVING THE BEST DREAM ABOUT EATING HOMEMADE CINNAMON rolls when someone woke me up by pounding on the front door. I squeezed my eyes shut, willing them to go away, but the noise only got louder.

And more painful.

I jerked awake and groaned.

No one was at the door. The pounding was in my head.

"Oh, fuck." I buried my face in my pillow.

Hangovers were a bitch. I'd partied quite a bit in my younger years, enjoying late nights out with the guys, boozing and picking up women. After a heavy night of drinking, I used to be able to wake up the next morning, guzzle some water, pop a few pain pills and be good to go.

But at thirty-three years old, my body didn't recover as quickly. The last time I'd been drunk, my headache had lasted for days.

My stomach rolled as I sat up and took a deep breath. I was still wearing my clothes from yesterday, but at least I'd kicked off my boots.

I looked around the room for some water, but all I found were three empty glasses on the nightstand. Something had died in my mouth, and my throat was screaming for a drink.

When I stood, I fought a dizzying wave but managed to stumble my way to the bedroom door.

I yanked it open and was immediately hit with a smell that nearly sent my ass to the floor.

Cinnamon rolls.

Mom used to make us cinnamon rolls on the weekends when she wasn't working. I hadn't eaten one in over three years. And since Mom didn't know where I lived, there could only be one person who'd brought that smell into my house. Piper.

I shuffled down the hallway to the kitchen. Under the smell of cinnamon, sugar and yeast, I caught a hint of bleach as I passed by the bathroom. I ignored it. First thing on the docket was drinking a gallon of water. Then I'd find out what Piper was doing in my kitchen.

Given my rumpled clothes, I doubted we'd had sex. Though it wasn't impossible. My brain was still too fuzzy to remember everything that had happened last night.

The light in the kitchen and living room was blinding. I groaned as I entered the main room, taking a break to lean on the fridge so I wouldn't pass out from the pain behind my temples.

"Morning." Piper was propped up against the counter with her phone in one hand and a steaming cup of coffee in the other.

"Got any more of that coffee?" My voice was hoarse and using it made my head throb even more.

She nodded, setting her mug aside to get me one of my own and fill it from the coffee pot in the corner.

I pushed off the fridge and stumbled toward the dining room table. I collapsed into a chair, rocking the legs a bit. Piper delivered my coffee and took the seat across from me.

I grunted my thanks before taking a first sip. The coffee scalded my tongue, so I set it down to cool. Then, with my elbows digging into the table, I propped my aching head into my hands.

"Are you going to live?" Piper asked.

"Maybe," I muttered, closing my eyes. "I just need a few minutes."

I kept my eyes closed as she stood and walked across the room. The unmistakable rattle of a pill bottle filled the kitchen, and at that moment, I would have married her.

She brought me some pain pills and a tall glass of water, setting them on the table before returning to her seat.

I forced my eyes open, popping the pills in my mouth and gulping the water. I still felt like shit. "Thanks."

"You're welcome."

I went back to my coffee, leaning back in my chair as I sipped it slowly. When that cup was empty, Piper got up and filled it for me along with my water. By the time I'd made it through my refills, I was nearly human again.

"Thanks for the coffee. And the water."

She shrugged. "Technically, it was your coffee and water."

"Still appreciated." My eyes wandered around the kitchen. "You cleaned?"

"Just a little," she spoke into her own cup.

It was more than a little. The dishes that had been piling up for two weeks were all cleared away. The counters were gleaming and the smell from the garbage can—the one that had driven me to the shop for countless long days—was now gone.

"I made cinnamon rolls." Piper smiled. "I hope that's okay."

"Yup. They smell great." I took another sip of my coffee,

the ache behind my temples beginning to fade. "How long have you been here?"

"Since about five. After you passed out, I went home but couldn't sleep much. So I came over to make sure you were alive."

"The jury's still out," I groaned, dropping my head back into my hands.

"Breakfast will help. My cinnamon rolls aren't magic, but they've been known to cure a hangover once or twice."

My stomach growled, then churned when I caught a whiff from my underarms. "Do I have time for a quick shower?" And to brush my teeth?

"Go for it. The rolls still need about ten minutes."

Taking my coffee cup with me, I disappeared into the bathroom, showering quickly, though my movements were all clumsy. My fingers fumbled over my bar of soap, dropping it twice, and I squirted way too much from my bottle of shampoo. There would be no working in the shop for me today. I didn't trust myself around power tools or sharp objects.

I climbed out of the shower and swiped a towel off the hook. That towel had been on the floor yesterday, but Piper must have picked it up. I dried and wrapped it around my waist, then raked my hands through my hair as I inspected myself in the mirror.

I looked like hell. My beard was scraggly and overdue for a trim. My eyes were bloodshot and my cheeks a little green.

But things weren't all bad. My shoulders weren't tense and balled up at my ears. My jaw was unclenched for the first time in weeks. It wasn't the hangover's doing.

It was Piper's.

Having her back in this house was settling.

I'd been a grumpy bastard ever since our dinner because I'd missed her dimpled smile. I'd missed her witty comments and knowing smirks. I'd missed the way she looked at me with those big, beautiful eyes.

I'd missed her.

The ding on the oven's timer pulled me away from the mirror and out of the bathroom she'd cleaned this morning. I went to my bedroom and pulled on some jeans and a gray T-shirt, then walked out with my coffee mug, surveying the living room with a more careful eye.

She'd picked up in there too and wiped away the accumulated dust. Under the cinnamon roll smell, there was a hint of my furniture polish.

"You didn't have to clean. But I appreciate it. I, uh . . . kind of let shit go these last couple of weeks."

Piper glanced over her shoulder. "I didn't mind."

My mouth watered at the pan resting in front of her on the stove. It was loaded with golden-baked rolls, oozing with cinnamon and sugar. Piper was drizzling white frosting over the top.

"You went to a lot of trouble."

She shrugged. "Not really. I've been wanting an excuse to make these. You've got a much better space to knead and roll dough than I do at the camper, so I decided to intrude on your kitchen. And since they took a while to rise, I just picked up. It wasn't much."

It wasn't much? I scoffed. "You cleaned my bathroom."

She smirked. "I had to pee. Cleaning it was necessary before I could go."

"Sorry." I grimaced. "And thank you. Again."

Someday, I'd make it up to her. Someday when my head wasn't swirling with whiskey fumes and my stomach wasn't growling like a bear. I hadn't eaten dinner last night, or lunch for that matter. It was no wonder I'd gotten so drunk off a half bottle of Jack.

"Want more coffee?" she asked.

"I got it." I carried my mug to the coffee pot, filled it and looked to hers between us. "Do you need a warm-up?"

"Sure." She smiled and pushed it closer at the same time I went to pick it up.

Our fingers brushed on the handle, sending an electric zing up my elbow. Her breath hitched and her cheeks turned rosy. But she didn't take her hand away.

The room got blurry before disappearing around us as our hands lingered on the warm ceramic. If I took one step, she'd be in my arms. She'd fill the hole I'd been missing for two weeks.

If I took one step, we could be naked on the couch in seconds.

But before I took that one step, she slid her hand free and tucked it into an oven mitt.

"I can't," she whispered, staring at her rolls.

"It's okay." I took her mug and filled it up. This morning wasn't about sex. Our casual relationship had burned us both. And this morning was her peace offering. "I get it."

"I don't want things to be awkward between us. Casual didn't work out. But how about something different? How about . . . neighbors?"

I nodded. "Neighbors."

Pushing down my attraction to her would take some getting used to. But it was better this way. Wasn't it? That's what I'd been telling myself for two weeks. I didn't need her in my bed. I'd just keep repeating it over and over until it stuck.

"I have a proposition for you," Piper said, dishing up her enormous cinnamon rolls on two plates.

"I thought you wanted to just be neighbors."

She giggled. "Not that kind of proposition."

"Damn."

She laughed again. "I was wondering if you'd be interested in building me a dining room table. I'm not sure what your availability is, but I wouldn't need it for a while. But you know how I feel about your furniture. A custom Kaine Reynolds piece is something I just can't live without."

I walked over to the table and sat down, sipping my coffee. "My wait list is two years out."

"Oh." Her shoulders fell. "I'm not surprised. Can you add me to it? I can just get something temporary in the meantime."

"Sure." I sipped my coffee again, hiding a grin.

I'd finished her table three days ago. I might have been doing my best to ignore her, but that table had called to me, begging to be finished. It was currently covered in a canvas cloth in a corner of the shop.

Maybe I'd wait until her house was done, then show up with a surprise delivery.

A stir of anticipation ran through my body. I hadn't given anyone a gift in years. I used to love giving presents, especially to Mom. She'd sacrificed so much, working long hours so we wouldn't go without. As soon as I'd been able to afford decent birthday and Christmas gifts, I'd always gone above and beyond. Usually, all Mom had wanted were pieces of my furniture, so I'd set aside time in my schedule to craft my finest.

I would have done anything for Mom.

Which was why it hurt so much that she'd chosen *him* instead of me.

"Here you go." Piper set a plate and fork in front of me, then sat with her own.

With the aroma of soft bread, sugar and spice wafting into my nose, all thoughts of the past and my mother disappeared. It was steaming, but I cut a huge piece of the cinnamon roll and shoved it in my mouth.

"Oh, Jesus," I groaned after swallowing the first bite and digging in for more. "This is going to save my life."

Piper giggled, covering her full mouth with one hand. "I'm glad."

I demolished that first cinnamon roll, then went back and polished off two more. "Magic. Maybe even better than the cake."

"No way," Piper scoffed. "But a close second."

"Where you'd learn to cook?" I asked, neither of us in a hurry to leave the table. The dirty dishes rested between us as we drank the last of the coffee. "You're good at it."

"Lots of places." She shrugged. "Most of my food comes from things I've tried and tweaked. Magic cake I learned to make from my aunt. The cinnamon rolls are my mom's recipe. In high school, I took a cooking class and learned how to make the best pie crust I've ever tasted."

"Pie?" My ears perked up. I'd take pie over cake any day of the week.

"If I promise to bring you a pie on a regular basis, will that move my dining room table up your waiting list?"

I chuckled. "It can't hurt."

The right thing to do would be to tell her no and not make her my pie slave. But there was no way I'd be turning down regular pies. Especially if they were anything like the rest of the food she made.

Piper settled deeper into her chair, bringing her coffee mug to those soft lips. I bet they tasted like the cinnamon roll frosting. The idea of running my tongue over the contours of her mouth made my cock jerk.

Even with a hangover, he was raring to go.

But that's not what we were anymore. We were neighbors, nothing more.

Piper looked so comfortable today. She was wearing green leggings and a loose-fitting long-sleeved black tee. Her legs were crossed, and instead of those fancy heels she normally wore, today she was in some plain, white tennis shoes.

She was even slouching for a change, and it was nice to see her so relaxed in her chair.

Her chair.

Her. Chair.

"Oh, fuck!" I flew out of my seat, spinning around for the front door. I ripped it open and stepped out into the mess on my porch. My hands dove into my hair as my eyes bugged out.

Piper may have cleaned the inside of my house, but she'd left the disaster outside for me to handle.

"Sonofabitch." The headache that those cinnamon rolls and cups of coffee had chased away was rearing its ugly face.

"Apparently, that chair was much too short," Piper dead-panned as she stepped outside with both of our coffee cups. She handed me mine, then took a seat in the chair I hadn't killed.

My eyes stayed glued to the carnage. "What the fuck was I thinking?"

"That using a hatchet would have taken too long?"

I frowned. "Smartass."

"Sarcasm is my weapon of choice. Unlike some people I know, who prefer to wield chainsaws against innocent lounge chairs for being the wrong size. A half inch was the problem, if I remember."

"I'm a perfectionist."

"Nooo," she gasped, clutching her heart.

A chuckle escaped my mouth. "What a damn mess."

"Yeah, you did a number on that poor thing. I'm just glad you didn't cut off your leg or arm in the process."

"I didn't hurt you, did I?" My eyes whipped to her in a panic, scanning her from head to toe.

But she waved me off. "I'm fine."

My shoulders sagged, and I walked over toward the porch stairs, sinking down in the same spot where I'd sat just last night with Piper. Only this time, instead of resting my head in her lap and staring into the forest, I sat sideways to face her.

Last night was coming into sharper focus, as were my drunken ramblings.

In my inebriated haze, I'd opened the door to my past. She had every right to an explanation, and a small part of me wanted to confess it all right then and there. Would things be easier between us—easier for me—if I finally unburdened how I'd come to live here in this forest?

No. I wasn't ready. Those memories had been bottled up for too long. Even after three years, the pain was crippling. Once I told the story, I'd no doubt get angry. And I didn't trust myself around her when I was in a rage.

Just look at what I'd done to her chair.

"About last night and what I said. I know I owe you an explanation, but—"

"Kaine." She cut me off. "Don't worry about it."

"Really?"

She nodded. "If you ever want to talk, I'm here to listen. But you don't owe me anything."

I nodded, looking at my lap, and whispered, "Thank you."

"Actually, I think I'm the one who needs to do some explaining. I'm sorry for leaving like I did after dinner."

"It's okay."

"It's not."

"You cleaned my house and made me breakfast. You also made sure I didn't decapitate myself with a chainsaw. It's all good."

She smiled. "Still, I'd like to explain. If you don't mind."

"Not at all."

Her eyes lost their humor as she looked out into the trees. This wouldn't be some light explanation or a bunch of nonsense excuses. She was about to tell me the reason she'd disappeared to Montana and sought refuge on our mountain.

"My ex-husband didn't want to get divorced. In fact, he fought it tooth and nail for nearly two years, contesting every agreement my attorney drafted. He kept saying it was because he loved me. Maybe that's true, but I also think he didn't want to be alone. He's used to getting undivided attention, and ever since the day I met him, he had all of mine."

I'd gathered as much from the one side of their phone call I'd overheard.

"We got married right after college," she said. "We were both really focused on our careers, and life was good. We were young. We were 'Happily Married'—that label everyone works so hard to get. But after a couple of years, I wanted more. I wanted to be 'Mommy.' So we started trying for a baby. One year passed, then another and nothing. I was so young, it shouldn't have been a problem, so we decided to see a fertility specialist."

The pain in her voice physically hurt to hear, but I stayed quiet, listening as she poured her heart out on my porch.

"We weren't . . . I wasn't able to have children." A lone tear slid down her cheek and she brushed it away.

"I'm sorry."

She forced a smile. "There are a lot of treatments and options for infertility. We could have kept trying. But still, the news was hard to hear, and I didn't take it well."

Piper twirled her mug, watching the dregs spin at the bottom. "Adam didn't take it well either. Instead of staying home to comfort his wife, he took his gorgeous costar out to dinner at my favorite restaurant. And then he kissed her and got caught."

My hands tightened around my mug. Talk about babies would normally send me running for the hills. The image of Piper holding a swaddled bundle was way more than I could handle this morning. So I forced it away, not letting painful memories shut me down. And instead, I focused on a different emotion. One that had gotten me through a lot of hard times. *Anger.*

What kind of a fucking asshole cheated on his wife? And under those circumstances? That motherfucker deserved to have his ass kicked. Repeatedly.

"He says he didn't sleep with her." Piper rolled her eyes. "But I don't know."

"You think he's lying?"

"Maybe." She sighed. "Yes, I do. But it doesn't matter now. The kiss was enough. I moved out and filed for divorce."

"But he still calls you?"

She nodded. "I asked him to stop. We'll see if he listens."

This guy didn't love her. If he truly did, he'd let her go. Maybe calling and harassing her was his way of getting even with the divorce. "What did he say to you during our dinner?"

"He asked if I was seeing someone. I told him yes. I know we were just casual, but you're the first man I've been with since Adam."

"He didn't like it, did he?"

"No." She smirked at me. "He didn't."

"Good." Though I didn't like that he'd upset her, I did like that it was because of me that the asshole ex-husband had gotten pissed off.

She flashed me a dimpled smile, then shook her head. "Regardless, I shouldn't have answered the call. I shouldn't have run out of here like that. I let him get to me when I should have just told you all about it over dinner."

"No big deal."

I wouldn't admit how good her apology felt. Because that would mean admitting how much it had hurt when she'd left.

"I've held all this in for a long time," she said quietly. "My parents don't even know about the infertility stuff. When I was married, they kept asking me when we'd give them grandchildren. My mom was so eager, she learned how to knit because she wanted lots of time to practice making baby blankets. I didn't have it in me to break their hearts, not when mine was broken too."

"Understandable."

"Maybe." She shook her head. "But I should tell them. I *will* tell them. Maybe. Eventually."

I wish I had some advice to give when it came to relationships with parents, but mine was so fucked up, it was better to keep my mouth shut.

Never in a million years would I have thought I'd go more than two days without talking to my mom. She'd once been my best friend. When I was having a rough day, she was the first person I thought to call. When I had good news to share, she was the person I wanted to take out to dinner and celebrate. She was the person I'd wanted to make proud.

But as it was, I hadn't spoken to Mom in three years. Anger had kept me away. And fear.

I was terrified to look at her face and see only disappointment for how I'd handled things.

Handled was too generous a term. I hadn't *handled* anything. I'd run away.

"It doesn't matter now, does it?" Piper asked rhetorically. "I've come to terms, or I am coming to terms, with everything. I'm lucky that Thea and Logan have three beautiful kids who I can spoil rotten as Aunt Piper. And I hope Owen settles down one day too and has some children I can love, even if it's from a distance."

"What about adoption?"

She shrugged. "I could look into it, but I don't know if they'd approve a single parent. And is that really fair to the kid? To live a life without a father?"

"I was raised by a single mom."

"Oh, yeah? Did you ever feel like you were missing something?"

"As a little kid? No. She was my everything. But as I got older, I became the man of the house. It would have been nice to have had a few years as just a teenager."

It would have been nice to have someone to lean on as an adult through the hard times.

Once I'd hit twenty-five, something in my relationship with Mom had changed. In a way, I'd become the parent. I'd fixed things around the house that were broken and made sure the oil in her car was changed regularly. I'd added her grocery list to my own and delivered food to her house on Sundays. I'd even started balancing her checkbook because it was the one task she'd always griped about in my youth.

Mom seemed glad to let me take the wheel. I didn't blame her. She'd put in so many long hours for so many long years, it was probably nice to have someone else drive for a change.

But when the world turned black and the numbness settled in, she hadn't been there to pull me through.

She'd made the wrong choice. She'd crushed me.

So I'd come here to suffer alone.

Then I'd gotten a neighbor.

twelve

PIPER

"I'M HERE." KAINE KNOCKED ON THE CAMPER DOOR WITH three hard thuds.

"Coming!" I hopped on one leg as I pulled my foot into a tennis shoe. "One sec!"

"Take your time," he called back.

I bounced over to the couch, sitting to tie up the laces. My fingers fumbled with excitement. Kaine was here to take me on a hike this afternoon and then I was cooking us dinner.

In the two weeks since my confession on Kaine's front porch, we'd settled into an odd sort of friendship. Well, odd for me. I'd never been friends with a man who I'd had sex with after the sex had stopped.

But friends we were.

I cooked dinner for us almost every night. I'd told Kaine it was no hassle since I had to cook anyway, so he'd come over to my camper, or I'd walk over to his place and we'd share our evening meals.

He'd taken me on a short after-work hike earlier in the week, and we'd found some huckleberry bushes. I'd never had huckleberries before since they were native to the Pacific Northwest, but after trying a couple, I'd been inspired. We picked a bunch, and on my table was the pie I'd baked for dessert.

After my confession on Kaine's porch, something had changed between us. Sexual tension still rippled between us when we got too close. Whenever we accidentally touched, the flying sparks were hard to ignore. But we both held fast to our nonsexual relationship.

What we'd found was a mutual adoration of good food. A love of this forest we called home. And the beauty of companionship.

I carried the bulk of the conversation, as I expected I would always do. Kaine wasn't one to speak just to hear his own voice, something that Adam had done more often than not.

It was refreshing for me to talk about my work, to share my excitement with someone who was just as excited to listen. Kaine might not share a lot of details about his life, but he was a willing confidant for the details of mine.

His face would soften as I spoke. Whenever I was feeling particularly sassy, he'd gift me with his quiet chuckle. And his vibrant eyes were always on mine whenever I spoke, telling me that he was completely engaged in our conversation.

I had his attention.

And he had mine.

After dinner, the two of us typically spent the evening together. Usually I'd accompany him to his shop, where I'd watch with rapt attention as he worked on a piece of furniture.

It was easy to get lost in the fluid movements of his hands and the strength in his arms as he turned a plain, rough piece of wood into something refined and graceful. It gave me tingles when he'd narrate the process in his deep, sexy voice. He'd whisper to the wood, and to me, as he worked, his unique lullaby the perfect end to my day.

When we weren't in his shop, we were inspecting my future home.

Kaine had taken such an interest in my remodel that he'd do regular walk-throughs with me to scrutinize the progress of my construction crew. One night last week, he'd found an issue with a window frame—something about it not being precisely level and how it might let in a winter draft. It had looked fine to me. But the following morning, Kaine had marched over first thing in the morning, his own level in hand, to have a word with the foreman.

I'd watched, laughing from my camper window, as my foreman followed Kaine inside. Ten minutes later, they'd come back out, shaking hands as the foreman promised to have the window fixed.

Kaine might not be ready to confide his past, but those little things told me he cared. They told me that this friendship was just as important to him as it was to me.

With my shoes tied, I swiped a baseball cap off the kitchen counter. It was a gift from Thea, one of the new red-and-white trucker hats she'd ordered for the bar.

"Hey." I opened the door and stepped down. "Ready?"

Kaine's forehead furrowed. "That's what you're wearing?"

"What?" I looked down at my clothes. I had on some denim cutoffs and a red racer-back tank top. It was also from the bar—I was basically a walking advertisement for Thea's business. It was cute, and I hoped to get some sun.

It was the middle of June and summer had finally came to Montana. I needed the sun since my regular spray tans from the city were now a thing of the past, as were manicures and pedicures. I'd taken to doing those in my camper since there wasn't a spa in town.

"We're hiking." Kaine frowned. "If you trip and fall, you'll skin your knees."

"Ah, yes," I said dryly. "That is a risk. One I mitigated by not wearing high heels."

Kaine's expression didn't change from underneath the brim of his own hat, though the corner of his lip twitched.

"I'll be fine." I smacked him in the stomach as I walked by, heading up the trail to the ridge. "Are you coming or not?"

He grumbled something under his breath, but his boots followed me up the trail. He was wearing his normal attire of Carhartts and a T-shirt. He also had on a small backpack, one he'd brought along on all of our excursions up the mountain. I didn't need to ask what was inside since Kaine was becoming predictable. He'd brought along two granola bars, four bottles of water, bear spray and a first-aid kit.

If I did trip and scrape a knee, he'd whip that thing out and have me slathered with anti-bacterial ointment and wrapped in Ace bandages before I could count to ten.

"Nice hat," Kaine said.

I stopped on the trail and turned, waiting for him to catch up. "Thanks. Thea gave it to me."

He walked right into my space, towering over me, so I had to tip my chin back. We weren't touching, but he was close enough that the heat from his chest warmed my bare skin. Or maybe that was the electricity crackling between us.

"You look good in hats," he said quietly.

"So do you."

The longer hair at the nape of his neck curled under the band. Those swoops were begging for some attention, but I used all of my willpower to keep my fingers by my sides.

My god, he had nice lips. His dark beard was such a contrast to the pale peach. My breath hitched as I remembered how it felt to have those soft lips on my own.

Kaine leaned in a fraction of an inch as the magnetic force between us tugged. It was tempting, *so tempting*, to do the same, but before I caved to the attraction, a bird squawked above us. The noise forced our bodies apart.

"Um . . . shall we?" I stepped backward, turning on the trail.

"Yup." Kaine took up the space beside me as we walked. We both hugged the edges of the trail so we weren't too close. But it was a narrow path, and the proximity of his hand to mine was noticeable.

The undercurrent between us was there, ever present and always flowing. It reminded me of the treetops today, and how they swished in the gentle breeze. They'd swing close to one another but just before they'd brush, the wind would ease and they'd whip in the opposite direction.

We continued up the trail until it got steep, and I took the lead. Kaine let me go first to set the pace. He took the hike to the ridge like it was a stroll through Central Park. I doubted his legs were straining or that his lungs were on fire. But the view from the top was worth breaking a sweat.

As we crested the trail, I breathed in the clean air, warmed up and ready for more. "Where are you taking me today?"

"I thought we could go east for a change." He pointed in the direction of his property. "There's a game trail that runs down the ridge. About two miles off, there's another ridge."

"Sounds great. I'll follow you."

He nodded and wasted no time in finding the path. It wasn't as wide or clear as the trail we took up to the ridge so occasionally the brush would scrape against my bare calves. Kaine took it slow, holding those long legs back so it wasn't too strenuous for me to keep up.

And though we were in dense forest, the view wasn't too bad.

Walking behind Kaine gave me a great view of his ass and broad shoulders. Months ago, I would have sworn up and down that a nice rear end was impossible to beat. But Kaine's shoulders were damn sexy. They were so big and brawny. They were so powerful and—*okay, that's enough.*

I'd had my moment to drool and now it was time for my thoughts to head back to the safe zone.

I opened my mouth to drum up some friendly, boring conversation and distract myself from the way his triceps bulged underneath the tight fit of his T-shirt, but Kaine stopped short on the trail and held up a hand.

I nearly ran into him. "What?"

He shook his head, and I clamped my mouth shut. Then he looked over his shoulder and pointed down the trail.

I followed his finger to where a grizzly bear was standing on its hind legs, staring at us with a crooked head.

I gasped, clinging to Kaine's shirt as my heart stopped.

I was going to be mauled and eaten by a bear today. There would be no huckleberry pie for dessert. Instead, I'd be this bear's treat.

And I wouldn't have any more nights with Kaine. When faced with an animal four times my size, that was the regret that popped to mind first. I wished I had gotten one more chance to kiss him.

"Don't. Run." He reached behind him and put a hand to my stomach, gently pushing me backward.

The bear watched us as we backed away with shuffled steps. It dropped down on all fours and took three steps in our direction. I nearly threw up my breakfast. Then finally, it let out a snort and ambled away in the opposite direction.

My sigh of relief rang through the forest.

Kaine didn't relax though, his eyes glued to the spot where the bear had been standing. He urged me on faster and, with one hand, reached into the side pocket of his backpack to retrieve the bear spray.

I had to spin around to keep from tripping as I hustled, though I was careful not to run. Every third step, I glanced over my shoulder to make sure the bear hadn't changed his mind about making me his afternoon snack.

It was only when Kaine turned, walking close to my side, that I began to breathe again. My hands didn't stop shaking until we were on top of the ridge and out of the trees.

"Is it gone?" I whispered.

"You can talk normally."

"No way," I whispered again.

He chuckled, shrugging off his backpack and dropping it on the ground. He dug out two bottles of water, handing me mine, and then surprised me by taking out a gleaming silver pistol.

I suddenly felt sorry for the bear.

"You're packing heat?" I teased.

"Better to be prepared." Kaine shrugged. "Bear spray is the best, but having a gun handy doesn't hurt either. I prefer to carry it in a holster on my hip, but I didn't want to scare you."

"It's fine. Owen insisted I take a handgun class after he joined the military. Guns don't scare me. Have you had that with us on every hike?"

He nodded. "Just the last couple. With the berries coming on like they have, it's not unusual to see more bears up here."

"How dangerous was that situation?" I asked, pointing in the direction of where we'd seen the bear.

"It was good that we didn't surprise him and we had some distance. But on the next hike, you'll have your own can of spray, and we're going to get some bells to make more noise."

"Seriously?" I was not feeling so hot about living in the forest at the moment. "Is it safe around my house?"

"Bears are mostly pests, like big raccoons. If one gets

comfortable around your house, they might make a damn mess of your garbage. So keep your lids on tight. But they normally live deeper in the woods. The only reason they're venturing closer to town now is because the huckleberries are so thick this year."

"I don't want to be eaten by a bear."

Kaine chuckled. "I won't let you get eaten by a bear. But no more hiking without me."

"Oh, I'm never hiking alone again," I declared.

Kaine flashed me one of his rare smiles. "Want to keep going?"

"Hell no. I'm locking myself in my camper for the rest of the weekend where it's safe and there's pie."

"Pie?"

"Huckleberry. I was going to surprise you after dinner."

His groan was nothing less than erotic, and it made my mouth dry. I took a drink from my water, then put it in his backpack, doing my best to erase that delicious sound from my memory.

Most days, it was easier to be around Kaine. But for some reason, today I was struggling to resist his temptation. After he left tonight, I'd probably be so wired, I'd have to take a shower and use my fingers to relieve some of the ache between my legs.

Kaine took a long drink from his own water, his Adam's apple bobbing as he gulped, then shoved it in his backpack. The bear spray stayed in one hand while his gun was tucked safely in his pocket as we descended the trail back to our homes.

If we did see another bear, Kaine would keep me safe. Out here, he was my protector.

A smile pulled at the corners of my mouth, and I looked down, hiding it from him with my hat. If my life was in danger, Kaine would wrestle a bear to the ground and kick its ass before making it his living room rug.

A giggle bubbled free.

"What?" Kaine asked over his shoulder.

I shook my head, coughing to hide another laugh. "Nothing."

Maybe Kaine would let me name the bear rug. It would have to be something manly, like the owner himself. A name like Boris or Baran or Boryenka. Apparently Kaine's imaginary rug was Russian.

Too busy brainstorming names, I didn't notice the shining black sedan parked behind my Mini. Not until a familiar voice startled me, and I knew exactly who I'd see as I peered past Kaine's broad shoulders.

"Who are you?" Adam was standing by the car, his hands fisted on his hips as he barked his question at Kaine.

"This is private property," Kaine answered. He might as well have said *move the fuck on, asshole.*

"I know whose property this is," Adam spat. "What I don't know is who you are."

"Adam," I snapped, moving up to Kaine's side. I went to take another step, but before I could, Kaine took my elbow in his grip and secured me by his hip.

At the gesture, Adam took two angry steps away from his car. "Piper, who is this guy?"

"My neighbor." The grip Kaine had on my arm tightened, almost as if he didn't like my answer. "What are you doing here, Adam?"

He shot a glare at Kaine. "Pip, can we talk in private?"

"No," Kaine barked.

I appreciated his protectiveness for the second time today, but there was no escaping a one-on-one with Adam. So I pulled on my arm enough that Kaine set me free. "Would you mind?"

He glowered. My eyes widened in a silent plea to not make

this worse, until he grumbled, "Fine."

I expected him to stomp down the path to the cabin, but to my surprise, he stalked across my driveway, right to the Airstream's door and let himself into my temporary home. The camper rocked as he slammed the door and went to the table, sitting down so he could watch us through the window.

"What are you doing here?" I asked as I walked over to my ex-husband.

Adam looked down with the blue eyes that had once held power over my every mood. They didn't inspire much loyalty anymore. His chiseled jaw was covered in a day's worth of scruff, something Adam did because it was popular in the industry, not because he liked it. He preferred to shave every morning and wouldn't be caught dead with a thick beard like Kaine's.

"I told you on the phone we needed to talk."

I crossed my arms over my chest. "And I told you not to come out here."

"Because of that guy?" Adam's jaw ticked as he glanced over to the camper.

Kaine was sitting at my dining room table with a fork full of huckleberry pie perched on his lips, simultaneously chewing another in an angry bite.

The bastard was eating my pie.

"Nice," I mouthed.

Kaine shoved another bite in his mouth. The look he sent me said, *If you want some pie, ditch the asshole and get in here.*

I rolled my eyes and looked back to Adam.

"Is that the guy you're seeing?" he asked through gritted teeth.

"No. He's my neighbor." And my friend. "That's beside the point. What are you doing here?"

Adam turned his back on Kaine and took me by the

shoulders. "I want you back. I'm miserable. I *need* you, Piper. Come home."

Adam had only gotten more good-looking with age. Not that long ago, he'd been irresistible. The wind caught a lock of his blond hair, settling it on his forehead. Out of habit, I almost brushed it back in place.

He was so handsome. And so out of place. He was built for the life he'd created in New York. He thrived on the fame and the fortune. He didn't need me, he just didn't know it yet.

"No." I shook my head. "This is my home now. Our marriage is over and you have to let it go. Let me go."

"All because of one stupid kiss?"

"No, Adam. Not just because of one kiss. We had more problems than either of us ever wanted to admit long before that kiss."

"If this is about getting pregnant, then—"

"It's about all of it," I interrupted. "Yes, the kiss. Yes, the wanting kids. And the fact that we rarely saw one another. I mean, in order to have sex twice a week, we had to schedule it for Sunday and Thursday mornings."

"Because we were trying to have a baby."

"No," I countered. "Because that was the only time when you didn't have morning rehearsal and I didn't have an early meeting."

"Don't you dare blame this on my work." He shoved a finger in my face. "You worked just as much as I did."

"You're right," I said gently, and he dropped his hand. "Because it makes me happy."

"Are you saying I don't make you happy?"

"I'm saying that you kissed your costar a week after we found out I couldn't get pregnant. Would that make you happy?"

"So it is the kiss." He tossed out a hand. "Just admit it was the kiss."

"Yes!" I shouted. "Of course it was the kiss. And a million other reasons, like the fact that I don't believe you when you said you didn't sleep with her. The man I married wouldn't have hurt me like that. I don't trust you."

He looked to the gravel beneath his shoes, refusing to meet my eyes. He'd done that every other time I'd confronted him about his affair with a costar.

"Well . . . did you? Did you sleep with her?"

He looked up and scowled, tossing a thumb over his shoulder in Kaine's direction. "Did you sleep with him?"

"Yes, I did."

Shock flashed across his face, but he schooled his features quickly. Then The Actor appeared, the one who was calm and collected in front of a packed theater. The man who could stand on a bright stage and charm an audience sitting in the dark.

I hated The Actor.

He always seemed to show up whenever we were fighting. It was Adam's self-defense technique, his way of shutting me out. The actor was the one everyone loved, but I'd always found him kind of ugly.

"This was a wasted trip," he said coolly.

I scoffed. "You think?"

"Good-bye, Pip." He brushed past me, going straight for his car.

"Adam?" I called.

He stopped and glanced over his shoulder. "What?"

"Did you sleep with her?" I asked again, one last time.

Maybe I asked because I sensed there was more to his story. Maybe I asked so I'd stop feeling so guilty about being the one to drive our marriage into the oblivion. Maybe I asked because if he denied it again, I was going to accept it as the truth.

"Stop asking me that," he snapped.

"Then tell me the truth."

With his chin held high, he turned and leveled his gaze on me. "Yes. I fucked her in the backseat of her car after we left the restaurant."

His truth knocked the air from my lungs. When I recovered my breath, I swallowed the burn in my throat, refusing to let Adam see one more of my tears. "Why wouldn't you just tell me when I asked? Why deny it?"

"Because I love you."

"Hmm. Funny kind of love." My eyes drifted to the ground. "Good-bye, Adam."

He yanked open the door to his car and slid inside. Gravel bits flew from his tires as he reversed out of the driveway and down the road.

I stood there, waiting until his car was out of sight, then I marched to the camper. Kaine's eyes tracked my movements as I stormed inside and ripped open the silverware drawer for my own fork. My ass had barely touched the bench seat before a bite was in my mouth.

With my cheeks full, I muttered, "You ate my pie."

"I needed some magic."

My mouth froze and the tears I'd fought outside came forward, though I blinked them away. I refused to cry for Adam. He'd gotten too many buckets of tears as it was. And surprisingly, it wasn't as hard as I thought to keep them at bay.

Maybe it was the huckleberry pie.

Maybe it was because deep down I'd always known the truth of Adam's betrayal.

Maybe it was Kaine's gentle eyes silently promising it would be all right.

By the time the pie was gone, so was the pain.

"I need to show you something." Kaine slid out of his seat and put his fork in the sink.

He grabbed mine and did the same before taking my hand and pulling me away from the table. As we walked out of the camper and across the path to his house, he didn't let go of my hand. He held it as we passed the cabin and continued down to his shop.

With his free hand, he opened the door and flicked on the lights. Then he pulled me through the labyrinth of incomplete projects in the center of the floor to something covered in the far corner with a canvas tarp.

"Grab that end," he instructed and let my hand go.

I went to the opposite end of the cloth, taking it in my hands like he'd done on his side. With a smirk, he whipped the cover off the table beneath, forcing me to do the same.

My jaw dropped as I let the tarp fall to the floor. My hands itched to touch the wooden top and they stretched for it but stopped an inch away as I looked to Kaine for permission.

He gave me a slight nod, and I dove in, pressing my palms against the smooth grain. The warmth of the wood soaked into my fingertips.

The edge of the table was rough—the live edge, as Kaine had called it. The contrast to the finished and flawless top gave the piece a rugged flair. And just like he'd promised, the stain brought out so many of the walnut's grains that I could study them for hours and never get bored.

"This turned out so . . ." I trailed off, without words to describe the masterpiece.

"It's yours."

My hands froze. "What?"

"I was going to wait until your house was done, but I decided to give it to you now. This is for your dining room."

"But what about the person you were making it for?"

He shrugged. "It was always for you."

Always? This was the unfinished table we'd had sex on over a month ago. Which meant he'd started making this for me long before I'd asked him to over cinnamon rolls.

All this time, I'd thought Kaine didn't know how to express his feelings. I'd thought that was why he hid so much and why he got embarrassed when I complimented his work.

I'd been completely and miserably wrong.

Kaine knew how to express his feelings just fine.

I stepped on top of the canvas cloth as I went to Kaine. He stood stoically, watching as I breached his space and tossed my arms around his sexy shoulders. Then, with my fingers threaded into the hair under the band of his hat, I stood on my tiptoes and pulled his mouth down to mine.

He flicked off my hat a split second before our lips fused.

His tongue swept across the seam of my lips. His arms banded around my back as he hauled me against his body.

The kiss was hot and frantic, the weeks' worth of pent-up tension sending us both into a crazed frenzy. The kiss led to Kaine stripping us both naked and making me whimper his name as he fucked me on my table.

The sex had been incredible, but it was the kiss that sealed my fate.

I was falling in love with my grouchy, tormented neighbor. I was falling in love with a man who was sweet and kind.

I was falling in love with a man who had a little magic of his own.

thirteen

PIPER

THE WAIT WAS OVER. ONE MONTH AND ONE WEEK AFTER Kaine and I went from being neighbors to lovers—again—I was moving into my new house. And the Kendrick crew had all come up to help.

"I'm hungry," Charlie told Thea.

"Again?" Thea gaped. "You just had a snack. I swear your leg is hollow."

Charlie just shrugged and gave me a shy smile.

"Good thing I've got lots and lots and lots of food in my new house." I walked over to the pantry, where I'd loaded the shelves with crackers and chips and cookies. My cart had been piled high at the grocery store this morning.

Charlie came to my side and her mouth dropped with a whispered, "Whoa."

I laughed. "Go crazy, kiddo."

"Me too! Me too!" Collin came racing in from the living room, where he'd been building a fort out of empty boxes.

"I swear I feed them." Thea shook her head. "Okay, what's next?"

I scanned the kitchen. There were a few odd dishes on the counter waiting to be washed before they were put away. But the rest of my drawers and cabinets were full. The furniture in the living room was in place, and we were just waiting for Kaine and Logan to bring over my table.

"I think we deserve a snack break too. Chips and salsa?"

"Definitely." Thea smiled and followed her kids into the pantry for the chips while I got out some bowls and the salsa.

The last month had gone by so quickly, it was hard to believe it was the middle of July and summer was halfway over. But it had been a wonderful summer.

Work had been hectic and crazed and rewarding, like always. As much as I enjoyed going down to Thea and Logan's house to work, I couldn't wait to break in my office. I'd miss hearing the kids playing in the other room while I shared an office with Logan, but the desk I'd ordered was just waiting to be covered in paperwork. The bookshelves were empty and desperate for binders and books.

It was going to be the room I finished decorating first, even before my bedroom.

Besides work, I'd spent the last month falling deeper and deeper into Kaine.

We spent most of our evenings together, eating dinner, then walking through the house. Most nights, there were a slew of decisions the foreman needed me to make, and with Kaine's input, I'd picked out doorknobs and window blinds and light fixtures.

The results were nothing short of stunning.

With the kids loaded up on crackers and cookies, Thea and I went into the living room and sank into my new couch. As I chewed a chip, I ran my hand over the camel leather. It was a bit stiff, but after a couple of months of me lounging here to watch the TV now mounted above the fireplace, it would soften.

"This place turned out so incredible." Thea looked around the open living room. "I'm so glad you had them vault the ceiling. Those beams make this room."

I smiled, letting my head fall back to appreciate the dark wood above us. "It turned out better than I ever imagined."

With the open concept, my living room, dining area and kitchen were all one giant room. There were large windows all along the far wall so I could look out into the trees while I was sitting at my dining room table. The fireplace in the living room was made of white stone with some rich built-in shelves on either side for my movies and books and whatever trinkets I found to showcase. The floors were all wooden, even in the kitchen, but I'd added rugs in each of the rooms to warm it up.

It was exactly what I'd been going for.

Warm. Bright. Inviting.

Home.

"I'm so happy to be here, but I'm going to miss the Airstream," I told Thea.

"You can borrow it whenever you want."

"It's so strange to think I'll be sleeping in my actual bed tonight."

I'd arranged for my New York belongings in storage to be transported out here. The truck had arrived yesterday with my furniture and more boxes than I'd remembered owning. So today, Thea and Logan had brought up the kids to help unpack. There were items that didn't work in this house that I'd swap out for others eventually.

But as of tonight, I was home. Permanently.

I took another chip from my bowl but hesitated before dousing it in salsa as my stomach churned. "Ugh." I gripped my stomach.

"Not feeling well?" Thea asked.

I closed my eyes and took a few long breaths, swallowing down the nausea. "No. I've just been queasy these last few days. I'm sure it's just the stress of the move."

"That's no good."

"It always goes away by dinner time, and I have my appetite back."

"Um . . . could you—"

The sound of truck tires crunching on my gravel driveway interrupted Thea, forcing us both off the couch. She grabbed Camila from where she was playing on a blanket with some toys on the floor, positioning her on a hip with a kiss to her cheek. Then we all went outside to see Kaine backing his truck up to the door.

"I'm so excited for this," I told Thea.

"From everything you've told me about this table, so am I."

I swallowed down another rush of nausea, refusing to let a stomach bug ruin this moment. Logan got out first, followed by Kaine. He shot me a quick grin before hopping up into the truck bed.

The motion of his long legs swinging into the truck, his muscled ass on display as he bent to undo a ratchet strap, chased away the sick feeling in my stomach.

My god, he is handsome. That thought crossed my mind daily. A wave of heat rushed down my spine.

Sex had become a key component in my evening routine with Kaine over the last month. We didn't have sleepovers, but Kaine left my bed later and later each night. The evenings we spent at the cabin, he'd walk me back to the camper after naked time under his sheets. I'd long since broken my rule about sex in his bed.

Why did I need boundaries when I'd already crossed them all?

Kaine had me whenever and wherever he wanted, and the pleasure was definitely shared. My heart, well . . . it was too late to add safeguards now. The man standing in the back of his truck had stolen it already.

I glanced over at Thea. She was drooling over her husband like I'd been with Kaine.

"If you keep looking at him like that, you're going to get another baby," I teased.

She laughed. "Oh no, we're done. Three is all I can handle." Her smile fell and she gave me a sideways glance before it moved to Kaine. She leaned in closer to talk under her breath. "Um, I was going to ask inside. But about the nausea. You couldn't be pregnant, could you?"

"Oh, uh . . . no." My heart sank. "No. I-I can't have kids." Not without major medical intervention.

"Oh." Her face paled. "I'm sorry. I didn't know. I didn't mean to ask if—"

"It's okay." I waved her off. "I don't talk about it much. One of these days I'll come down to the bar while it's quiet and we can talk about it." Now that I'd confided my issues to Kaine, I didn't feel so protective about my secrets.

She smiled. "I'd like that. I didn't mean to pry. It's just that when I was pregnant with all three kids, I'd get these waves of nausea that would make my skin gray like yours was on the couch. Then every night by dinner, I was starving. Still, I shouldn't have intruded. I'm so sorry."

"Really." I squeezed her arm. "It's fine. You didn't know."

Our whispered conversation was stopped short when Logan positioned himself at one end of the table. With Kaine at the other, the pair carefully unloaded my table, bringing it through the door.

When it was situated in the center of the dining area, Kaine whipped off the canvas tarp. All of us converged around the table, even the kids, admiring its beauty.

"Whoa," Thea whispered, stealing Charlie's word from earlier.

Logan came to her side, throwing an arm over her shoulder. "You should see some of the pieces in Kaine's shop. When we were loading up the truck, I made a mental list of things I'm going to have him build for the house."

Thea smiled. "Charge him double, Kaine. He can afford it."

Kaine's eyes just dropped back to the table.

As expected with new acquaintances—one of whom was the misanthrope Kaine Reynolds—things had been slightly awkward today. Though I'd talked about Logan and Thea constantly to Kaine, and vice versa, everyone was still feeling each other out.

Kaine was his quiet self, as I'd anticipated. His charm wasn't as forthcoming as Logan's, who'd spent years working ballrooms to raise funds from the rich. Kaine captured your heart more slowly, like a moss that took months to claim the bark of a forest tree. In time, he'd win over the Kendricks, and they'd learn he was the strong, silent type.

Awkwardness aside, I was calling today a win. Despite the forced conversation, everyone was in a cheerful mood and Kaine hadn't run away to hide in the cabin until the company was gone.

Was it strange that in all the time we'd spent together, he was just meeting my friends? Considering how rarely he left the mountain, I guess it wasn't that odd. Neither of us cared to go into town much for dinner, not when I enjoyed cooking.

Did he have any friends still in Bozeman where he'd grown up? Because he didn't have a single one here in Lark Cove besides me. Was it just his nature to keep to himself? Or had his past driven him to isolation?

Another wave of nausea hit, and I gripped the edge of the table, willing the chips I'd eaten to stay in my stomach.

"You okay?" Kaine asked, coming to my side.

"Fine," I lied. "Just so happy to have this table. Thank you."

"You're welcome."

"Are you going to let me pay for it?" Every time I'd asked over the last month, he'd pretend like I hadn't asked him the question. Kaine's method of saying *no* was apparently to not answer at all.

And per usual, he ignored my question, left my side and went over to shake Logan's hand. "Thanks for your help with this."

Logan grinned. "Anytime."

"Nice to meet you, Thea."

"You too." She nodded, bouncing Camila on her hip. The baby tried to shove her fingers in Thea's mouth. "Stop that." Thea laughed, jerking her chin away. It just made Camila giggle, a sound so precious it melted your heart.

I looked around the table, seeing Logan smiling at his daughter. Charlie and Collin were laughing too.

When I got to Kaine, I expected to see that soft smile I got after making him a special pie, but instead, he was glaring at his boots. His hands were fisted at his sides like he had bamboo shards shoved under his fingernails.

"Kaine?"

He looked up, his face suddenly cold and impassive. "I need to do a couple things in the shop today."

"Oh, okay." I thought he'd planned to spend the day helping me get furniture in place and boxes unpacked. "We're all going down to the bar for pizza later. Want to come?"

He shook his head, already heading for the door. He held up one arm in a wave, then crossed the living room like his boots were on fire. It didn't take long for his truck to rumble to a start and pull away from the house to go down the mountain road on my side, only to come back up again on his.

Luckily, his strange behavior went unnoticed by the Kendrick family, who were all still enraptured by the youngest member.

What was Kaine's problem? Were things more uncomfortable for him than I'd guessed? Did he not like children? As I thought back to the introductions earlier, he'd seemed fine around Charlie and Collin. But I didn't remember him even looking in Camila's direction.

Did he not like babies? It wasn't unreasonable for some men to be wary of babies. My brother wasn't particularly fond of them, something both my mom and I figured would change once Owen had his own.

Maybe Kaine had the same apprehension when it came to little ones.

My stomach did another round of acrobatics, so I retreated to the kitchen for a glass of the ginger ale I'd bought earlier, hoping it would settle things down.

As I sipped my soda, Thea came to the kitchen. "If you're not up for pizza, we can reschedule."

"No! I'll be fine." I smiled wider. "It always passes. And the ginger ale helps."

"Good. That always helped me too," she said, looking toward her children.

My eyes followed her to where Logan was helping Collin build a tunnel out of the empty boxes.

There was no way I could be pregnant. Right? I hadn't had my period lately, but that was normal for me. It wasn't uncommon for me to go four or five months without a cycle. On top of that, my cervical mucus was abnormal. It basically murdered sperm that dared get close enough.

No, there was no chance I was pregnant. The test results

were definitive.

The day our fertility specialist had called to deliver the results, I'd been so nervous, I'd made Adam take the call. He'd listened intently, nodding along as the doctor spoke, and after he'd hung up, he'd told me everything.

Then he'd held me as I'd fallen apart on our living room couch.

So even though Kaine and I barely kept our hands off one another, there was no way I could be pregnant, not without a doctor to implant a fertilized egg into my uterus.

Kaine was no doctor.

I was definitely not pregnant.

"You are pregnant, Ms. Campbell. Your blood tests confirm it."

It was the third time the doctor had said those three words. *You are pregnant.*

"I don't understand." My mouth was flapping open. "Are you sure that's my blood sample you're looking at?" I peered around the doctor's shoulder, pointing to the file in her hand as I double-checked the name.

She just laughed, showing me that it was in fact my name at the top. "I'm sure."

My hands dove into my hair. "I cannot believe this."

"Congratulations." She smiled as I sat stunned on the exam table. "If your nausea continues, keep up with the ginger ale. Saltine crackers help some women. And if it persists or gets unmanageable, your OB can prescribe something stronger."

I managed a nod as she congratulated me again and left the room.

Pregnant.

Thea had been right after all.

In the past three days, my nausea had gotten worse, so much so that I couldn't concentrate on work this morning. Not wanting to give the Kendrick kids a stomach bug, I'd made a trip up to Kalispell to hit an urgent care and get checked out.

And after sitting in the doctor's office for three hours, answering questions and having tests done, it was official.

I was pregnant.

Me. *The Infertile One.*

It took me almost thirty minutes to come unstuck from my exam room. A nurse came in three times to check on me—and kick me out—but I just stayed on the table, staring at the gray walls in disbelief. Finally, after the nurse's fourth visit, I collected my purse and walked through the clinic in a daze.

I passed the doctor again and she gave me another *congratulations.* I nodded my good-bye, then went out to my car where I sat for twenty minutes, my hands frozen on the steering wheel.

Pregnant. I was pregnant.

With a baby.

I was having a baby.

This was a dream, right? Or was it a nightmare? Would I wake up, only to find myself alone in bed and the one thing I'd always wanted taken away from me again?

My hand drifted to my belly, and a tear dripped down my cheek. I felt both. This was no nightmare. This was the dream. This was real-life magic.

How many hours had I wished for this? How many times had I prayed for a miracle?

A smile cracked my frozen face and another tear fell.

"I'm having a baby." The words filled the car and my heart with so much joy, I collapsed against the steering wheel, laughing and crying.

When I pulled myself together, I sat up and flipped down my visor's mirror. My mascara was glommed on my wet eyelashes. The blush I'd carefully applied to my cheeks was streaked with tear trails. My face still held a tinge of green from the nausea.

Who the hell cared what I looked like, because I was pregnant.

"Oh my god." I giggled. "Yes!"

I felt like hopping out of the car to do a jumping heel click. Instead I sat there, blissfully wiping away the tears. But as my face dried, the euphoria dulled.

Had the doctors in New York gotten my diagnosis wrong? That just couldn't be. We'd gone to one of the best fertility specialists in Manhattan.

I'd been sitting right there next to Adam as he'd listened to the latest test results, so it wasn't like some detail had been lost over time. It wasn't like he'd had hours to confuse or forget important aspects of the report.

Sure, I hadn't seen the results in person, but neither had he. The doctor was booked solid, so we'd opted for the results over a phone call instead of waiting a week for an appointment window to open up.

The clinic hadn't minded giving us our results over the phone, because in their world, diagnosis was just the beginning. Our doctor had been determined to give us a child.

When we first met with the specialist, she decided the first course of action was to correct my missing cycles. She gave me a hormone shot in the ass, handed over a box of ovulation sticks and prescribed lots and lots of sex.

She also told me to do whatever it took to reduce my stress levels, so I got weekly massages and cut back at work. I eliminated wine and chocolate and everything delicious.

Three months, countless shots and no pregnancy later, the

doctor ordered another set of tests.

The results from those tests were the ones Adam had taken over the phone. And something had to have gotten lost in translation.

I dove into my purse, rifling around for my phone at the bottom. After looking up the fertility clinic's number, I waited through a few minutes of transfers until I finally reached the nurse who'd been on our case.

"Hey, Patrick." I smiled as he answered. "This is Piper Campbell. Formerly, Piper Hall. Do you remember me?"

"Piper. Of course, how could I forget those dimples. So good to hear from you." His warm voice had always soothed my nerves when I was bare-assed, waiting for the needle pokes. "Though it's about three years later than I'd expected."

"Yeah." I sighed. "Adam and I got divorced so we didn't really need that consultation for in vitro."

He hummed. "I'm sorry to hear that. Unfortunately, that happens with some of our clients. People always say time is the true test of marriage. I say it's infertility. What can I do for you today?"

"Um . . ." I took a deep breath, not really even sure how to say this out loud. "I'm pregnant."

"You're pregnant! All right!" He clapped, the noise echoing into the phone. "Congratulations! You'll be one heck of a mama."

"Thank you. So much. But the reason I'm calling is, well . . . *because* I'm pregnant. Based on the last tests you guys ran for us, I was under the impression that I'd never be able to conceive without some help. I'm shocked, to say the least, and I guess curious how it could have happened."

"Hmm. That doesn't seem right off the cuff. But let me go back and check your file. Give me a second." A keyboard clicked in the background as he typed.

My fingers ran up and over the steering wheel as I waited. After they'd made about five loops, he came back onto the phone.

"Okay. So let me just refresh myself here. We started with some basic hormone injections to get your ovulation back on track. And when those didn't result in a pregnancy, we tested both you and your husband for abnormalities. I'm seeing here that your vaginal pH was slightly acidic, but nothing that couldn't be corrected. But we recommended IVF because of your husband's poor sperm quality. The doctor made a note that your chances of natural conception would be less than ten percent."

The phone fell out of my hand and landed on my lap, and I scrambled to pick it back up. "Patrick, I think I must have heard you wrong. I thought I was the one with the abnormalities, not Adam."

"No," he said gently. "You both had challenges. Without intervention to match sperm and egg, you likely wouldn't have conceived. He has a low sperm count and limited motility. The doctor said that there was a high chance the quality was too poor for in vitro. Our recommendation for the best chance at fertilization was to explore external donors."

My mind whirled, and the only word I came up with was "Huh?"

"Didn't the doctor explain all of this to you when she delivered your results?"

"I'm sure she did." To Adam. My blood started to boil. "I guess I must have missed it. Thanks so much for your time today."

"My pleasure. And again, congratulations. I'll expect to see a baby announcement."

"You got it." I ended the call, then tossed my phone into the passenger seat.

Poor sperm quality? Limited motility? *Adam* had a fertility problem?

"Gah!" I screamed, my hands strangling the steering wheel.

How could he have kept this from me? How could he have led me to believe that it was all my fault we couldn't have children?

I cranked the key in the car, revving the engine as I screeched out of the parking lot. I was fuming mad, but I resisted the urge to stomp on the gas and speed down the highway toward Lark Cove.

All through the divorce, I'd been plagued with guilt, and at the time, I'd felt defective.

"Damn you, Adam." *Damn you.*

How could he deceive me like this, yet claim to love me? He'd held me in his arms those nights I'd cried myself to sleep. He'd dried my tears with his thumbs. He'd kissed my puffy eyes, telling me I was still the most beautiful woman in the world.

Had that all been a lie too?

I pulled up his number on my phone, fuming as it rang twice.

"Hel—"

"You're an asshole!" I shouted before he had a chance to utter another syllable. "How could you have lied to me about this? How could you have kept something like this from me?"

"What are you talking about?"

"You told me it was my problem. That I was the reason couldn't have a baby. But that's not exactly true, is it? A know how I know it was all a lie? Because I'm p

"You're-you're pregnant?" he stuttered.

"Is this why you wanted to get back togeth

you fought so fucking hard for our divorce? So I wouldn't learn the truth?"

"Pip—"

"Don't," I snapped, cutting him short. "I don't want to hear anything you have to say. I want to hate you for doing this to me. I want to hate you for the way you've made me feel for the last three years. I want to, but I won't."

The anger in my voice disappeared as my free hand went back to my belly. "Because of your lies, I get the greatest gift I could have ever dreamed of. I get to be a mother. I won't hate you, but I will never think of you again."

My thumb squashed the button to end the call, and I immediately pulled over on the side of the road so I could retrieve my phone lying on the other seat. With fast strokes, I pulled up Adam's name and blocked his number.

In a deceptive and cruel way, Adam had given me a gift.

In an accidental way, so had Kaine.

Kaine.

"Oh, hell." My stomach rolled for the first time since I'd left the doctor's office and it had nothing to do with morning sickness.

I had to figure out a way to explain to Kaine that I could, in fact, have children.

And that I was having his baby.

fourteen

KAINE

SHUT OFF THE BELT SANDER AND POPPED MY SAFETY GLASSES UP
on my head. Then I brushed away the dust on the board in
front of me, testing its texture with a swipe of my fingers.

"Not quite." This piece of white oak would be the top to an
end table, so the finish needed to be as smooth as satin.

I flipped my glasses back down, but before I could start up
the sander again, a voice rang through the shop.

"Knock, knock." Piper was standing in the large bay door
that I'd opened this afternoon to keep the shop from getting too
hot.

"Hey." I slid my glasses off and wiped my dusty hands on
my pants. "Not working today?"

She shook her head and stepped inside. "Got a sec?"

"Sure. What's up? Feeling any better?"

"Um . . . not really." Her hand went to her stomach and her
face got green. She lifted a finger. "Be right back."

"Can I hel—"

She shook her head, then spun around and darted out of
the shop.

I hurried after her, reaching the door just in time to see her
hurl in a bush.

"What can I do?" I asked.

"Get me a water. And don't come over here." She retched again.

"Okay." I went back inside and to my mini fridge. I took out a bottle of water and waited for her to come back.

I hadn't seen Piper much since the day I'd helped move her into the new house. She'd been sick, so I'd given her some space. One thing I'd learned was that she did not like me to see her vomit. And if I was being honest with myself, I'd used her stomach bug as an excuse to avoid her.

It had been a strange day, getting her moved into that house. Mostly because it was the first time I'd met her friends. The Kendricks were nice people, but something about meeting them had been too intimate. Piper had introduced me as her neighbor, which was true. But I hadn't missed the way Thea looked at us. She saw Piper and me as a couple.

Because we looked like a couple.

There was nothing casual about our relationship. We'd drifted from occasional hookups in an Airstream to me stopping by Piper's house last night to make sure she was drinking enough water because I didn't want her to get dehydrated.

The right thing to do would be to take a step back, talk to Piper about establishing some boundaries.

She didn't need to cook for me every night. I didn't need to be included in activities with her friends.

Especially when Thea and Logan had their kids along.

Seeing their baby daughter had brought on a slew of emotions I just wasn't ready to deal with yet. Over the last couple of months, Piper had shifted my focus. Instead of dwelling on the past and reliving the pain each day, she'd consumed my thoughts. She'd made me feel and, in a way, forget.

Then Camila Kendrick had brought it all back. That little girl was gorgeous with her dark eyes and dark hair. My daughter would have been just as beautiful. She would have had that same mesmerizing laugh. Her chubby fists would have looked so perfect clinging to the collar of my shirt, like Camila's had to Logan's. I would have bought her tiny shoes and an adorable pink romper too.

Camila was painful to be around, so I'd escaped to my shop. Piper had noticed, but she hadn't brought it up.

Should I tell Piper about my baby girl? If I were to confide in anyone, it would be Piper. She'd become the best friend I'd ever had.

She laughed a lot. She made *me* laugh a lot. And I trusted her.

"Sorry." Piper shuffled into the shop, her face pale. She'd pulled a piece of gum from her mouth and was chewing it furiously.

"It's okay." I took her the water and escorted her to the replacement chair I'd made for my porch. It was finished, flawless this time around, and I only needed to stain it to match its companion. "Sit down and just take it easy."

She sat and took a few deep breaths as she sipped her water. When she lifted her eyes to mine, the fear in them kicked my heart into overdrive. "I, uh . . . I've been trying to think of the best way to tell you this."

"What?"

She blew out a long breath and dropped her gaze to her lap but didn't speak.

My stomach plummeted in the silence. She must be here to talk about our relationship. Maybe she wanted more, or maybe she was going to end it. Either way, my defensive instincts roared to life.

If she wanted to end us, I was going to do it first. And if she wanted a commitment, I was shutting that down immediately.

I refused to put myself in a position where I could lose everything again. Where another person had the power to destroy me. Piper was approaching that line already and it was time to push her back.

"We should talk about us."

Her chin lifted. "Huh?"

"Us. We should talk about us." I took the glasses off my head and tossed them over to a table. "That's what you're here for, right? I mean, I've been thinking about it too. We've drifted too far from casual. It's been fun, but maybe the best thing would be for us to spend some time apart. Get some distance."

The bullshit spewed out of my mouth so fast I shocked myself.

Piper blinked a couple of times, her mouth slightly agape.

"I'd like to stay friends, if you're good with it. But I don't want to make you uncom—"

She held up a hand. "Please, stop talking."

I shut up.

"Could you sit down?"

I grabbed the old office stool that I wheeled around the shop and sat next to her side.

"I didn't come here to talk about our relationship." She swallowed hard. "I need to tell you something." Her chest rose as she inhaled, then caved as her breath came out in a whoosh. "I'm pregnant."

My muscles went limp. Every single one of them, and I fell off my stool, my ass slamming onto the concrete floor.

"Kaine!" Piper shot out of her chair, rushing over to me. "Are you okay?"

I shook off the paralyzing shock and let Piper help me up onto unsteady legs, then onto the stool again. It took a few moments for my brain to come unscrambled. "You're pregnant?"

She nodded. "I went to the doctor this morning."

"I thought you couldn't get pregnant."

"Neither did I," she whispered.

"It's mine?"

She frowned, crossing her arms over her chest. "I'm going to pretend you didn't just ask me that question."

I huffed. She was pregnant. *With my baby.* A rush of panic hit, chasing away the remaining shock. I shot off my stool, sending it flying sideways. "What the fuck, Piper!"

"Don't you yell at me."

I ran a hand over my beard, pacing back and forth. "How did this happen?"

"Adam lied to me about my fertility test results. I had some problems, but so did he. That was why we couldn't get pregnant. Because of him. I didn't know."

"You didn't know?" I scoffed. "You expect me to believe that?"

"It's the truth."

I stopped pacing and shot her a glare. "You said we were covered."

"And I was wrong."

Wrong? Wrong was so mild a word for this situation. This was my worst nightmare. This was everything I never wanted to feel again barreling down on me so fast I couldn't breathe.

How could she have let this happen? How could I have let this happen? I should have taken more precautions. I should have insisted on condoms.

I should have never trusted Piper.

"Did you do this on purpose?" I asked. "Did you just use me because your husband couldn't give you a kid?"

My words slapped her so hard, her entire body flinched. "You *asshole.* How could you even think that about me?"

"Can you blame me? It seems awfully convenient for you. You use me and get what you always wanted."

"Fuck you." Her face turned hard as stone. The spark in her eyes died, and she looked at me like I was nothing but the dust under her expensive shoes.

She could glare at me all she wanted because I didn't give a fuck. I had a right to ask these questions. I had a right to know the extent of her betrayal.

Because after all, that's what everyone did, didn't they?

They betrayed me.

"I didn't plot this." Her voice was cold. "Do you think I want to have a baby with a man who I've known for only months? A man who I know nothing about? A man who is so determined to keep me out that he won't even sleep in my bed after he fucks me? This is not the ideal situation, believe me. But it's happening."

It was happening.

It was happening all over again.

"I'm sorry for dropping this on you." Piper squared her shoulders. "It was just as big a shock to me. But I won't lie and say I don't want this baby. I'm going to give you some time. We can talk later."

Her footsteps grew distant as she made her way to the door. When they disappeared, I gave into the crushing pain and dropped to my knees.

I couldn't go through this again.

I couldn't.

So I shut it all out, like I'd taught myself to do years ago. I let the numbness soak into my bones. I let the darkness chase away the fear and pain. I let the light Piper had brought into my life be smothered by the black.

My knees were bruised by the time I shoved myself off the floor, then mindlessly walked home. I pushed open the door, but my feet wouldn't go inside. The haven I'd built up here wasn't safe anymore. It was tainted with memories of Piper.

I saw her sitting at my table, eating magic cake. I saw her in my living room, appraising my furniture with a quiet smile. I saw her in the kitchen, making me cinnamon rolls.

I pictured her, pregnant with our child, trapped in a crumpled car as life seeped out of her body in a crimson stream.

The need to flee hit me hard and I backed away from the door.

The same need had consumed me three years ago, after a funeral.

I'd left my entire life behind in the middle of the night, never looking back. I drove aimlessly until I got so tired, my drooping eyelids forced me to stop. I slept in my truck on the side of the highway, and the next morning when I woke up, I saw the sign welcoming me to Lark Cove.

It was as good a place as any to get lost.

For weeks, I ignored countless messages from Mom begging me to return home. I asked a buddy to take care of my house. Rent it. Sell it. Burn it down. I didn't care. And I begged the landlord of my former shop to get out of my lease, then ship me my tools.

I used their pity as leverage. It made running away all too easy because they all agreed to help me without question.

I endured being a part of society for as long as it took to find and close on my house. Then I shut out the world for the worst few months of my life.

Eventually, the phone calls, texts and emails from Mom stopped. Friends forgot about me, or at least, they clued into the fact that I wasn't coming back. People stopped trying to rescue me and just left me to my grief.

When it subsided to the point where I was able to breathe

again, work became my first priority. I needed the familiar tasks, the distraction—the money. So I called some old clients, drummed up some business and got busy.

Work and solitude weren't going to save me this time, but that didn't stop me from getting in my truck and driving the hell away from Lark Cove.

I was lost in my own fears. I didn't think about the road or where I was headed. I just drove and let the memories from the past keep my foot on the gas pedal.

No matter how many miles I drove, the voices in my head haunted me.

I'm pregnant.

One statement but two different voices. Shannon's voice had been so soft. Piper's had been strong and sure, even though she'd been nervous.

There was an accident.

I'd hardly recognized Mom's voice as she'd called from the hospital.

We tried to save the baby, but we lost them both.

The doctor's hoarse voice was burned into my brain. I heard it in my nightmares. Just like I heard the muffled sounds of a hospital floor as I sat behind a closed door with a lifeless baby in my arms.

I'd begged the doctor to let me hold her, just once. He'd hesitated at first because of how small and discolored she'd looked, but when I'd pleaded again, he'd ultimately relented.

She'd been so tiny and precious. Most of her face had been hidden in that pink blanket, but she'd been so peaceful as she'd rested against my chest. She would have been a beautiful child.

Oncoming headlights on the black highway caught my attention. I'd driven for so long that the sun was just disappearing behind the horizon. I shifted in my seat, switching hands on the steering wheel as the other car came my way.

Its low beams flashed as they crested a bump, and the flicker was enough to catch a streak as it bounded for the road.

A deer.

It ran full speed, barely crossing the centerline as the other car whizzed by. Its hooves and spindle legs staggered on the asphalt as it scrambled to get out of my lane. But I was going too fast and it wasn't fast enough.

My truck crushed its innocent body.

"Goddamn it." I pressed the brake, slowing down and veering off to the shoulder. I shoved the truck in park, unclipped my seatbelt and hustled outside. Behind me, the carcass was lying in the shallow ditch that ran along the highway.

I approached, knowing exactly what I'd find. Even in the twilight hour, I saw blood sprayed across the pavement. Raw guts and broken bones were not in their rightful place.

"Son of a bitch." I cursed and walked back to inspect my truck, leaving the animal for the varmints.

There was a clump of hair wedged into a joint of the grill guard, but the thick steel bars had served their purpose. Deer were a major hazard on Montana roads, and it was better to hit one than swerve and risk crashing into another car or rolling your own.

That didn't make it any easier to stomach.

I hung my head and climbed back in my truck, continuing down the road. Another life lost. The guilt of killing that animal gnawed at me as I drove. It took the place of the fear and pain I'd been reliving for hours.

Where was I? I didn't have my phone—I didn't have anything, not even my wallet. I was lucky that I'd run away with a full tank of gas. A green sign came into view and my headlights reflected the white letters.

Ahead was a junction. If I took a right, it would wind me around to Lark Cove. If I took a left, it would take me somewhere I'd avoided for too long.

Home.

I turned left.

I arrived in the dead of night, standing outside the house where I'd grown up. The porch light cast a soft glow my direction. The trees in the front yard, the ones I'd planted in high school as saplings, were nearly as tall as the power lines. The siding that had been white when I'd left was now gray. The front door was a dark red instead of denim blue.

But the placard above the door was the same as it had been for decades. It was the one I'd welded together my junior year in shop class, spelling *Reynolds* out of bolts and nails and screws.

I walked up the sidewalk, noticing new cracks. The grass was creeping over the edge where I used to come and keep a straight line. I went to the door, inspecting a yellow rose bush in bloom that hadn't been there years ago.

I knocked on the door, nerves shaking my limbs. Did she hate me for leaving her? Did she hate me for how I'd abandoned our family? If she did, she had every right.

The sound of shuffling footsteps came from inside and I held my breath. The door opened and she stepped closer, her face tired and eyes hazy with sleep. She was wearing the same plush, green robe I'd bought her for Christmas five years ago.

"Kaine?" She gasped, a wrinkled hand covering her mouth. "Is that you?"

"Yeah, Mom. It's me."

She stepped closer. Then with a deafening crack, she slapped me across the face.

"I'm sorry for hitting you."

I chuckled. "For the last time, it's fine."

"I used to feel so guilty whenever I'd have to give you a spanking." Mom sighed. "You were such a good kid and most of the time you'd shape up if I threatened to get out my wooden spoon. But there were a few times you'd push me over the edge. You'll see."

I nodded at Mom in the passenger seat.

We'd spent the last two days talking. She knew all about Piper and the pregnancy. She knew that I was terrified of losing another child. She knew exactly what to tell me to put some of those fears to rest.

And to my surprise, she knew where I'd been these last three years. She'd just chosen to let me stay hidden until I was ready to be found.

Mom had hurt me. But I would rather have her in my life than hold on to that old pain. To have her back in my life, I was willing to move past the choices she'd made after Shannon and the baby had died.

"Thanks for coming with me."

Her eyes softened. "I'm always here for you."

I drove us through town, dreading every inch as we got closer to our destination.

I'd realized on my drive to Bozeman that I had to stop running. I was going to be a father. By accident or by choice, it was happening. And if I was going to be worthy of my child, I had to put old ghosts to rest.

Mom's idea was for me to start at the source.

We pulled up to the gates of the cemetery, and I crept inside, parking along the loop that circled through the green grass.

Mom gave me a reassuring smile before opening her door. I swallowed down the urge to hurl and got out of the truck too.

It smelled the same, like cold stone and wet grass. The one and only time I'd been here had been for the funeral. But my feet remembered the way to Shannon's family plot.

Mom and I sidestepped headstones and sculptures as we wound our way toward a grove of trees. Her parents had insisted on burying her here, in the place where they could visit. I'd agreed on one condition.

That I could pay for our daughter to be buried with her.

Except for the short minutes after she'd been taken from Shannon's body to try and be saved at the hospital, our baby had only lived in her mother's womb. I wanted her to have Shannon's comfort in the grave too.

I didn't want my daughter resting alone.

As we got closer to their place, I noticed a bundle of fresh-cut yellow roses by their tombstone.

They were the same yellow roses growing outside Mom's front door.

"You come here?"

She nodded. "Every week."

She visited them. She cared for them.

When I hadn't been here, she'd tended to them instead.

A lump clogged my throat. "Thank you."

Mom's hand slipped into mine, and we stopped at the base of the grave. The marker only had Shannon's name on the stone along with her dates of birth and death. But in the lower corner, I'd asked that they carve something for our child.

A tiny pair of angel wings.

Shannon had been eight months pregnant, but we still hadn't picked out names. We had narrowed down the boys' names but had struggled with options for a girl.

And since I hadn't been able to put her name on the granite, I'd given her wings instead.

Tears dripped from my eyes and into my beard. I didn't even bother wiping them away. I just stood there, holding Mom's hand, and let go.

Like Piper had once told me on the ridge, sometimes you just needed to cry.

The tears lasted a while, but when they stopped, I closed my eyes and spoke to the ghost I'd tethered to me for years.

Good-bye, sweet angel.

A breeze blew past, lifting her up to fly free.

"Thanks, Mom."

She squeezed my hand. "You're welcome."

I took one last look at the grave, smiled at Shannon's name, then turned away and escorted Mom back to my truck. Maybe I'd visit again. Maybe this would be my farewell. I wasn't sure. But one thing I did know was that I had work to do before I went back to Lark Cove.

Talking to Mom had helped me deal with my fears for Piper's pregnancy. They were still there, they probably always would be. But Mom's excitement about becoming a grandparent had broken through. She'd helped me see things from a different angle.

I was getting another chance. I hadn't destroyed the first one. *He* had.

But if I didn't pull my head out of my ass, I would ruin this one.

"Kaine," Mom said as we left the cemetery's gates. "I'm proud of you for going there today. I know it wasn't easy. I hope it gives you some closure."

"It did."

"Good. We-we should talk about—"

"No," I cut Mom off.

"But—"

"No." My voice left no room for argument. "We won't talk about him. Ever. If you want to be in my life, you won't bring him up."

Her shoulders fell, but she nodded. "Okay."

Just the idea of him made my jaw clench. I didn't want to be so forceful with Mom, but he was a no-go topic. If I was going to forgive Mom and get over what had happened three years ago, I had to block him out.

I'd made some peace with Mom. I refused to let him take that too.

"What are your plans? How long can you stay?" she asked, changing the subject.

I rubbed my beard with a hand, forcing the tension out of my jaw. Then I took a deep breath, releasing the anger and concentrating on what had to be done. "I need to deal with my old house. I have no idea what's become of my stuff. I wouldn't mind stopping by and saying thanks to my landlord at the old shop. And I'd like to fix your fence. Maybe get your car into the mechanic."

"Oh, Kaine. Don't worry about those things. I can manage."

"I know," I told her. "But I want to."

It was time to make up for the years we'd lost. It was time to finish the things here I'd left undone.

Because when I went back to Lark Cove, I'd be staying for good.

I was done running.

fifteen

PIPER

STANDING IN FRONT OF THE WINDOW IN MY GUEST BEDROOM, I stared out at Kaine's cabin. It sat there, empty, just like it had for the past nineteen days.

It had been almost three weeks since I'd told Kaine I was pregnant and he'd thrown such awful accusations in my face.

Just like I'd promised him, I left the shop after dropping the baby bomb and gave him a night to come to grips with our situation. I came home, got sick—again—and tried my best to get some rest. Though with how angry I was at Kaine, sleep was fitful. So I got up early the next morning, did some work, and puttered around the house until I decided his time was up.

By all rights, *he* should have come to *me*. But one thing I'd learned in our months together, that man was damn stubborn. He could brood like no one I'd ever met. And since I knew he wouldn't come to me, I pushed aside my own stubborn tendencies and meandered along the path to his place.

I found the cabin empty. There were no dishes in the sink. His bed was made. And something about the air, so undisturbed and too quiet, told me he hadn't been there in hours.

His silver truck was gone from its normal place in his driveway, and I doubted I'd find him in the shop, but I went to check anyway.

All of the lights were on and the large bay door was open—to the building he locked up religiously. The cold night air had crept inside and taken away the shop's normal warmth. I closed it all up so the animals couldn't get inside, then went back to my house.

I kept a careful eye on his place all day. Waiting. Stewing. Then I began to worry.

Was he okay? Was he hurt? I didn't know his family or friends, so I couldn't call to check with them. And it wasn't like I could call the man himself because I didn't have his phone number.

So I waited. For days, I came to this window and checked to see if he was home. I spent hours standing here, watching his house. And after days without any sign of Kaine Reynolds, I got mad.

Really, *really* mad.

Because my sexy, caring, shy, *dumbass* of a neighbor had just disappeared.

He'd clearly severed ties with his former life before coming to this mountain. What was stopping him from doing it again? It certainly wasn't me or the baby I was carrying.

The bastard was so chicken-shit scared he'd run away.

For nineteen, almost twenty days, I'd nursed my anger. I'd coddled it and let it grow. Because if Kaine ever set foot on my mountainside again, I wanted to be prepared. I had a few things to say about his behavior, and if he came back, he was going to hear it.

Sipping my decaf tea, I kept my glare on his house. It was a dick move for him to leave without telling me, and one day, I desperately wanted to say that to his face.

Along with something else I'd learned in the last nineteen days.

Tires crunched gravel, and I abandoned my post by the

window. I'd left the front door unlocked this morning because Thea was coming over. In Lark Cove, I didn't have to fear leaving a door unlocked for a few hours here and there, unlike in the city.

"Hello!" Thea opened the door.

"Come on in!" I shouted down the hallway as I hurried to greet her.

We hugged as she came inside, though she was missing her normal entourage. "Where are the kids?"

"I left them home with Logan." She smiled. "He wanted some extra time with them since he's got to fly back to New York next week."

"Ah." The foundation was having a quarterly board meeting, and as the chairman, Logan was going back for the week.

Since I'd started as Logan's assistant, I'd never missed a board meeting. Even though flying was supposed to be safe, I wasn't taking any chances with this pregnancy, especially during the first trimester, when the risk of miscarriage was high.

"It feels weird not to be going back with him."

"He understands," Thea said. "Trust me. He'd never push you to do something that made you uncomfortable."

"Don't tell him I told you this, but he really is the World's Greatest Boss."

She winked. "Your secret is safe with me."

After Kaine had left, I'd gone down to the bar and told Thea everything. She knew all about Adam, our infertility and how Kaine had gotten me pregnant. She listened to my confession for hours between occasionally serving her customers. Maybe it was because she was a bartender and she was well practiced at lending an ear, but she was an incredible listener.

And a wonderful friend.

I was terrified about a miscarriage. Pregnancies were lost all the time and mine could be taken away. This dream might end. So I'd prepared myself for the worst, not wanting to get my hopes up. I hadn't let my thoughts wander to nursery decor or baby names.

But then Thea and Logan had me over for a celebratory dinner. They were so excited about my pregnancy, it calmed my nerves exponentially. And I let myself be happy too.

I was keeping faith.

"Want some coffee?" I asked as we walked into the kitchen. "Or decaf tea that is supposed to help with nausea but tastes like tree bark?"

"The tree bark is tempting." She smirked, dropping her purse on the island. "But I'll pass. How are you feeling?"

I shrugged. "Good."

That wasn't entirely true, but I refused to complain about this pregnancy.

Sure, I was tired. I was going to bed before dark and waking up each morning with bags still under my eyes. The nausea hadn't let up either. But I was so overjoyed to even be having these babies, I wouldn't let the ill effects of pregnancy get me down.

Every moment I carried these twins was a moment I'd enjoy.

I'd gone in for an exam two days ago and my doctor had given me a vaginal ultrasound. She'd claimed it was because of my infertility history, but I think she'd been able to sense my fears and wanted to put them at ease.

Learning I was pregnant with twins was only slightly less shocking than learning I was pregnant in the first place.

Kaine's sperm was magic.

It was difficult to pinpoint, but I think he got me pregnant the night we had sex in his shop after he'd surprised me with my table. Though, with how much we'd been together after that, I couldn't be certain. But in my mind, I gave credit to that night.

Because that was when I'd realized how I was falling for Kaine.

I liked the idea that my children were conceived in love.

By the time I reached my due date in March, I was going to look like a whale. I didn't care. I was going to be exhausted caring for two newborns alone. I couldn't wait. Life was going to get messy and chaotic and crazy. Bring it on.

"I brought you a present." Thea smiled and dug into her purse. She pulled out two small woodpeckers and handed them over.

"Oh my god," I gasped. "Did you make these?"

She nodded. "I thought they'd go with your woodland theme and were gender neutral."

"They're incredible."

She'd sculpted the birds from old silverware. The feathers were made from fork tongs. The back was done with layered spoons. And the face and legs were made from the silverware's etched handles.

"Those holes in the feet are for screws so you can hang them on the wall."

"Okay." I nodded, unable to tear my eyes away. I wasn't sure where she got her inspiration, but Thea's ability to make art from articles most would consider trash was truly a gift. "Where'd you get this idea?"

"I made a frog from some old forks a while back for Charlie. And before that I made a bird's nest from old spoons. I hadn't made anything from silverware for a while and had some still in my workshop, so I thought I'd give these a try. They turned out kind of cute."

"Cute is an understatement. I can't wait to get the nursery painted and hang them up."

"How's it coming along in there?"

"Good! I'll show you." I led her down the hallway, taking the woodpeckers too. They'd get added to the growing collection of baby things amassed in the middle of the room. "It seems strange to paint a room that I just had painted, but the color I picked out for the guest room just wouldn't work for a nursery."

I'd picked a dark, nearly charcoal gray for the room originally. But now that the babies were coming, I wanted something lighter and softer. The nursery would be full of whites and creams and beige, and after I found out the babies' genders, I'd add some colorful accents.

Coral and pink for girls.

Green and brown for boys.

"Uh . . . I see you've been busy online shopping." Thea stared at the stack of baby clothes on the dresser.

"That would be my mother." I rolled my eyes. "She's basically had a package sent to me every single day since I told her I was pregnant. If she keeps this up, they'll grow out of all the newborn stuff before they can even wear it once."

Thea laughed. "You're probably right. Though I always underestimate the amount of puke and poop babies create."

"I never thought I'd be so excited at the prospect of poop." I giggled. "My parents are so excited, I don't have it in me to tell them to stop shopping. If they want to spoil their grandkids, I'm going to let them. My mom is already making plans to come and stay here for a month after they're born. And they'll be here for Christmas."

My parents would be wonderful grandparents, even from a distance. When I'd called to tell them the news, they'd been delighted. Even though I wasn't married and lived on the other side of the country, they'd been nothing but supportive.

I'd finally found the courage to tell them about the problems with my marriage, and how I'd gone years believing I probably wouldn't have children. When I'd told them about Adam's betrayal, they'd taken a page from his family's playbook and disowned him immediately.

My mom had begged me to move home so she could be closer and able to help. After my argument with Kaine, I'd considered it seriously for a few days. But when I pictured what life would look like in New York, it wasn't where I wanted the babies to call home.

I wanted them to splash around in Flathead Lake every summer. I wanted to teach them how to walk in these hallways. I wanted them to play outside under the trees. And when—if—Kaine returned, I wouldn't take his children to the other side of the country.

According to the doctor's estimate, I was due in early March, if I went full term. Kaine had months and months before these babies came into the world. I was pissed as hell at him, but I hadn't lost hope that he'd get his shit together and decide to be a father.

Because he had the potential to be one of the best. He kept his heart hidden, but it was full of goodness and grace.

"Any word from . . ." Thea asked, pointing out the window toward Kaine's house.

I shook my head. "Nothing."

"Sorry."

"It's okay." I shrugged, setting a hand on my stomach. "I'm making the best of this. I'm trying not to think about all of the idiot men in my life. Though I did get an interesting email from Adam yesterday."

"Oh, really." She frowned. "And what did he have to say?"

"Ugh." Why had I even opened that email in the first place? "The subject line was *CONFESSION*. That should have warned me away."

Instead, his shouty caps had enticed me to read the message

that should have been sent straight to the trash.

"First, he scolded me for blocking his number. Then, he scolded me for not returning the messages he'd left from other numbers. After that, he went on and on for five paragraphs, telling me that the fertility news hit him hard. He blames his lies on shock. And once he started that lie, he didn't know how to unravel it."

"Was there an apology in there somewhere?"

"He admits that how he reacted was wrong. But he asked me to look at it from his point of view. We'd been under the assumption that I was the reason we couldn't have a baby. He knew how badly I wanted to get pregnant. So the news that *he* had the problems and *he* couldn't give me a child was devastating. He realizes he should have talked it through with me, but instead, he made some stupid mistakes."

Thea scoffed. "Putting your dick inside a woman who is not your wife a week after lying to her about fertility test results would definitely qualify as a mistake."

"But according to him, totally justifiable," I deadpanned.

The rest of his email was another plea for me to reconcile. He had yet to grasp that his mistakes were unforgivable. As much as I'd wanted to respond, reinforcing that we'd never be together again, I'd simply moved the email to the trash.

Silence would speak louder than a reply.

I'd considered blocking him but just hadn't been able to click that button. Why, I wasn't sure. Maybe because he'd been in my life so long, and though I was furious at him, blocking him felt too . . . extreme.

"After a while, he'll move on," Thea reassured me.

"I hope so." I shrugged. "I loved him for a long time, and even though he hurt me, I still want the best for him."

"You're a better person than I am. I kind of want him to get a receding hairline and beer belly."

A fate akin to death for Adam. His vanity had grown throughout our marriage in steady increments. Something I'd noticed, but like a lot of things, I'd adjusted to. Now I saw that he was more worried about being handsome on the outside than making sure he was beautiful on the inside.

"Anyway, enough of him." I waved that conversation away and picked up the book of baby names I'd left in here. "I think I've got boy names already picked. But I'm struggling with girl names. Feel like helping me make a list of possibilities?"

"I'd love to."

The two of us retreated to the living room, where we settled into my cozy furniture. I went through the baby book, reading off names I liked while Thea kept track in a notepad. Then the two of us ate lunch, gossiping about things in town, until she decided to head home and let me catch a nap.

I stood on the front stoop, waving as she backed away from the house. It was strange to look outside and not see the Airstream or my Mini. Logan had come to collect their camper last week, and three days ago, my Mini had been supersized to the white Tahoe parked in my garage. With two babies on the way, I needed space and four-wheel drive for the winter roads.

I went inside, deciding to spend time in the office before I lazed on the couch for my Saturday afternoon nap. With Logan leaving for New York, I wanted to double-check all of the meeting materials and items for his trip were ready to go.

Hours later, I'd missed my nap and had eaten my favorite summer pasta dish for dinner at my desk. I'd found spelling errors in three of the presentations, so I'd gone through the entire week's worth of slide decks to check for more.

I was halfway through a small stack of Oreo cookies when the doorbell rang.

Smiling to myself, I hurried for the door. Mom's daily delivery of baby items was coming in late today. Normally, my packages came about six in the evening, including Saturdays. John, my deliveryman, stopped here last on his way home to his wife and three kids. But I guess he had more packages than normal today.

"Hi, Joh—"

It wasn't John on my doorstep.

It was Kaine.

"Hi," he rumbled.

My jaw dropped.

In nineteen days, Kaine had changed. He'd trimmed his beard shorter than I'd ever seen before. His hair, which I loved to comb my hands through at night, was shorter too and brushed away from his forehead. And for the first time ever, he was wearing something other than a T-shirt.

His navy, button-down shirt went all the way to his wrists. He'd tucked the hem into jeans and was wearing a leather belt. Its brown color matched his polished boots.

His image was so different, he could be an imposter if not for the same colorful swirl in his eyes I'd memorized months ago. Still, it took me a good minute before I clamped my mouth shut and crossed my arms over my chest.

I was so angry at him for leaving, and our argument in the shop. But could I remember a single thing I wanted to say to him? No. The ass chewing I'd been practicing was gone. Poof. Vanished.

All I really wanted to do was give Kaine a hug.

What *was* that? Why did he always make me want to hug him? I closed my arms tighter across my chest because there would be no hugging until I got an explanation. And an apology.

"I'm sorry." His eyes pleaded for my forgiveness.

Now I just needed the explanation.

I opened the door wider, stepping to the side to let him in. He nodded, then crossed the threshold. His eyes raked over the room, taking note of the changes I'd made since he'd been here last.

While he ran his fingertips across an end table by the couch, I had the perfect view of his backside. Why did he have to look so good? It made summoning my lecture even harder.

"Place looks good." He took a seat on the edge of the couch, his forearms resting on his knees.

I shrugged, then went to the chair opposite him. I waited for him to speak first, but instead of giving me the explanation I was due, he slid the baby names book across the coffee table.

As he stroked the cover, his shoulders rolled inward. His entire frame slumped deeper into the couch. "I have a confession to make."

Ironic word, that.

It was also ironic that I seemed to have the propensity to fall in love with men who ran away from their problems. When things had gotten too hard in our marriage, Adam had run into the arms of another woman. Had Kaine done the same?

My spine stiffened at the idea of him with someone else. It had crushed me to find out that Adam had cheated, but my heart had healed—quicker than I would have imagined.

If Kaine had spent the last three weeks with someone else, I'd be destroyed.

"Will you hear me out?" he asked, setting the baby name book aside.

I waited a beat, then another, finally giving him a nod.

His broad chest caved in with a deep sigh. "I said some awful things to you that I didn't mean. It's not an excuse, but I was scared and let my fears get the best of me. I'm sorry."

"Apology accepted."

"Thanks."

I waited for him to continue, but he just sat there looking at me with those vivid eyes.

My eyes narrowed. If he thought *that* qualified as a confession, he was sorely mistaken. The air in the room grew tense and heavy. My lungs seemed to be working twice as hard, but I couldn't take a deep breath. The rage I'd been nurturing bloomed inside my chest, flaring like a campfire doused with gasoline.

"That's it?" I asked. "That's your confession? You were scared?"

He held up a hand. "I—"

"No." I shot off my chair. "I'm talking now."

Wisely, he dropped his hand and closed his mouth.

"You don't think I was scared?" I pointed to my chest as I began pacing between my vacated chair and the coffee table. "Do you have any idea how big of a shock that was for me? Do you think it was easy for me to come into your shop and tell you I was pregnant when I was the one who had assured you we were safe? That was my mistake and that is on me. But your reaction? That's on *you*."

He nodded. "You're right."

"Damn right, I'm right. You disappeared for nineteen days. That's almost three weeks! And you couldn't even manage to pick up the phone and let me know."

"I didn't take my phone. And I don't have your number."

I stopped midstep, shooting him a glare that could level one of the hundred-year-old trees outside. "Not a good excuse."

"I should have called." He held up his hands. "But I didn't want to have this conversation over the phone. I've got—would you please sit down?"

"Fine." With a harrumph, I recrossed my arms and sank into the chair.

"There's a lot about my past I need to explain. I'm hoping when you hear me out, you'll understand why I got scared. But—"

"There's always a *but*, isn't there?" I huffed. Kaine had avoided his past over and over and over again. When was I going to learn that he didn't trust me enough to confide in me?

"But," he said, his jaw ticking, "I'd like it if you weren't seething when we had that conversation."

"That might take a while."

"I'll let you cool off and come over later." He stood from the couch. "Is that okay?"

I nodded, letting him see himself out.

The door closed behind him and I didn't move. My heart was pounding, my pulse booming through every vein. I took a few deep inhales, calming myself down because getting this worked up couldn't be good for the babies.

When my shoulders finally relaxed, I stared at the place where Kaine had been sitting. Would he explain? Would I finally understand what haunted him so deeply?

I guess we'll see. When he came back from his cabin, I'd do my best to shove my anger and frustration aside and listen to his story. When he came back from his cabin—

My stomach plummeted.

"Oh, shit!" I leaped out of my chair, racing across the room. I reached the door just as a very large, very male, very angry fist pounded on it from the other side.

I opened it, this time expecting Kaine's face.

He had his own fury going. "What the fuck happened to my house?"

"Yeah, about that." I winced. "I kind of, um, accidentally . . . set it on fire."

sixteen

KAINE

"LET ME GET THIS STRAIGHT. THE MORNING AFTER I LEFT, you came over to my house and saw I was gone. So you went to the shop, locked it up for me, then came home. You waited a week for me to come back, and when I didn't, you came back to the cabin. And cleaned?"

Standing on the other side of the island in her kitchen, Piper shrugged. "It was dirty. And I was mad at you."

"So you cleaned and did my laundry?"

Her cheeks got red as she muttered, *"Tried* to do your laundry."

"Even though you were mad at me."

"Yes, I was. *Am,*" she corrected quickly. "I decided to kill you with kindness, or whatever that saying is. And your garbage was starting to grow creatures. I didn't want one of them to sneak over and smother me in my sleep."

This woman. She never stopped surprising me.

While I was gone, she'd gone over to do her revenge cleaning. She unloaded my dishwasher, took out the garbage and found a load of laundry in my washer that had been sitting wet for a week. So she rewashed the clothes and put them in the dryer.

Except she didn't know that the sensor in my dryer was

broken. She didn't know that I wasn't great about cleaning out the lint trap.

Piper turned on the dryer, then came home, assuming it would stop on its own.

It stopped all right. After catching fire.

The fire destroyed my laundry room and about half of my living room. Luckily, she had her windows open, and when she smelled smoke, she called the fire department. They were able to save the house but there was a lot of work to be done to get it back to rights.

"I guess this makes us even for the fight," I teased.

"Even?" she gaped. "No way."

"You set my house on fire."

She raised her chin. "You accused me of getting pregnant on purpose."

Fuck. "Okay. Not even."

Her shoulders fell. "I really am sorry about the fire."

"It's only a house. I'm just glad you weren't hurt."

If she hadn't noticed the smoke, it could have started a forest fire. Something of that magnitude would have consumed both our homes. The idea of her and our baby trapped here in a blaze made my stomach churn.

But she was okay. My house could be repaired. And to be honest, I wasn't even that mad.

"My contractor is just finishing up a job," she said. "Then he promised to get his crew up here to fix it. He said it could be as soon as next week."

I nodded. "Sounds good. I'm sure the motel has a room open."

"Or you can stay here." She said it so quietly, I wasn't sure I'd heard her right.

"I thought you were mad at me."

"I am."

I rubbed my beard, looking outside at the fading evening light. It had been a damn long day, and the longest part was yet to come. I'd gotten up early, spent the morning finishing a couple of projects on Mom's house. Then I'd showered, hugged her good-bye and hit the road. The five-hour trip from Bozeman to Lark Cove had been tense, mostly because I'd had no idea how I was going to explain everything to Piper.

"Where were you?" she asked.

"I went to see my mom."

"For three weeks?"

I nodded. "I hadn't seen or spoken to her in three years. We had a lot to talk about."

The last nineteen days had been filled with apologies and honest conversations. Mom knew all about what I'd been doing these last three years. I'd learned about her new job as the office manager at a law firm and the man she'd just started dating. We talked about everything, except for the one topic that we avoided completely. And as far as I was concerned, we'd never talk about *him* again.

Piper didn't know it, but she was the reason I'd reconnected with Mom. If not for this pregnancy, I don't know if I ever would have returned home. I liked to think I would have pulled my head out of my ass eventually, but the truth was, it had become easier to hide out.

But the day Piper had come to the shop and told me she was pregnant, everything had changed. It had taken me these last nineteen days to close the book on my former life.

The friend I'd called to deal with my house had actually worked with Mom to get it rented. But boxes and boxes of my things had been shoved in storage, so I'd had to go through them all. Sorting through the nursery items had been the hardest. The clothes and old mementos had been easier, just time-consuming. The same was true with my old shop.

I'd spent the last two and a half weeks selling some items, tossing others and donating the rest. On top of that, I'd met with the tenant in my house and worked out an agreement for them to purchase the place.

Everything from my former life was being put to rest. Once I told Piper about the accident, I wanted to leave it behind for good.

"Come sit down." I retreated to the living room and took one end of the couch while she took the other.

She tossed her knees up into the seat between us, and the lights above us cast a soft glow on her skin. Hardly an hour had passed over the last nineteen days when I hadn't pictured her face. But my mental image hadn't done her beauty justice.

"You look beautiful," I told her, earning a blush. "How are you doing? Feeling okay?"

She nodded. "A little sick here and there, but nothing I can't manage."

"Everything check out with the doctors?"

"I'm good. The babies are good and should be arriving around March eleventh."

"March eleventh," I repeated, penciling that date into my mental calendar. Unless we had an off winter, we'd be surround-ed by snow. "The roads might still be icy then, but if we plan— wait. Back up a minute and say that again. The *babies*?"

She raised a shoulder. "You have magic sperm."

Magic sperm. "How many babies are we talking about here?"

Piper laughed, flashing me those dimples. "Just two."

"Just. Two." My head fell back into the couch as it raced. Twins. We were having twins.

It was hard enough to wrap my head around the idea of

one kid, let alone two. But in seven months, we'd be parents. To twins.

There were so many things to figure out by then, like where they'd sleep and which car seats to choose and if we'd be those parents who assigned each of their twins a color so we could tell them apart.

Twins.

"It kind of blows your mind, doesn't it?" she asked.

I made an explosion sound.

Piper laughed again, shifting in her seat to reach for a blanket.

I sat up straight, helping her cover her legs. She was in leggings that went to her ankles, the tight black material wrapping around her curves, much like the fitted gray T-shirt she was wearing. She didn't look pregnant, but that was how Shannon had been too. She hadn't looked pregnant until around the fifth month.

"About four years ago, I met a woman in a bar. Her name was Shannon. We hit it off right away. One thing led to another, and I took her home. Neither of us wanted anything serious. We had our fun, then I drove her home the next morning. I figured I'd never see her again. She came back about six weeks later and told me she was pregnant."

Piper flinched and the sound of her gasp filled the room.

"It was never meant to be something serious with Shannon, but plans change when you're having a baby. Suddenly, this woman who I'd spent less than a day with was going to be in my life for good."

Just like it would be with Piper. The thought of having Piper in my life felt right, but things with Shannon had never really fit.

"She was a nice person. She was beautiful and smiled all the time. She was so excited about the baby. I swear, Shannon was never anywhere without a pregnancy book in her hands."

"You keep saying *was*. Shannon *was*."

"She was." I met her eyes. They were full of dread. She'd mentally skipped ahead of my explanation. "Shannon moved in with me because we thought it would be easier with the baby coming. I'd even asked her to marry me, but she turned me down."

"Did you love her?" Piper asked.

"No." I sighed. "It would have been easier if I had, but those feelings weren't there. We tried to date for a while, but something was always missing. We both felt it. She just wasn't the one. But we were having a baby and living together just made sense. At least at the beginning."

In hindsight, we should have kept our distance. She should have stayed in her own apartment instead of moving into my house.

"She decorated the nursery. I made the baby a bassinet. We were still picking out names when she was about eight months pregnant, but neither of us was in a hurry to decide. We had time."

I stared blankly across the room, unable to look at Piper for this next part. I'd never told this story before. And if I saw Piper cry or her face twist in sadness, I didn't know if I could get through it all.

"Shannon was out to dinner one night. It was Memorial Day weekend and it was crazy in town. She'd already gone to the parade that morning and spent the afternoon hanging out with some friends. I asked her to just stay home and take it easy. But she wanted to go to this new restaurant downtown."

She hadn't invited me to go along. Shannon had stopped asking me out to dinner months before that night. When she'd first moved in, we'd gone out together all the time. I'd figured she'd stopped asking because those dinners had felt too much like dates.

It should have been my first clue that something was different. But I'd been too busy to notice. Plus, I'd been relieved. All I'd wanted to do for Memorial Day was stay home, cook myself a cheeseburger on the grill and drink a beer to relax.

"She never made it home. A drunk driver ran a stop sign going forty in a twenty-five and was T-boned by a truck."

Piper gasped. "Oh, god."

"The doctors had already lost Shannon by the time I arrived at the hospital. They delivered the baby, hoping to save her, but . . . I lost her too. They let me hold her for a few minutes after they cleaned her up. To say good-bye."

"Kaine, I-I'm so sorry."

"It broke me," I whispered. "I was so excited about the baby. We all were. It wasn't the ideal situation, but still, I wanted to be a father. A *good* father. And I just . . . I loved her. I'd never even met her, but I loved her."

Piper kicked off her blanket and scooted closer to me on the couch. Then, without warning, she climbed into my lap and hugged me.

Her arms wound tight around my shoulders. Her hair hung loose and brushed against my cheek as she buried her nose in my neck.

It was the embrace I hadn't even known I'd been craving, the one that would stitch together so many of those open wounds. So I wrapped my arms around her back and held her just as tight.

"You got scared," she whispered.

"Terrified," I whispered back. "When you told me you were pregnant, it brought back a lot of pain that I'd buried deep. I know I shouldn't have left, but I just couldn't deal with all of it. I needed some time to work it out."

I'd needed some time to talk it through with someone who'd been just as devastated.

The days I'd spent with Mom had been healing. More times than I could count, I'd kicked myself in the ass for running away. Coming up to this mountain, to live alone, hadn't helped me process my grief in the slightest. But after uncovering those wounds and letting them breathe, I was starting to feel some much-needed closure.

But I'd never regret finding my mountain. It was where I'd found Piper.

Or maybe she'd found me.

Piper leaned back and sniffled, then scooted off my lap. But instead of going back to her corner of the couch, she settled into my side and rested her head on my shoulder. I threw an arm around her back, keeping her close.

"I'm sorry, Kaine. I'm so, so sorry."

I rested my cheek on her hair. "So am I."

We sat quietly for a while, leaning on one another until Piper broke the silence with a question I was hoping to avoid tonight.

"Why didn't you see your mom for three years?"

"It's a long story. Let's just say that after Shannon and the baby died, she made some choices I couldn't live with. I was hurting and felt like she'd betrayed me, so I left. I cut off all ties and came up here to disappear."

"What choices?"

I sighed. "Just . . . family stuff."

Piper stiffened. The air in the room, which had been so warm with her curled into my side, dropped ten degrees. She pushed off the couch and left the room, walking down the hallway that led to a guest bedroom, her office and the garage.

Fuck. I'd promised her an explanation, but my vague answer had just shut her down. She didn't know it was for the best. This was the part of my story I refused to talk about, even with my mother. There was too much rage there. Too much pain. I hadn't let go of those emotions and until I could handle them myself, I wasn't going to unload them on her.

I stayed on the couch, letting my head fall backward again, and gave Piper a few minutes. But as I listened to her slam cupboard doors and stomp around, I realized space was only making things worse.

Pushing off the couch, I went down the hall and found her in the guest bathroom, setting out some towels on the countertop. Her eyes met mine through the mirror as I leaned against the doorjamb.

"I'm sorry," I told her. "There are still some things I'm working through myself. Can we save the rest for another day?"

She sighed and looked down at the sink. When she looked up, her eyes saw right to my core. She must have seen the pain there because she gave me some grace with a small nod.

"Thank you."

Piper's gaze dropped to the towels. Her hand slipped off the cotton and splayed over her belly. "With everything that happened to you. I can't imagine. Do you . . ." She took a deep breath. "Do you want—"

"Yes." I stepped into the room. "I want them."

Them. Her. Us.

I wanted it all.

"Okay," she breathed and her shoulders dropped.

Leaving Piper again would be nearly impossible. She'd ingrained herself into my life. And I'd missed enough of this pregnancy. Though it scared me, a spark of excitement was there too. I was getting the chance to be a father again.

I was getting the chance to try this again with Piper.

I'd cut her deep with that argument in the shop. I was a

top-grade asshole for the things I'd said and then leaving for so long. I'd always be sorry for how I'd reacted. Now that she knew why I was scared, would she forgive me?

I sure as hell hoped so. Because then we could start over. Go back to the beginning and try our best not to fuck it up again.

"Where do we go from here?" I had my ideas but wanted to hear hers first.

She shrugged. "Let's just take it slow."

Slow. "I can do that."

"If you need anything else in here, just let me know." Piper patted the towels, then shooed me out of the bathroom.

I followed her out of the room and down the hallway, back into the living room. She went right for the couch, covering a yawn with the back of her hand, before snuggling right back underneath her blanket.

"Can I show you something?"

She nodded. "Sure."

"Okay. Hang tight." I went right for the door, hustling outside. Then I jogged over to the cabin, noticing the charred backside that had escaped me before.

There was one more thing I wanted to do tonight. One more thing to bring me closure. And now that Piper knew about Shannon and the baby, I wanted to do it with her by my side.

Rushing inside the house, I went straight to the bedroom closet, retrieving the box I'd stashed there. I tucked it under one arm, then grabbed the duffel bag I'd dropped earlier on the couch. It was full of the clothes and toiletries I'd bought in Bozeman for my stay there. I took it all back to Piper's, leaving the duffel by the door and settling next to her on the couch.

"Sorry." She jerked when my weight hit the cushions, her eyes popping open.

I set the box on the coffee table. "We can do this later. Why don't you go to bed?"

She shook her head, sitting up a bit. "No, it's okay. What's in the box?"

Leaning forward, I flipped off the lid. "When I left Bozeman, this box was the only thing I brought with me other than my truck."

Piper sat up just as I lifted out the pink baby blanket. Then I pulled out one item at a time, handing them to her to see. Beneath the blanket was a grainy black and white ultrasound photo. Next to it was the list of baby names Shannon and I had been debating.

Ten on her side. Ten on mine. All but two had been crossed off.

Morgan and Beckett.

"Shannon didn't want to know if we were having a boy or a girl. We'd been in the middle of narrowing down names." She never got to know that we'd had a girl.

The last item in the box was a pair of tiny, pink work boots that were the same style as the ones I wore every day.

I grinned as I pulled them from the box. "My mom bought these. She told me that even if we had a boy, he'd have to wear them because she couldn't find blue."

"They are so cute." Piper smiled. "I'm glad you kept them."

"Me too." I leaned into her side, and she leaned back. "I haven't looked at all this in years. I just boxed it up and set it aside. Kind of like I have with a lot of things. But . . . I'm trying."

"I know you are," she said softly.

"Thanks for letting me show you."

She rested her hand on my knee. "Anytime."

We stared at the items for a few moments, then Piper and I both carefully repacked the box. When the lid was closed, a weight had been lifted.

Piper lay out on the couch again, righting her blanket. I bent down and untied my boots, then kicked them off and relaxed into the seat, stretching my legs under the coffee table.

My eyes landed on the book of baby names. "I told my mom about you and the baby. I'll have to call her tomorrow and tell her we're having twins."

"My parents are excited too. My mom keeps sending me baby gifts." Piper shifted, trying to get comfortable. But she was doing her best to keep her feet off my side of the couch.

I took both of her ankles in my hands and pulled them across my lap. When her bare feet were resting on my thighs, I took one and began massaging the arch.

"My god," she moaned, the sound going straight to my dick.

"Have you picked out any names?" I asked, hoping it would distract me enough I wouldn't get hard.

She hummed. "I was thinking about Robert and Gabe if they're boys, after both of my granddads."

"I like those." I relaxed deeper into the seat. "I've always liked traditional names."

"I'm stuck on girl names though. Any ideas?"

I'd thought of a million baby girl names over the last three years. "Hope and Faith."

"Hope and Faith," she whispered. "I love those."

"We didn't—me and Shannon—we didn't pick out girl names. We thought we had time."

"Robert and Gabe for boys. Hope and Faith for girls."

Her statement was quiet but firm. I needed those names picked out. I needed to know if something bad happened, my kids would have names. And Piper knew I needed it too.

"Will you do something for me?"

She nodded, her eyes falling shut as I continued to rub her feet.

"Would you go out to dinner with me?"

"Are you asking me on a date?"

"Yes, I am."

She smiled. "We're doing everything backward."

I was taking that as a yes.

The night got still and darkness settled. Piper fell asleep on the couch, and I carried her down the hall and into her bed.

Just like the rest of the house, her room was stylish and warm. As I settled her under her maroon comforter, I swiped the hair from her eyes and bent to kiss her forehead.

She hummed, snuggling deeper into her pillow.

Fuck, but I wanted to curl up next to her. I wanted to fall asleep with her in my arms. Not once in all of our nights together had we slept in the same bed.

I'd always left. I'd always maintained that line in the sand.

There were no lines anymore. I would cross them all.

Piper Campbell had broken past all of my walls and made me fall in love with her. She'd worked her way into my broken heart, filling the black holes with light.

"Kaine?" Piper's soft voice stopped me right before I shut her door. Her head was still resting on the pillow, but her dark eyes were open.

"Yeah?"

"Yes, I'll go on a date with you."

I grinned. "I wasn't going to take no for an answer. Night."

"Good night."

As I padded down the hall, I shut off the lights and locked the front door. Then I went to my room, stripped off my clothes and climbed into bed, staring up at the ceiling as I replayed our conversation.

We're doing everything backward.

Piper had been right about that.

Maybe backward was the only way we'd end up forward.

seventeen

PIPER

"DO YOU WANT TO GRAB PIZZA AT THE BAR FOR DINNER?" Kaine asked. "Or hit the diner for a burger?"

I took in his profile from the passenger seat. He was driving my Tahoe, relaxed and sexy behind the wheel. His hair had grown out in the last two months since he'd come back, but he'd kept his beard trimmed short and it made his lips look soft and full.

The sweater he'd pulled on this morning was bunched up, revealing his forearms. His wrist hung carelessly over the steering wheel while his large fingers dangled above the dash. The sight of him in that seat, driving me around, was one I'd never get sick of.

He looked over and raised an eyebrow. *Busted.* I drooled over him a lot these days and most times he caught me.

I smiled but didn't look away. "Let's just go home."

Over the last two months, Kaine and I had been playing house. From the outside, we looked like a happy couple blissfully awaiting the arrival of our twins. The inside wasn't far off from that image either.

Kaine had even lifted his ban on socializing. He took me to the bar to hang with Thea and Logan on the weekends when they were working. When I didn't feel like cooking, we went to the only other restaurant in town, Bob's Diner. And on occasion, Kaine and I would drive to Kalispell for dinner at a nice restaurant.

Just like he'd done for our first date.

He'd flirted with me over candlelight and pasta at this quaint Italian restaurant. Then he'd taken me to a movie. It was simple and sweet, a cliché even. Dinner and a movie. Kaine hadn't planned anything extravagant or over-the-top. He'd just planned an evening where I was the center of his attention.

It was the best date I'd had in my life, and I'd had a near-constant smile on my face ever since. There hadn't been another time in my life when I'd felt so cherished.

Kaine cherished me.

I forced my eyes away from his handsome profile and looked outside to the trees covered with ice crystals. My first winter in Montana hit earlier than normal for the region. It was only the middle of October and every day this past week had been below freezing. We hadn't gotten a huge snowfall yet, but the thought of it made me shiver.

Kaine saw my shoulders shimmy and turned up the heat on my side of the car.

Cherished. I wasn't all that cold, but I left the dial alone.

"What do you want for dinner?" I asked.

He shrugged. "Whatever. We can just scrounge around for leftovers."

I rubbed my belly. I didn't look pregnant yet, just more like I'd eaten too many large meals for the last month. Which, of course, I had. Now that I was past the first trimester, my appetite had come back with a vengeance. I'd gained all the weight I'd lost from my months of puking and surviving on saltine crackers.

"I'm hungry."

Kaine chuckled and reached into one of the bags he'd put

on the floor behind his seat. His hand came back holding a granola bar. Then he dug around and found a bottle of chocolate
milk.

"Where did you get these?"

"I went to the little coffee shop in the mall."

"You went to the coffee shop? When?"

"While you were trying on your hundredth pair of maternity jeans."

"Ahh." I nodded and tore into the wrapper of the bar. "Good
thinking."

"Gotta make sure you're fed every hour, on the hour. Like
a bear."

I just smiled and tore open the wrapper. A minute later, the
bar was gone and I was still hungry. We'd gone to the doctor for
an exam and ultrasound today, then gone to the mall to shop for
nursery things. I'd spent an hour in the dressing room of the one
and only maternity store, getting acquainted with more spandex
than I'd owned in my life. With all the activity, I was famished.

"How much do you want to bet that my mom overnights us
a package of blue onesies?"

Kaine reached across the console and took my hand, threading his fingers in mine. "She already did."

"What? When? We just found out we were having boys
three hours ago."

I'd called my parents right after we'd left the doctor's office.
And though my mother was surely best friends with the clerks
at the shipping store by now, I was certain even she couldn't get
something to Montana from New York in under three hours.

Kaine's thumb stroked the back of mine. "She sent me a
box the size of Texas last week full of boy and girl clothes, along
with a note to hide it from you until today. Then I could give you
the right ones and send the rest back."

With my free hand, I clutched my heart. Not only was my mom incredibly thoughtful, but I loved that she and Kaine talked. He talked to my dad too. And my brother. It wasn't for long stretches, but they all knew him and on occasion, they'd chat if he answered my phone or we called them together.

"We should try your mom again," I suggested. "You can tell her about the mini toolboxes you found."

They were by far the cutest toys I'd ever seen. The boys wouldn't be able to play with them for a while, but Kaine had bought them from the toy store anyway.

"Maybe I should have waited on those," he muttered.

"Why?"

"No reason."

There was a reason. Kaine was worried that something bad might happen to the babies. I'd caught him lost in thought many times over the last two months. I'd find him in the nursery, holding a white baby bootie or a soft blanket, staring blankly at a wall. He'd be completely lost in his own head, battling his fears.

Every time, I did the only thing I could think of.

I hugged him.

Not once had I promised him that everything would be okay. Life was unpredictable and harsh—something he understood better than anyone.

"Call her." I knew talking to his mom would help ease some of his fears.

Suzanne Reynolds had become a solid presence in our lives. I'd never met the woman. I'd never seen her picture, so I had no idea what she looked like. But she'd become one of the most important people in my life.

Because she was so important to Kaine.

He called her every day, trying to make up for the years lost. He talked to her about the babies and his work. He'd introduced her to me on a phone call the day after he'd told me about Shannon and their daughter.

Kaine brought up his phone on the Tahoe's system. He drove it so often, it was basically his vehicle. Whenever I had to go down to Logan's house for work, he drove me and would then come and pick me up. He took me to dinner or to the grocery store. Thea teased me about being the only person in Lark Cove who had a chauffeur.

The sound of a dial tone filled the cab. We'd tried Suzanne after leaving the doctor's office but hadn't gotten ahold of her. I was afraid we'd miss her again when the fourth ring came, but at the last second, she answered.

"Hello," she panted.

"Hey, Mom. You busy?"

"Hey! No, I was just out in the garage, putting the flower pots away before it snows."

Kaine frowned. "I should have done that for you when I was there."

"The mums were still blooming. And it's not like I haven't done it before."

"Sorry." Kaine tightened his grip on the steering wheel. I'd lost count of his apologies these last two months.

"Hi, Suzanne," I chimed so she'd know I was there.

"Piper! What a nice surprise. So . . . did you guys find out?"

I smiled and looked at Kaine. He was smiling too as he delivered the good news. "Boys."

"Boys!" Suzanne cheered. "Twin boys. Having two boys is so much fun."

My head tilted to the side, replaying her words. Suzanne sounded like she knew what it was like to have two boys, but as far as I knew, Kaine was an only child.

I opened my mouth to ask, but Kaine cut me off.

"Sounds like you're busy, Mom. I'll let you go and call you later."

"No, I'm—"

He hung up on her. His eyes stayed glued to the road as I gaped at him. With one push of a button, he'd thrown a wet blanket on the special day.

In so many ways, he'd been remarkable these past couple of months. He was opening up and talking more. He didn't brood or sulk like the man I'd met this summer. When we hadn't seen one another for a few hours, he'd seek me out.

He'd come into my office and say hello. If I was cooking dinner, he was sitting across from me at the island, listening to me talk about work. Each night, we'd sit on the couch together, watching television, and when I'd inevitably fall asleep an hour into a movie or show, he'd carry me to bed.

In so many ways we were a couple. We didn't have sex. We didn't kiss. But Kaine touched me often. He held my hand. He massaged my shoulders or my feet when I was tired. He was still the rugged mountain man I'd fallen for, but he was showing me his softer side, the one that was caring and attentive and present.

Things would have been perfect, except for the fact that he didn't trust me. He was holding something back.

Which meant I was holding back something too. *My heart.*

How could I trust him with my heart when he didn't trust me with his past? How could I love him completely when he kept his secrets locked away?

I'd let myself believe that my marriage had been blissful and happy, ignoring the problems piling up at Adam's and my feet. I wasn't doing that again.

I'd given Kaine time—two months, to be exact. I'd been patient, hoping that the rest of his confession would come. But after this long, I was giving up hope. There were times when

Kaine would talk to his mother in hushed whispers from the guest room. Just like now, he never let me speak to her for long. Whatever he was hiding had everything to do with his family.

What had happened to them? Why had he disappeared to the mountain for three years?

I refused to beg for answers. *Refused.*

I'd asked once and he'd blown me off. He'd hung up on his mother to shut me out. Well, I was fairly adept at staying silent too.

I slipped my hand out of Kaine's and crossed my arms over my chest. As I turned to the side window, he just sighed.

But did he speak up? *No.* He just drove us to my house.

When he parked, I didn't wait for him to open my door like he usually did. I pushed it open myself and hurried inside. I went to the kitchen pantry and dug around my cracker stash for another snack.

My mouth was full, chomping angrily on Cheese Nips, when he came through the door. His arms were overloaded from our shopping haul.

"Seriously?" I rolled my eyes, swallowing my bite. "Take two trips."

"I can get it all in *one.*"

"Whatever." I shoved more crackers in my mouth.

Kaine would do just about anything to avoid multiple trips from the car. When we got groceries, he'd load up every single plastic bag on his forearms, then cradle a gallon of milk and a box of ginger ale against his chest. He risked my groceries' well-being on a regular basis because he didn't want to take two trips.

He took the bags down the hall to deliver them to my bedroom and the nursery. I continued to work out my frustration with the man by eating.

When Kaine returned to the kitchen, an apology was written on his face. "She was busy."

I glared at him, telling him exactly what I thought about his bullshit excuse. "You have to give me something, Kaine."

"I'm trying." He braced his hands on the counter. "Things are complicated with my family."

"And things were complicated with me, but I told you everything. I opened up to you about all of that stuff with Adam."

He cringed at my ex-husband's name but didn't say anything.

"Fine." I went back to the pantry in search of more food.

The space was big enough I could stand inside the door. I was scanning the cabinets for something sweet when two strong arms wrapped around my shoulders and the heat from Kaine's hard chest pressed against my back.

"Ask me something," he said softly.

"No."

"Please."

I sighed. "Why didn't you talk to your mom for three years?"

"Ask me something else," he murmured into my hair.

Disappointment settled on my shoulders, but he didn't let me go. So I asked another one of my unanswered questions. "Where is your dad? You never talk about him."

"He and Mom got divorced when I was just a kid. He was a good dad when he lived in Bozeman, but then he moved. He worked for a company that did some development overseas. He was living and traveling through Asia a lot but did his best to call and check in. It was just too expensive for him to come home and visit much. When I was thirteen, he got pancreatic cancer. He died eight months later."

"I'm sorry." My heart broke for him, and I wished I hadn't asked.

"It was a long time ago." He let me go, and I followed him

out of the pantry.

All of the skeletons in Kaine's closet caused him pain. Did he have any pleasant memories from his past? Because I couldn't think of a single happy story he'd told me from his youth.

"I'm sorry."

"It's okay." He shrugged. "If I didn't want to talk about it, I wouldn't have told you."

No kidding. I'd figured that out the hard way. When Kaine wanted to avoid a topic, he did so wholeheartedly.

"So . . . dinner?" I asked.

He held out his hand. "Take a walk with me first."

I placed my palm in his and let him guide me to the door. I hadn't bothered to take off my coat or my shoes when I'd come inside, so we went right out into the cold. I gripped his hand harder as we started down the path between our houses. My heels weren't ideal for traipsing in the forest.

Kaine grumbled, letting go of my hand so he could take my arm. "You and your damn heels."

"I like to look cute for the doctor."

"You're always beautiful, no matter what you wear. I don't know why we need to risk breaking your neck with those extra three inches."

I leaned into his side. "Soon I won't be able to even see my feet. You can pick out my shoes for me."

"Thank fuck."

I giggled, letting my bad mood slip away as we walked. It was hard to stay mad at him when he called me beautiful and fussed over me.

"Should we check on progress?" I asked, pointing to the cabin.

He nodded and escorted me up the porch steps. Since his return from Bozeman, he'd finished staining the chair he'd built to replace the one he'd murdered by chainsaw. It was now situated by the other, both facing the trees.

He opened the door and we were assaulted by the smell of fresh paint as we stepped inside.

"Looks like they got done early today." Kaine let me go and went to the laundry room while I inspected the living room.

The couch had been trashed because of the fire, along with one of his end tables. Most of his other belongings had been saved, including his clothes, which had been safe in the closet along with the box of his daughter's things. Though I'd had to wash all his pants and shirts about five times to work out the smell of smoke.

"Looks good." Kaine stepped up behind me, inspecting the new walls and flooring.

The crew had completely rebuilt the exterior and interior walls on this side of his house. It would probably always be obvious where the new logs had been placed from the outside because their color was brighter than the original ones. But inside, you couldn't tell what was new.

"Looks like they're almost done." I frowned, hating the idea of him moving back here. I'd gotten used to him in my house. "Not long now and I guess . . . you'll be home."

"Yeah." Kaine scowled.

His angry look gave me butterflies. Did he not want to come home? Because that would be awesome.

"I'm going to be sad when you move back here." I was fishing now. I might not beg for him to share information from his past, but I wasn't above begging to keep his incredible woodsy scent in my home.

"Me too." He stepped closer and cupped my jaw in his hands. "I like being at your place."

"What are we doing?" I whispered.

"Going backward."

My eyebrows came together, but before I could ask what he meant, Kaine leaned in and kissed my forehead. "Let's get you out of here. It smells. Got something to show you in the shop."

I savored the smell of fresh paint, taking every breath a bit deeper, but he'd deemed it unhealthy. He'd kicked me out of the house the day he'd painted the nursery, delivering me to Logan and Thea's house for the day.

Kaine took my arm and led me outside, then down the slope to the shop, letting us in through the side door. "I've been working on these for a couple of weeks."

I reveled in the smell of sawdust as he flipped on the lights. "Working on what?"

"You'll see. I still need to sand them and get them stained, so use your imagination for what they'll look like when they're done."

"I can do that." I walked behind him to a canvas tarp at the back of the shop.

He gripped the cloth and paused with a long breath. Then he met my eyes before whipping the tarp clear.

My hands flew to my mouth, my eyes instantly filling with tears.

He'd made bassinets for our babies.

Each cradle was rounded, like an oval nest. They reminded me of nutshells, but with slots. They sat on pedestal bases that allowed the top to rock and sway.

"Kaine," I whispered, trying to blink the tears away, but they were too overwhelming.

His face softened as he came over and pulled me into his arms.

"Damn hormones." I sniffled into his sweater. I'd cried more in the last few months than I had in the last few years, including all the nights I'd cried during my divorce.

Kaine rubbed my spine gently until I got the tears under control. Then I stepped out of his arms and gingerly touched each of the bassinets.

"They're perfect."

"I was going to do a darker wood to match the changing tables you ordered online."

"That sounds great." I nodded. "Now I know why you told me to wait on ordering the cribs."

He chuckled. "I wanted to have them completely finished before I showed you, but I could tell you were getting antsy. I didn't want you ordering cribs tomorrow when I wasn't looking."

I smiled. "You know me too well. How did you come up with this design?"

I'd looked at probably a hundred different crib and bassinet designs over the last couple of months, and nothing had this much character.

"I made one of these when Shannon was pregnant."

My god, this man was strong. How hard had it been for him to make these for our babies? How many painful memories had he relived just to give our boys something special?

My love for him doubled in that moment. Maybe even tripled. And I realized that I had to cut Kaine some slack.

He was still dealing with the grief of his baby's loss. He was still coming to terms with us becoming parents. So what if I didn't understand the complexities of his family dynamic? I'd learn about it in time. When he was ready.

Walking to his side, I slid my arms around his waist. His arm automatically snaked around my shoulders.

Our babies will be okay.

I didn't say the words, but I felt them. I just hoped he could feel them too.

We stood there for a while, holding one another until the rumbling of my stomach was so loud we both laughed.

"My boys are hungry," he declared. "Let's get some dinner."

As we walked back to my house, I felt the craving for a cheeseburger. So instead of eating leftovers like we'd planned, Kaine took me down the mountain to Bob's Diner. After a huge meal that would last me at least two hours, we came back home.

I changed into my pajamas, then settled into the couch next to Kaine, letting my feet go into his lap. He worked his hands on them both, digging his thumbs into the arches.

"Magic hands," I murmured.

Magic hands. Magic sperm. *Magic man.*

When Kaine touched me, I wasn't able to think about much else. My worries melted away with the tension in my muscles, and I drifted off to sleep not twenty minutes into the movie he picked.

Hours later, my eyes fluttered open as he carried me to bed, but they didn't stay that way for long. He set me down on the bed, tucking me under the heavy blankets. Kaine's fingers brushed away a lock of hair from my forehead right before his lips took its place.

"Love you," I murmured into the pillow.

I was asleep by the time Kaine had backed out of the room.

Asleep and dreaming that he said it back.

eighteen

PIPER

TWO WEEKS WAS ALL IT TOOK FOR MY BLISSFUL STATE TO disappear. My pregnancy mood swings were becoming a real bitch.

So was I.

At the moment, frustration was my disposition of choice. Sitting next to Kaine on the couch, the scowl on my face felt permanent.

Work had been long and hard over the last week. The foundation board had made the decision to completely revamp the process in which proposals were reviewed and approved. I'd been lobbying to streamline the process for years and they'd finally agreed.

I'd been ecstatic when Logan had shared the news. That excitement had died when he'd told me about the ambitious timeline. The change, which would have been smooth and flawless over six months, was crammed into three so the bulk of the expense would be incurred before the end of the year.

Logan and I were leading the charge on the project, but it meant the two of us had been putting in long hours. I knew we'd get it done. We'd push fast and hard and get our win. But I'd be exhausted by the time we hit December.

My only saving grace was Willa. As the director of a summer

camp, her winters were quiet months, and she'd begun working for Logan part-time a few years ago. She'd stepped up and taken a huge workload off my shoulders so I could focus on our project.

The results of this project would be amazing. It was going to save us all time and make the most deserving charities float to the top of the stack. It would be my career's crowning jewel.

But it meant I'd be stressed and snappy and grumpy for a while.

Kaine drew the short straw as my neighbor, my friend, and the father of my children. He was bearing the brunt of my frustration.

Except his presence only made the frustration worse.

His house was complete, and he could move home at any time, but he hadn't. Weeks ago, that would have sent me over the moon, but instead, it frustrated me to no end.

Why? Because we hadn't talked about anything. I had no idea how to classify our relationship. And as a perpetual planner, living in limbo made me twitchy.

Dealing with work and the uncertainty with Kaine was manageable. Or at least, it would have been if not for the fact that I'd turned into a raging heap of hormones.

My sexual frustration was about to send me over the edge of sanity.

The movie on the screen was an action movie, but the hero was kissing the heroine. It was long and hot and the camera zoomed in on their locked lips. The hero's cheeks were hollowed—his costar was definitely getting the good tongue. My core pulsed as I watched the scene, and I squirmed, squeezing my thighs together in an attempt to relieve some ache.

This happened every night.

Kaine and I would sit side by side on the couch. The heat

from his bulky arm warmed the skin on my side. His scent surrounded me, seeped into the blanket I kept draped over my lap. And his hard thighs would occasionally bump up against mine.

On the screen, the hero was stripping off the heroine's clothes. God, I wanted to be stripped naked. I wanted to feel Kaine's hands run up and down my skin while he fucked me hard.

One thought about his cock filling me up and I groaned, shifting again on the couch.

I hoped Kaine would think I was uncomfortable and not combustible. What would he do if he knew I was thinking about sex? Would he want me again?

Now that I was in the middle of my second trimester, there was no mistaking I was pregnant. Nothing about me was attractive at the moment, and as much as I wanted to beg Kaine for just one night, I didn't want a pity fuck.

Liar. I'd take anything at this point to take the edge off.

I didn't feel all that sexy right now. My belly had taken on a life of its own. My old clothes didn't fit, and I'd embraced the stretch of maternity pants with a vengeance. Stretch marks were happening, no matter how much cocoa butter I rubbed on at night.

I still felt beautiful, but a different kind of beautiful. Pregnancy, becoming a mother and creating a life was a beautiful act. But standing in front of the mirror was a shock each morning. Every day there were new changes, and it was an adjustment to take them in. Just when I'd gotten used to the larger breasts and widening hips, something new would pop up.

I wanted something—or someone—to make me feel desired. I wanted to be reminded of what it had felt like when Kaine couldn't keep his hands off me. I missed his hands digging into my curves, worshipping them as his mouth kissed across my bare skin and his cock split me in two.

My face flushed, the throbbing in my center getting worse. I desperately needed an orgasm.

"Ugh," I groaned again, recrossing my legs the other way.

The couple on the television were naked now, sandwiched together underneath a flimsy sheet. The heat in the room was sweltering, so I whipped the blanket off my lap, fanning my face.

My eyes zeroed in on the coffee table to avoid the screen. Kaine's bare feet were propped up on the edge. They were long, not unlike his cock.

Seriously? My thoughts were taking on a life of their own. The frustration was suffocating me, so I shoved a fist in the couch cushion to propel myself up.

"Do you need something?" Kaine asked, his hand coming to my elbow to help me.

"I—" *My god.* The sexiest man alive was sitting on my couch. Sitting beside him meant I'd only gotten a sliver of the view. Now I had the whole thing and it only made the tension coil tighter.

"I, what?"

"I-I need you to have sex with me." My hand flew to my mouth as my eyes bugged out. *Shit.* I actually said that.

How many times had I heard girlfriends talk about pregnancy brain? I'd been skeptical. But now I knew it wasn't just an urban legend. The babies were sucking the intelligence right out of me.

"Sorry." I covered my scarlet face with my hands and peeked between the slats of my fingers.

Kaine reached for the remote, shutting off the television as he stood. Then he tossed it aside before grabbing my hand and pulling me down the hallway. His simple gray sweatpants only did good things to the globes of his ass.

"What are you doing?" I asked, tearing my eyes away from

his backside.

He shot a grin over his shoulder. "Having sex with you."

"What? No!" My feet stopped, and I pulled my hand free. There were moments in my life when I wish I had a rewind button. This was one of them. If I could only go back a minute, I'd keep my butt on the couch and forget all about propositioning Kaine for sex.

"I thought you wanted me to have sex with you."

"Not like this." I shook my head. "I'm just . . . it's the hormones. I'm horny. But I don't want you to have sex with me because you're on a mission to appease my every whim."

"Piper." He tucked a lock of hair behind my ear. "I'm going to fuck you because I've been desperate to be inside of you since the last time. I'm going to fuck you because you're more beautiful now than you've ever been. And because sitting next to you on the couch, trying to hide a hard-on, is getting really old."

My heart swelled. "Really? This isn't a pity fuck?"

"Hell no." He swiped my hand again and continued down the hall, his pace faster this time.

We crossed the threshold to my bedroom and Kaine swept me up into his arms. But instead of tossing me onto the bed like he'd done time and time again, he cradled me in his arms and gingerly set me on the mattress.

"Good?" he asked.

"Yeah." I nodded, reaching for the elastic waistband of his sweats. But he stepped back before I tugged them down.

He shook his head. "Go slow."

Slow? Slow was not our thing. I'd be up for trying it one day, but not right now. Where was the ferocious and rough lover I'd come to expect?

With the lightest touch, Kaine stripped me of my clothes, one article falling to the floor at a time. The way he slid down my panties so carefully was pure torture. When I was naked, he bent down and cupped my jaw, tilting it up so he could plant the slightest kiss on my lips.

I leaned in, craving more, but he pulled away before I even got a hint of tongue.

I huffed in frustration. The gentle caress and the careful strokes could be saved for another day. Tonight, Kaine needed to tear at my clothes before doing the same to his own. He needed to give me bruising fingertips and kisses with bite.

He made short work of his clothes, scattering them with a whoosh and whir and thud. His frantic stripping gave me hope that he was as anxious for my touch as I was his.

I inched backward on the bed, propping myself up on my elbows. Past my protruding bump, I caught a glimpse of Kaine's erection bobbing free as he knelt on the bed.

He took my knees in his hands and spread them apart. The look in his eyes was feral but his touch was just a whisper.

"Yes," I moaned as he came closer, the heat from his cock soaking into my center.

He lined himself up, barely working inside the tip before pulling back. When he pushed back again, he only went an inch deeper. His hesitant moves didn't come close to satisfying the ache.

I breathed, trying to relax and let him be in control. Kaine had never once disappointed me in the bedroom, and maybe this slow approach was his way of delaying for amplified gratification.

He pushed in again, this time sinking deeper. It wasn't all the way, but it was better than only getting his crown. I closed my eyes, savoring the moment of bliss before he pulled out again.

Over and over, he barely penetrated before backing off. I was dripping for him but he didn't sink to the root. I opened my eyes in another frustrated huff only to find his closed. His jaw was tight, his lips pursed like he was furious. He'd dropped his hands from my knees and they were fisted at his sides.

He was the picture of physical restraint.

"Kaine," I whispered. "You're not going to break me."

When his eyes popped open, they were full of fear.

I reached for him, pulling him lower. "We can have sex. It's perfectly safe for me and the babies. I promise."

He sighed, his forehead dropping to mine but careful not to put any pressure on my belly. "God, I want you."

"Then have me." I brushed my lips against his in a wicked grin. "Have me like you want me. Like I want you. Fuck me, Kaine. Hard."

He paused for a moment, then pushed back up, settling on his knees. "Are you sure?"

I nodded, then cupped my breasts, pushing them together. I massaged the flesh and toyed with my nipples because Kaine loved it when I gave him a show, and I wanted to drive him over the edge.

As I tweaked a nipple harder, a deep groan filled the room at the same time Kaine thrust forward, burying himself deep.

"Yes," I cried out, arching my hips into his.

His hands gripped my thighs, digging into my flesh as he lifted them higher. Our connection deepened. "Fuck, you feel good."

"I missed you."

He grunted his agreement as he pulled back. But instead of slamming into me like I'd hoped, he carefully slid in deep all the way to the root.

"Harder."

"No." Kaine shook his head, his jaw clenching as he moved in another measured stroke. His cock stretched me, but it wasn't enough. It wasn't the punishing thrusts we were both craving.

"Please," I begged. "Harder. I need you, Kaine. Don't hold back."

He fought to keep his control, gritting out another "No."

"You're not going to break me!" I shouted.

He froze, his expression a mix of surprise and frustration.

I threw an arm over my eyes, embarrassed for my outburst. "You're not going to break me," I repeated again. "I need you. You. The Kaine who tossed me onto the couch the second time we met and fucked my brains out. I need the Kaine who was never afraid to let loose in the bedroom. I need that Kaine because he made me feel wanted and sexy. I need to work out some hormones, and I need you to make me feel beautiful."

Kaine dropped the grip he had on my thighs and leaned forward. His breath floated across my cheek. "You are beautiful. You're so beautiful it takes my breath away. Seeing you on this bed, my boys growing inside of you, there isn't a more beautiful sight in the world. But I can't hurt you."

I put my palm on his jaw. "You won't."

"I c—"

My thumb silenced his protest. "You won't. I trust you. I know you'd never do anything to hurt me or the babies. But I need this. Please? Please show me that we still have this."

The indecision on his face broke my heart. Here was a man so worried about the fate of this pregnancy that he wouldn't even let himself enjoy sex.

"We'll be okay," I whispered. "*They* will be okay."

It was the first time I'd said those words. I'd told myself I wouldn't promise him things would work out, because in this world, who knew what could happen? But I believed it to the depths of my soul.

From the first moment I'd felt the twins move a couple of

weeks ago, I'd known it would be okay. They'd be a joyous addition to this world, and they'd become my entire universe. I knew it.

"They will be okay." My words rang in the air for a few long moments, until the worry on Kaine's face finally faded.

My heart soared when he bent down, capturing my mouth in the kiss I'd been longing for. It was raw and mind-numbing. His tongue worked in and out of my mouth, sweeping against my bottom lip before his teeth nibbled in its path. Then his cock began to rock in and out.

The rhythm was slow at first, but not like before. This time, it held the promise that more was to come.

As his hips picked up speed, Kaine abandoned my mouth, leaning back on his calves. My body shook, my breasts bounced, as his strokes became booming thrusts.

The swaying of the bed's frame filled the room until my gasps and moans drowned it out. The buildup was nearly unbearable. The explosion coming was going to wreck me. But I held on, nearly in tears that Kaine and I were finally back to this point. That we'd found this connection again.

In a flash, my orgasm ripped through me, stealing every sensation until all that was left were stars. I jerked and writhed. I pulsed and shuddered. I was a boneless and panting, limp mess by the time I came down. I barely had the energy to crack my eyes open, blink away the white spots and focus on the second-best part of sex with Kaine.

The man himself.

His eyes were closed, his long, dark eyelashes forming perfect swoops above his cheekbones. His mouth was open, just slightly, and his bottom lip swelled to a perfect pout.

The sight of him on the edge made my inner walls clench. His brawny shoulders and chiseled arms reminded me of the wooden pieces he made. Soft to the touch, but solid and un-breakable beneath the silken exterior.

The ends of his hair curled at the nape of his neck and were damp with sweat. Perspiration beaded by his temples as he rammed into me, harder and harder, exactly like I'd asked. This was the lover I knew, the lover I worshipped.

A new orgasm began to build, this one not as sharp as the last. It came over me like a wave, stealing away my breath as it pulled me under. I gasped, getting Kaine's attention.

He opened his eyes just as it broke, then gripped my thighs harder, pulling me onto his cock as he planted deep and let go. His hot spurts slid between us, coating my sex.

Kaine came down from his high, looking as dizzy and delirious as I felt. He collapsed next to me on the bed, and we both stared at the ceiling, unable to move. The world was spinning faster in this bedroom and gravity weighed heavy on my limbs. It was a rush, like being drunk. I was afraid my heart might beat out of my chest and my brain might scramble.

But then Kaine reached over and took my hand, and the rush faded.

As his fingers laced with mine, the spinning stopped. Gravity wasn't quite as heavy. And my world was right again.

"Thank you," I whispered.

Kaine's thumb stroked my knuckle. "Thank you back."

I smiled, slipping my hand from his to go clean up. I attempted to sit, but my abs weren't what they used to be and it was a struggle. I was getting in the habit of swinging my legs over the side of the bed, using an arm to push myself up. But before I could, Kaine was there behind me, helping me to sit up.

He hopped off the bed first, helping me stand. Then he gathered up my clothes so I wouldn't have to bend down. With them piled in my arms, I made my way to the bathroom. I did my business, then put back on my pajamas, using the last bit of energy I had for the day.

As I came out of the bathroom, I expected to see Kaine dressed and ready to retreat to his room. But instead, the bed had been turned down and a deliciously naked Kaine was lying underneath the top sheet.

"You're sleeping here?"

"Yup."

"What if I don't want you to sleep here?" *Why am I asking such stupid questions?* Of course I wanted him to sleep here.

He chuckled. "Too bad."

I was giddy with renewed energy as I crossed the room, shut off my bedside lamp and slipped under the sheet. What did this mean? What did any of this mean? Kaine and I had been living together for months. Now sex was back in the mix.

Were we a couple? Were we friends having twins together?

I rested my head on my pillow, took a long deep breath and worked up the courage to start asking questions.

"I—whoa!" My hands flew to my belly.

"What?" Kaine was at my side in a flash, his hands immediately diving under my tank top. "Are you hurt?"

"No." I giggled as the twins kicked. It was like a bag of popcorn was popping inside me. "Can't you feel them?"

His hands stilled, his palms hot against my skin. One of the babies kicked it, and Kaine's face transformed.

Gone was the fear I'd seen in his eyes since the day I'd told him I was pregnant. For the first time, he looked completely in awe. Our babies would be okay.

"See?" I reached up and toyed with a lock of hair by his ear. "They're excited."

Kaine's hands roamed my stomach, chasing kicks and punches. When he looked at me, I got one of his rare, gleaming smiles that made my heart double in size.

The babies were on a roll, literally, shifting and moving inside me. "I look like an alien."

"It's beautiful." Kaine's voice was full of wonder.

"I guess they like sex."

His hands stilled. "What?"

"Sex." I laughed. "They like it. Maybe an orgasm is like a hug for them. We should hug them more."

"Oh, Jesus." He rolled his eyes, dropping his forehead to my stomach as he laughed. I laughed even harder, loving this carefree side of him that I rarely saw.

As our laughter died down, Kaine shifted onto his back, sliding a hand underneath my neck. The movement forced me into his side, curling my back against his chest.

We'd never cuddled before. We'd have sex and lie next to one another. Sometimes I'd drape myself over his bare chest while we caught our breath. But there was never this intimacy. There was never the promise he would stay.

"What are we doing, Kaine? You and me?"

"Going backward."

"I don't understand that." I looked over my shoulder, begging for an answer that made sense. "I hate to be cliché, but I really need a label."

"A label, huh?" His eyes softened, and he kissed my hair. "I guess you could say we're a couple."

"I like that label."

"So do I. We missed all of this. Before the boys, we missed the nights together. The you and me and getting to know one another. I want to go back and do it all. I want the hand-holding. The kisses. And I was waiting for you to be ready for the rest."

"The rest?"

He nodded. "The rest. Sharing this bed. Sharing these boys.

Sharing a life."

"You want that?"

"I want you. I've wanted you for months." He brushed a lock of hair off my shoulder. "Somewhere along the line, you stole my heart. I'm going to steal yours in return. Just wait and see."

My breath hitched. Was this happening? Had Kaine Reynolds, a man dedicated to keeping his emotions locked up behind a dozen padlocks, just confessed his feelings? This sounded a lot like . . . love.

"You really mean all of this?"

"You're important to me," he said quietly. "The most important person in my life."

"You're important to me too."

"Then let's go backward." His arms banded around me tighter. "Let's do all those things I should have done from day one."

Yes was right on the tip of my tongue, but I held it back.

"Where is it all coming from?" The sex between us had been amazing, but for this kind of confession? One of us should have blacked out.

"It's been there for a long time. I guess . . . I didn't want to spring it on you. I won't say that the babies didn't change this. We both know it doesn't work like that in real life. But I'd like to think that even without them, this would have happened eventually."

I liked to think that too. I liked to believe that eventually he would have confided in me. And I had faith that eventually I'd hear the rest of his family's story. It wasn't easy, but I'd give him more time.

"So?"

I snuggled deeper into his arms. I knew what he was asking

but messing with him was too much fun to pass up. "So, what?"

"Are we going backward?"

I smiled, holding in my answer.

"Piper," he grumbled.

I still didn't say anything.

"Jesus, woman. Yes or no?" He shook my shoulders until we were both laughing. "Answer me, damn it."

"Yes!" I giggled. "Yes. I like backward."

"You drive me crazy." He smiled. "But I wouldn't have it any other way."

Kaine kissed my hair again and shifted his arms so one was resting under my neck and the other was over my belly. Then for the first time, I fell asleep in his arms with his scent surrounding me and his heartbeat as my lullaby.

"Morning," I yawned as Kaine kissed my hair. My first thought when waking up was how nice it was to have him in my bed. The second was how badly I'd embarrass myself if I didn't get to the bathroom and pee.

I whipped off the covers, pushing myself off the mattress and scurrying to the bathroom. Getting out of bed was the fastest I moved these days.

I did my business on the toilet, emptying my bladder and sighing with relief as the pressure eased. I had a smile on my face as I stood to pull up my pants. But then it dropped, and I stumbled against the wall as I looked down to the porcelain bowl filled with red.

"Kaine!" I shouted, then I started to cry as panic set in. "I'm bleeding."

nineteen

KAINE

PIPER SHOOK HER DOCTOR'S HAND. "THANK YOU SO MUCH."

"My pleasure." The doctor smiled. "I'll let you get changed. If you have any other concerns, just call or come on in. Otherwise, I'll see you at your checkup in two weeks."

"Thank you again." Piper waved as the doctor let herself out of the exam room. As soon as the door closed behind her, Piper rested back on the table, the paper crunching underneath her back. "Everything is okay."

It sure as hell didn't feel okay. As many times as the doctor had reassured us, what I was feeling right now was not *okay*. The image of Piper standing beside the toilet this morning was on a loop in my head.

Her face so white as she looked down at the water tinged red with blood.

The terror in her eyes, her unsteady hands as we hurried to get her dressed.

The sound of her panicked voice on the phone with the doctor.

Piper had been on hold with the doctor's office as I'd thrown on some clothes, then loaded her into the car. The nurse had assured us that things were likely fine but to come in just in case. I'd already been racing down the highway at that point.

The thirty-minute drive to Kalispell had only taken twenty. If not for a few patches of early morning frost causing me to slow, I would have made it in fifteen.

A nurse had waited inside the door as we'd walked into the clinic. She'd taken us to an exam room where Piper had stripped off her clothes in a frenzy, donning an ugly, faded gown. As she'd climbed up on the table, I'd stuck my head out the door and hollered that we were ready.

The doctor had come in with a smile. It hadn't helped steady my shaking hands. Neither had the good results from the exam, or the sound of the babies' heartbeats on the monitor. My foot wouldn't stop bouncing on the speckled linoleum, and the lump in the back of my throat wouldn't stop choking me.

Things were definitely not *okay*.

The doctor suspected the blood was a normal side effect of sex. Piper had likely developed a polyp of sorts that had burst when we'd been together. It was normal. Everything was normal. The doctor had said *normal* about a hundred times.

Except this was un-fucking-normal. I couldn't breathe. I stood from the stiff chair and went to the door.

"You're leaving?" Piper's head came off the table.

"Get dressed," I ordered before escaping the room.

A nurse passed me in the hallway, smiling brightly. Most expectant fathers probably smiled back. She'd have to settle for a curt nod as I scanned the walls for an exit sign.

I found an arrow pointing to the left and followed it to another, making my way back to the waiting room. I let myself out of the clinic and jogged down the hallway that led me to the parking lot. Piper's doctor's office was attached to the hospital, and beyond the glass doors, an ambulance drove by.

The moment I pushed outside, the cold air assaulted my face. It froze the hairs in my nostrils and cooled the blood in my ears. The pressure in my chest was crushing, and the thin air wouldn't fill my lungs. I spotted a bench on the sidewalk and stumbled toward it, collapsing on the icy boards.

Then I dropped my head into my hands and tried to breathe.

The darkness was coming back. The sun was rising, lighting a new day, but the black was creeping in on me. I could have lost it all again. Except it wasn't someone else's fault this time. There had been no accident. The person responsible was me.

I could have lost my boys. I could have lost Piper. And why? Because I'd wanted to have sex with her.

The entire reason we were here—why I was here, outside another hospital panicked and alone—was because I couldn't keep my dick in my pants.

"Sir?" A voice hovered above me. "Sir? Are you okay?"

In front of me, hot pink scrubs came in and out of focus. A nurse placed her hand on my shoulder, repeating her question.

The world was spinning too fast, and the air wouldn't stay in my chest. The bench beneath me swayed like a ship riding out an ocean storm. I gripped the edge, holding on for dear life so I wouldn't drown.

"I think he's having a panic attack."

"Oh my god." Piper's voice broke through the static buzz in my ears. "Kaine? Kaine, take a breath."

I nodded, trying to breathe as she sat at my side. But my lungs, they just wouldn't work right.

"Breathe." Her hand rubbed up and down my back. "In and out. Breathe."

The nurse's hot pink scrubs disappeared from my periphery, but I didn't turn. My eyes were locked on the blurry sidewalk beneath my feet.

I sucked in a gasp but it wasn't enough oxygen. My heart was racing, and I was seconds away from blacking out when the nurse's pink scrubs were back in front of me.

She shook out a brown paper bag and handed it to Piper, who put it over my face.

My hands covered hers, my eyes squeezing shut as I dragged in a ragged breath. The bag crunched and crackled as it constricted on my inhale, then expanded on my exhale. Seven more huffs into the paper sack and I finally had enough oxygen back in my bloodstream to open my eyes.

The nurse wasn't alone anymore. Three others from the hospital had gathered on the sidewalk, crowding Piper and me on the bench.

I shied away from their attention, focusing on Piper while pulling the paper bag away from my face.

"Are you okay?" She hadn't put on her coat in her rush to follow me outside.

I frowned, pushing off the bench. My legs were unsteady but not enough that I couldn't stand or walk.

Piper stood too, and I yanked the coat out of her arms. Then I pulled the purse off her shoulder and held it while I handed her the coat. "Put this on."

"Sir, do you—"

I shot the nurse a glare before pushing past her and the others. It was bad enough that Piper had to see me like that. I didn't need a fucking audience as my life spiraled out of control.

Piper rushed to catch up while simultaneously putting on her coat, carrying her purse and saying thank you to the nurse. But I didn't slow down.

Getting the hell away from the hospital was priority number one.

We got to the car and I didn't open the passenger door for Piper like I normally did. I let her climb in herself while I hopped in the driver's side, turned on the engine and got us gone.

The cab of the Tahoe was silent, much like the drive up had been. But my mind was whirling faster than the tires on the pavement.

One or two.

If we had lost the boys, I would have had to decide again. I would have had to put them in the ground.

One. We'd bury them together. Brothers should be together. And at least Piper and I had picked out names. Their headstones wouldn't be unmarked.

"Kaine!" Piper hollered. "I said slow down."

I blinked, glancing at the speedometer between my white knuckles. Then I backed off the gas. "Sorry."

It would be ironic if I crashed this car, for more than one reason. Leaving the house was tempting fate. But staying home wasn't safe either.

"I'm sorry." Piper sighed. "I didn't know this would happen."

My silence was deafening. It sounded a lot like blame.

"I can't help you if you don't talk to me."

Talk? If she only knew what she was asking. She had no idea how impossible it was for me to talk about everything that had happened. I'd lose my temper. I'd lose the control I'd worked so hard to keep. And she'd be right there in my warpath.

Look at what had just happened at the hospital. I couldn't even control my own body.

Mom had been begging me for weeks on our phone calls to open up. She thought it would be healthy for me to talk about it with her or Piper, then let it go. She wanted me to find forgiveness and move forward.

How did you forgive someone who stole a piece of you? How did you forgive someone who you loved and trusted completely but hadn't hesitated when the time came to stab you in the back?

Forgiveness? Not happening. Mom didn't know what she was asking for either. Three years and the pain and rage I'd felt was as strong as ever. I'd just managed to bury it deep. If I let it go, I didn't know what would happen. The last time I'd thought about him, I'd taken a chainsaw to a chair.

I could have killed myself or Piper that night.

"Where do you go?" Piper whispered. "When you get so lost in your own head, where do you go?"

Where did I go?

To the past. To the places and people who haunted me.

I broke my eyes away from the road as Piper swiped a tear from her cheek. The sadness on her face made everything worse. I was hurting her. I'd promised to care for her, and instead I was causing her pain. I wasn't doing right by her or the boys.

When you were broken, breaking others wasn't all that difficult.

Maybe it would be best if I kept my distance for a few more months. My stomach churned at the idea of leaving them. But what other choice did I have?

A few days apart would do us both some good. Things had happened so quickly; our lives had changed so much these past few months. We could each use time to process it all.

Piper swiped another tear. I hadn't answered her question.

There was nothing to say.

I focused on the road, driving us safely home as Piper dried the occasional tear. When we pulled into the garage, she was out of the door before I shut off the engine. She slammed it closed behind her, then did the same with the door that led inside.

"Son of a bitch."

I was ruining this. Just last night I'd told her that she was the most important person in my life. She'd asked me for a label, and I'd given her one. But who was I kidding? I didn't know the first thing about being part of a couple.

I shut off her Tahoe and went inside. I'd expected to find Piper in the living room or kitchen, but as I passed the guest bedroom, the sound of sniffling and rustling clothes caught my attention. When I reached the doorway, I found Piper running back and forth between the closet and the bed.

She was taking my clothes out of the closet and putting them into the duffel bag that they'd come over in.

"What are you doing?"

"I think you need this." She grabbed the stack of jeans she'd folded for me two nights ago when we'd been at the kitchen island, folding laundry. She tossed them on the bed, undoing all the folding.

Undoing us.

"Need what?"

"To run away."

"What? No." I stepped into the room, stopping her before she could go back to the closet for more. "I don't want to run away."

"But maybe you should." She looked up at me with glassy eyes. "I mean, you just had a panic attack, Kaine."

"No. I just . . . I just needed a second." *Panic attack* sounded so serious. "It was just a shock." Wasn't it?

"No, it wasn't. And it's my fault. I've been pushing so hard, wanting you to open up to me on my timeline. But my timeline doesn't matter. *You* matter. So maybe you need to run away. Get some space and get okay with everything. When you're ready to talk, I'll be here. If you decide you don't want to talk, I'll still be here."

This woman. She'd figured me out so quickly.

Except she was dead wrong. *I* was dead wrong. I didn't need space to come to terms with my past. What I needed was *her*.

I wanted her to have all my pieces, even the ugly, misshapen ones.

"I'm scared."

"I know," she whispered. "I'm scared too. I wake up every morning, wondering if this was a dream. I worry that I could lose it at any time. This is everything I've ever wanted, and it terrifies me because it could all be gone in a flash."

"You don't know what it feels like." Piper might be scared, but her imagination couldn't conjure the magnitude of fear I was living with. The pain of losing a child was unthinkable.

"No," she said gently. "I don't know the kind of pain you went through. I hope to God I never do. And I'm so sorry you went through that. But I do know what it feels like to lose someone you love."

She did? "Who?"

Her eyes held mine. "You. I'm losing you."

I sat on the edge of the bed, tugging her hand so she'd sit down next to me. "You're not losing me."

"I'm not?"

"Never. And I'm sorry. About last night, I shouldn't have been so rough. And—"

"Stop. Please, stop," Piper begged. "It wasn't your fault. It wasn't my fault. I won't feel guilty for last night, and I won't let you either. You heard the doctor. Everything is normal."

"It still scares me. I-I don't know how to deal with some of these feelings. But I'd like to try if you'll listen."

She nodded.

I took her hand and stood from the bed. For this conversation, I wanted to be in a bigger room. I needed more space because the rage would inevitably return, and I wanted room to let it breathe.

Piper followed me without a word to the living room and

took a seat on the couch. But instead of sitting next to her, I went to the chair across from the coffee table. As much as her touch calmed me, to look in her eyes did so much more.

"Remember how I told you Shannon was in a drunk driving accident?"

She nodded. "Yes."

"Well, she wasn't the one driving. And she wasn't the one drunk. My brother was."

Piper flinched. "You have a brother? All this time, you never . . ."

She trailed off, her brain getting ahead of her questions. Then her eyes got wide and her hand slapped over her mouth, muffling a gasp.

"My brother is five years younger than me. My parents got divorced just a few months after he was born. He wasn't exactly planned since they were already separated at the time."

I didn't remember much from that time, other than Mom being exhausted a lot and falling asleep on the couch while I played. I remember Dad coming over to take me fun places, like the park in the summer or the sledding hill in the winter. I don't think he'd ever really bonded with Isaiah before moving to Asia.

"Mom did her best to raise two boys on her own, but she worked a lot. And as I got older, I took on more responsibility, especially with Isaiah. It was just him and me at home after school and on Saturdays until Mom got home from work. He was younger, but he was my best friend too."

"Was?" Piper whispered. "Did he—in the accident, did he . . ."

"Die? No. He made it out without a scratch."

Piper sat on the edge of the couch, her hands resting on her stomach, waiting for me to continue.

"I should have known something was going on with Isaiah and Shannon. They were closer to the same age and had a lot of the same interests. He was always hanging around the house when she was home. They'd watch TV together or cook dinner together. I didn't think anything of it at first. I thought he was just getting to know her for my sake."

"But it was more?"

I nodded. "They were dating behind my back. Mom knew. Her parents knew. Even some of my friends." Former friends. I hadn't kept in touch with them after I'd moved to Lark Cove.

"Why wouldn't they tell you?"

"I don't know." I sighed. "Maybe they thought I'd be mad or jealous. But they hid it and snuck around for months."

They'd meet for meals or movies. They'd gone away for a couple of weekends together. Shannon had been complaining because she was too big to fit behind the wheel of her car comfortably, so Isaiah had started driving her places when I couldn't. I'd thought it was nice of him, but it was just another one of their lies.

"He took her to dinner the night of the crash. Had too much to drink and still got behind the wheel. He wasn't paying attention and ran a stop sign. They got T-boned by a one-ton truck. There was hardly anything left of her side of the car."

The person who'd hit them hadn't been injured either. But the incredible force of the collision had sent her compact car through the intersection and partway down the next block.

"Kaine," Piper whispered. "I'm so sorry."

"He should have fucking protected them." My hands fisted and I stood from the chair. "They were mine, and he should have taken more care. He should have told me from the beginning. And he should have just made her drive."

Putting the blame on Shannon was impossible since she'd

lost her life. Isaiah got the blame since he was the one to walk away.

It was his fault I'd lost my daughter.

And it was mine too. I'd been so consumed with work that I'd missed the signs. I'd worn rose-colored glasses where Isaiah was concerned.

His whole life he'd been reckless, and I'd been there to clean up his messes.

When he was eight, he spent an hour tossing a football against a window, sure it wouldn't break. When it shattered, I boarded it up before Mom got home and told her it was just an accident.

When he was fourteen and got in a fight with one of the neighborhood kids that summer, I let him crash on the couch in my apartment to hide his black eye and busted lip for a week.

When he was seventeen and got busted at a party for drinking, I was the one who took him down to the courthouse and paid for his minor-in-possession ticket. Mom never knew.

I was the man who talked to him about sex. I was the man who taught him how to drive. I was the man who tried to make *him* a man. A good man.

Instead, he'd taken everything I'd had and then some.

I paced the room as the anger seeped into my veins. "He wasn't just my brother. He was my friend. He was . . . I trusted him. And he betrayed me. In every possible way, after everything I did for him, he betrayed me."

"And that's why you didn't tell me about him?" Piper asked. "Because you were hurt?"

"No. I don't talk about him because I *can't* talk about him. Not without going into a rage. You saw what I did with the chainsaw. What you didn't see were the holes I punch in walls whenever I think about him. The countless broken dishes I've thrown against the floor. I never want to lose my control in front of you. Talking about him, thinking about him . . . it's just better that I keep it in. Talking about him only brings out the worst in me."

"Is that why you didn't talk to your mom for all those years?"

I nodded. "She defended him. She said it was just an accident. She chose him over me. After that . . . I just couldn't be around her."

"So you left."

"I came here. Did my best to shut out everything from that life. Me and Mom, we're still trying to figure things out. We talk about neutral topics. Her job. You. The boys. But whenever the rest of it comes up, things turn red."

"And where is your brother?"

"In prison." Right where he belonged. Where he couldn't destroy any other lives. Isaiah had been charged with vehicular manslaughter while under the influence and was currently serving a five-year sentence.

I had no idea how I'd deal with his release. I had no desire to see his face again or listen to his excuses. Mom would undoubtedly take his side, meaning I'd lose her again too. Isaiah would take and take and take, just like he always had.

My heart rate spiked as the rage spread through me cell by cell. I took a few deep breaths, wishing it away, but what I really wanted was to smash something. I needed something to crumble, like my world had crumbled all because of my brother.

"Kaine." Piper's soothing voice broke through the haze. "You have a right to be mad."

"I hate him. He took *everything* from me."

"I know." She stood from the couch and crossed the room. Her arms wrapped around my waist as she pressed her ear to my heart. Her embrace chased the anger away. "But it's not everything anymore."

She was right. Now that I had Piper and the babies, *everything* took on a whole new meaning. I hated my brother. And I was still angry at my mother, though we were working on our relationship.

Except without my past, I wouldn't have Piper. I wouldn't have come to this mountain. I wouldn't have fallen in love with my gorgeous neighbor.

"It almost killed me losing my daughter," I admitted. "It broke my heart that Mom made excuses for Isaiah and took his side. It crushed me that he'd do something like that to me. And I didn't love her, but losing Shannon was awful. But somehow, I lived through it. If anything ever happened to you or the boys, I wouldn't . . . I wouldn't survive it."

"They're going to be okay, Kaine. They'll be incredible."

I held her tighter. "Not just them. *You.* I wouldn't survive without you."

She looked up at me, tears welling in her eyes. "I'm not going anywhere. And neither can you."

"I'm here for good. Promise."

"Don't promise," she whispered. "Prove it."

Prove it.

I'd spend the rest of my life proving it. Starting today. "I love you."

Surprise flashed across her face. "You—you do?"

"I want to marry you."

Her mouth fell open.

"I want to share this life with you, Piper. Raise these boys. Live on this mountain together." And that would be a hell of a lot easier if we were married. As soon as she agreed, we'd go pick out a ring. We had some work to do and some trust to build, but we'd get there in time.

"Seriously?" Her eyebrows creased. "You want to get married?"

"Is that a yes?"

A slow grin spread across her lips just before she laughed. "No."

"No?" I jerked back.

"No. I'm not going to marry you." She cupped my cheek, standing on her toes to brush a kiss across my mouth. Then she patted my stomach and walked to the kitchen. "I'm starving. Want to share some popcorn?"

"Popcorn? I just asked you to marry me."

"And I said no." She opened the refrigerator, getting out a carrot stick. She crunched one bite, then smiled. "I love you too, by the way."

"Gee, thanks," I muttered.

Piper took her carrot stick with her as she rounded the counter and walked toward the guest room. "Will you help me move all your clothes into my closet?"

"Yes. See how easy that is to say?"

She giggled, smiling at me again before disappearing down the hall. "Are you coming or not?"

"Coming," I grumbled.

We weren't done with this conversation. She wanted me to prove it?

I'd prove it.

I'd keep asking her to marry me until I got the answer I wanted.

twenty

PIPER

"WE'RE HEADING OUT!" KAINE'S VOICE RANG DOWN the hallway.

"Wait!" I yelled, hiking up the band of my maternity jeans as I came out of the bathroom.

When you had to go every three minutes, pants like this were a must. My plan was to keep enjoying the abundance of spandex and Lycra for as long as possible post-pregnancy too.

I had the huge band back in place as I came down the hallway.

Kaine was grinning as he stood by the door. He had his winter coat on and a beanie over his hair. He wore knee-high snow boots that laced all the way up his calves. They made his already bulging thighs look even beefier.

A shiver ran down my spine as I walked into his arms. He wrapped me up, kissing my hair before whispering in my ear, "Marry me."

"No," I whispered back.

He grunted. I'd decided it was his way of cussing without words.

It had been a month since he'd told me about his brother and asked to marry me the first time. He must have asked at least three hundred times since.

And each time, I'd turned him down.

I stepped out of his arms and looked up at his handsome face. "Please watch out for creatures with big teeth."

"It's winter. Most of them are asleep." He patted the holstered pistol on his hip. "But I have this just in case."

"Stop worrying, Piper. We're not going far." Logan walked over from the kitchen, wearing attire similar to Kaine's. Though his pants didn't have a dark stain on the knee from the wood shop, and his coat was rip-free.

I looked back up at Kaine. "Make sure my boss doesn't get lost in the woods."

"You say that like you'd actually miss me." Logan feigned shock. "Does this mean you've finally realized how much you need me?"

"Only to sign my paychecks. But I'm this close to perfecting your signature." I held my thumb and index finger an inch apart. "After that, you're dispensable."

Logan laughed and rolled his eyes. "Let's go, Charlie!"

His daughter came running out of the guest bathroom, zipping up her black snow bibs. Thea followed behind her, carrying a neon-green winter coat that matched her snow boots.

"Happy hunting, guys." The three of them were heading up toward the ridge to cut down a couple of Christmas trees.

"Logan Kendrick, I'm begging you to get a reasonable tree this year." Thea tugged a gray stocking cap over Charlie's head. "Six feet. Seven, tops. I can't have another ten footer like last year's."

"Sure, baby. We'll get a smaller one." Logan winked at Charlie, who winked back. He'd be coming back with a nine-and-a-half-foot tree, no doubt.

"Don't do that winking thing with each other." Thea crossed her arms. "I won't decorate anything over the seven-foot mark."

"I'll do it," Charlie chimed in.

"Problem solved." Logan kissed Thea's cheek and shuffled Charlie outside into the snow.

"I'm doomed." Thea laughed, going to check on Collin and Camila, who were playing in the living room.

"Do you have any requirements?" Kaine asked.

"Green."

"Done." Kaine brushed another kiss on my lips. "Love you."

"Love you too. Be safe."

About three weeks ago, he'd seen signs of a mountain lion around the area during a hike. I liked cats, but cougars were not on my list of animals to see up close and personal. Kaine had called the game warden to come up and see if they could relocate the animal, but their search had turned up empty.

There hadn't been any signs since and it was unlikely the animal would come anywhere near us, but Kaine wasn't taking any chances. Which meant any time I went outside, even to check the mailbox, he was my escort. He'd also decided we were getting a dog—one the size of a wolf.

But for now, Kaine carried his pistol with him everywhere and they weren't wandering far from home.

With axes in hand, Kaine and Logan set out up the trail toward the ridge. Charlie trudged behind them, dragging a blue sled so she could collect her own mini tree for her bedroom. I waved at them all, then closed the door before too much cold air could seep inside.

"How are you doing?" Thea asked as I sat on the couch beside her.

"Good." I rubbed my obliques. For once in my life, they were rock solid. "Things are starting to get tight though, and I can't tie my shoes anymore. Kaine's been sweet and puts them on for me."

"Has he kept up with the proposals?"

I smiled. "He asks me at least five times a day. He even upped his game last night and produced a ring."

"What!" Her eyes got wide. "Where is it?"

"I'm not sure. When I said no, he pouted and hid it somewhere. But it is gorgeous."

He'd bought me an eternity band. The entire thing was made up of diamond halos set in rose gold, and it was truly a piece of art. The stones weren't enormous and the ring wouldn't weigh heavily on my finger. I didn't need a huge jewel to flaunt or dazzle people with its brilliance. It was the perfect ring because it was just so . . . Kaine.

It was understated but powerful, much like his furniture. It was simple and beautiful, much like our relationship.

"So he keeps asking you to marry him," Thea said. "He loves you. You love him. He bought you a ring. Remind me why you keep saying no?"

"We need time." I shifted on the couch, trying to get comfortable.

"Just to play devil's advocate here, is that because you don't think you'd accept after you got to know him?"

"Logan is rubbing off on you," I teased. "He thinks playing devil's advocate is the best job ever."

"Right?" She laughed.

"But no, to answer your question. I want to marry Kaine. I love him more than I've ever loved another person."

This real love, this deep and profound feeling of being with *the one*, wasn't something I'd understood with Adam. We hadn't had true love, we'd had convenience. It had been easier to stay together than break apart. Adam and I had been content but never truly happy. Never truly in love. We'd never had the passion I had for Kaine.

I wanted to make an everlasting commitment with Kaine. Just not yet.

"I want time for things to settle." I blew out a long breath as one of the babies pushed against a rib. "There is no rush. I'm not walking down the aisle pregnant, so we can enjoy this time together and just . . . be."

I didn't want any new labels slapped on us right now. Wife. Husband. We'd get to those in time. First, I wanted some time to just accept things as they were. Label-free. Then, we'd tackle being parents. After that, we could decide what was right for our family. Together.

The past month since Kaine had confessed everything about his brother had arguably been the best thirty days of my life. And without secrets looming and me pushing Kaine too hard to reveal them, it was the best month the two of us had ever had together.

Kaine laughed and talked to me while we made dinner. He touched me and kissed my hair while we were watching TV. He held me in his arms at night with one arm under my head and another resting over my belly.

He was proving to me his love, whether he knew it or not. His simple gestures, like taking out the trash or making me bedtime tea or massaging my lower back when it ached, were more meaningful than any of the marriage proposals.

"I know it seems crazy," I told Thea. "But things between Kaine and I have gone so fast from the beginning. When I was with Adam, we dated for years before we got married. I knew all about him. And that didn't turn out well, but there's something to be said for knowing what kind of toothpaste your partner likes best. Or how much cereal they eat in the morning. Or how long it takes them to shower. I just want to know Kaine and settle in together before the boys are born."

Thea nodded. "That makes sense."

"We're getting there. And it's been nice living together."

A few days after Kaine's confession, I'd come home from working the morning at Logan's to find everything from the cabin here. The coffee table from the cabin was in the living room, the one I'd bought now at the cabin. His clothes were in my closet, his tennis shoes and boots were next to my heels. And he'd declared the garage was now his domain.

He hadn't asked me to move in, he'd just done it. Because this was *our* life. Our home.

"Has he told you more about his brother?" Thea asked.

"Some." I nodded. "It's hard for him to talk about."

Though he was talking about Isaiah. To me. It was by far the best of the simple gestures he'd made over the last month. I trusted him to talk when he was ready. He trusted me to listen. He trusted himself not to go into a rage.

He still got angry whenever he spoke about his brother, but he kept himself in check. There were no porch chairs hacked to pieces. No dishes had been shattered on the floor. Kaine would ball his fists and pace the room as he spoke through gritted teeth, but he wouldn't shut down.

I didn't blame him for his anger, and I understood why he'd kept it all from me. The way his muscles would bunch and his normally loving eyes would turn cold, he was a different man when that pain and anger took over.

He didn't trust himself when he was so mad, but I did. Kaine would sooner cut off his own hand than lift it to me in anger.

"He's so hurt, Thea. About his brother and all that happened. I wish there was something I could do to help him find some peace."

Thea knew all about Kaine's past. He'd shocked me by suggesting I share it all with a friend. He didn't want me carrying the burden alone, and while his tendency was to keep things bottled up, he knew I wasn't wired that way. So he'd driven me down to the bar one afternoon and left me there to eat pizza and confide in Thea.

"Logan and his sister went through a rough time right after we got together."

"I remember that," I told her.

Thea sighed. "I don't know if I handled it right or not, but I just tried to be supportive. I let him vent when he needed to get his frustrations off his chest. And when they eventually made amends, I never held anything against her."

Logan's younger sister, Sofia, was a spoiled brat. Or at least, she had been. Logan had told me that Sofia had been trying harder lately to become more responsible. She was finally growing up.

But the issues between Kaine and his brother were in an entirely different stratosphere than the squabbles Logan had with Sofia.

"I doubt Kaine will ever forgive Isaiah. Making amends isn't something I think he'll be able to do. And I don't blame him for it. But I do want him to find some peace with it. Not for Isaiah's sake, just his own."

The death of his daughter had tainted all of Kaine's memories of Isaiah. I didn't expect the brothers to work through their issues, especially while Isaiah was in prison, but I did want Kaine to get some closure.

"It'll fade," Thea promised. "You have these babies. You two live your life. The anger will fade."

"I hope you're right." I smiled, then shook off my heavy heart. "Are you guys all set for Christmas?"

"Ready as I'll ever get. Logan's family gets here next week so that's always hectic. But it will be nice to see everyone. When does your family arrive?"

"Same. Next week. I'm really excited to see them. This year has gone by so quickly with the move and the remodel. Then everything with Kaine and this pregnancy. It feels like I haven't seen them for years, not months."

I'd never been this excited for a Christmas as an adult. One nice thing about having Kaine's cabin empty was it gave my parents a nice getaway spot for their two-and-a-half-week vacation. My brother would sleep in the guest room here when he arrived the following week.

"Is Kaine nervous about meeting them?"

I shrugged. "If he is, he's not telling me. I think he's more nervous that his mom has a nice time."

Suzanne was coming up on Christmas Eve to spend the holiday with us. She'd had three years of holidays without her children. When we'd called to invite her up, she'd been so happy we were including her in the festivities that she'd cried.

He wouldn't admit it out loud, but Kaine was overjoyed too. He'd been busy this last week making her Christmas gifts. He'd built Suzanne these beautiful wooden cutting boards and candleholders. I think he was anxious to show her how his talent had grown over these last three years.

My phone on the coffee table chimed. I groaned, summoning the energy to get up. Getting off the couch was as difficult as hot yoga these days. And I'd end up just as sweaty.

"Don't." Thea stopped me, handing over the phone. "Here you go."

"Thank you. Speak of the devil." Suzanne's name was on the screen. "Hi, Suzanne."

"Hi, Piper." Her voice sounded off, not as cheery as when she normally talked to Kaine and me. There was a whirring in the background too, like she was driving. "Is Kaine there?"

"He went out hiking to get us a Christmas tree and didn't take his phone. Is everything all right?"

"I need to talk to him. And I'm so sorry, but I won't be able to come up for Christmas."

"What? He's so excited you're coming."

"I was excited too." She sniffled. "But I won't be able to come now. I, um . . . I just really need to talk to Kaine."

"I can have him call you as soon as he comes back."

"Thank you. And I'm so sorry to be missing your family. Please give them my best."

"O-okay," I said, stunned. "Bye."

She hung up, and I turned to Thea. "Well, that was weird. Kaine's mom isn't coming for Christmas after all."

"Why not?"

I shook my head. "She wouldn't say. Which was the odd part. But it sounded like she was upset and driving someplace. Kaine needs to call her."

"Do you want me to go and find them?" Thea offered.

"No. I doubt they'll be gone too long. She didn't say it was an emergency so we'll just give it time."

I summoned the energy to push myself off the couch, then I went to the kitchen and made the kids a snack, getting Thea and me each a bottle of this delicious cream soda I'd found at the grocery store.

Suzanne's phone call put a damper on my time with Thea and the kids. As we watched them play, my eyes were constantly drifting to the door. Finally, an hour and a half later, it opened and three red-nosed and huffing faces came inside.

"Daddy!" Collin raced across the room to his dad.

Thea was right on her son's heels, peering around them to see the trees outside. Her face fell into a frown when she saw the massive tree strapped on top of their SUV. Its tip hung over the front windshield and the trunk extended well past the bumper.

"Seriously, gorgeous. You're killing me." As she rolled her eyes, Logan just grinned as he stomped the snow from his boots.

Kaine grinned as he came inside. The tree he'd gotten for us was propped against the house. Frost on his beard wet my skin as he bent to kiss my cheek. "I'll put it in a stand later this afternoon."

"Okay." I nodded, though the excitement for our first Christmas tree had also dimmed because of Suzanne's call. I stepped out of the way so they could all come inside.

Thea helped Charlie out of her snow gear as the guys shrugged off their coats.

"Your mom called a while ago," I told Kaine as he pulled off his hat. "She wants you to call her, but she said she can't come for Christmas."

"What?" His forehead furrowed. "Why not?"

"She didn't say."

He frowned, then walked over to the kitchen to get his phone. His boots left small globs of snow along the wooden floor. He lifted my bottle of cream soda off the island and took a sip, then grimaced. "I don't know how you can drink this. It's liquid sugar."

"It's yummy." I rubbed my belly where the babies were jiving. "Your boys love it."

His eyes softened, then he dialed up Suzanne and said hello. But his good mood fled as she spoke, and his shoulders stiffened.

Thea and I shared a look as she guided the kids through the living room to give him some quiet.

While they sat at the dining room table, I walked to Kaine and leaned against the counter, trying to catch his gaze. But he was silently fuming, his grip on my soda bottle getting dangerously tight.

"What's wrong?" I whispered, but he ignored me.

The next moment, Suzanne must have said something shocking. His entire body flinched before stringing as tight as a rubber band.

Had someone died? Was Suzanne having health problems? My mind was imagining bad scenarios, one right after the other, when Kaine slammed the bottle in his hand down on the granite island. The bottle shattered, sending fizzing soda and glass shards flying.

I jumped and the kids screamed at the deafening noise.

Logan came my way with worry etched on his face. He stood by my side, but I kept my focus on Kaine.

"He was supposed to get five years," he gritted into the phone.

My heart dropped. This was about his brother.

Suzanne's voice grew louder on the phone, her pleas coming through loud enough for me to hear. "Kaine, please. Don't get angry."

"He deserves to be punished!" Kaine roared. "But I see nothing has changed. You're still taking his side."

Thea scooped up Camila and grabbed Collin's hand, nodding for Charlie to follow her out of the dining room and down the hallway to the other side of the house. Logan watched them go, then refocused on Kaine as he inched closer to my side.

"No," Kaine snapped. "He earned two more years for what he did. And to hell with you both if you're going to defend him. I'm done with all this. You. Him. And if the justice system isn't going to teach him a lesson, if his own mother won't hold him responsible, then maybe I'll teach him that lesson myself. He *killed* my daughter!"

My heart raced frantically at his words. Kaine had never threatened anyone before, and he'd never talked about revenge or retribution. Rage rolled over his shoulders, filling the kitchen like a dark fog. His hatred infected the air, chilling it to ice.

This was the side of Kaine he'd been trying to hide. The man out of control and so full of anger he was blind to the world around him.

Maybe if I touched him, I'd be able to bring him back.

I stepped closer, lifting a hand to Kaine's forearm, but with one long stride, he paced out of my reach. Before I could take another, Logan gripped my elbow and held me back.

And then the phone went flying across the room. It crashed into the thick, wooden door and fell with a loud clang.

"Kaine," I gasped. "What happened?"

He didn't say a word. The look in his eyes was feral as he swiped his truck keys from the dish on the counter and went right for the door. He stepped on his phone with a boot heel and destroyed it completely.

"Kaine!" I wanted to rush after him, but I wasn't wearing shoes and the floor was covered in glass from the broken soda bottle. If I could just touch him, if I could just get him to look at me, he'd calm down. He'd take a breath and snap back to reality.

But he was on a mission, striding out the door and into the cold without a backward glance.

"Kaine!" Logan called after him too, but it did no good.

Kaine's truck engine rumbled to life. Then he was gone.

I sidestepped a piece of glass, only to step on a smaller one. "Damn it!"

"Where's he going?" Logan asked.

"I don't know." I picked the glass off my foot and backed away. I ran my hands through my hair. "I don't know. Maybe to drive around and blow off some steam. Or . . ." My stomach fell. "Or he's going to confront his brother."

I might not have heard the entire conversation, but it didn't take much to piece it together. Isaiah had been released from prison. Or he was being released. Suzanne wasn't coming to Christmas here because she'd be spending it with her other son.

I went to my phone and pulled up Suzanne's number. It rang immediately to voicemail. I tried it again, only with the same result.

If Kaine was going to find Isaiah, I had to get there first. I had to stop him. But I had no idea where Suzanne lived or where I could find them.

"I need your help," I told Logan.

"Anything."

"I need to find out where Kaine's mother lives. I need to know when his brother, Isaiah Reynolds, was released from prison. What time. Where. Any information you can get me."

"I'll call Sean." Logan whipped out his phone, dialing his personal assistant's number. Sean had been a systems hacker in his former life before Logan had hired him. He'd get answers to my questions and then some in a matter of minutes.

While Logan talked on the phone, I rushed to the hall closet, pulling on some shoes and a coat. Just as I was zipping it over my belly, Thea came rushing to my side.

"What's happening? Are you okay?"

I shook my head. "I have to go after Kaine."

"Is that safe?"

"He won't hurt me. He just needs to calm down."

This wasn't like his panic attack, where Kaine had needed space to come to terms with the changes in our life. This was something else, something I'd seen time and time again when the fury from his past was taking over. He didn't need space to get through this.

What he needed was me.

"Sean's digging," Logan said, joining us. "He'll call you as soon as he finds out what's happening."

I nodded and grabbed my purse from the kitchen counter. "I'm going."

"Piper—"

"He needs me." I cut off Thea's protest. "He's going through so much. He needs me. And I need to be there to help him through this."

"But—"

Logan placed a hand on his wife's arm. "Call us if you need anything."

"Thank you." I went right down the hallway toward the garage where the Tahoe was parked. But before I could disappear from sight, a chilling thought settled in my mind. My heart plummeted.

"Logan?" I called over my shoulder.

"Yeah?"

"Did Kaine take off his gun?"

twenty-one

KAINE

THE COLLISION WAS INEVITABLE.

Things between Isaiah and me had been left unsettled for far too long.

A blind rage had sent me storming out of the house, and hours later as I sat behind the wheel of my truck, it hadn't eased in the slightest.

My brother was supposed to get five years. Five. Years. I'd accepted his sentence. I'd accepted that five years of his life would be payment for taking the life of my baby. He'd lose five years for taking Shannon away from her family and friends.

Five years. Not three. He owed me two more years.

After the accident, Isaiah had been taken to the hospital too. While I'd been holding my daughter's lifeless body, while Shannon's parents had cried over her corpse, he'd been getting treated for some minor cuts and scrapes.

Then he'd been arrested.

Isaiah had sat in a jail cell as I'd arranged a funeral with Shannon's mom and dad. My mother had pleaded with me to visit him, but I'd refused.

He needs to talk to you, Kaine.

It was an accident. He was barely over the legal limit.

He's devastated.

I'd finally heard enough and left. I'd shut out the world, but not so completely that I hadn't kept tabs on his case. Isaiah had pleaded guilty and been sentenced to three to five years in the state penitentiary.

How did a murderer get away with just the minimum sentence? Isaiah owed me two more years, and if the government wasn't going to collect his punishment, then I would.

My foot pressed harder into the gas pedal. I was doing my best to stay close to the speed limit because I didn't need a cop stopping me right now, not while I was this angry. But the miles were rolling by too slowly.

I wanted my retribution, then I wanted to forget I even had a brother.

Piper would be worried. I should have stopped an hour ago and called her from a pay phone, but I'd kept my eyes on the pavement and my truck roaring down the interstate to Bozeman.

An exit came up on my right, then flew past. It was better that I take care of this on my own. Piper didn't need the stress, and until I confronted my brother and collected retribution, this anger would always loom over us.

I wanted her to marry me, but what the hell kind of husband would I make? I'd scared her today. I'd scared the Kendrick kids.

"Fuck." I pounded my fist on the dash.

This had to stop. I had to end this. I couldn't feel this way around Piper or my boys. They didn't need to see their dad go fucking crazy over a phone call.

Today, I was ending this. And then I'd leave it all behind and never look back.

When I'd called Mom earlier, she'd been driving to pick up Isaiah. She'd claimed that his early release was a surprise to us all, but I didn't know if I believed her anymore.

Ironically, the state penitentiary was between Lark Cove and Bozeman, in a town called Deer Lodge, along the interstate. When I'd driven past Deer Lodge before, I'd smiled to myself, knowing that Isaiah was behind the tall gates and barbed wire fences. This time as I drove by, I gripped the wheel harder, letting my teeth grind together.

My boot pressed the pedal faster. The speed limit was shattered now, so my only hope was not crossing paths with a cop. Mom had Isaiah with her and they were likely heading home. They were probably just an hour ahead of me, maybe less.

The afternoon light was already fading by the time I reached the Bozeman city limits. It wasn't even four o'clock yet, but the sun was on its winter descent. Navigating the town streets didn't take long, even though they were covered in patches of ice and snow. When I pulled up to Mom's, two sets of footprints led up the snow-covered sidewalk toward her front door.

I threw open the door to my truck and stepped outside, ice crunching underneath my boot. The chill from the air did nothing to cool my blood—it had been boiling for hours, simmering for years.

The moment I rounded the hood, the front door to the house flew open. Mom rushed outside, pulling her sweater over her chest. Her dark hair was pulled back, the gray strands by her temples showing.

Before the car accident, she hadn't had any gray hair. Her face hadn't had as many lines around her mouth or wrinkles in her forehead.

"Kaine, calm down." She raised her hands, but I didn't stop as I marched for the house, plowing right past her on the sidewalk.

"Is he in there?" I jerked my chin to the house.

"We just got home," she said, following on my heels. "He

just got out of *prison*. Let him be. You two can have it out at a different time."

"Let him be?" I turned and glared down at her. "Let him be? I'm not going to feel sorry for the bastard for being in prison. He deserved to be locked away. He should still be locked away for another two fucking years!" My voice boomed across the frozen yard.

"Kaine—"

"Damn you for choosing him," I spat. "Damn you."

"He's my son."

"So am I."

A tear dripped down her cheek and she wiped it away. "You'll understand when you're a parent."

"I was a parent. Until *he* took her away from me."

Her face paled and another tear fell. I ignored it and spun back around for the door.

Isaiah was standing behind the screen, staring outside.

Mom gripped my elbow, trying to hold me back, but I easily shook her loose.

"Still hiding?" I called out.

Isaiah dropped his shoulders and pushed through the door. He walked slowly down the stairs, then met me on the sidewalk. His chin rested on his chest, his eyes aimed to our feet.

"Look at me," I ordered, my fists clenching.

He lifted his eyes, and I staggered back an inch. Because the man in front of me was not my brother.

This was not the carefree, fun-loving young man who'd come into my shop and keep me company while I worked. This wasn't the cocky, charismatic man who'd charm all the ladies whenever we were out for beers at a local bar. This wasn't the boy who'd come home from school each day with a new joke for the dinner table.

This was not my brother.

This was a shrunken version of the boy I'd tried to raise into a good man.

Isaiah's frame, which had always been leaner than my own, had withered. His jeans, probably the ones he'd worn to prison, now hung from his hips. His black Nike hoodie was baggier on his shoulders than it had been when I'd given it to him as a birthday present five years ago. He'd worn it so often back then that the color had faded to a dark gray.

His hands were shoved in his jeans pockets, and his shoulders were hitched up to his ears. His hair, which he'd always worn longer to be like mine, was now sheared short. Behind his ear, a black tattoo trailed down his neck.

But it was his eyes that had changed the most. They were dead. Completely void of anything but pain and loneliness.

My hands unfisted. One lifted toward his shoulder, ready to set it there before assuring him he'd be all right. Habit screamed for me to comfort him. But I dropped my hand back to my side.

He's a killer.

I wouldn't let his starved frame or hollowed cheeks make me forget who he really was.

He was a killer.

"You took my daughter. You owe me two more years for the ones she never got to live."

Isaiah nodded, tears welling in his eyes.

Those tears made me hate him even more.

In a flash, I raised my fist and plowed it into his face. I felt a bone in his nose crack under my knuckles before I heard it.

"Kaine!" Mom screamed and tried to push past me to Isaiah.

"Shit," he cursed as his hands went to his nose to catch the blood. He shuffled a few steps backward.

"Fuck you." I closed in on him again, unwilling to let him

escape. He'd earned that punch. And the one I threw next that sent him onto his ass.

I bent down and gripped the collar of his sweatshirt and hauled him up to his feet. With one hand, I held him up while the other pummeled into his cheek.

"Kaine! Stop!" Mom cried. "Please, stop!"

She pulled at my elbow again, jerking as hard as she could. But I was solid and unmoving. The rage I'd had for so long was loose, thirsty for more blood.

I shrugged Mom off, blocking her with my back, then hit Isaiah again. He stumbled on the icy ground, his arms flailing sideways to get his balance. But with my grip on his sweatshirt, he couldn't fall.

His nose was bleeding, and I'd opened up his cheek. An eyebrow was split in two and the blood was seeping into his eye. But he didn't make a move to fight back. He just looked at me with more of those *fucking* tears.

He looked at me and begged me to keep hitting.

I raised my fist again, ready to punish him over and over again until I didn't have to see the pain in his eyes. Until some of the pain in my heart ebbed. But before I could drive my knuckles into his skin, a sound broke through the blood rushing in my ears.

"Kaine." It wasn't Mom's voice.

I lowered my fist, glancing over my shoulder.

And there it was. The calm.

Piper stepped closer and slid her hand up my arm, pulling it down and away from Isaiah's face. "Let him go."

The grip I had on Isaiah's sweatshirt released immediately.

He fell to his knees, and Mom rushed past me to kneel at his side.

Piper held my gaze and inched even closer to my side. Her

touch extinguished the bloodlust I'd felt just seconds ago. And with it gone, all that was left was pain.

Agonizing, brutal, crippling pain.

I hadn't just lost Shannon and the baby when they'd died. I'd lost my brother too. I'd lost my best friend and the person I'd loved second only to our mother.

I'd lost them all.

"Fuck." I ran a hand through my hair as tears welled in my eyes. I gripped the strands hard, hoping the sting would keep the tears at bay. "I fucking hate this."

Three years of pain slammed into my chest like a sledgehammer and the tears wouldn't stop. I blinked furiously, willing them away, but the moment Piper wrapped her arms around my waist and pressed her body into mine, I lost it.

She rested her cheek against my heart, and I collapsed onto her. With the babies between us, I clung to her like a drowning man did a buoy.

"Piper." My voice cracked.

"I know," she whispered, her arms gripping me tighter.

The tears flowed off my face and into her hair. A sob wracked my chest, shaking us both. And she just held on tighter.

I wanted to have my baby girl back. I wanted Shannon to be alive, living a happy life. I wanted to hate Isaiah for taking them both. But the hate, it just wasn't there. The rage was gone. With Piper in my arms, all I felt was the immense sadness I'd buried for so long.

So I cried.

And cried.

Finally, after there were no more tears left, I pulled myself together and let Piper go. I ran my hands over her hair, smoothing it down as I inspected her from head to toe.

"What are you doing here?"

She shrugged, swiping away a tear of her own. "I followed you when you left. I was worried."

"How did you find me?"

"Logan helped. His other assistant, Sean, got your mom's address for me. I guessed you'd come here and, well . . . I got lucky."

I frowned at the idea of Piper behind a wheel, especially on a long drive through icy roads. "I'm sorry. I lost it and I shouldn't have. I'm sor—"

She put a finger to my lips. "It's okay."

"Are you?"

"I'm fine. We're fine." She rubbed her belly, then looked past me to where Mom and Isaiah were standing. Piper smiled, then reached out to shake Mom's hand. "I'm Piper. It's nice to finally meet you."

"You too." Mom took Piper's hand but kept a wary eye on me. I didn't miss the way she was shielding Isaiah's body with her own.

"I know this is a bad time," Piper said. "But I really, *really* have to pee. Can I use your bathroom?"

This woman. How could she make me laugh at a time like this? I let out a dry chuckle, then gripped her hand and led her past Mom and Isaiah into the house.

The minute she caught sight of the bathroom, she ran toward it, pulling down her pants without even closing the door. I shook my head, pulling it closed as she moaned a sigh of relief on the other side.

For her to arrive not long after me, it meant she hadn't stopped along the way either. And she had to have been driving too fast. Normally, I would have scolded her for speeding, but in this case, it might very well have saved my brother's life.

I stood sentry by the bathroom door, waiting as the toilet

flushed and Piper came out.

"Phew." She sighed. "Much better."

"Good." I tugged her into my arms again. "I'm sorry I left like that."

"I know." She rested her ear against my chest. These days, with her belly protruding out so far, she stood kind of sideways to hug me.

I wrapped one arm behind her shoulder and let my other hand rest on her stomach. *Kick. Please, kick.* I needed some kind of reassurance that the boys were okay. That I hadn't caused them and Piper too much stress.

"Here." Piper took my hand, sliding over to the far side. And just like that, a small tap hit my palm.

Thank you. "I love you. All three of you."

"I know that too," she whispered. "But we can't stay in this hallway forever. You've got to go out there and face him. We have to put the past to rest so you can live for the future."

"I can't forgive him."

"I'm not asking you to. I'm just asking you to do whatever you can today to put it behind us."

I blew out a long breath, then nodded.

Her arms squeezed me tighter before letting go to follow me down the hallway.

In the living room, Isaiah was sitting in a recliner, his head tipped to the ceiling and a rag pressed to his nostrils. Mom came rushing out of the kitchen with a bag of frozen peas for his cheek.

While she fussed over him, I led Piper to the couch to sit. Across from us, a fire was burning in the fireplace, making the room toasty and too hot. But Mom always kept a fire going this time of year, even when the furnace kept the house plenty warm.

Mom shot me a glare as she pressed the bag of vegetables to

Isaiah's face. She could be pissed at me all she wanted, but I refused to feel guilty for kicking his ass. If not for Piper, he would have gotten all that and more.

"I really thought you were going to shoot him." Mom's angry voice filled the room.

"What? Shoot—"

My gun. I was still wearing my gun from hiking earlier. No wonder she'd looked so panicked.

"I wish you had," Isaiah whispered.

The air in the room turned ice-cold.

"Isaiah, don't say that." Mom covered her mouth with a hand, sinking down to the ledge of the fireplace. She reached over and covered one of his hands with hers—and the string of prison tattoos running up each of his fingers.

Isaiah slipped his hand free, pulling the bag of peas off his eye before sitting up. The rag to his nose was soaked.

"I broke your nose."

He nodded. "Yeah. But I learned how to set it back in prison."

With the rage no longer in control, it was harder not to feel bad for my brother. Just hours ago, I'd wished him two more years in prison. But now that I looked at him—really looked at him—I knew he wouldn't have survived it.

Had he been tortured by other inmates? Or did the haunted look in his eyes come from torturing himself?

"How long?" I asked. We both knew I was asking about Shannon.

"Since the beginning." He met my eyes. "I loved her since the beginning. After she moved in, we just hit it off. But with the baby and all that, I didn't know how you'd react."

"You should have told me." It wouldn't have mattered that they were together. He had to know that I didn't have feelings like that for Shannon. Didn't he? I'd told him. Hadn't I? The only reason we'd been living together was because of the baby.

"We were going to tell you. We were just waiting for the right time." A tear slid down Isaiah's face. "I asked her to marry me. That night. She said yes, and I had three beers instead of two to celebrate."

I closed my eyes, forcing a few breaths.

"Then I killed her."

"It was an accident," Mom corrected. "A tragic accident."

"No, Mom. I killed them." Isaiah's shoulders collapsed. "I killed them, and I have to live with that."

It wasn't just me who'd lived these last three years in pain and anguish. One stupid mistake had cost us all.

I'd escaped to my mountain and found the beautiful woman at my side. I was getting a second chance to be a father and to live with the love of my life.

But Shannon was gone. Isaiah wouldn't get a second chance.

No punishment I could ever deliver would be worse than the one he was inflicting upon himself.

As I looked into his eyes, the ones with the same colors as my own and Mom's, the hatred I had for Isaiah disappeared.

"It was an accident."

He shook his head. "No. I shouldn't have had those beers. I wasn't paying attention. I leaned over to kiss her and the next thing I knew, we were flying. Then they were dead."

"Isai—"

"I killed them. I killed Shannon. I killed your daughter." His words physically hurt to hear. "You deserve to hit me as many times as you want. I fucking hate me too."

Hearing the self-loathing in his voice struck a nerve. The agony on his face was too much to bear. I stood from the couch and crossed the room. Mom shot up too, standing guard, but I sent her a look asking for some trust.

Isaiah watched me with wide eyes as I hauled him out of the recliner by his sweatshirt. And just like Piper had done with me so many times, I hugged him.

I hugged the five-year-old boy who fell off his bike and scraped the shit out of his knee, all because he'd been trying to keep up with me and my friends as we'd peddled around the neighborhood.

I hugged the ten-year-old kid who'd begged me to help him practice fielding grounders before a baseball game.

I hugged my brother, the one who'd always looked at me like I was his Superman.

Isaiah collapsed into my chest, gripping the back of my sweater as he broke down. He cried in my arms, sobbing his apology over and over again.

I clung to him, holding him upright. Because that was my job. I was his big brother. I was supposed to be there for him. Despite everything, the pain and hurt, he needed me.

I'd been so lost these last three years. I realized as I held Isaiah, so much of my floundering was because I'd missed him. I'd missed our family. Me and Mom and Isaiah had always leaned on one another. Without them, I'd just been drifting—until a beautiful woman came into my world and saved it with her magic cake.

I glanced behind me at Piper. She swiped a tear with the back of her hand and wiped her nose dry as she sniffled.

Would things have been different if Isaiah and I had talked years ago? *Probably not.* After the accident, I'd been in too much pain to listen to anyone. The only thing I could do to keep on living was to block it out. To run and deal with the grief alone. To be numb.

Then Piper had made me feel again.

It took a while for Isaiah to get his emotions under control. Even then, I suspected it was only temporary. For all the pain I felt, it had dulled these last few months. But for Isaiah, it seemed as fresh as it had been the night of the accident.

I let him go and he sank down in the chair. Mom's hand went right back on top of his, and as I sat by Piper's side on the couch, I realized why Mom had chosen him.

It wasn't about choosing at all. It was about loving us both.

Isaiah had made the worst kind of mistake. The type that had forever changed the course of his life.

Maybe Mom had known I'd recover. Maybe she'd known I had the strength to move past it all. Maybe she'd known Isaiah needed all she had to pull through.

Maybe if I let go of my anger toward them, we'd all make it through.

"Breakfast tomorrow? Perkins?" It was Isaiah's favorite from when we were kids.

Mom nodded. "I'd like that."

Isaiah looked at me like I'd grown two heads but eventually blinked and nodded too.

"Meet you there at eight." I stood from the couch again and took Piper's hand to help her up.

"Nice to meet you both. See you in the morning." Piper waved good-bye and followed me outside. She'd parked the Tahoe right behind my truck so I led her to the passenger door and helped her inside.

"What about your truck?"

"I'll get it later. I want to show you something before it gets too dark."

Once we were both buckled, I drove her across town and right to the cemetery. There was barely enough light left as I led her past snowy graves.

"There." I pointed to the headstone.

"Oh, Kaine." Her hand went to her heart. "It's beautiful. Those angel wings. Thank you for bringing me here."

"I wanted you to see it. I want you to see everything."

Piper leaned into my side, wrapping an arm around my back. "I'm glad you brought me here."

"Me too." I held her close.

When I'd come here with Mom months ago, I hadn't been sure if I'd return again. But now, I knew this was it. This was good-bye. Starting now, I was putting all of this pain behind us.

I'd never forget Shannon. I'd never forget the precious baby who I'd laid to rest by her side.

But it was time to stop letting a tragedy run my life. It was time to stop moving backward.

It was time to let the beautiful people in this one grave rest knowing I'd found my peace too.

PIPER

"PIPER!" KAINE BELLOWED.

"What?" I yelled back.

"Come out here a sec."

I set down the plate of crackers I was eating in the kitchen and walked down the hall to the garage, where Kaine had been building shelves and organizing all morning.

It had been weeks since our frantic trip to Bozeman and Isaiah's release from prison. And it had taken until now for life to go back to some semblance of normalcy.

The night after Kaine and I left his daughter's grave, we made a quick stop at Target for some toothbrushes, pajamas and clean underwear, then we checked into a hotel, ordered room service and stayed in bed the rest of the night.

The next morning, we met his mom and Isaiah for breakfast.

I had hoped that after a restful night's sleep, emotions would have settled and our meal might be a happy one. I had hoped that both Kaine and Isaiah would find something easy to discuss over our meal and begin down the long road of repairing their relationship.

Unfortunately, my hopes were dashed ten minutes into breakfast.

Kaine was his usual quiet self, and Isaiah looked as miserable as he had the previous day. When Kaine asked Isaiah about his future now that he was on parole for two years, Isaiah just shrugged and drank his coffee.

After that, conversation at the table was nearly nonexistent. Suzanne and I chatted a bit about the twins, but the tension over eggs and pancakes was stifling, and eventually, we all just ate in silence before leaving with fast good-byes.

Though we invited them to Lark Cove for the holidays, I was relieved when Suzanne and Isaiah chose to stay in Bozeman.

So Kaine and I returned home just in time to prepare for my family to arrive. My parents got here just a week after we returned home. We'd barely had time to clean, do laundry and decorate the tree before it was time to play host and hostess.

But it was wonderful seeing my parents and brother. They were overjoyed to spend time in my new home and get to know Kaine. While Mom and I spent days baking and relaxing in front of my fireplace, Dad and Owen thought Kaine's shop and its plethora of power tools was heaven on earth.

For Christmas, Kaine surprised me with weekly massages until the boys were born. He'd bought enough so I could have one after each doctor's appointment. And I'd given him a new pair of boots since his were about shot.

My parents showered us with gifts for the boys, as expected. I'd told them not to get Kaine and me anything, and to my surprise, they'd listened. Instead, they'd bought plane tickets to come and see us again after the babies were born.

It was the best Christmas I'd had in ages. Mom and Dad told Kaine countless stories from my childhood. My brother told us all about the woman he'd been dating for the past six months. We laughed. We ate. They drank.

My family embraced Kaine like he'd been a part of our family forever, and I didn't miss how they were seemingly more comfortable with him than they'd ever been with Adam.

When we took them to the airport, Mom kissed Kaine's cheek and told him he'd make a wonderful father. Dad hugged him, thanking him for taking such good care of me. And my brother had already requested a week off work next summer so he and Kaine could take a backpacking trip into the mountains.

I was sad to see them go but ready for us to just be alone.

After weeks of chaos, we finally had the house to ourselves. Kaine had decided to skip work in the shop today to do some organizing in the garage. And I'd just finished working in my office, trying to catch up from only putting in short days while my family had been in town.

"You summoned me?" I teased with a smile from the doorway of the garage.

But my smile dropped when I saw what Kaine was holding in his hands. He'd found the painting Thea had given me months ago.

The painting I'd hidden in my garage, then forgotten about. *Damn pregnancy brain.*

"What's this?" he asked.

"It's, uh . . . a painting. Thea made it for me." I crossed the concrete floor and stood by his side. "It's of the day we saw you on the ridge. The first day we met."

"Huh."

I waited for what felt like hours for another word, but he just stared at the painting.

"I can give it back to Thea if it bothers you," I offered. Though the idea of losing it made my stomach churn.

"No," he said quietly. "You should hang it in your office."

I loved this painting and how Thea had captured his raw emotions, but I didn't want to see it every day. "Oh, no. That's okay. We can just tuck it away out here or in a closet."

"Why don't you want to hang it up?"

"Because." I gave him a sad smile. "I don't want to be reminded of you in pain."

"And I want you to always remember that you saved me." He set the painting down, resting it against his leg. Then he brushed a lock of hair behind the ear I'd always thought was too big. "Please?"

I might have saved him, but he completed me. And if he wanted this painting up, it would look incredible in my office. "Okay."

Kaine kissed my forehead, then picked up the painting. He took a hammer out of the tool bench he'd brought over earlier along with a nail. Then he walked inside.

I stayed in the garage, listening to a few thuds from the hammer as he hung up the painting in my office.

"I love you," I told him when he came back into the garage.

He set the hammer down and came to me for a hug. "Love you too."

"Do you, um . . ." I hesitated.

"Do I, what?"

Still want to get married?

The question had been on my tongue for weeks. And just like I had time and time again, I chickened out before letting it slip free. "Do you want tacos or pasta for dinner?"

"Either one. You choose."

"Tacos." I brushed my lips to his, then walked to the door.

Kaine went back to his shelves, making this place his own. And I went inside to cook dinner with a heavy heart.

Our visitors were gone. We were getting back into our routine where I worked in the office while Kaine created masterpieces in his shop. Where we ate dinner, relaxed on the couch and made love before going to sleep.

Life was going back to what it had been before Kaine's clash with Isaiah.

Except Kaine didn't ask me to marry him five times a day anymore. His proposals had stopped completely. The last time Kaine had asked me to marry him was before he'd gone out Christmas tree hunting.

I guess I'd said *no* one too many times.

"What are you doing here?" Logan asked, looking up from his laptop.

I held up a large envelope. "Getting your John Hancock on this contract."

He'd told me to take the week between Christmas and New Year's off, but I ignored him since there was just too much to do before my maternity leave.

Logan frowned and stood from his desk chair. He came around the desk and took the folder from my hand while simultaneously pulling out my chair. At least, *I'd* dubbed it my chair. It was the one I sat in whenever I came down to work in his office.

"Thanks." I sank into the seat, grateful to have the weight off my cankles.

"You know, I could have come up to you."

I shrugged. "I had to come down anyway. I thought I'd just hang out here until I need to meet Kaine at the bar."

It was New Year's Eve and the Lark Cove Bar was having a party. Thea and Jackson had pulled out all of the stops, decorating the bar. Now it wasn't just rustic, it was sparkly rustic. They'd ordered two cases of champagne and an extra half dozen bottles of tequila. Thea had even invented a special New Year's Eve pizza, which was just pizza with the year spelled out in pepperoni.

I couldn't think of a better way to ring in the new year than laughing and enjoying the evening with friends. And I couldn't wait to kiss Kaine at midnight, though with how badly my feet hurt these days, I probably wouldn't last until nine.

"What's Kaine up to?" Logan asked, resuming his seat.

"He had to run up to Kalispell for the day to pick up some supplies he ordered from the lumberyard."

"He's coming for the party though, right?"

I nodded. "He promised to be back by five."

Logan opened the envelope and signed the page marked with the little green flag. Then he slid the papers back into the envelope and handed it back. With a snap, he shut his laptop and signaled that work was done for the day.

I listened for sounds of the kids from the other room—my favorite part about working at Logan and Thea's—but it was quiet. "Where are the kids?"

"Already at Hazel's for the night. I told her I'd bring them over, but I guess I was taking too long because she came over after lunch and kidnapped them."

I smiled. "They'll have fun."

And I hoped next year, I could talk her into taking the twins too. Though, I doubted it would take much convincing. Hazel might be a grandmother to Logan and Thea's kids, but she'd already laid claim to my boys. On more than one occasion, she'd insisted on babysitting for us after their birth because newborns were her specialty.

"So . . ." Logan sighed. "I got an email today."

I sat straighter, not liking Logan's uneasy tone. "From?"

"Adam."

"Seriously?" I grumbled. "He's getting desperate if he's emailing you now. What did it say?"

"He just asked if I'd pass along a request for you to call him."

Adam had been emailing me for months. It wasn't often, but about every three weeks, I'd see his name pop up in my inbox. I'd hoped that in time, he'd realize I wasn't going to respond. I still hadn't blocked his email address, mostly because his messages were a minor irritation I forgot about immediately after hitting delete. But if he'd resorted to hassling Logan, then my avoidance tactics weren't going to work.

"Ugh. I'll call him later."

"He's, um, also getting a call from Kaine."

"What?" If not for the fact that I moved like a sloth these days, I would have shot out of my chair. "You told Kaine?"

He held up his hands. "If Thea's ex-husband were emailing her boss after she'd already told the guy to piss off, I'd want my friend to tell me about it too."

When I'd called Kaine earlier, he'd been cryptic, saying we had something to talk about later. Now I knew what that something was. He'd gotten tipped off to the emails I'd been hiding from him. *Busted.*

"Is this how it's going to be now?" I asked Logan, holding back a smile. "You're always going to be on his side."

"Hey, it's about damn time." He grinned. "You and Thea gang up on me constantly. And that's just with stuff around here. Let's not even talk about all of your alliances at work. This was my shot to take back some of my power and I took it."

"Whatever." I crossed my arms, pretending to be mad. It lasted about five seconds before I broke into a laugh.

The truth was, I was happy that Logan and Kaine were friends. I'd been nervous after Kaine had blown a fuse the day of the Christmas tree hunt. I'd figured that Logan would go all overprotective, worrying about my safety with Kaine and warning me about getting involved with a man who had anger issues.

But like he often did, Logan Kendrick surprised me. He'd

never once mentioned Kaine's outburst. He'd simply asked if things were okay. I'd told him and Thea all about the incident in Bozeman, and they'd been nothing but supportive.

They understood that Kaine's anger had all stemmed from pain. And slowly, he was healing.

I was proud of how Kaine had taken the lead in his family's dynamic. He talked to his mom almost daily. And he'd had two phone calls with Isaiah in the last few weeks. Though they had both been short, mostly just saying hello, followed by uncomfortable silence before hanging up.

It was progress. Still, I didn't like that Kaine had any kind of animosity in his life, especially from someone he clearly loved.

"What's that look for?" Logan asked.

I unfurrowed my forehead. "Oh, I was just thinking about Isaiah. And Kaine."

"Give them time. From what I can tell, Kaine's put a lot of this behind him. Mostly because of you. I think the question now is not whether Kaine will ever forgive Isaiah. It's whether *Isaiah* will forgive Isaiah."

"I wish I could help."

"You can't fix this one, Piper."

"You're right." I nodded and waved it off. "Anyway. I didn't mean to talk about something so serious. It's just been on my mind." And the fact that ever since their confrontation, Kaine had stopped proposing.

He still kissed me and touched me at every opportunity. He made love to me almost every night. He told me he loved me. He looked at me and the rest of the world disappeared, just like I'd always wanted. So why, when I was so desperate to say yes, had he stopped asking me to be his wife?

I'd found the ring he'd bought for me hidden the other day. I'd just happened to be doing his laundry—and snooping. I'd found it tucked into the pocket of a pair of jeans he never wore.

He hadn't gotten rid of the ring, so why had he stopped asking? Had this entire debacle with his family changed his mind?

Today was the last day of the year, and I didn't want to go into the next with so many unanswered questions and loose ends.

I needed to call Adam and put an end to his emails once and for all. Then Kaine and I would need to have a serious conversation. I pushed up and out of my chair, determined to make the last hours of this year count.

"That look is scaring me," Logan teased.

"I have a phone call to make." First, I was going to deal with the man I'd divorced. Then I'd deal with the man I wanted to marry.

"Don't tell Adam I said hello."

I giggled and waved good-bye to Logan. "See you at the bar."

"Are you going straight there?"

"Uh, yeah. Why?"

"No reason." He shrugged. "I'm just heading down right behind you."

"Okay. See you there." I let myself out of his house and waddled carefully across their driveway to my SUV. I climbed inside and let the heater run for a moment before pulling up Adam's number on the dash.

It only rang once before he answered. "Pip?"

"Adam." I sighed. "You can't email my boss."

"I needed to talk to you."

"Five minutes." I put the Tahoe in reverse and backed out of the driveway slowly. I'd give Adam the time it took me to get to the bar.

"I'm sorry," he said. "That's it. I just wanted to say I was sorry."

My foot hit the brake and I waited a few seconds for the excuses. But he said nothing. "Are you there?"

"I'm here."

"That's it? Just . . . you're sorry?"

"Well, I had more, but your boyfriend called me earlier and told me that if I said anything other than *I'm sorry*, he'd be on the first flight out to New York to rearrange my face. He was . . . convincing."

I snorted a laugh. Kaine's threat had to have been quite colorful for Adam to actually hear it.

"He also informed me that if you did call, it would be the last time we spoke."

"No more emails either," I warned.

"No more emails."

I lifted my foot off the brake, navigating down the narrow road that led to the highway. Divorcing Adam had nearly broken me. But in a small way, I was grateful. Because here I was.

Home.

I'd found the love of my life, and even if we didn't get married, the commitment we had for one another was stronger than the bond I'd worked a decade to build with Adam.

"Good-bye, Adam. I wish you the best."

"Same to you, Piper. Take care."

I ended the call right as I reached the stop sign to turn onto the highway. But before I did, I pulled up Adam's contact one last time. And hit delete.

"One last thing to do this year," I told the empty car, then drove it to the bar.

Kaine's truck was in the parking lot, which was a surprise. I thought I'd beat him here and kill some time helping Thea with whatever decorating she wanted to do. When I pushed through the door, he was sitting at the bar with a glass of ice water in front of him and a second waiting in front of the stool at his side.

"Is this for me?" I asked, taking the seat. "You're here early."

"Hi." He leaned over and kissed my cheek. "Yeah, finished up fast. Got here a couple of minutes ago."

"Where is everyone?" It was still early, but I'd expected to see at least Thea or Jackson behind the bar.

"Kitchen. Thea's prepping pizzas. Jackson went to change a keg of beer."

"Ahh." I sipped my water and glanced around the room. Since I'd stopped in yesterday, Thea had added more streamers to the iron beams that ran across the ceiling and she'd sprinkled confetti on all the tables.

"How are you feeling?" Kaine ran a hand up and down my back. He always managed to find the tight spots with one pass, and his fingertips began working out a sore spot underneath my shoulder blade.

"Good." I leaned closer. "I hear you talked to my ex-husband today."

He grunted. "If he calls or emails again, I'd better hear about it from *you*. Not Logan."

"He won't be calling again. But if he does, you'll be the first to know."

Kaine kissed my temple. "Got a surprise for you today."

"Hmm." I closed my eyes as his hand kept massaging. "I like surprises."

"You can have it after the party."

"Okay. Maybe we could duck out of here early. I need to talk to you about something in private."

His hand froze. "What's wrong?"

"Nothing."

"People don't say they need to talk about something in private when everything's good. So what's wrong?"

"Nothing!" I insisted, shying away from the scowl on his face.

Damn it. I should have kept my mouth shut. But pregnancy only allowed my brain to function until four in the afternoon, and since it was close to five, strategic thinking was a crapshoot.

"Piper."

"Kaine." I mimicked his angry tone.

He stared at me, waiting, but I just stared back. There was no way I was going to talk about his proposals—or lack thereof—when my boss was due to arrive in seconds and the entire town of Lark Cove would soon be crowded around us to toast the new year.

"It's nothing," I lied, patting his leg.

He huffed. "God, you're a shit liar."

Before I could protest—because I wasn't a bad liar, just an unpracticed one—he bellowed toward the back. "Thea!"

"What?" she called back.

"We're going to skip the party."

"Kaine! No, we're not, Thea!" I yelled as she came out from the back, wiping her hands on a towel.

"Okay. You guys have a happy New Year's Eve. Call me tomorrow."

"Seriously?" I asked as she rounded the bar. She wasn't mad that we were missing the party she'd been planning for a month?

No, she isn't. Thea smiled and hugged me tight just as Logan walked in the front door.

"Leaving already?" Logan asked with a smirk as Kaine helped me off my stool.

"Kaine, I'm not missing this party."

His answer? Silence.

"Do you think ignoring a hugely pregnant woman is wise?"

He grunted.

The man was lucky he was so hot. It was impossible for me to stay angry at that face.

With one hand gripping my elbow, he waved good-bye to Thea and Logan, then to Jackson, who'd also come out from behind the bar—laughing.

"I told you it was nothing," I snapped as we walked outside and to my car. "Can we just go back inside now? I have to pee."

"What did I just tell you about lying?"

Damn it again. I didn't have to pee.

"I got all dressed up for this party."

He raised an eyebrow. "Trying to impress someone other than me?"

"Women dress up to impress other women," I informed him as he opened up the passenger door to the Tahoe.

"And I'm sure Thea was impressed. Up you go."

"What about your truck?"

He answered by slamming the door.

I crossed my arms over my chest, resting my forearms on my belly. Then begrudgingly buckled up.

There was no way we'd be staying for this party. Kaine thought something was wrong, which it kind of was, and he was on a mission to solve my problems.

I pouted the entire drive up the mountain until he pulled into the driveway. Then I gasped. Because in my driveway—our driveway—was an Airstream.

"You bought a camper?"

"No, I got *our* camper. Logan and I made a trade. Thea's got a new bedroom set waiting when she gets home tonight."

"Oh my god." I stretched my arms for Kaine's face, framing it and pulling him closer for a kiss. The minute his soft lips touched mine, I melted. "I'm not upset about the party anymore."

"There's something else I want to show you." He kissed me again before getting out and coming around the Tahoe. He helped me down and then led me to the Airstream's door.

The generator behind the camper was running so I wasn't surprised when the inside was toasty warm.

"It feels smaller than I remembered. Though that's probably because I've turned into a hungry-hungry hippo."

"Hey." He stepped inside behind me, wrapping his arms around my chest. "Don't say bad things about my wife."

"It's tru—" Wait. *Did he say wife?* "Did you just say wife?"

"Yup."

"But you stopped proposing."

"Did I?"

With his hard chest against my back and one arm trapping me tight, he used the other to pull something from his pocket. It was my ring.

He spun me around, then dropped to a knee. "Marry me?"

"Yes."

He grinned and slid the ring on my finger. "It's about damn time."

"I love you."

Kaine surged to his feet, framing my face with his hands. "I love you. I'll love you every day for the rest of your life."

I leaned closer, smiling against his lips and whispered, "Prove it."

epilogue

KAINE

Two and a half years later . . .

"WHERE DID PIPER GO?"

Piper's mom shrugged from the leather couch. Her dad did the same from the armchair I'd made last summer. Both of them were too busy cooing over my baby niece playing on the floor to even look up and answer my question.

Earlier today, Piper had been right here too, sitting in her corner of the couch. But even with the baby in her arms, she'd been off this morning. She'd been quiet and distant. I'd figured it was just because she was tired. We'd had company for the past week, and on top of that, the twins had been up and down all last night. Gabe and Robbie had just learned how to crawl out of their cribs, so we'd gotten late-night visitors in our room three times.

But when I'd left the house an hour ago, taking Isaiah with me to the shop, Piper had been smiling in the kitchen. She'd seemed back to her normal self.

Except now I couldn't find her, and I had a sinking feeling in my gut that something was wrong.

Since her parents were of no help, I left them and continued through the house. I'd already checked the boys' room and our bedroom without luck. I peeked into the guest room but she wasn't there. Her brother and his wife were both zonked out on the bed, taking advantage of a nap while Grandma and Grandpa were babysitting their three-month-old daughter.

I crept down the hall, treading lightly toward the laundry room.

"Damn." She wasn't anywhere in the house.

I went outside through the garage's back door and scanned the yard. All I saw were toys scattered across the grass and a stack of lumber next to the far side of the fence.

The yard was a new addition to our home. We'd brought in a skid steer last summer and graded a level spot to put down some sod. Then we'd swapped out the dining room windows for French doors and built a porch, and now we had a place where the boys could play outside.

I was in the middle of building them the mother of all tree houses in a grove of trees in the far corner of the yard. It was going to have stairs and a ladder. The house itself would be big enough for them no matter how old they got. With four walls and a sturdy roof, they'd be able to camp out here when they got older.

I walked through the yard, gathering up squirt guns, footballs and a plastic yellow baseball bat. After dumping them in the outdoor toy box, I walked over to the gate and let myself out to head toward my old cabin.

At the same time we'd cleared an area for the yard, I'd also decided that the footpath between the cabin and our house wasn't enough. So I'd bulldozed a narrow gravel road between them. Now, if someone came up one side of the mountain to go to one of the houses, you didn't have to drive all the way back down to get to the other.

Halfway across the road, I smiled as laughter and barking echoed from inside the cabin. The squeals and giggles got louder as I approached.

I bounded up the stairs, grinning at the chainsaw marks on the porch boards. I'd replaced the chair that I'd hacked to pieces, but the marks had stayed. They reminded me of how miserable and lonely my life had been. They reminded me of how lucky I was now.

Without knocking, I opened the door to my former home.

In the middle of the floor, Robbie and Gabe were climbing all over Koda, our dog.

We'd bought him as a puppy not long after the boys were born. He'd started off small, but full grown, he was a beast. He weighed just over a hundred pounds and resembled a wolf, though the boys treated him more like a horse and were constantly riding him around.

Robbie was currently draped over Koda's back while Gabe was doing his best to wrestle the braided rope toy from Koda's mouth. The dog looked up at me, acknowledging my presence, then tugged harder on the rope, sending Gabe crashing to the floor in a heap of laughter.

I hadn't believed that dogs could smile before I'd watched Koda play with the boys. But he was grinning ear to ear, happy to be with his two favorite humans.

Meanwhile, Mom was sitting on the floor with them, her phone out and camera clicking as she took probably the thousandth photo of the day.

"Have you seen my wife?" I asked.

"No." She smiled. "Sorry. I've been busy trying to keep these two alive."

I chuckled. "It's a full-time job."

Except for the deep-brown eyes that matched Piper's, the

boys were my spitting image. With my dark hair and their own mischievous smiles, Robbie and Gabe found trouble faster than Koda could chase a squirrel up a tree.

At two years old, safety wasn't a concept they'd grasped yet. If there was a table to climb and jump off of, they found it. If there was a drawer or cabinet in the house with sharp objects, they'd open it. If there was a staircase or hill they could throw themselves down, away they went.

They sought out danger, all while roughhousing with each other. One or both always had a bruise or black eye. Knees were always skinned and elbows scraped. They pushed and wrestled constantly.

"Daddy!" Gabe finally noticed me and abandoned the rope toy. He pushed up onto his feet and raced my way. His feet couldn't keep up with his head as he ran my way and he dove into my legs. I caught him before he could fall, just in time to catch his brother.

"How are my boys?"

"Goot," Robbie declared as I hoisted them each on a hip.

They were slow to talk, but over the last month, their words had come like a flood, though they replaced *d* with *t* most of the time and sentences were spoken slowly.

"Where. Mommy?" Gabe asked, a clear break between his words.

"I don't know where she went."

He frowned. "Want. Nack."

Snack.

"Nack!" Robbie squirmed out of my grip, dropping to the floor. He fell to his knees but quickly scrambled back up, leading the race to the cabinets as Gabe wiggled his way down too.

"I'll help." Mom stood from the floor, going over to the cabinets.

She'd come up two weeks ago to stay in the cabin. We used it for any guests, but she was our most frequent visitor. She'd come for a couple of weeks every few months, and each time, she'd bring a haul of snacks for the boys. They knew right where she kept the Fruit Roll-Ups and Goldfish crackers.

"I'm going to find Piper. Are you good?" I asked. Babysitting the boys could be exhausting, and I didn't want her to get too worn out.

She waved me away. "We're great. I'll bring them over later."

"Thanks, Mom." I left them to their snacking and went back outside. Koda stood to follow, but I motioned for him to stay. At least with him there, Mom had a helper.

My relationship with Mom had gotten easier since the boys were born. The animosity I had for her just . . . disappeared. I guess I never wanted Robbie or Gabe to see any strife between their father and their grandmother. They loved her so completely, and she them, that it wasn't worth holding on to my anger toward her.

From the cabin, I walked down to the shop. I'd just come from there, but I was running out of places to search for Piper. And with both of our properties, there was a chance that she'd come while I was going.

But when I opened the door, it was only Isaiah inside. He was still tinkering on the engine to the wood lathe that had quit on me last week.

"I don't suppose Piper stopped by here, did she?"

He looked up, his hands covered in grease. "No. I haven't seen her since breakfast."

I frowned. "How's it coming?"

"Good." Isaiah reached for a rag to clean off one hand, then flipped the switch on the lathe. It spun to life without the squeak I'd gotten used to over the last year and sounded as good as the day I'd bought it.

"Fixed." He grinned. "Told you I could save you a couple grand."

"Damn. Then I guess I'll just have to pay you instead."

"Nah." He shut off the lathe and finished wiping his hands. "It's just a hobby."

"You've always liked engines. Maybe you should look for a job as a mechanic."

Isaiah sighed and looked at his feet. This was about the time that I expected him to shut down.

Whenever I brought up the future or things he could make of himself, he'd go quiet. He still hadn't told me what had happened to him in prison. I'd only asked once and I'd gotten silence for three months as an answer. Eventually he'd returned my phone calls, but since, I hadn't pushed.

Isaiah had changed since the accident. He was still living with pain and regret. Piper's theory was that he didn't want to think about the future because he didn't think he deserved one. Maybe she was right.

But like with Mom, the last couple of years had changed my feelings toward Isaiah. I didn't hold ill will toward my brother. He deserved to find some of the happiness that I'd been lucky enough to find in my life.

Stocking shelves at night at Costco didn't make him happy. It paid for his portion of the grocery bill at Mom's and some utilities. But he wasn't happy.

"I've been thinking about that," Isaiah said. "I, um . . . I actually got offered a job working at a garage in Clifton Forge. They do a lot of remodels on old classics. Pay isn't great but it sounds like a cool gig. One of the guys I was inside with contacted me about it."

"Really?" I asked, trying to hide the shock that he'd just

willingly confided in me. "Are you going to take it?"

He shrugged. "Maybe."

Isaiah didn't say anything more, and I didn't press. We were still feeling each other out, still redefining our relationship. Maybe one day things would be back to the easy friendship we'd had once.

"I'd better try and track Piper down. See you back at the house."

He waved as I turned and left the shop. I walked back home and did another pass through the house but still couldn't find her. So I went to the last place she might have gone without leaving me a note.

The Airstream.

We parked it alongside the garage rather than in the driveway. There, it was out of the way and could be hooked up to the power from the house rather than a generator. We'd offered it to her parents for the week they were visiting, but they'd decided to rent a place on the lake for a change. They'd also rented a boat and tomorrow I was going to teach Piper how to water-ski.

The moment I rounded the garage, I spotted a light on inside the Airstream.

"There you are," I said as I opened the door. She was sitting at the small table across from the kitchen, the same one where we'd shared our first meal together. "I've been look—what's wrong?"

She sniffled and wiped her eyes dry. "It's nothing. I'm just tired."

"Piper," I warned.

She rolled her eyes, still swiping at the tears. "I'm fine."

As I stepped into the camper, I saw dishes in the sink. The oven was on and it smelled like chocolate.

"Are you baking?"

She nodded just as a sob burst loose.

My heart broke as I crossed the floor in two long strides, pulling her out of the bench seat and into my arms. "What's wrong?"

"I forgot how to make my magic cake," she cried into my shirt.

"Magic cake?"

She nodded. "The last five times I've tried to make it, something has gone wrong. The cake isn't dense enough. The frosting doesn't taste right. They've all been bad."

As the taste tester for these alleged failed cakes, I had no idea what she was talking about. "Can't you just follow the recipe?"

"No!" She leaned back and glared. "You don't make magic cake from a recipe."

"Right." *Sorry I asked.* "Can you call your aunt?"

"I already did." She huffed and stepped back, walking to the small oven and peering through the glass window. "I'm doing everything right. It's just not working. So I came in here to try a different oven. It worked in here when I made it before."

There was more going on here than a need for chocolate. She only made that cake when something was wrong. And as far as I knew, things in our life couldn't be more right.

Nine months after the boys were born, Piper and I had gotten married in a small ceremony at a guest ranch in Kalispell. From the day she'd walked down the aisle in that fancy rustic lodge wearing a white-lace, strapless gown, I could count on one hand the number of bad days we'd had compared to the good.

"Why do you need magic cake?" I asked gently.

"Because," she turned from the oven, "I'm pregnant."

I swayed on my feet. "We're pregnant?"

"Yup." She nodded, her eyes filling with more tears.

"That's . . . fuck. Yes!" I clapped and let out a whoop, my

excitement too big for this small camper. "Hell yes! I hope it's a girl." I fist pumped, then swiped Piper's arm and pulled her back into my chest. "I love you."

But instead of saying it back or smiling, she burst into tears.

"This is amazing news. Why are you crying?"

"Because I'm worried we used it all up."

"Used what up?"

"Our magic," she whispered.

Our magic. Now I understood why she was so worried.

While the beginning of Piper's pregnancy with the boys had gone smoothly, the last month had been unbearable. She'd been placed on bed rest due to high blood pressure. But after two weeks of only getting up to use the bathroom, it hadn't helped. Things only got worse.

The doctors had monitored her closely, but five weeks before her due date, they'd decided to induce because she was showing other signs of preeclampsia.

The boys had spent their first ten days in the hospital, being monitored. The ten days after we brought them home, I hadn't slept. I'd convinced myself that if I fell asleep, something would happen to them.

Basically, I'd gone crazy.

Until finally, my body had shut down. I'd dropped, dead on my feet, in the kitchen one day. Piper had been so worried that she'd called an ambulance.

They'd tried to keep me in the hospital overnight, but I'd refused.

That had been the low point.

Logan had picked me up from the hospital and brought me home. Thea had been here, helping Piper when I walked through the door. My mother had shown up two hours later. Piper's mom six hours after that, courtesy of the Kendrick private jet.

That night, I'd confessed to Piper how terrified I was that something would happen to our family. I'd let my fears from what happened with Shannon and my daughter drive me insane.

Then I'd promised never to let her down like that again.

This time around, I'd do better.

"It's going to be okay," I promised. Then I took her face in my hands and gazed at her beautiful face. The face that started and ended my day. "We've got a lifetime of magic left."

"How can you be so sure?"

"Because it was never the cake." I brushed my lips against hers. "The magic is us."

One year later, as our daughter Grace rested in my arms, Piper stood in the doorway of the nursery, watching as I rocked our baby girl to sleep.

"You were right," she whispered, her dark eyes sparkling with the moonlight. "It was never the cake."

I smiled at my wife and kissed Grace's forehead.

Magic.

Enjoy this preview from *Tinsel*,
book four in the Lark Cove series.

tinsel

prologue

SOFIA

Kindergarten

"POP! LOOK IT!" WITH A SMILE STRETCHED ACROSS MY face, I slid my drawing down the table toward Grandpa's seat.

His black-rimmed glasses were perched on the tip of his nose as he bent over my brother's homework. "So when you're changing a percentage to a whole number, all you have to do is move the decimal two places."

"Like this?" Logan asked, drawing a dot on his paper between some numbers.

"Exactly." Pop clapped him on the shoulder. "And then to change a whole number into a percentage, just—"

"Pop!" I shuffled my drawing, the paper swishing on the wooden table. "Look what I did."

That got his attention. He looked away from Logan's homework and picked up the drawing I'd done of our family, adjusting his glasses higher on his nose as he took it in. "Now what's this?"

"It's our family." I beamed with pride at the picture I'd drawn. "My teacher said we could draw our families on this paper, and then we get to hang them on the big board in my classroom tomorrow."

"Very nice."

"That's me." I pointed to the smallest person on the page. I'd used everyone's favorite color to draw them, so mine was in pink. "And there's Mommy in green. And that's Daddy in blu—"

"Pop, can you help me with my math too?" Aubrey shoved her way in between me and Pop.

"Sure, sweetheart."

I frowned when he slid my drawing away and shifted his seat to make room for my sister's homework.

"I did you in red, Pop. See?" I pushed the drawing back.

"Looks beautiful, princess," he said, though his eyes were locked on Aubrey's textbook.

I pouted. "You didn't look."

He sighed and met my gaze. "It's wonderful. Now you keep coloring while I help Logan and Aubrey with their important homework. Okay?"

"Okay," I muttered, taking *my* homework back. Then I slipped off my chair, which was quickly filled by Aubrey, and left the dining room.

Third Grade

"Daddy, are you coming to my recital?" I asked, standing in the doorway to his office.

He glanced at me, then looked back at the mirror as he adjusted his tie. "I can't tonight. I have a meeting."

"You always have meetings," I muttered.

"Enough of that pouting, Sofia." The line between his eyebrows deepened as he scowled. "Adults have to work. Someday you'll understand."

I might only be eight, but I understood already. Daddy

worked all the time. If we wanted to spend time with him, we had to come into his office.

I *hated* this room.

I hated the dark bookshelves that bordered the walls. I hated the leather couch that faced the gas fireplace. I hated the smell of his cigars that would stick to my hair. I really hated the desk in the middle of the room that sat on an ugly, expensive rug Mommy had picked out special last year.

I hated it all because Daddy spent more time in here than anywhere else in this house, including his own bedroom. If he was even home.

His fancy office in the city was even more hated than this one.

Because when he wasn't here, he was there. Or at dinner meetings, missing my important things. He didn't miss Aubrey's or Logan's things. Last week he'd gone to one of Aubrey's school debates. And he'd been at Logan's last soccer game.

I dropped my chin so he wouldn't see it quiver. "You miss all my recitals."

I'd been practicing my dance routine *so* hard for this recital because I got to be the leader of the chorus in front of all the other girls. My teacher had picked *me* to be first, and Daddy was going to miss it. But dance wasn't important to Daddy, not like the stuff Aubrey and Logan did at school. Ballet wasn't *practical*.

Daddy sighed, something he did a lot with me, and finished with his tie. Then he crossed the room to bend down in front of me. "I wish I could go to all of your recitals. But I have an important job."

"I never want to have an important job."

He chuckled and tipped my chin up. "Then you never have to. You can do whatever you want, my darling. Now give me a hug and then I've got to go."

I looped my little arms around his neck and squeezed him hard. Then I watched as he went out one door to work, and I went out the other to my recital.

One that he missed, along with all the others.

Sixth Grade

"But, Mom!" My voice echoed through the limousine.

"No, Sofia. You're not going."

I crossed my arms over my chest and scowled at the back of the driver's head. "This isn't fair."

"If you want to go to fashion week, I'll take you in a few years. But right now, I don't have the time to plan a trip to Paris."

I rolled my eyes. She didn't have time? *Yeah, right.*

She just didn't want me to go with Regan because her mom—an interior decorator—had called our house *out of touch.* Which was why Mom had acted on a sudden "whim" to redecorate. We'd been dealing with her own interior decorator coming in and out of our house for the last two months with painters and flooring specialists and construction people in tow.

"Logan gets to go to Washington DC later this year," I reminded her. "And you let Aubrey fly across the country to Seattle, like, a month ago."

"Logan is almost eighteen and going to DC for his senior-class trip. Aubrey went to Seattle for a Future Business Leaders of America national conference. Fashion week for an eleven-year-old is a bit different, don't you think?"

"Whatever," I mumbled. "Maybe fashion is what I want to do when I grow up."

Logan and Aubrey were already poised to take over the

Kendrick family empire. Dad had plans for them both. And me? I could do whatever I wanted, just like he'd always told me.

What I wanted was to go to fashion week in Paris with my friend so we could come back home and brag about it at school.

"You're not going."

I hunched my shoulders forward, casting my eyes down to my lap. Then I let out a deep breath and lowered my voice. This pout was something I'd been practicing lately. It worked on Daddy like a charm, but so far, my luck with Mom had been hit or miss.

"Okay, fine. But would you take me shopping?" I asked. "Regan told me that she overheard Louisa Harty in the bathroom call my clothes *old lady*. I was hoping to pick up some tips from fashion week so she wouldn't make fun of me anymore."

"What?" Mom gaped, turning in her seat next to me.

I held back a smile that my fib had worked.

"Your clothes are not *old lady*," she said. "Everything you wear is this season and on trend."

I shrugged. "I thought so too, but . . ."

"We'll go together." Mom dug into her purse for her phone. "Besides, you're right. If this is what you want to do for your career, then you might as well get started early."

Before we made it home, she'd planned a trip for the two of us to Paris and gotten front-row seats along one of the most exclusive runways at the event, something Regan's mom would never have been able to secure.

As we pulled into the courtyard in front of our estate, a pang of regret poked my side for tricking Mom. Fashion wasn't all that interesting and certainly not something I wanted to do as a *job*.

Logan was the smart Kendrick child, the golden boy who would become a business tycoon like our father Thomas. Daddy was always taking time to mentor him. Aubrey too. She constantly earned praise for how *bright* she was. She'd be right behind Logan, going to work with Daddy in the city every day.

My role in the Kendrick family was different. I wasn't going to get a job and miss out on the fun stuff. I wasn't going to spend more time in my office than exploring the world. I wasn't going to just let my money pile up in the bank when I could use it for an adventure.

Logan could be the future leader of the Kendrick family and Dad's right-hand man. Aubrey could be the gifted daughter Mom bragged about in her weekly society club meetings.

I had my own path in mind.

I was going to be the princess.

one

SOFIA

"Sofia, you're gorgeous." Malcom kept the camera pressed to his face as he moved behind me to shoot at a different angle.

I held my pose, keeping the pensive look frozen on my face, though I was smiling on the inside. Malcom didn't need to tell me how beautiful I looked today. I felt it.

My hair was pinned up in a billowing crown of espresso curls that had taken my stylist nearly two hours to perfect. My makeup had been applied by two artists who'd contoured and highlighted me so expertly I wouldn't need Photoshop touch-ups. And the outfit the magazine had chosen for me was straight off the runway.

My dress was a white strapless piece that fit snuggly to my chest. The sweetheart neckline plunged deep, giving me the illusion of cleavage. The A-line, tulle skirt poofed wide at my hips, making my waist look impossibly tiny.

It was freezing now that the sun was setting on this deserted corner of Central Park. We'd gotten an early snowfall this November, and the trees around us glittered with ice crystals and tufts of snow.

But I was surprisingly warm thanks to the white fur wrap looped over my arms and strung across the middle of my back.

My bare shoulders were still exposed to the cold, but excitement and anticipation kept the chill from soaking in.

I was going to be in a magazine. Me. Sofia Kendrick.

I'd made the society columns countless times. My name graced their pages whenever my family made a sizeable donation to a local charity or whenever one of my relationships failed. The press had spent weeks speculating why both of my marriages had ended. But this magazine article wasn't about my family or my failures. It was a feature about me and four other New York socialites, showcasing our unique lifestyle.

The reporter had already interviewed me for the piece, and after the photo shoot was complete, I'd only have to wait six short weeks until I could show off my magazine.

"Tilt your head down and to the left just slightly."

I did as Malcom ordered, the clicks from his camera telling me I'd gotten it right.

"Damn." He came to my side, showing me the display screen on the back of his camera.

This time my smile couldn't be contained.

He'd nailed it.

Malcom had captured me in profile, finding just the right angle so my face was in shadow compared to the bare skin on my shoulders. The late-afternoon light cast a golden glow on my already flawless complexion, accentuating the long lines of my neck. My Harry Winston earrings dangled from my ears and matched the ring on my right hand, which Malcom had delicately positioned in front of my chin.

Malcom's assistant nosed in next to him to see the camera. "That's your cover."

"The cover?" My mouth fell open.

"Ultimately the magazine has final say," Malcom said. "But this is the best picture I've shot for this project. Once I do some minor edits, it'll be the clear choice."

A feature in the magazine's interior was definitely worth boasting about. But the cover? That was on par with my sister's accolades.

Aubrey was always being mentioned and discussed in Fortune 500 magazines or in periodicals like the *Wall Street Journal*. This feature would be in *NY Scene* magazine, and though it was a lesser-known publication, it had been gaining a lot of popularity lately. People were calling *NY Scene* the next *New Yorker*.

And I was going to be on the cover for their New Year's edition.

Maybe the lifestyle I'd chosen wasn't such a mockery after all.

Maybe I'd finally be seen as something more than the *other* Kendrick child, the pretty one who hadn't amounted to much.

"Sofia, how could you not tell me about the article? You know we have to be careful around the press."

"I wanted it to be a surprise. And I didn't say anything bad. She took everything I said and twisted it around!" I wailed into the phone as I sat in a crumpled heap on my living room floor.

Tears coated my cheeks. Snot dripped from my nostrils. My normally tan and bright skin was a blotchy mess, and my eyes were too puffy. I was the definition of an ugly cry.

All because of that miserable magazine.

I'd been so excited an hour ago when my doorman had brought up ten copies of *NY Scene*. I'd ordered extra so I'd have some to give to my parents and some to get framed.

But that was an hour ago, before I'd read the article.

Now I was dealing with the aftermath of another classic Sofia mistake. It never got easier to hear that I'd let down my father. It always hurt to read one of my sister's condemning texts.

Seriously? Could you at least try not to embarrass us?

It stung, though the pain was just a dull ache compared to my own agonizing humiliation. The words the reporter had used to describe me were cruel. Reading them had been like taking a lash to my skin.

Instead of stylish, she'd called me superficial and gaudy.

Instead of charming, she'd called me naïve and phony.

Instead of witty, she'd called me flighty.

Clearly, the woman had mixed up notes between interviews. That, or my self-image was off a touch.

"Sofia." Daddy sighed, his disappointment seeping through the phone. "I'll see if there is anything we can do, but since you didn't run this by me first, I doubt we'll be able to pull a retraction."

"O-okay." I hiccupped. "I'm s-sorry."

"I know you are. But next time you're asked to give an interview, I think you'd better have one of our lawyers come along too."

So basically, Daddy thought I needed a babysitter to speak. My sobs returned full force, and I barely heard him say his goodbye before hanging up.

I tossed my phone onto the carpet next to me and my ten magazines then buried my face in my hands.

Everything was ruined. The reporter had been thorough in her portrayal of my life. She had found every unflattering detail and put them front and center in the article.

She'd written about both of my failed marriages and how

I'd rushed into each, only dating my former husbands briefly before walking down the aisle in multimillion-dollar ceremonies.

She'd made sure to tell the world that I'd never had a job, and rather than dedicating my time to my family's charitable foundation, I spent my days shopping for new clothes and handbags.

She'd even interviewed my ex-boyfriend Jay to exploit the nasty details of our breakup. We'd been together for almost five years but had never married. I'd thought I was being smart, not hurrying into another marriage. Turns out, matrimony would have been better.

My ex-husbands had both signed confidentiality agreements as a condition of our divorce settlements. If the reporter had called them, they'd been forced to stay tight-lipped. But not Jay.

He'd told her I threw tantrums worse than a two-year-old when I didn't get my way and that I hadn't been supportive of his career.

Lies.

Jay hadn't loved me, he'd loved my trust fund. He'd been determined to win the World Series of Poker—except he wasn't good at poker. When I'd stopped covering his tournament fees, he'd picked a fight with me.

My *tantrum* had been me shouting at him in one of the dressing rooms at Bloomingdale's. He'd barged in on me, demanding I give him money. When I'd refused, he'd threatened to tell the tabloids I'd cheated on him with his scumbag manager. Again, another lie. But I'd lost it all the same and security had been called to escort us both out of the store.

The reporter had zeroed in on the fight and security escort.

Her feature read more like an exposé, and her words had tainted Malcom's beautiful photograph on the cover.

But at least I wasn't alone. The reporter had ripped the other four socialites in her feature to shreds too. The five of us were a joke. A drain on society. We weren't princesses in five royal American families. We were silly women parading around a city of intellect and culture, infecting it with our shallow existences.

A part of me wished my father were more vindictive. Or at least more protective of his baby girl. He could easily buy *NY Scene* and ruin that reporter's career.

Except he wouldn't do that. Because she hadn't really told a lie, had she?

That reporter had sat across from me on my cream couch in this very room, smiling and sipping a cappuccino while asking me her questions and taking notes.

I'd told her how I'd gotten an interior design degree from an art institute in Manhattan, but by the time I'd graduated, I'd hated interior design. I'd told her I'd been unlucky in love, sparing her the details that were none of her or anyone else's business. I'd told her my preference for Fendi over Gucci. When she'd asked what accomplishment I was most proud of, I'd told her it was finding Carrie, my personal chef.

I'd told her about *me*.

And she'd turned me into a hideous fool.

"Oh my god." I sobbed harder into my hands.

Was I the person she'd portrayed? Was that how everyone saw me?

If it was, I couldn't stay here in the city. I couldn't stomach walking past people, wondering if they'd read the article.

I dried my eyes and picked up my phone, then pulled up my older brother's number. He lived in Montana with his wife Thea and their three kids. They didn't sell *NY Scene* in Lark Cove, but there was no doubt he would have heard about the article by now.

News traveled fast across the country when the topic was my epic failures. I was sure Logan would be just as disappointed as Daddy. He'd told me on more than one occasion to grow up.

Whatever. I dialed his number anyway. I didn't expect or need his sympathy. What I needed right now was an escape, and Montana was the first place that came to mind.

"Hi, Sofia." He sounded annoyed. Aubrey had probably called him after sending me that text.

"Hi." I sniffled, wiping my nose with the back of my hand. "Look, before you lecture me, I know I screwed up. I trusted that reporter when the smart thing to do would have been to keep my mouth shut."

"Probably."

"I didn't mean to disparage our family. I just . . ." *Wanted to make you all proud.* "I just made a mistake."

"It happens." His voice softened. "Dealing with the press can be tricky."

"Yeah. It sucks."

"What can I do?"

"I was actually wondering if your boathouse was empty for New Year's."

"Sure. We'd love to have you. Just let me know when you'll be here, and I'll pick you up from the airport."

"Thank you." I pushed myself up off the floor, stepping on one of the magazines as I walked out of the living room. "I'll be there tonight."

"Good morning," I said on a yawn, walking into the kitchen.

"Morning." Thea, my sister-in-law, was standing by the coffee pot. "You're up early."

I shrugged. "I'm used to meeting my trainer at seven, which

is five Montana time."

"Coffee?" She took another mug from a cupboard.

"Yes, please." I slid into a barstool at the island in their kitchen. "Thank you for letting me come out here on short notice."

She delivered my mug, then brought over her own and sat two barstools away. "You're welcome here anytime."

Was I? Her tone wasn't convincing.

Thea and I hadn't gotten off to a good start, which was my fault entirely. She'd come to New York with Logan about five years ago, just after they'd started seeing one another. Well, they'd actually met years before in the hotel bar where Thea had been working. They'd hooked up and gone their separate ways, but not before Thea had gotten pregnant with no way of tracking Logan down.

Lucky for them, fate had intervened and delivered Logan here to Lark Cove and back into Thea's life. And he'd met five-year-old Charlie—his daughter.

But fate wasn't something I believed in, so when he'd brought her home to meet our family, I'd been skeptical, to say the least. Actually, I'd been a total bitch, certain that Thea's story was full of holes and that all she really wanted was to steal our family's fortune.

I'd thrown one of Logan's ex-girlfriends in Thea's face. I'd treated her like trash and dismissed Charlie completely. I'd judged her solely on her occupation as a bartender.

Ugh, I'm the worst.

I'd been trying ever since to get into Thea's good graces. But since I only saw them two or three times a year, my progress had been slow. Especially because Thea and I had nothing in common except our last name.

Most would call us both beautiful. Thea certainly was with her long dark hair, sparkling eyes and blinding smile. But she had an inner beauty that catapulted her to a different level. She worked hard, running her own business. She was an artist, creating sculptures and paintings that spoke to the soul. She didn't care about material things or social status. Her goal in life was to raise happy children.

She probably agreed with everything that reporter had written.

Silence loomed in the kitchen as we drank our coffee. "It's, um, quiet this morning."

"The kids were up late last night. I'm sure they'll sleep in."

"Sorry." They'd stayed up late because my flight hadn't gotten in until nine. With the thirty-minute drive from the airport to Lark Cove added on top, they hadn't gotten tucked into bed until almost ten.

"Don't worry about it. A late night isn't going to hurt them."

"I can't believe it's already been six months since you guys came to the city. The kids sure have grown since this summer."

Charlie, Collin and Camila were eleven, four and two, respectively. While Charlie was still the same tomboy she'd always been, Collin and Camila were developing their own personalities. Collin was a bundle of energy, never stopping as he explored the world. And Camila wasn't the baby she'd been last summer. Now she was talking and doing her best to keep pace with her older siblings.

Maybe she'd have better luck than I had.

Did they think their aunt was a complete failure too?

With talk about the kids out of the way, there wasn't much else to discuss at five in the morning. So we sat there, listening to the refrigerator hum. Halfway into my coffee, I wished I'd stayed in bed. There was an elephant in the room, and it was named *NY Scene*.

"You think it's true."

"Huh?" Thea asked.

"The magazine. You think what she wrote was true."

"The truth?" She sighed. "Yes and no. Yes, I think they captured the facts. No, I don't think you're all of the things she called you."

"Thank you." My chin quivered. That was maybe the nicest thing she'd ever said to me. "I, um . . . I feel kind of lost. I don't want to be that person." Useless. Spoiled. Petty.

Thea was quiet for a few moments, then reached across the granite counter and covered my wrist with her hand. "I have an idea."

"What's that?" I looked up, my hopes skyrocketing that she'd help me out.

"You're going to have to trust me."

"I do." I nodded. "I trust you."

"Good." Thea smiled and went back to her coffee. I waited for her to tell me her idea, but she didn't say a word. She just kept sipping from her mug for a few minutes and then got up and went to the fridge for eggs.

"Uh, are you going to tell me your idea?"

She grinned over her shoulder, then cracked the first egg on the edge of a bowl. "Just trust me."

I frowned at the dingy building outside the car window. A few hours after breakfast, Thea had loaded us all up in their SUV and ordered Logan to drive to the Lark Cove Bar.

"Are we getting lunch here or something?"

"No, I've got to get a few things organized before we can go."

"Where are we going?" Logan asked.

"Paris. We're leaving this afternoon."

"What? Paris?" I looked between them both in the front seat of their SUV. "Why didn't you say anything at breakfast? Or when I called you yesterday?"

"Um, because I didn't know," Logan told me then turned to his wife. "We're going to Paris?"

She nodded. "Isn't that what you gave me for my Christmas present?"

"Well, yeah. But we can go whenever you want."

"And I've decided I want to go for New Year's Eve. You can kiss me underneath the Eiffel Tower."

"Gross, Mom." Charlie groaned in her seat next to me. Collin and Camila just giggled from their car seats.

"I've already arranged for the kids to stay with Hazel and Xavier," Thea told Logan, earning a cheer from the kids that they'd be staying with their gran. "The jet is already here since Sofia flew over last night. We just have to pack and go."

"But what about the bar?" he asked. "Your New Year's Eve party is in two days. You really want to miss it?"

She shrugged. "They can party without us this year."

"But—"

"I rarely do anything spontaneous, gorgeous. I'm stepping way outside my comfort zone here. Just go with it."

His entire frame relaxed, and he reached across the car to take her hand. "Paris is what you want?"

"Paris is what I want." She nodded. "Ten days. Just the two of us."

"Okay. Then we'll go to Paris." He leaned across the car and planted a firm kiss on her lips, getting more groans and giggles from the kids.

"Is this your idea?" I asked. "For me to house-sit while you're gone?"

Thea gave Logan a grin that could only be described as diabolical. "Sort of."

"Wait. What do you mean—"

Before I finished my question, she opened the door and started unbuckling the kids.

I rushed to get out of the middle seat and follow, hurrying to catch up as she crossed the snow-covered parking lot. "Thea, what do you mean sort of?"

"Trust me."

"I'm starting to fear those two words."

She laughed and kept walking, Camila perched on her hip while Charlie and Collin raced around in the snow, kicking and throwing it at one other.

"Inside, guys!" Logan hollered, getting to the door first and holding it open for us.

Stepping inside and out of the cold, I took a few seconds to let my eyes adjust to the dark interior of the bar. Even with the blinds on the front windows open and the winter sun streaming inside, the bar was dim.

The kids rushed past me, bringing clumps of snow with them.

This was only the third time I'd been to Thea's bar and restaurant. All of my previous trips to Montana had been for family gatherings, so my time in Lark Cove had been confined to Logan and Thea's house on Flathead Lake. I didn't know this bar well, but it didn't take much of an inspection to know that it hadn't changed a bit since I'd been here last.

The ceilings were high with iron beams running the length of the open room. The bar ran in an L along the back walls. Behind it were mirrored shelves crowded with liquor bottles. The wooden plank floors matched the wooden plank walls, except while the dark floors were battered and covered in peanut shells, the dark walls were battered and covered in framed photos and the occasional neon sign.

Nothing else matched. Not the chairs or the stools or the tables. It was a mishmash of collectibles and went against every single one of the design principles I'd learned in college.

A strange twinge ran up my neck. It was the same feeling I'd had the other three times I'd been here, the same prickle I'd gotten when I'd ridden the subway once in high school for "fun." I was convinced that the next black plague would originate from those tunnels.

Maybe that twinge was my body's way of warning me of danger. Like it knew my immune system wouldn't be able to ward off the germs in places like this.

Not that the bar was dirty or grimy. It was actually quite clean and dust-free. The bar was just . . . old. And battered. Some might call it rustic. But the only kind of rustic I enjoyed was the brand-new kind you found in Aspen estates.

I'd give Thea one thing: her bar was unique. The jukebox in the corner was ancient, filled with old country music I'd never heard of. There was a set of antlers hanging on one wall with a bra draped from the horns.

As the kids chased each other around a cocktail table in the middle of the room, Logan and Thea took turns grabbing them one by one to help them out of their winter coats.

The twinge in my neck was gone. The clean and refreshing smell in the room had chased it away. I guess this place wasn't like the subway—not even a little.

Bleach lingered in the air, hinting that someone had scrubbed the bar top not too long ago. They must not have gotten to the floors yet.

Beneath the cleaner, the air was infused with citrus. I spotted a cutting board and a knife on the bar next to the slotted tray of bar fruits. It was overflowing with lemon, lime and orange wedges.

"Hey." A smooth, deep voice echoed in the empty room as a man emerged from the hallway behind the bar. His long, tanned fingers were wrapped around a white dish towel as he dried his hands. "What are you guys doing here?"

"We're going on a vacation." Thea smiled and walked behind the bar. "So I need to grab a couple of things before we leave."

"Vacation? Like, today? That wasn't on the calendar."

She laughed. "I know. I'm being spontaneous."

"Something you are not." The man chuckled and a shiver rolled down my spine.

This bar might not have changed since I'd been here last, but this man was definitely new. And definitely sexy.

His onyx hair was short on the sides and longer on top with wide swoops through the silky strands like he'd combed it out with his fingers. His face had this beautiful, odd symmetry that I felt the urge to sketch. His eyes were narrow and set in a harsh line above the wide bridge of his nose. His jaw was made entirely of hard, unforgiving angles. His cheekbones were so sharp they could cut glass. The only thing soft about this man's face were his full lips.

Apart, the features were all too strong and too bold, but mixed together, he was magnificent.

"Have you met Dakota before?" Logan caught my attention and nodded to the man I'd been blatantly studying.

"Pardon?"

"I'll take that as a no," he muttered. "Dakota Magee, this is my sister Sofia Kendrick."

Dakota jerked up his chin.

"Hi." I swallowed hard, finding it difficult to breathe when he was looking my way.

Those black eyes scrutinized me from head to toe, giving nothing away about what he found. He didn't blink. He didn't move.

I'd had my first boyfriend at thirteen and plenty of others since. I'd been married—and divorced—twice. I'd been on the receiving end of more pick-up lines and catcalls than a stripper headlining a Vegas show.

I knew when a man found me attractive. I knew when I stirred a man's blood.

But Dakota's stare gave nothing away. It was empty and cool. He looked right to my core, making my heart boom louder and louder with every passing second that I failed his inspection.

"So since I'm leaving on this last-minute vacation, I had an idea." Thea's voice came to my rescue, forcing Dakota to break his stare. "Sofia can help you out while I'm gone."

"I don't need help."

"I don't think that's such a good idea."

Dakota and Logan both spoke at the same time my stomach dropped. She wanted me to help? Here?

"With New Year's Eve, it'll be busy," Thea said.

"Then I'll call Jackson if I can't keep up," Dakota shot back.

Thea shook her head. "He and Willa made plans to go to Kalispell for New Year's."

"Fine." His jaw clenched, the angles getting angry. "Then I'll handle it. Alone."

"Listen. I feel awful leaving you here alone on one of the biggest days of the year when I'd planned to help out. But this will be perfect. You can teach Sofia the ropes for a couple of days, and then she can help during the party. It's a win-win."

He grumbled and crossed his arms over his chest. But he didn't argue with his boss.

"Thank you." Thea smiled, knowing she'd won. "Thank you both for doing this. It'll be great."

How could she think *me* working in her bar would ever be *great*? I had no experience, let alone desire, to mix other people's drinks.

Dakota's stern expression turned arctic as he leveled his gaze on me again. It was no secret he didn't want me here as much as I didn't wish to stay.

I inched backward, hoping to make an escape while I had the chance, but my foot caught on the edge of a chair. My feet slipped in the puddle of melted snow that had collected underneath my boots. My arms flailed as I tried to keep my footing, but when one heel went skidding sideways, I was doomed.

A cluster of peanut shells broke my fall as my ass collided with the floor.

"Ouch." My face burned with embarrassment as Logan rushed to my side.

"Are you okay?"

"Fine." I nodded, letting him take my elbow to help me back up. When my feet were steady, I rubbed the spot on my butt that was sure to bruise.

"Those peanut shells can be slippery," Thea told me. "My first two weeks here, I slipped constantly. But you'll get used to walking on them. And I guess you might as well start work by sweeping them all up."

"Sweep?" My mouth fell open. "I don't know how to sweep."

Dakota scoffed and turned on a heel, striding out of the room.

"Broom's in that closet over there." Thea pointed to a door next to the restroom, then followed Dakota down the hallway.

Logan's mouth was hanging open like mine as he stared at the spot where Thea and Dakota had disappeared. He shook it off, blinked twice, then unglued his feet and hustled after them both.

Which left me in a *rustic* bar, surrounded by peanut shells, while my nieces and nephews played like this was just another normal day in paradise.

What kind of fresh hell was this?

acknowledgments

Thank you for reading *Tragic*! I hope you've enjoyed Kaine and Piper's story. Because of readers like you, I get to do my dream job, and I am so very grateful.

Special thanks to my amazing editing and proofreading team. Elizabeth Nover. Ellie McLove. Julie Deaton. Kaitlyn Moodie. Thank you to Sarah Hansen for *Tragic*'s beautiful cover and to Stacey Blake for the incredible formatting work you do on each and every book. And a huge thank you to Danielle Sanchez, my publicist, for all of your work, love and support—and for being one of my absolute favorite people on the planet.

I can't say thank you enough to all of the awesome bloggers who read and spread the word about my books. THANK YOU! To my ARC team and Perry Street, thank you for loving my stories. Your excitement for them gives me life!

And lastly, thank you to my friends and family. I couldn't do this without you!

also available from
DEVNEY PERRY

Jamison Valley Series
The Coppersmith Farmhouse
The Clover Chapel
The Lucky Heart
The Outpost
The Bitterroot Inn

Maysen Jar Series
The Birthday List
Letters to Molly

Lark Cove Series
Tattered
Timid
Tragic
Tinsel

about the author

Devney is a *USA Today* bestselling author who lives in Washington with her husband and two sons. Born and raised in Montana, she loves writing books set in her treasured home state. After working in the technology industry for nearly a decade, she abandoned conference calls and project schedules to enjoy a slower pace at home with her family. Writing one book, let alone many, was not something she ever expected to do. But now that she's discovered her true passion for writing romance, she has no plans to ever stop.

Don't miss out on Devney's latest book news. Subscribe to her newsletter!
www.devneyperry.com

Devney loves hearing from her readers.
Connect with her on social media!

www.devneyperry.com
Facebook: www.facebook.com/devneyperrybooks
Instagram: www.instagram.com/devneyperry
Twitter: twitter.com/devneyperry
BookBub: www.bookbub.com/authors/devney-perry

Made in United States
North Haven, CT
24 January 2024

47845639R00217